Praise for *This Time, That Place*

"Fiction writers are foreigners, no matter where we live or where we're from. We're born outsiders. Clark Blaise is the maestro of our aloneness. 'The infinite perversity of life' is his subject. These stories will break your heart. As the narrator of 'Words for the Winter' puts it: 'I who live in dreams have suffered something real, and reality hurts like nothing in this world.' No one does heartbreak like Clark Blaise."

—John Irving

"A wonderfully rich, warmly populated gathering of Clark Blaise's short stories, a dazzling gallery of portraits of North American lives rendered in Blaise's emotionally evocative style. His characters are so specifically present to the reader, so fascinating in their quirks and oddities, it's something of a shock when a story comes to an end—for the lives of Blaise's characters are so palpable, like our own, we understand that they must continue beyond the (mere) ending of a story. These are tightly constructed stories fueled by what one of Blaise's characters recognizes as 'his fundamental Quebec Catholicism, the Jansenist belief that there is no end to the implications of a single act.'"

—Joyce Carol Oates

"A life's work from one of the most important short story writers to ever live in North America. No artist before Blaise, and nobody since, has moved through the continent with so much sensitivity, compassion, and intelligence. Most at home when they are lost, Blaise's characters search hardest for belonging when the conditions are least hospitable. For fifty peripatetic years, his beautifully crafted stories have shown us a way though. In our desperation, whenever we ask: 'Where am I now?' Clark Blaise provides the honest answer we need: 'Right here.'"

—Alexander MacLeod,
Scotiabank Giller Prize-nominated

T0015425

THIS TIME,
THAT PLACE

This Time, That Place

SELECTED STORIES

CLARK BLAISE

FOREWORD BY MARGARET ATWOOD

INTRODUCTION BY JOHN METCALF

BIBLIOASIS
WINDSOR, ONTARIO

FIRST EDITION

Library and Archives Canada Cataloguing in Publication
Title: This time, that place : selected stories / Clark Blaise.
Other titles: Short stories. Selections (2022)
Names: Blaise, Clark, author.
Identifiers: Canadiana (print) 20220203849 | Canadiana (ebook) 20220204071 | ISBN 9781771964890 (softcover) | ISBN 9781771964906 (ebook)
Classification: LCC PS8553.L34 A6 2022 | DDC C813/.54—dc23

Edited by John Metcalf
Text and cover designed by Gordon Robertson

 Canada Council for the Arts   Conseil des Arts du Canada

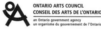 ONTARIO CREATES | ONTARIO CRÉATIF

Canada

ONTARIO ARTS COUNCIL
CONSEIL DES ARTS DE L'ONTARIO
an Ontario government agency
un organisme du gouvernement de l'Ontario

Published with the generous assistance of the Canada Council for the Arts, which last year invested $153 million to bring the arts to Canadians throughout the country, and the financial support of the Government of Canada. Biblioasis also acknowledges the support of the Ontario Arts Council (OAC), an agency of the Government of Ontario, which last year funded 1,709 individual artists and 1,078 organizations in 204 communities across Ontario, for a total of $52.1 million, and the contribution of the Government of Ontario through the Ontario Book Publishing Tax Credit and the Ontario Media Development Corporation.

The publication of *This Time, That Place: Selected Stories* has been made possible through the support of Tim and Elke Inkster of The Porcupine's Quill, who first gathered most of these stories across four separate volumes: *Montreal Stories; Pittsburgh Stories; Southern Stories;* and *World Body.* We at Biblioasis are grateful for their assistance with this project.

PRINTED AND BOUND IN CANADA

MIX
Paper
FSC® C100212

CONTENTS

FOREWORD

I MET Clark Blaise in the fall of 1967, when we were both twenty-seven and teaching in the lower ranks at Sir George Williams University in Montreal. Clark had arrived in Montreal in 1966, and had been teaching English as a Second Language to recently arrived citizens—the real-life experience that informed his now much-anthologized story, 'A Class of New Canadians.' He was therefore an old hand at the city by the time I got there, so he was a fount of information and I was a newbie, even though I was five months older than he was.

Sir George was named after the founder of the YMCA— this information from Clark, an amazing accumulator of information—and was later to be subsumed into Concordia. In 1967 it was a curious place—certainly not anyone's idea of a venerable ivy-covered grove of academe. It was housed in a great big brand-new block of a building, with escalators and fluorescent lighting. You taught a course in the daytime to a group of sullen, silent nineteen-year-olds who resented not having got into McGill; then, in the evening, you taught the same course to a clutch of beady-eyed adult 'returning students,' who wanted a degree in order to climb up a rung on whatever ladder they were on. They were highly motivated and not afraid to speak their minds. They plunged in, they discussed everything, they demanded extra reading.

On the days I was teaching both day and night, I'd eat in the cafeteria and drink a lot of coffee there, and that's where I'd see Clark. Though we were not teaching 'creative writing'—that particular entity had not yet manifested itself in Canada, except for a single example in British Columbia—we were both known to be writers, though I had published only a volume of poetry and Clark's first book of stories, *A North American Education*, was six years in the future. Nonetheless, he'd been appearing in various prestigious literary magazines, most but not all of them in the United States, and I had a nascent novel. We were promising young writers—in the eyes of others, it seems, and also in our own eyes—so writing is partly what we talked about.

The rest of the time Clark was very amusing on many subjects, himself and his double-jointedness and his fractured, peripatetic childhood and his various travels and dislocations included, but especially about the many different languages he spoke. He would give examples, transforming his body language and timbre of voice for each. At that time he was learning Russian; his eyes would become shrewd and mistrustful, his shoulders would rise, his hands would open, his smile turn falsely genial. 'Tovarich! sdelay mne odolzheniye, pozhaluysta! ('Comrade, do me a favour, please!') The Soviet Union was still in full swing, so the effect was sinister.

But then he'd morph into a restrained Frenchman, then into an unbuttoned, casual Québeçois: his father had been from Quebec, so his accent was spot-on. German was also on offer, as I recall, as was a Southern drawl. When you've been dragged around as a child as much as Clark had been, you become adept at camouflage. Think of him as a cuttlefish: when in a clump of seaweed, look like seaweed. He could 'do' someone from almost any background. And of course, in order to blend into a background, you need to observe that background closely: its textures, its smells, its symbols, its furniture. Perhaps the richness and accuracy of detail and the attention to the nuances of dialogue for which Blaise has been so justly praised has come in part from these early experiences. To avoid being prey, how do you hide in plain sight?

For a fiction writer, such a talent can be both an asset and a liability. If you don't have just one single 'identity,' you aren't confined to it: your range is cosmopolitan. But when you have so many possible identities at your command, where is the centre? Are you a trickster figure, wandering the margins like Odin in disguise, always observing but never fully rooted? Is your 'identity' the fact that you aren't definable by your membership in a single group? Are you a shape-shifter like were-wolves and gods? Are you a conglomerate, like Walt Whitman, who announced, 'I contain multitudes?' Was he a part of all that he had met, like Tennyson's Ulysses, or was all that he had met a part of him, as is the case with devouring dragons? Where was the boundary line between self and surround? Were roots a good thing to have, or did they render you parochial and xenophobic? What is 'belonging,' and why exactly would you want it? If you 'belong,' do the demands of others exceed anything you may expect to gain from them in return? What do 'national boundaries' mean, anyway? In asking such questions, Clark was well ahead of his times. This clutch of themes was to preoccupy him in his fiction, appearing in many variations and through many personae over the next fifty-odd years.

Clark had been through the University of Iowa's writing program (worshipped like a god by those few who actually knew about it), and had attended approximately twenty-five schools when growing up, and had met a lot more writers than I had, and had also read more modern novels, though I had the edge when it came to obscure Victoriana. He was like a sort of slot machine: you inserted a question about writers or writing, and out would come the answer.

This next factoid may seem bizarre in retrospect, but Clark was an early reader for the manuscript of my first novel, *The Edible Woman,* which I was revising, having written it back in 1964–5. In return, I sometimes baby-sat for his two adorable sons, Bart and Bernie, when he and his sophisticated wife, the writer Bharati Mukherjee, also a writer, wanted the odd evening out.

In 1967–8 we were living through a time of rapid transformation, though of course we didn't quite grasp the extent of it. The sixties had already seen many tumults. The Cuban missile crisis and the assassination of John F. Kennedy had frightened us in the early sixties; the Civil Rights movement in the United States was ongoing, and was to impact Sir George in the winter of 1969, when students occupied the computer centre and destroyed equipment in a race-related protest. The Vietnam War had spurred a flood of war-repudiating refugees coming to Canada—200,000 of them by the end—but that too was in its early stages. Quebec separatism was simmering behind the scenes, but was not to burst forth for a couple of years, complete with bombings, kidnappings, a murder, and the War Measures Act. It was thus still possible to publish bilingual poetry anthologies in Canada, with anglophone and francophone poets sharing the pages. Similarly, the second wave of the women's movement was still subterranean: the first I would hear of it would be in 1969, when I was no longer in Montreal. The Summer of Love had not yet happened. Drugs were around—marijuana and LSD, as I recall—but they were not endemic, and people were not dying en masse of overdoses. The Moon Shot was a year and a half in the future.

Despite crises and percolating uproars, 1967 was an oddly hopeful year, especially in Montreal. Expo 67, an international 'World's Fair,' was being held there—I arrived just in time to see it—and contrary to low expectations and advance doomsaying, it had been a great success. Little Canada had pulled it off! In the fifties and early sixties we'd got used to Canada being decried for its provincialism or else just ignored: this, after a brief moment of wartime prominence during which Canada had punched well above its weight.

This international-triumph optimism coincided with an energetic mood among young writers, both anglophone and francophone, that diverged from that of the generation preceding them, especially among fiction writers. Those earlier writers—few in number though they were—had gone to the UK or to the United States, or to Paris, it being a truism that there was no action in backwater Canada since hardly anyone was interested in reading, and certainly they were not interested in reading second-rate, moose-ridden, pallid Canadian writing, and if you wanted to make yourself known or even get published, you had to do it in a culturally central place.

But suppose you relocated, what were you to write about? You could hardly pretend to be English or French. 'American' was a little more possible, but then you'd be competing with giants. And if you wrote as a Canadian, who in the United States or England or France would want to hear from you? Who even in Canada wanted to read about boring old mediocre Canada? A couple of years after 1967, a US editor—I had one by then—asked me if I knew any well-known writers who might provide a quote for my book. I said I knew some in Canada. He replied, 'Canada is death down here.' That was the dilemma.

The sixties generation of Canadian writers responded by forming magazines and publishing houses, largely as a means of publishing themselves and their fellow writers. There were a few branch plants—offshoots of larger international publishers—that did a bit of Canadiana once in a while, and one house—McClelland and Stewart—that had recently decided to specialize and become 'the Canadian publishers,' but a lot of us were poets and experimental short fiction writers, and those forms—then as now—were hard sells if you were looking at more than a few hundred copies. The House of

Anansi—co-founded by Dave Godfrey, known to Clark via Iowa, and Dennis Lee, known to me via Victoria College at the University of Toronto—had just begun. (Coach House preceded it by a year or two; others were to follow.)

Many who would later become preeminent as story writers had not yet published: Alice Munro, for instance; Carol Shields; David Bezmozgis; Austin Clarke. Mavis Gallant was publishing in the *New Yorker*, but none of us knew she was Canadian. We did have Robert Weaver's *Canadian Short Stories in English*, with Morley Callaghan and Stephen Leacock, for instance, but those people seemed very old to us. We had literary magazines, a few. How did young writers of that time find one another? We were passed along by letter, often through the editors of small ventures; or through bookstores; or through readings, which did happen then. We sought one another out.

The first books the House of Anansi published were poetry collections and books of stories, because that's what young writers were producing then. Novels were full-time commitments, and how to support yourself while composing one? But you could write poems and stories while studying or holding down some other kind of day job. (The 'grant economy' and the 'creative writing school job' were not yet available to us.) Then you'd submit your poems and stories to small magazines—you did this yourself, as none of us had agents—mailing them out with a self-addressed, stamped envelope, every page numbered and with your name at the top in case someone dropped your priceless work of art on the floor and the pages got mixed up. Then you waited for the reply. Mostly it would be a rejection letter, but sometimes not.

We didn't expect to make much money doing this, but sometimes you did make a bit. Clark recalls how, in the early 1970s, he was able to publish a story in *The Fiddlehead* (a literary magazine) for $40, and have it broadcast on CBC Radio on Robert Weaver's program *Anthology*, for the (then) large sum of $125, and also read it aloud via the Montreal Story Tellers Fiction Performance Group, for a further $40. Print, audio, in-person: platform diversification had already set in.

The Montreal Story Tellers deserves a paragraph all to itself. This enterprise seems impossibly quixotic, but in this it was of its time—a time of quixotic enterprises. There, in the midst of Quebec Separatism, were five anglophone writers, going about to English Catholic secondary schools in Montreal and reading their stories to the doubtless bemused students. The outfit was the brainchild of John Metcalf—himself from England—and included Hugh Hood (from Toronto), Ray Smith (Cape Breton), Ray Fraser (New Brunswick), as well as Clark Blaise himself (North America). Ironically, Blaise from 'everywhere' (in Hank Snow terms) was the closest thing to a Montrealer that the group could proffer. According- xvii ing to Blaise, 'We proudly wrote the kind of stories that wouldn't make it into any anthology ... then on the market. I've got to give the priests credit: they never questioned our sex-and-liquor-heavy plots. In fact some of the priests invited us back to their offices, opened a desk drawer and pulled out a whiskey bottle and glasses.'

How long ago such a situation now seems: what high school teacher, priest or not, would take such a risk today? You'd turn up on social media as a corrupter of fiction writers, if not of students—exposing them to such unchained, let-it-rip fiction. But as Clark and I sat chit-chatting and drinking our evil coffees in order to crank up our energy for the evening classes, the Montreal Story Tellers had not even been dreamed up. What were we thinking, those two twenty-seven-year-olds of over fifty years ago? What reasons had we proposed to ourselves for doing what we were doing? Why had we given up other possibilities (he as a geologist, I as a biologist) to devote ourselves to the fickle gods of word and story? It was not a choice that anyone made easily, back then. Fame and fortune were not assumed to await us. There was not a long queue of youngsters longing to be writers, or certainly not in Canada. It was an eccentric thing to be doing, and pretentious, if not morally suspect and perhaps a little insane. We were at least partly aware of the dangers, as I recall: apprentice yourself to the craft, chain yourself to the sullen art, eat your heart out, achieve a bit of success, go down in flames amidst bad reviews and derision and the fallout from literary feuds, or else just waste away in obscurity. Why would you not wish instead to be a doctor or a lawyer or something safe and respectable?

So why did we feel that glittering possibilities awaited? Because we did on some level feel that. Cultural space was opening up; the elders, though few in number, were taking an interest; we had a peer group of sorts; a reading audience was possibly forming. Bliss was it in that dawn to be alive, as Wordsworth famously said; though he also said, 'We Poets in our youth begin in gladness; But thereof come in the end despondency and madness.'

I'll leave us there, in the over-lit cafeteria of Sir George Williams University, beginning in gladness, dreaming our writerly dreams, exchanging our writerly gossip. (We had not yet encountered the despondency, not in any serious form; we have escaped, so far, the madness.) Did Clark know he would become one of the preeminent story writers of his generation? Probably he did not. But probably he intended to bust himself trying. We were nothing if not dedicated.

'What was that writing thing I was doing, then? Why was it so important?' another writer—an octogenarian—said to me recently. It's a good question, especially now; in the midst of so many crises—environmental, political, social—why write? Isn't it a useless thing to be doing? Maybe, but so maybe is everything else. We know what we know about the Great Mortality of the fourteenth century because some people wrote things down. They bore witness.

Let's suppose that this is what Clark Blaise has been doing.

So, future readers—or even present-day readers—if you want to understand something about what life was like in the restless, peripatetic, striving, anxiety-ridden, simmering cultural soup of the late twentieth and early twenty-first centuries, read the stories of Clark Blaise. He's the recording angel and the accuser, rolled into one. He's the eye at the keyhole. He's the ear at the door.

Margaret Atwood
Toronto, November 2021

INTRODUCTION

'VE ALWAYS considered Clark Blaise's first two books, *A*
North American Education (1973) and *Tribal Justice* (1974),
to be two of the best collections of stories ever published in
Canada. The stories are as rich in texture and as compelling
now as they were when first written. They are wearing well.
The wealth of detail and the gorgeous sensuality in the stories are pleasures which are inexhaustible. Significantly, both
books are much admired by other writers but still lack the
general readership they deserve. These two collections remain
among the most underrated books in Canadian literature.

Whimsically, wistfully, in the years since, I've often wondered if Clark's standing in the fervent anti-American seventies would have been firmer with the academic drongoes
had *A North American Education* been entitled *A Canadian
Education* and had the narrator of the title attempted to satisfy
his urgent adolescent sexual curiosity not in Florida but in
Prince Albert, Saskatchewan, on a snowbank in the alley below
the dentist's office.

Blaise wrote of himself in relation to his stories in *World
Body* (2006):

Fate, family and marriage have conspired to make me into a hydroponic writer: rootless, unhoused, fed by swirling waters and harsh, artificial light. In Canadian terms, a classic un-Munro. A Manitoba mother and a Quebec father; an American and Canadian life split more or less equally, can do that to an inquisitive and absorptive child. I never lived longer than six months anywhere, until my four-year Pittsburgh adolescence and fourteen years of Montreal teaching. As a consequence, when I was a young writer, I thought that making sense of my American and Canadian experience would absorb my interest for the rest of my life.

But a five-minute wedding ceremony in a lawyer's office in Iowa City forty-two years ago delivered that inquisitive child an even larger world than the North American continent. I married India, a beautiful and complicated world, and that Canadian/American, French/English, Northern/Southern boy slowly disappeared. (I wonder what he would have been like, had the larger world never intervened.) The stories in *World Body* reflect a few of those non-North American experiences. I now live in California, but my California, strangely, presents itself through Indian eyes.

When I first knew Clark fifty years ago as a member of the Montreal Story Tellers I was a young English immigrant from a still-insular England. We gathered from his stories that he had spent his childhood among redneck crackers having chigger-like worms removed from his feet with the aid of carbolic acid and pouring fresh quicklime down the seething, hissing squatty-hole. In Cincinnati he attended school with Israelites and 'the coloured,' elementary school students either balding or with moustaches. He spoke French; even more impressive, he understood *joual*. His mother had studied art in Germany during Hitler's rise to power; his father, a thuggish, illiterate womanizer was, in Clark's words, 'a salesman, a violent, aggressive, manipulative man specializing in the arts of spontaneous misrepresentation.' Bernard Malamud was his friend. He had been at Iowa in much the same years as Raymond Carver, Andre Dubus, and Joy Williams. And to top off all this outré richness, he was married to Bharati Mukherjee, a novelist and story writer of great beauty who dazzled us with saris. I found him (and her) exotic.

When my son Daniel married Chantal Filion, Clark said to me, 'At last your people have joined my people.' But by then I was less clear who my people were. I was no longer, as I had been, simply a part of the Metcalf diaspora from Wensleydale in North Yorkshire. I had acquired another country, another citizenship. My first wife was of Lebanese origins, her people from a village not far from Mount Hermon, so my daughter is half British, half Lebanese-Canadian, though American in upbringing. My wife is Jewish as, therefore, is my stepson. My wife connects me to Quebec where she was born and to Romania, Poland, and Israel. My younger son and daughter are from Tamil Nadu State. My wife and I were the guardians of boat children, a brother and sister from Cholon in Saigon. Over the fifty years I've known Clark, my life, I realized slowly, had become a Clark Blaise life, a Clark Blaise story.

Thirteen years is the longest, by far, that I lived in a single place; Montreal will remain my city for life. Predictably enough, the city did take the place of my warring parents—Montreal is my parents; I am once again their baffled son in its presence. I worked for both Neil Compton and Sidney Lamb (Renowned teachers at Sir George Williams University, now Concordia). I heard my own voice pumped out over the CBC. Later, in Toronto, I sat one night at Massey College high table beside Northrop Frye, across from Marshall McLuhan. In Canada election to Olympus is possible. The myths have touched me, I met my whole generation of Canadian writers and aged with them. I was there when the exiles returned. I got to know the others before they passed away. I started a writing program in Montreal and taught in others in Toronto and British Columbia and Saskatchewan; I think I did find the next generation of talent, in classrooms or through the mails, and with John Metcalf edited four books of 'the best' in Canadian stories. More of my stories have been anthologized than I ever thought possible, from my Iowa origins. And it all started by joining a group, The Montreal Story Tellers, the only conscious *gathering* of English-language prose writers in Montreal this century.

Clark wrote of the group in the memoir he contributed to the book by J.R. (Tim) Struthers, *The Montreal Story Tellers* (1985):

> The Montreal Story Tellers is now a part of Canadian literary history. For me, it was the public manifestation of inner maturing. I learned in the group that I still needed an ensemble; despite my immodest flights of fancy, I wasn't yet ready to stand alone. I always had the sense that of the five, I was the one the audience hadn't heard of, and I was the one they had to endure after the famous Hugh Hood and the sexy Ray Smith and the satiric John Metcalf and the whack-o Ray Fraser. So I learned to tame myself, to wait.
>
> We are now at the age of the rock stars of the Sixties; we've had to change, or run the risk of becoming absurd. The easy work is all behind us—that fire and passion— but I have to feel our best work is yet to come.

We all knew that the stories Clark was writing in those years were extraordinary. His first nationally published story, 'Broward Dowdy,' which appeared in the American magazine

Shenandoah in 1964, was, when I came to read it, a flare that hung in the night sky illuminating and revealing a way forward. We all knew that his stories held a sudden place in the barrens of Canadian writing. We all knew that Clark was writing Canada's *Dubliners* or *Bliss.*

Of these stories, Clark wrote:

I was writing very openly, in the late sixties, of Montreal. The city was drenched with significance for me—it was one of those perfect times when every block I walked yielded an image, when images clustered with their own internal logic into insistent stories. A new kind of unforced, virtually transcribed story (new for me, at least) was begging to be written—stories like (from my first two books) 'A Class of New Canadians,' 'Eyes,' 'I'm Dreaming of Rocket Richard,' 'He Raises Me Up,' 'Among the Dead,' 'Words for Winter,' 'Extractions and Contractions,' 'Going to India,' and 'At the Lake' were all written in one sitting, practically without revision. I'd never been so open to story, so avid for context. I was reading all the Canadian literature I could get my hands on, reading Canadian exclusively; there was half a silent continent out there for me to discover.

I was still discovering the city, or, more precisely, discovering parts of myself opened up by the city. I was respectful if not worshipful of all its institutions. I defended its quirks and inconsistencies as though defending myself against abuse; I was even charmed by things I would have petitioned against in Milwaukee like separate Catholic and Protestant schools, Sunday closings, and male-only bars. 'The Frencher the Better' was my motto to cover any encroachment on the aboriginal rights of the English.

I once heard Clark introduce one of his own readings by saying rather sadly that he was being paid more for reading aloud for one hour than he received in royalties for a year. It's

5

sometimes impossible not to feel angry about this. We all of us would have preferred to sit at home and receive royalties. We would have preferred readers to listeners. Readers work harder and stand a chance of getting more. But as the principal of a school in which I once worked used to murmur when it was reported to him that children had again emptied their free milk into the grand piano, 'We live in an imperfect world.'

None of us was ever seduced, so far as I know, by the idea of performance. We all realized that writing and performing were entirely distinct activities and that for us, writing was the sterner and more valuable task.

Clark's stories ran on wheels, as it were; Clark gave the impression that he was merely the almost invisible track on which they ran. The stories are so beautifully crafted and balanced in terms of their rhetoric that Clark seemed almost to disappear behind them. This was, of course, an illusion. Clark was never openly dramatic, never given to gesture, but he read fluently and *urgently* and with a fierce grip on the audience which tightened relentlessly. It was rather like watching an oddly silent pressure-cooker which you knew was capable of taking the roof off at any moment.

I said the Montreal Story Tellers was united only in its desire for honoraria. As a bond, that never loosened. But now, looking back, I think that we were held together by much more. We *grew* together. I don't think the group would have worked as it did unless we were getting from the association something more important than money. Four of us, at least, were writers obsessed by the idea of excellence, crazy about craft. The group gave us an association where craft was recognized and didn't have to be discussed; we were at home with each other, at home in the way that perhaps the disfigured are or the lame, that exiles are in a hostile land.

In my own case, at least, there was a sense in which membership in Montreal Story Tellers was a way of helping to *define* myself; the company of other writers I respected helped to confirm that I was a writer indeed. We were all younger then, of course, and our hilarity and arrogance masked an unease about our possible futures.

It is still received opinion that short stories are the apprentice work that a writer undertakes before tackling the really serious work of the novel, where the big bucks are. Imagine then how liberating and reinforcing it was for me as a young writer of short stories to read Blaise in the little mags and to listen to him as Hugh Hood drove the Montreal Story Tellers to our readings. Clark often proposed that the short story, far from being fiction's Cinderella, was actually *superior* to novels.

Most novels are watery, diluted, and bloated, and they do not have anything like the richness of a short story.

What, he asked, was the difference between a Mavis Gallant story and someone else's novel? It's that in comparison, 'the novel becomes smaller and thinner than her story.'

For me, the short story is an expansionist form, not a miniaturizing form. To me, the novel is a miniaturizing form. I think of the story as the largest, most expanded statement you can make about a particular incident. I think of the novel as the briefest thing you can say about a larger incident. I think of the novel as being far more miniaturist—it's a miniaturization of life. And short fiction is an expansion of a moment.

I think the job of fiction is to view life through a microscope so that every grain gets its due and no one can confuse salt with sugar. You hear a lot about cinema being a visual medium—this is false. It *degrades* the visual by its inability to focus. It takes the visual for granted. Only the word—for me—is truly visual.

I've always favoured the short story for its energy, a result of its confinement, and for the fact that its length reflects the author's ability to hold it entirely in his/her head like a musical note. You can't do that with a novel. Holding everything, meaning the syllables, the rhythms, the balance of scene and narration, long sentences and short...

Such were the intense and radical niblets tossed over from the front passenger seat to the two Rays and me, the peanut gallery in the Lada's cramped back seat.

Critic Barry Cameron wrote of the kinship of Blaise stories with poetry quoting from Blaise's now famous essay 'To Begin, to Begin':

> The sense of a Blaise story as poem is reinforced by his theory of the function of first paragraphs and first sentences in fiction. No matter how skilful or elegant the other features of a story may be, the first paragraph should give the reader 'confidence in the power and vision of the author.' Genesis is more important to Blaise than apocalypse, for a Blaise story is often, if not always, its beginning amplified or expanded:

>> The first sentence of a story is an act of faith—or astonishing bravado. A story screams for attention, as it must, for it breaks a silence. It removes the reader from the everyday .... It is an act of perfect rhythmic balance, the single crisp gesture, the drop of the baton that gathers a hundred disparate forces into a single note. The first paragraph is a microcosm of the whole, but in a way that only the whole can reveal.

>> It is in the first line that the story reveals its kinship to poetry. Not that the line is necessarily 'beautiful,' merely that it can exist utterly alone, and that its force draws a series of sentences

behind it. The line doesn't have to 'grab' or 'hook' but it should be striking.

Blaise pursued this vision of stories as a form of poetry in the following:

> When I 'see' a story it is always in terms of its images and situation, the tone and texture and discovery that seems immanent in that situation—and very rarely do these intimations demand a thirty-eight-year-old spinster or a college drop-out on an acid trip. I try to work out a voice that will allow for a simultaneity of image and action. Sometimes it is 'second person,' frequently first person, commonly present tense. Sometimes it will have no time-referent beyond the present moment. In my book *A North American Education,* most of the Montreal stories—'Eyes,' 'Words for the Winer,' 'Extractions and Contractions,' and 'Going to India'—follow, at least in part, this pattern. Those are stories of texture and voice—details selected with an eye to their aptness but also to their 'vapour trails,' their slow dissolve into something more diffuse and nameless.

In one sense, Blaise's books are one book. Some critics have accused him of doing nothing much more than writing versions of his autobiography over and over again: the fat child, the English-Canadian mother, the French-Canadian father, life as the son of a salesman in Florida, Pittsburgh, Cincinnati…I've never understood the point of this criticism. It is as if such critics believe that the stories are somehow lesser because autobiographical, less imaginative, taking less effort. But the stories are all different in emphasis and detail and each is a wonderfully crafted unique artifact. I suspect that for Blaise there really isn't a clear dividing line between auto-biography and fiction; he blurs the idea of genres. We might consider the travel book *Days and Nights in Calcutta* (1977) that he wrote with his wife, Bharati Mukherjee, as fiction, too, because in writing it he uses all the devices of fiction. Read the wonderful section in which he describes attending a lecture on the poetry of Rabindranath Tagore during which the electricity fails; it would require only a nudge of this piece of 'non-fiction' to become 'fiction.' Blaise explores the relationship between autobiography and fiction in his third collection, *Resident Alien* (1986), which includes stories and essays and which is essential reading in any consideration of his work. The story 'Identity' from *Resident Alien*, as so often in Blaise, could be regarded as a story or an essay or a memoir. What do these labels really mean or matter? What matters is that, once read, these pieces will never leave your mind.

> What I *knew,* at the age of twenty, was suburban life in Pittsburgh in the mid-fifties; I knew it cold. I knew the retail trade in furniture, paper routes, baseball, the charms and terrors of women and gobs of facts in astronomy, sports, archaeology and geography. Those were the elements, in fact, of many later stories and my first novel, but if I had tried it as an undergraduate—and probably I did—it would have come out like warm, flat soda water.
>
> It's alchemy, taking the facts, the common language, the world and characters we know and transforming them into something never before seen, hitherto unknown and forever fresh.

And that, of course, is the point: alchemy. In Blaise's writing the autobiographical is transformed, *transmuted* by art into stories 'forever fresh.'
Base metal into gold.

John Metcalf
Ottawa, June 2021

BROWARD DOWDY

W E WERE LIVING in the citrus town of Orlando in 1942, when my father was drafted. It was May, and shortly after his induction, my mother and I left the clapboard bungalow we had been renting that winter and took a short bus ride north to Hartley, an even smaller town where an old high school friend of hers owned a drugstore. She was hired to work in the store, and for a month we lived in their back bedroom while I completed the third grade. Then her friend was drafted, and the store passed on to his wife, a Wisconsin woman, who immediately fired everyone except the assistant pharmacist. Within a couple of days we heard of a trailer for rent, down the highway towards Leesburg. It had been used as a shelter for a watermelon farmer, who sold his fruit along the highway, but now he was moving North, he said, to work in a factory.

A Mrs Skofield was renting the trailer. She was a fat, one-eyed woman who gave me a bottle of Nehi grape without my asking, then led us down the highway from her tiny gas-station-general-store to the trailer. As we walked she explained that the trailer wasn't exactly hers, but she reckoned she was entitled to what she could get from it, since a no-count farmer had skipped off in the middle of the night, owing her money and leaving the trailer behind. My mother asked if it had water, or electricity, and Mrs Skofield snorted, 'What y'all expect, honey? Weren't no tourist livin' there.'

It was blisteringly hot inside. Even the swarm of fruit flies buzzing around the mounds of lavender-crusted oranges were anxious to escape. The furniture was minimal: two upturned crates, a card table, a coverless bed, a wood-burning stove, and an icebox. Behind the trailer, away from the highway and facing the forest of live oak and jack pine, someone had built a porch foundation of planks and cinder block.

'We'll take it if you finish that porch,' my mother said.

'Screens is hard to come by,' Mrs Skofield said, 'but we got heaps of gunnysack. I'll get my brother to put up some curtains you can roll up and down that'll be better than any screens ever was.'

'What about—' my mother started, then looked out the door.

'The brother'll dig y'all a squatty-hole. And you can have five gallon of water a day from the store. We'll sell y'all ice cheap.'

'What about people?' I asked. 'Is there any kids?'

'Ain't nobody now, hon, but just you wait you a couple weeks and you'll have all the company you want.'

'How come?'

'Fambly named Dowdy lives down that there trail,' she said, pointing to a narrow cleft in the trees. 'They ain't come down yet, but they'll be here. Come down from Georgia.'

'They white?' my mother asked.

Mrs Skofield snorted, then said, 'Y'all just spot you a nigger in them woods and my Seph'll fix it. A single white lady can't take no chances.'

'My Billy is fightin' Japs,' my mother said. 'Leastways he will be.'

Mrs Skofield went on to describe the lake that lay behind the trees, and how it was world famous for fishing. We moved in that day, and by evening I had already discovered a quiet inlet where I caught sunfish with just a blade of grass on my hook. And even before the Dowdys came, I knew the woods. My tender feet itched maddeningly with tiny thread-like worms my mother kept removing with carbolic acid, but at last my feet toughened and I was no longer bothered. By July, when our neighbours finally came, I was lean, brown, and lonely, and craving friendship that would free me from my mother's needs.

Then on a muggy day in July the Dowdys' rusting truck loaded with children, rattling pans, and piles of mattresses in striped ticking churned down the sandy ruts I had come to call my trail. I helped them spread their gear on the floors of a pair of tarpaper shanties, and watched their boy my age, Broward, pour new quicklime down last summer's squatty hole. Within hours, he had shown me new fishing holes, and how to extract bait worms from lily stalks.

13

A few weeks later, Broward and I were fishing from a half-sunk rowboat in the inlet, merely dabbing the hook and doughball in the water to attract a swarm of fish, and snapping it out fast enough to avoid hooking another one. It was hot and lazy, and we didn't talk.

'Brow'd, Brow'd,' came a cry from the shanties. It was his mother, whom we could see, sitting on the floor of the kitchen where a door should have been.

'Your mother's calling you, Broward,' I said, attempting to head off a showdown.

'I'm fixin' to come,' he answered. 'She ain't gettin' supper less'n I'm there anyhow. She ain't fixin' to whale me before dinner.'

'Brow'd,' she shrieked, 'you git the hell over here 'fore I tear the skin off'n your back, you hear?' We saw her get off the floor and disappear inside.

'See, I tolt you so,' he said, flashing his nervous smile. 'Here, got another doughball so's I can bait up?' I took a slice of bread from the cellophane package—the one my mother had sent me up to Skofield's to get—moistened it in the warm muddy water and shaped it into a ball the size of a marble. Broward thanked me as he always did, then formed it around the tiny hook that dangled on the end of the string tied to the long cane-pole. The instant it touched the water, a school of bream rose to meet it; Broward snapped the bait and two tiny fish— one hooked and one caught by the gills—were sent flying to the bank. I jumped ashore and dropped the new acquisitions into the reeking flour sack that half floated by the boat, attached to a flaking oarlock. Then I stretched my legs their full length to get back into the boat, for Broward suspected that under the old deserted landing where I had been standing, swarms of water moccasins made their nest.

'You watch you don't never leave your catch in deep water,' he cautioned. 'Once I lost me a whole day's catch to turtles that was just snappin' off their heads soon's I throwed them in. I hate them critters,' he said, untying the sack. 'Ever time you catch you even a li'l one, don't forget to chop off his head.' He leaped ashore, and pulled the sack after. 'I gotta go now. She's sent my brother down to fetch me.'

One of Broward's younger brothers was scampering through the tall swamp grass towards us. It was Bruce, about three, blond and blue-eyed like all the others. And like the rest of the family, his stomach was bloated out like a floating fish's. Bruce wore only a filthy pair of underpants, with large holes cut around his rump and penis. As dirty as the cloth was, it was difficult to distinguish where it left off and Bruce began. Bruce, Broward explained to me, was 'shy—real shy. He don't take up with strangers much.' He threw his grimy little arms around Broward's equally soiled knees, and whined, 'C'mon, Brow'd.' Broward set the sack down to disentangle his brother's buried head and hugging arms, then took it up again—the precious, unrationed fish that fed us all that summer—and taking Bruce's hand, trudged back through the grass and mud to their two shanties.

'Why don't y'all eat with us?' he asked. It was the first time, after a month's daily fishing, that he had invited me home even though I passed through the clearing in front of their shanties twice a day.

'I can't, Broward,' I replied. 'You got all those others to feed as it is. Anyhow my mother's expecting me.'

'Set real quiet and they won't even see you,' he said, and I laughed. 'You gotta do what she says, I guess,' came his stock reply, accompanied with a shrug of his bone-sharp shoulders. 'Nobody's gonna eat less'n I fix it. Sure like to have you over. I ain't never had a friend to dinner.' We took a few more steps toward the Dowdys' in silence.

'Okay,' I said.

There was a slight clearing in the sawgrass in front of their shanties. On either side of the trail there was marsh, and the shanties had been elevated on stilts, with ladders leading to the interiors and planks forming a network of safe paths. One shanty was for cooking and eating, and the other for sleeping. Usually there were equal numbers in each shanty, either sleeping, or playing by the boards in what passed for a yard. The interior of each shanty was dim. They depended on the light that filtered in through the numerous cracks in the tarpaper framework. One particularly large rip just over the stove served for both the overhead light and the escape hole for smoke and the fumes of cooking. The flour sack, the same as Broward's fish sack, slumped next to the stove like a dumpy old man. The humidity in the central Florida air caused the top half-inch of flour to cake over. The bulging bottom was gnawed open and here and there lay conical deposits, like anthills. Broward set the still-flopping sack on the floor by the stove. The flies that had followed us from the inlet and those that had been waiting, blackening the pools of watermelon juice on the table, now bombarded the sack. Broward's mother, who had been in the other shanty when we arrived, came back.

'You get them things the hell out of here, you hear?' she shouted from her slumped position at the head of the ladder. 'And you hand me my pack of Luckies on the table.'

'Yes, ma'm,' Broward answered softly, and slid the cigarettes across the floor.

'When I say I want my cigarettes, I mean for you to *hand* them to me, if you ain't too stupid, that is. Ain't you worth nothin'?'

'Yes, ma'm,' he replied quietly as he ripped a brown paper bag open and spread it on the table. 'Hand me them fish,' he directed.

'On the table?' Flies settled in my eyes.

'Sure.' I laid it on the table.

'Now dump 'em,' he said. I opened the top and tilted the sack downward, and the fish came sliding and squirming out. A little turtle, clamped onto the largest fish, started to walk away, dragging his prize behind. 'Goddamn it,' Broward hissed, 'that right there's just exactly what I was sayin'.' He scooped it up and shook the fish from its beak. He slammed it furiously to the floor, as though it were a tiny coconut, then fired it against the wall until at last, mercifully, the bottom shell snapped off. I couldn't bear the sight; it looked, I imagined, like a frog turned belly-up, white and helpless; but then an almost nauseating vision of the secret nether-parts of the turtle, half frog, half snake, took hold and when he asked me to come over and look, I only waved my arms frantically around the fish and around my head, to clear my face of flies. He tossed the remains underhand into a clump of sawgrass.

'Here,' he said, handing me his pocket knife. 'While's I'm lightin' the fire y'all scrape the leeches off and start choppin' up the fish.'

'How?' I asked. My father had been an angler, with artificial lures and a casting rod. He loved to fish and my mother had always done the cleaning.

Broward laughed. 'Y'all just watch. First stick the knife under here, see,' indicating the area under the gills, 'and then just cut through. Then you slit his belly and dump out all this. Got it? Then make sure there ain't no leeches in the meat.'

'Y'all get a mudfish?' his mother asked.

'No, ma'm.'

'Then how the hell you expect to feed your fambly? How can anybody be so goddamn dumb is what I want to know.'

'Don't get mad. We couldn't help it. I ast everbody that come in from the lake if they got anythin' they was throwin' out, like a mudfish, and there weren't nobody even heard of one. They was all Yankees anyhow.'

'If you wanted to get one, you could have,' his mother retorted.

'Ma, I tried, honest. Now I got me a friend to dinner.'

'Ain't enough you don't bring home no food, but you gotta bring home another mouth to feed. Tell me this—you see him invitin' us up there? Not for nothin'.'

'They would. Maybe not all of us, but me anyhow, and you and Pa too.' He looked to me for support.

'Sure,' I said weakly. My mother would die, cooking for migrants.

'Anyhow we ain't losin' any food. Val said she's sick again and she don't want nothin'.'

'She ain't sick any more'n I am. She's fixin' to run off is all. I know what she's sick from,' she laughed. 'They gets to be her age and all of a sudden they's regular ladies they think and their fambly ain't good enough for them no more and this place just don't suit them—it ain't elegant like Waycross is. Or they starts thinkin' how grand they can live in Leesburg and go to pitcher shows ev'ry night. Well, that ain't the way you was raised, and it ain't the way anybody was intended to be raised, and they all gone to the devil, ever single one. There ain't no more my children goin' to school, you hear that, Mr Smarty? Any body thinks they're too good for this house is free to sashay out and all it means is they ain't any goddamn good theirselves.'

While she was speaking Broward had been stacking wood around the burning paper. Then he came back to the table and took the knife from me.

'I'll go, Broward. It's not fair.'

'Now you're stayin'. Now it's fer sure you ain't leavin."

After the fish had been cleaned, or at least cleaned to his standard, Broward took out a cleaver from inside the flour sack and began chopping the fish into half-inch squares. Then he dusted the diced fish with a handful of grey flour and dropped the pieces into the oiled skillet. They spattered and spewed and smoked and occasionally the flames from under the skillet curled around and ignited the oil. The flames shot roofward, nearly lapping the paper ceiling. He smothered them with the wet fish sack, and then the frying settled down to the noisy gurgle of flour in boiling oil.

The smell of frying fish never changes no matter how you cook it. You forget how you cleaned it, what kind of sorry fish you caught, and begin to look forward to eating it. Broward took the stack of dishes from the end of the bench by the table— plates with bright purple designs, the kind you get at service station openings—and placed them evenly, seven to a side.

Meanwhile, the odour of frying fish had attracted the other Dowdys to the kitchen entrance. They seemed not to notice me, as though I were one of them, and Bruce even wad-dled up and hugged me around the legs. By the time the fish was lifted and in its place at the centre of the table, the fam-ily had all assembled in an evidently prearranged pattern on the benches. Broward stood at the end nearest the stove, while Bruce and I occupied the last seats on either side.

They all sat quietly about the table. All eyes were on the tall, thin, and red-cheeked father. His face was lined from sleep and his weak blue eyes were bleary from the light. He rose, bowed his head, and folded his hands piously. The children remained seated, but also folded their hands and closed their eyes as hard as they could, so that each face was a mass of folds and wrinkles.

'Lord,' the father shouted as though He were sleeping in the next shanty, 'Thou hast been truly good to thine sheep. We thank Thee that we have this delicious food on our humble table, health in our fambly, and that Thee, that guards all our blessings, hast kept our name and blood untainted.' All the family followed with an 'amen'.

'Brow'd, you take care of Bruce's food, now, hear?' his mother ordered. 'You know he ain't fixin' to eat less you cut it up. I reckon your friend there can handle his own.'

'Yes, ma'm.' Bruce looked up at his brother and smiled his thanks.

'Here, y'all hold your fork like this and bring it up to your mouth.' As soon as Broward let Bruce's hand go, the fork clattered to the floor. 'Oh, it just ain't no use,' Broward said, looking at his mother. Bruce looked up smiling, with his mouth open.

'You feed that baby, you no good—'

'Wayc, you do it,' Broward pleaded. 'He don't remember from one meal to the next and anyhow I got me a friend to dinner.' Waycross Dowdy, who was fourteen and already taller than his father, and blubbery, scowled at Broward, then down at Bruce. Then he picked up the fish on Bruce's plate and stuffed it into his own mouth, and no one said a word.

On Wayc's other side sat Stuart. He never looked up from his plate, and was eating his fish with his fingers, cleaning them with a smack, then a swipe against his pants. Stuart often fished with Broward and me, and of the children, he bore the closest resemblance to Broward. Next to Stuart sat Starke, one half of a twin combination. Though much younger, he was built on the order of Wayc, with a low forehead and wide neck, and muscles already thick on his arms and shoulders, that jumped with the slightest movement of his hands. As I looked from the children to the parents, particularly to the mother, I noticed something of the final maturity of Waycross Dowdy in nearly all of them, made all the more terrible for its softened femininity. Starke's twin sister, Willamae, the only girl at the table except for a baby in her mother's arms, was a wisp of a girl whose eyes never focused on any object for more than a few seconds, and whose speech was so heavily 'cracker' that I couldn't understand it. She wore a pair of purple earrings which she kept swinging with a flick of her long red fingernails. Next to her was Henry, still wearing the cutout underwear of infancy. He was loud, a brat, and particularly antagonistic to his sister, whose earrings he kept trying to pull off.

'Wayc, you make Henry quit pickin' on Willamae,' Mrs Dowdy ordered. Wayc swung over the bench and lumbered up to his brother. Henry's fingers were on Willamae's earrings when he was sent headfirst into the edge of the table by a slap on the back of the head. He shrieked, Willamae's earring now lay in his hand, and Willamae, seeing it, shrieked with pain and delayed outrage. She dashed from the table, out of the kitchen, towards the other shanty, holding both hands over her ear. Henry's forehead, scraped a watermelon-red, was already purple in a long narrow band. Waycross went back to his seat, and Broward went over to Henry, whose face was red from crying. He looked down, then ran his finger across the cut. Then he took Willamae's plate and dumped her uneaten fish into his own.

'Take a little?' he asked Henry, who didn't reply.

Broward came back to his seat and offered some more to me, which I refused. Then he scraped half the remaining fish into the skillet and kept the rest for himself. After a few minutes Henry quit crying and shuffled over to his mother.

'Ma—Wayc, he hit me.'

His mother looked at the bruise. 'You know he didn't mean to go and do it,' she comforted. 'Y'all go back and eat up your dinner.'

As he walked back, he stopped for a moment behind Wayc, who didn't turn. I thought he was going to hit him back, and half hoped, half feared that he would. Henry waited for everyone to quit eating before he said, 'Anyhow, you didn't hurt me at all.'

Letters from my father came once a month, from Somewhere in the Pacific. During the sweltering nights of my ninth summer, my mother and I sat on the porch in the dark, with the burlap rolled up, listening to the Orlando station on the battery radio, to the network news.

Her face aged that summer, and her body grew thin on the fish I caught. She would read me parts of the letters and told me when to listen closely to the news, and very slowly I realized that the Pacific Theater was a battleground and not what it sounded like, and that men were dying all over, everywhere but home, and I would cry out to my mother, 'Why doesn't he come back to us?' and she would answer, 'Pray that he will.'

My memory of him blurred, although now we had a picture of him holding a coconut in his hand and grinning just like he did at home—looking happier in fact—surrounded by much younger men in shorts, wringing out their shirts. In his letters he called me 'little soldier' and always ended with an order for me to look out for my mother, and not to forget him, and he said that he missed us very much. Those orders I took seriously, and the fishing every day with Broward became in my imagination something of a tactical manoeuvre.

Broward knew nothing of the war, and asked me many times where my father was but never understood. He merely fished for food, but I reconstructed assaults and casualties. Turtles became tanks, and were thrown on tiny fires until— half cooked—the retracted parts surrendered; dragonflies were Zeros, and downed with a deluge of water; and the endless wriggling hordes of bream were Japs and their numbers hacked with glee. My father had been a driver for the citrus trucks going to port, and every so often he'd write that 'this island I can't name' would be a great place for growing oranges.

But the summer was an idyll. Whenever Broward and I roamed the woods we felt that unutterable sensation of being the first who had ever felt or heard the music of the place. For hours we would run along the beaches of the lake, prying our way through the twisted vines and stunted underbrush, skimming the ankle-deep run-offs, and building lookout blinds along the beach where we could watch the Yankees in their rowboats and hear their strange accents plainly over unruffled water. Alone, I would gaze over the water; the sun, piercing the calm surface of the lake, fluoroscoped the top two or three feet of lime-tinted water, often exposing a gator drifting like a log, or schools of bream dancing in the warm water like swarms of mayflies. I would think that there was just the lake, the beach, and me; then I would be startled by the splash of water from the swamp behind, and turning quickly, I'd often catch a glimpse of brown and know that I, or a prowling cat, had disturbed a deer and sent it in fearful bounds deeper into the forest. Then September arrived, and we received notice from the government that we were to be resettled in South Carolina in special quarters for servicemen's dependents. And with September came time for the Dowdys to leave the summer moss-picking grounds and head back up to the pecan-fields of Georgia.

'You know, this is the time of year I like best,' Broward confided the last time I ever saw him. 'When we get up north, we're right near a big city and all kinds of things happen that don't happen here. Last year they made Wayc and me go to school and I can almost read now. Pa says there ain't no reason to go to school, but I know there ain't nothin' you can't do if you can just read and write, ain't that so?'

Before the Dowdys could leave, they had to get their sole possession, the old Dodge truck, ready to roll. Over the humid summer months, rust had set in and a thorough oiling was needed. Naturally it was Broward who had been ordered under the truck to oil the bearings. The last I saw of Broward Dowdy were his legs, pale and brilliant against the sour muck, sliced cleanly by the shadow of the truck and the shanties beyond.

A NORTH AMERICAN
EDUCATION

E LEVEN YEARS after the death of Napoleon, in the presidency of Andrew Jackson, my grandfather, Boniface Thibidault, was born. For most of his life he was a *journalier*, a day labourer, with a few years off for wars and buccaneering. Then, at the age of fifty, a father and widower, he left Paris and came alone to the New World and settled in Sorel, a few miles downriver from Montreal. He worked in the shipyards for a year or two then married his young housekeeper, an eighteen-year-old named Lise Beaudette. Lise, my grandmother, had the resigned look of a Quebec girl marked early for a nursing order if marriage couldn't catch her, by accident, first. In twenty years she bore fifteen children, eight of them boys, five of whom survived. The final child, a son, was named Jean-Louis and given at birth to the Church. As was the custom with the last boy, he was sent to the monastery as soon as he could walk, and remained with the brothers for a dozen years, taking his meals and instructions as an apprentice.

It would have been fitting if Boniface Thibidault, then nearly eighty, had earned a fortune in Sorel—but he didn't. Or if a son had survived to pass on his stories—but none were listening. Or if Boniface himself had written something—but he was illiterate. Boniface was cut out for something different. One spring morning in 1912, the man who had seen two child brides through menopause stood in the mud outside his cottage and defied Sorel's first horseless carriage to churn its way through the April muck to his door, and if by the grace of God it did, to try going on while he, an old man, pushed it back downhill. Money was evenly divided on the man and the driver, whom Boniface also defamed for good measure. The driver was later acquitted of manslaughter in Sorel's first fatality and it was never ascertained whether Boniface died of the bumping, the strain, or perhaps the shock of meeting his match. Jean-Louis wasn't there. He left the church a year later by walking out and never looking back. He was my father.

The death of Boniface was in keeping with the life, yet I think of my grandfather as someone special, a character from a well-packed novel who enters once and is never fully forgotten. I think of Flaubert's *Sentimental Education* and the porters who littered the decks of the *Ville-de-Montereau* on the morning of September 15, 1840, when young Frédéric Moreau was about to sail. My grandfather was already eight in 1840, a good age for cabin boys. But while Frédéric was about to meet Arnoux and his grand passion, Boniface was content to pocket a tip and beat it, out of the novel and back into his demimonde.

I have seen one picture of my grandfather, taken on a ferry between Quebec and Levis in 1895. He looks strangely like Sigmund Freud: bearded, straw-hatted, buttoned against the river breezes. It must have been a cold day—the vapour from the nearby horses steams in the background. As a young man he must have been, briefly, extraordinary. I think of him as a face in a Gold Rush shot, the one face that seems both incidental and immortal guarding a claim or watering a horse, the face that seems lifted from the crowd, from history, the face that could be dynastic.

And my father, Jean-Louis Thibidault, who became Gene and T.B. Doe—he too stands out in pictures. A handsome man, a contemporary man (and yet not even a man of this century. His original half brothers back in France would now be 120 years old; he would be, by now, just seventy); a salesman and businessman. I still have many pictures, those my mother gave me. The earliest is of a strong handsome man with very short legs. He is lounging on an old canvas chaise under a maple tree, long before aluminum furniture, long before I was born. A scene north of Montreal, just after they were married. It is an impressive picture, but for the legs, which barely reach the grass. Later he would grow into his shortness, would learn the vanities of the short and never again stretch out casually, like the tall. In another picture I am standing with him on a Florida beach. I am five, he is forty-two. I am already the man I was destined to be; he is still the youth he always was. My mother must have taken the shot—I can tell, for I occupy the centre—and it is one of those embarrassing shots parents often take. I am in my wet transparent underpants and I've just been swimming at Daytona Beach. It is 1946, our first morning in Florida. It isn't a vacation; we've arrived to start again, in the sun. The war is over, the border is open, the old black Packard is parked behind us. I had wanted to swim but had no trunks; my father took me down in my underwear. But in the picture my face is worried, my cupped hands are reaching down to cover myself, but I was late or the picture early—it seems instead that I am pointing to it, a fleshy little spot on my transparent pants. On the back of the picture my father had written: 'Thibidault et fils Daytona—avr/46'.

We'd left Montreal four days before, with snow still grey in the tenements' shadow, the trees black and budless over the dingy winter street. Our destination was a town named Hartley where my father had a friend from Montreal who'd started a lawn furniture factory. My father was to become a travelling salesman for Laverdure's Lawn Laddies, and I was to begin my life as a salesman's son. As reader of back issues, as a collector of cancelled stamps (the inkier the better), as student and teacher of languages.

Thibidault et fils: Thibidault and son. After a week in Hartley I developed worms. My feet bled from itching and scratching. The worms were visible; I could prick them with pins. My mother took me to a clinic where the doctor sprayed my foot with a liquid freeze. Going on, the ice was pleasant, for Florida feet are always hot. Out on the bench I scraped my initials in the frost of my foot. It seemed right to me (before the pain of the thaw began); I was from Up North, the freezing was a friendly gesture for a Florida doctor. My mother held my foot between her hands and told me stories of her childhood, ice-skating for miles on the Battleford River in Saskatchewan, then riding home under fur rugs in a horse-drawn sleigh. Though she was the same age as my father, she was the eldest of six—somewhere between them was a missing generation. The next morning the itching was worse and half a dozen new worms radiated from the ball of my foot. My mother then consulted her old *Canadian Doctor's Home Companion*—my grandfather Blankenship had been a doctor, active for years in curling circles, Anglican missions, and crackpot Toryism—and learned that footworms, etc., were unknown in Canada but sometimes afflicted Canadian travellers in Tropical Regions. Common to all hot climes, the book went on, due to poor sanitation and the unspeakable habits of the non-white peoples, even in the Gulf Coast and Indian Territories of our southern neighbour. No known cure, but lack of attention can be fatal.

My mother called in a neighbour, our first contact with the slovenly woman who lived downstairs. She came up with a bottle of carbolic acid and another of alcohol, and poured the acid over the worms and told me to yell when it got too hot. Then with alcohol she wiped it off. The next morning my foot had peeled and the worms were gone. And I thought, inspecting my peeled, brown foot, that in some small way I had become less northern, less hateful to the kids around me though I still sounded strange and they shouted after me, 'Yankee, Yankee!'

My father was browned and already spoke with a passable Southern accent. When he wasn't on the road with Lawn Laddies he walked around barefoot or in shower clogs. But he never got worms, and he was embarrassed that I had.

Thibidault and son. He was a fisherman and I always fished at his side. Fished for what? I wonder now—he was too short and vain a man to really be a fisherman. He dressed too well, couldn't swim, despised the taste of fish, shunned the cold, the heat, the bugs, the rain. And yet we fished every Sunday, wherever we lived. Canada, Florida, the Middle West, heedless as deer of crossing borders. The tackle box (oily childhood smell) creaked at our feet. The fir-lined shores and pink granite beaches of Ontario gleamed behind us. Every cast became a fresh hope, a trout or *doré* or even a muskie. But we never caught a muskie or a trout, just the snake-like fork-boned pike that we let go by cutting the line when the plug was swallowed deep. And in Florida, with my father in his Harry Truman shirts and sharkskin pants, the warm bait-well sloshing with half-dead shiners, we waited for bass and channel cat in Okeechobee, Kissimmee and a dozen other bug-beclouded lakes. Gar fish, those tropical pike, drifted by the boat. Gators churned in a narrow channel and dragonflies lit on my cane pole tip. And as I grew older and we came back North (but not all the way), I remember our Sundays in Cincinnati, standing shoulder to shoulder with a few hundred others around a clay-banked tub lit with arc lamps. Scummy pay-lakes with a hot dog stand behind, a vision of hell for a Canadian or a Floridian, but we paid and we fished and we never caught a thing. Ten hours every Sunday from Memorial Day to Labor Day, an unquestioning ritual that would see me dress in

my fishing khakis, race out early and buy the Sunday paper
before we left (so I could check the baseball averages—what
a normal kid I might have been!), then pack the tackle box
and portable radio (for the Cincinnati double-header) in the
trunk. Then I would get my father up. He'd have his coffee and
a few cigarettes then shout, 'Mildred, Frankie and I are going
fishing!' She would be upstairs reading or sewing. We were
still living in a duplex; a few months later my parents were
to start their furniture store and we would never fish again.
We walked out, my father and I, nodding to the neighbours (a
few kids, younger than I, asked if they could go, a few young
fathers would squint and ask, 'Not again, Gene?'); and silently
we drove, and later, silently, we fished.

Then came a Sunday just before Labor Day when I was
thirteen and we didn't go fishing. I was dressed for it and the
car was packed as usual, but my father drove to the county
fair instead. Not the Hamilton county fair in Cincinnati—we
drove across the river into Boone County, Kentucky, where
things were once again Southern and shoddy.

I had known from the books and articles my mother was
leaving in the bathroom that I was supposed to be learning
about sex. I'd read the books and figured out the anatomy for
myself; I wondered only how to ask a girl for it and what to do
once I got there. Sex was something like dancing, I supposed,
too intricate and spontaneous for a boy like me. And so we
toured the fairgrounds that morning, saying nothing, reviewing the prize sows and heifers, watching a stock-car race and
miniature rodeo. I could tell from my father's breathing, his
coughing, his attempt to put his arm around my shoulder, that
this was the day he was going to talk to me about sex, the facts
of life, and the thought embarrassed him as much as it did
me. I wanted to tell him to never mind; I didn't need it, it was
something that selfish people did to one another.

He led me to a remote tent far off the fairway. There was
a long male line outside, men with a few boys my age, jok-

ing loudly and smelling bad. My father looked away, silent. So this is the place, I thought, where I'm going to see it, going to learn something good and dirty, something they couldn't put on those Britannica Films and show in school. The sign over the entrance said only: *Princess Hi-Yalla. Shows Continuously.*

There was a smell, over the heat, over the hundred men straining for a place, over the fumes of pigsties and stockyards. It was the smell of furtiveness, rural slaughter and unquenchable famine. The smell of boys' rooms in the high school. The smell of sex on the hoof. The 'Princess' on the runway wore not a stitch, and she was already lathered like a racehorse from her continuous dance. There was no avoiding the bright pink lower lips that she'd painted; no avoiding the shrinking, smiling, puckering, wrinkled labia. 'Kiss, baby?' she called out, and the men went wild. The lips smacked us softly. The Princess was more a dowager, and more black than brown or yellow. She bent forward to watch herself, like a ventriloquist with a dummy. I couldn't turn away as my father had; it seemed less offensive to watch her wide flat breast instead, and to think of her as another native from the *National Geographic*. She asked a guard for a slice of gum, then held it over the first row. 'Who gwina wet it up fo' baby?' And a farmer licked both sides while his friends made appreciative noises, then handed it back. The Princess inserted it slowly, as though it hurt, spreading her legs like the bow-legged rodeo clown I'd seen a few minutes earlier. Her lower mouth chewed, her abdomen heaved, and she doubled forward to watch the progress. 'Blow a bubble!' the farmer called, his friends screamed with laughter. But a row of boys in overalls, my age, stared at the woman and didn't smile. Nothing would amaze them—they were waiting for a bubble. The she cupped her hand underneath and gum came slithering out. 'Who wants this?' she called, holding it high, and men were whistling and throwing other things on the stage: key rings, handkerchiefs, cigarettes. She threw the gum toward us—I remember ducking as it came my way, but someone caught it. 'Now then,' she said, and her voice was as loud as a gospel singer's, 'baby's fixin' to have herself a cigarette.' She walked to the edge of the stage (I could see her moist footprints in the dust), her toes curled over the side. 'Which of you men out there is givin' baby a cig'rette?' Another farmer standing behind his fat adolescent son threw up two cigarettes. The boy, I remember, was in overalls and had the cretinous look of fat boys in overalls: big, sweating, red-cheeked, with eyes like calves' in a roping event. By the time I looked back on stage, the Princess had inserted the cigarette and had thrust baby out over the runway and was asking for matches. She held the match herself. And the cigarette glowed, smoke came out, an ash formed . . .

I heard moaning, long low moans, and I felt the eyes of a dozen farmers leap to the boy in overalls. He was jumping and whimpering and the men were laughing as he tried to dig into his sealed-up pants. Forgetting the buttons at his shoulders, he was holding his crotch as though it burned. He was running in place, moaning, then screaming, 'Daddy!' and I forgot about the Princess. Men cleared a circle around him and began clapping and chanting, 'Whip it out!' and the boy was crying, 'Daddy, I cain't hold it back no more!'

My father grabbed me then by the elbow, and said, 'Well, have you seen enough?' The farm boy had collapsed on the dirt floor, and was twitching on his back as though a live wire were passed through his body. A navy-blue stain that I thought was blood was spreading between his legs. I thought he'd managed to pull his penis off. My father led me out and he was mad at me for something—it was *me* who had brought him there, and his duties as my father—and just as we stepped from the tent I yelled, 'Wait—it's happening to me too.' I wanted to cry with embarrassment for I hadn't felt any urgency before entering the tent. It seemed like a sudden, irresistible need to urinate, something I couldn't hold back. But worse than water; something was ripping at my crotch. My light-coloured fishing khakis would turn brown in water, and the dark stain was already forming.

'Jesus Christ—are you *sick?* That was an old woman—how could *she . . .* how could *you . . .*' He jerked me forward by the elbow. 'Jesus God,' he muttered, pulling me along down the fairway, then letting me go and walking so fast I had to run, both hands trying to cup the mess I had made. Thousands of people passed me, smiling, laughing. 'I don't know about you,' my father said. '*I think there's something wrong with you,*' and it was the worst thing my father could say about me. We were in the car. I was crying in the back seat. 'Don't tell me someone didn't see you—didn't you think of that? Or what if a customer saw *me*—but you didn't think of that either, did you? Here I take you to something I thought you'd like, something any *normal* boy would like, and—'

I'd been afraid to talk. The wetness was drying, a stain remained. 'You know Murray Lieberman?' my father asked a few minutes later.

'The salesman?'

'He has a kid your age and so we were talking—'

'Never mind,' I said.

'Well, what in the name of God is wrong with two fathers getting together, eh? It was supposed to *show* you what it's like, about women, I mean. It's better than any drawing, isn't it? You want books all the time? You want to *read* about it, or do you want to see it? At least now you *know*, so go ahead and read. Tell your mother we were fishing today, okay? And *that*—that was a Coke you spilled, all right?'

And no other talk, man to man, or father to son, ever took place.

I think back to Boniface Thibidault—how would he, *how did* he, show his sons what to do and where to do it? He was a Frenchman, not a North American; he learned it in Paris, not in a monastery as my father had. And I am, partially at least, a Frenchman too. My father should have taken me to a *cocotte*, to his own mistress perhaps, for the initiation, *la déniaisement*. And I, in my own lovemaking, would have forever honoured him. But this is North America and my father, despite everything, was in his silence a Quebec Catholic of the nineteenth century. Sex, despite my dreams of something better, something nobler, still smells of the circus tent, of something raw and murderous. Other kinds of sex, the adjusted, contented, fulfilling sex of school and manual, seems insubstantial, wilfully ignorant of the depths.

At thirteen I was oldest of eighty kids on the block, a thankless distinction, and my parents at fifty had a good twenty years on the next oldest, who, it happened, shared our duplex.

There lived on that street, and I was beginning to notice in that summer before the sideshow at the county fair, several girl brides and one or two maturely youthful wives. The brides, under twenty and with their first or second youngsters, were a sloppy crew who patrolled the street in cut-away shorts and bra-less elasticized halters that had to be pulled up every few steps. They set their hair so tightly in pin curlers that the effect, at a distance, was of the mange. Barefoot they pushed their baby strollers, thighs sloshing as they walked, or sat on porch furniture reading movie magazines and holding tinted plastic baby bottles between their knees. Though they sat in the sun all day they never tanned. They were spreading week by week while their husbands, hard athletic gas-pumpers, played touch football on the street every Sunday.

But there were others; in particular the wife next door, our two floors being mirror images of the other, everything back-to-back but otherwise identical. What was their name? She was a fair woman, about thirty, with hair only lightly bleached and the kind of figure that one first judges slightly too plump until something voluptuous in her, or you, makes you look again and you see that she is merely extraordinary; a full woman who was once a lanky girl. She had three children, two of them girls who favoured the husband, but I can't quite place his name or face. Her name was Annette.

She was French. That had been a point of discussion once. Born in Maine, she would often chat with my father in what French she remembered while her husband played football or read inside. By that time I had forgotten most of my French. And now I remember the husband. His name was Lance— Lance!—and he was dark, square-shouldered, with a severe crewcut that sliced across an ample bald spot. He travelled a lot; I recall him sitting in a lawn chair on summer evenings, reading the paper and drinking a beer till the mosquitoes drove him in.

And that left Annette alone, and Annette had no friends on the block. She gave the impression, justified, of far outdistancing the neighbourhood girls. Perhaps she frightened them, being older and, by comparison, a goddess. She would sit on a lawn chair in the front yard, on those male-less afternoons of toddling children and cranky mothers and was so stunning in a modest sundress that I would stay inside and peek at her through a hole I had cut in the curtains. Delivery trucks, forced to creep through the litter of kids and abandoned toys, lingered longer than they had to, just to look. At thirteen I could stare for hours, unconscious of peeping, unaware, really, of what I wanted or expected to see. It was almost like fishing, with patience and anticipation keeping me rooted.

My parents were at the new property, cleaning it up for a grand opening. I was given three or four dollars a day for food and I'd spend fifty or sixty cents of it on meaty and starchy grease down at the shopping centre. I was getting fat. Every few days I carried a bulging pocketful of wadded bills down to the bank and cashed them for a ten or twenty. And the bills would accumulate in my wallet. I was too young to open an account without my parents' finding out; the question was how to spend it. After a couple of weeks I'd go downtown and spend astounding sums, for a child, on stamps.

While I was in the shopping centre. I began stealing magazines from the drugstore. The scandal mags, the Hollywood
parties, the early *Playboy* and its imitators—I stole because I
was too good to be seen buying them. I placed them between
the pages of the *Sporting News*, which I also read cover to
cover, then dropped a wadded five-dollar bill in the newspaper honour box, raced home, and feasted. Never one for risks,
I burned the residue or threw them out in a neighbour's garbage can, my conscience clear for a month's more stealing and
secret reading. There was never a time in my life when sex
had been so palpable; when the very sight of any girl vaguely
developed or any woman up to forty and still in trim could
make my breath come short, make my crotch tingle under my
baggy pants. In the supermarket, when young mothers dipped
low to pick a carton of Cokes from the bottom shelf, I dipped
with them. When the counter girl at the drugstore plunged
her dipper in the ice cream tub, I hung over the counter to
catch a glimpse of her lacy bra; when the neighbour women
hung out their clothes, I would take the stairs two at a time
to watch from above. When those young wives hooked their
thumbs under the knitted elastic halters and gave an upward
tug, I let out a little whimper. How close it was to madness;
how many other fat thirteen- and fourteen-year-olds, with a
drop more violence, provocation, self-pity or whatever, would
plunge a knife sixty times into those bellies, just to run their
fingers inside the shorts and peel the halter back, allowing the
breasts to ooze aside? And especially living next to Annette
whose figure made flimsy styles seem indecent and modest dresses maddening. Her body possessed the clothes too
greedily, sucked the material to her flesh. She was the woman,
I now realize, that Dostoyevsky and Kazantzakis and even
Faulkner knew; a Grushenka or the young village widow, a
dormant body that kindled violence.

The duplexes were mirror images with only the staircases
and bathrooms adjoining. In the summer with Annette at

home, her children out playing or taking a nap, her husband away, or just at work, she took many baths. From wherever I sat in our duplex watching television or reading my magazines, I could hear the drop of the drain plug in her bathroom, the splash of water rushing in, the quick expansion of the hot water pipes.

I could imagine the rest, exquisitely. First testing the water with her fingers, then drying the finger on her shorts and then letting them drop. Testing the water again before unhooking the bra in a careless sweep and with another swipe, peeling off her panties. The thought of Annette naked, a foot away, made the walls seem paper-thin, made the tiles grow warm. Ear against the tiles I could hear the waves she made as she settled back, the squeaking of her heels on the bottom of the tub as she straightened her legs, the wringing of a facecloth, plunk of soap as it dropped. The scene was as vivid, with my eyes closed and my hot ear on the warm tile, as murders on old radio shows. I thought of the childhood comic character who could shrink himself with magic sand; how for me that had always translated itself into watching the Hollywood starlets from their bathroom heating registers. But Annette was better or at least as good, and so available. If only there were a way, a shaft for midgets. It wasn't right to house strangers so intimately without providing a way to spy. I looked down to the tile floor—a crack? Something a bobby pin could be twisted in, just a modest, modest opening? And I saw the pipes under the sink, two slim swan-necks, one for hot, one for cold, that cut jaggedly through the tile wall—they had to connect! Then on my hands and knees I scraped away the plaster that held the chromium collar around the pipe. As I had hoped, the hole was a good quarter-inch wider than the pipes and all that blocked a straight-on view of the other bathroom was the collars on Annette's pipes. It would be nothing to punch my way through, slide the rings down, and lie on the tile floor in the comfort of my own bathroom and watch it all; Annette bathing! Ring level was below the tub, but given the distance the angle might correct itself. But detection would be unbearable; if caught I'd commit suicide. She was already out of the bath (but there'll be other days, I thought). She took ten-minute baths (how much more could a man bear?), the water was draining and now she was running the lavatory faucet which seemed just over my head. How long before she took another bath? It would seem, now that I had a plan, as long as the wait between issues of my favourite magazines.

I rested on the floor under the sink until Annette left her bathroom. Then I walked down to the shopping centre and had a Coke to steady myself. I bought a nail file. When I got back Annette was sitting in her yard, wearing a striped housedress and looking, as usual, fresh from a bath. I said hello and she smiled very kindly. Then I turned my door handle and cried, 'Oh, no!'

'What is it, Frankie?' she asked, getting up from her chair.

'I left my key inside.'

'Shall I call your father?'

'No,' I said, 'I think I can get in through the window. But could I use your bathroom first?'

'Of course.'

I checked upstairs for kids. Then I locked myself inside and with the new file, scraped away the plaster and pulled one collar down. Careful as always, aware that I would make a good murderer or a good detective, I cleaned up the plaster crumbs. I'd forgotten to leave our own bathroom light on, but it seemed that I could see all the way through. Time would tell. *Take a bath*, I willed her, as I flushed the toilet. It reminded me of fishing as a child, trying to influence the fish to bite. It's very hot, sticky, just right for a nice cool bath ... My own flesh was stippled, I shivered as I stepped outside and saw her again. She'd soon be *mine*—something to do for the rest of the summer! My throat was so tense I couldn't even thank her. I climbed inside through the living-room window that I had left open.

I took the stairs two at a time, stretched myself out under the sink to admire the job. I'd forgotten to leave *her* light on, but I thought I could see the white of her tub in the darkened bathroom, and even an empty tub was enough to sustain me. How obvious was the pipe and collar? It suddenly seemed blatant, that she would enter the bathroom, undress, sit in the tub, turn to the wall, and scream. Do a peeper's eyes shine too brightly? In school I'd often been able to stare a kid into turning around—it was now an unwanted gift.

You're getting warm again, Annette. Very very hot. You want another bath. You're getting up from the chair, coming inside, up the stairs . . . I kept on for hours till it was dark. I heard the kids taking baths and saw nothing. The white of the bathtub was another skin of plaster, no telling how thick. I'd been cheated.

Another day. There had to be another link—I had faith that the builders of duplexes were men who provided, out of guilt, certain amenities. Fans were in the ceiling. Windows opened on the opposite sides, the heating ducts were useless without a metal drill. Only the medicine cabinets were left. They had to be back-to-back. I opened ours, found the four corner screws, undid them, took out the medicines quietly (even my old Florida carbolic acid), then eased the chest from its plaster nest. It worked. I was facing the metal backing of Annette's medicine chest. The fit was tight and I could never take a chance of tampering with hers—what if I gave it a nudge when Lance was shaving and the whole thing came crashing down, revealing me leaning over my sink in the hole where our medicine chest had been?

The used-razor slot. A little slot in the middle. I popped the paper coating with the nail file. I darkened our own bathroom. If Annette opened her chest, I'd see her. But would she open it with her clothes off? Was she tall enough to make it count? How many hours would I have to stand there, stretched over the sink, waiting, and could I, every day, put the chest back up and take it down without some loud disaster? What if my father came home to shave, unexpectedly?

I waited all afternoon and all evening and when eight o'clock came I ended the vigil and put the chest back up. With a desire so urgent, there *had* to be a way of penetrating an inch and a half of tile and plaster. When she was in her bath I felt I could have devoured the walls between us. Anything *heard* so clearly had to yield to vision—that was another natural law— just as anything dreamt had to become real, eventually.

I became a baby-sitter; the oldest kid on the block, quiet and responsible. I watched television in nearly every duplex on the street, ignored the whimpers, filled bottles, and my pockets bulged with more unneeded cash. I poked around the young parents' bedrooms and medicine cabinets, only half repelled by the clutter and unfamiliar odours, the stickiness, the grey- ness of young married life in a Midwest suburb. I found boxes of prophylactics in top drawers and learned to put one on and to walk around with it on until the lubrication stuck to my underwear. Sex books and nudist magazines showing pubic hair were stuffed in nightstands, and in one or two homes I found piles of home-made snaps of the young wife when she'd been slim and high-school young, sitting naked in the sun, in a woods somewhere. She'd been posed in dozens of ways, legs wide apart, fingers on her pubic hair, tongue curled between her teeth. Others of her, and of a neighbour woman, on the same living-room sofa that I was sitting on: fatter now, her breasts resting on a roll of fat around her middle, her thighs shadowed where the skin had grown soft, *This is the girl I see every day*, pushing that carriage, looking like a fat girl at a high school hangout. Those bigger girls in my school, in bright blue sweaters, earrings, black curly hair, bad skin, black corduroy jackets, smoking. They become like this; they *are* like this.

These were the weeks in August, when my mother was leaving the articles around. Soon my father would take me to the county fair. There were no answers to the questions I asked, holding those snapshots, looking again (by daylight) at the wife (in ragged shorts and elastic halter) who had consented to the pictures. They were like murder victims, the photos were like police shots in the scandal magazines, the women looked like mistresses of bandits. There was no place in the world for the life I wanted, for the pure woman I would someday, somehow, marry.

I baby-sat for Annette and Lance, then for Annette alone, and I worked again on the lavatory scheme, the used-razor slot, and discovered the slight deficiencies in the architecture that had thrown my calculations off. I could see from their bathroom into ours much better than I could ever see into theirs. Annette kept a neat house and life with her, even I could appreciate, must have been a joy of lust and efficiency, in surroundings as clean and attractive as a *Playboy* studio.

One evening she came over when my parents were working, to ask me to baby-sit for a couple of hours. Lance wasn't in. Her children were never a problem and though it was a week night and school had begun, I agreed. She left me a slice of Lance's birthday cake, and begged me to go to sleep in case she was late.

An hour later, after some reading, I used her bathroom, innocently. If only I lived here, with Annette over there! I opened her medicine chest to learn some more about her: a few interesting pills 'for pain', Tampax Super (naturally, I thought), gauze and adhesive, something for piles (for him, I hoped). And then I heard a noise from our bathroom; I heard our light snap on. My parents must have come home early.

I knew from a cough that it wasn't my mother. The Thibidault medicine chest was opened. I peered through the razor slot and saw young fingers among our bottles, blond hair and a tanned forehead: Annette. She picked out a jar, then closed the door. I fell to the floor and put my eye against the pipes. Bare golden legs. Then our light went out.

I looked into our bathroom for the next few seconds then ran to Annette's front bedroom where the youngest girl slept, and pressed over her crib to look out the window. She was just stepping out and walking slowly to the station wagon of Thibidault Furniture, which had been parked. She got in the far side and the car immediately, silently, backed away, with just its parking lights on ...

And that was all. For some reason, perhaps the shame of my complicity, I never asked my father why he had come home or why Annette had been in our bathroom. I didn't have to—I'd gotten a glimpse of Annette, which was all I could handle anyway. I didn't understand the rest. *Thibidault et fils*, fishing again.

Jean-Louis Thibidault, twice divorced, is dead; buried in Venice, Florida. Bridge of Sighs Cemetery. I even asked his widow if I could have him removed to Sorel, Quebec. She didn't mind, but the *prêtre-vicaire* of my father's old parish turned me down. When my father was born, Venice, Florida, was five miles offshore and fifty feet underwater. The thought of him buried there tortures my soul.

There was another Sunday in Florida. A hurricane was a hundred miles offshore and due to strike Fort Lauderdale within the next six hours. We drove from our house down Las Olas to the beach (Fort Lauderdale was still an inland city then), and parked half a mile away, safe from the paint-blasting sand. We could hear the breakers under the shriek of the wind, shaking the wooden bridge we walked on. Then we watched them crash, brown with weeds and suspended sand. And we could see them miles offshore, rolling in forty feet high and flashing their foam like icebergs. A few men in swimming suits and woollen sweaters were standing in the crater pools, pulling out the deep-sea fish that had been stunned by the trip and waves. Other fish littered the beach, their bellies blasted by the change in pressure. My mother's face was raw and her glasses webbed with salt. She went back to the car on her own. My father and I sat on the bench for another hour and I could see behind his crusty sunglasses. His eyes were moist and dancing, his hair stiff and matted. We sat on the bench until we were soaked and the municipal guards rounded us up. Then they barricaded the boulevards and we went back to the car, the best day of fishing we'd ever had, and we walked hand in hand for the last time, talking excitedly, dodging coconuts, power lines, and shattered glass, feeling brave and united in the face of the storm. My father and me. What a day it was, what a once-in-a-lifetime day it was.

THE SALESMAN'S SON
GROWS OLDER

CAMPHOR BERRIES popped underfoot on a night as hot and close as a faucet of sweat. My mother and I were walking from the movies. It was late for me but since my father was on the road selling furniture, she had taken me out. She watched the sidewalk for roaches darting to the gutters. They popped like the berries underfoot. I was sleepy and my mother restless, like women whose men are often gone. She hadn't eaten supper, hadn't read the paper, couldn't stand the radio, and finally she'd suggested the movies. Inside, she'd paced behind the glass while I watched a Margaret O'Brien movie. The theatre was air-cooled, which meant the hot air was kept circulating; even so the outdoors had been formidable under a moon that burned hotly. The apartment would be crushing. She'd been a week without a letter.

I think now of the privileges of the salesman's son, as much as the moving from town to town, the postcards and long-distance calls; staying up late, keeping my mother company, being her confidant, behaving even at eight a good ten years older. And always wondering with her where my father was. Somewhere in his territory, anywhere from Raleigh to Shreveport. Another privilege of the salesman's son was knowing the cities and the routes between them, knowing the miles and predicting how long any drive would take. As a child, I'd wanted to be a Greyhound driver.

The smell of a summer night in Florida is so strong that twenty years later on a snowy night in Canada I can still feel it. Lustrous tropical nights, full of roaches and rats and lizards, with lightning bugs and whippoorwills prickling the dark and silence. I wanted to walk past our apartment house to the crater of peat bogs just beyond, so that the sweat on my arms could at least evaporate.

'Maybe Daddy'll be home tonight,' I said, playing the game of the salesman's son. There was a cream-coloured sedan in our driveway, with a white top that made it look like my father's convertible. Then the light went on inside and the door opened and a drowsy young patrolman with his tie loosened and his Stetson and clipboard shuffled our way.

'Ma'am, are you the party in the upper apartment? I mean are you Mrs Thee ... is this here your name, ma'am?'

'Thibidault,' she said. 'T. B. Doe if you wish.'

'I wonder then can we go inside a spell?'

'What is it?'

'Let's just go inside so's we can set a spell.'

A long climb up the back staircase, my mother breathing deeply, long *ah-h-h's* and I took the key from her to let us in. I threw open the windows and turned on the lights. The patrolman tried to have my mother sit. She knew what was coming, like a miner's wife at a sudden whistle. She went to the kitchen and opened a Coke for me and poured iced tea for the young patrolman, then came back and sat where he told her to.

'You're here to tell me my husband is dead. I've felt it all night.' Her head was nodding, a way of commanding agreement. 'I'll be all right.'

She wouldn't be, I knew. She'd need me.

'I didn't say that, ma'am,' and for the first time his eyes brightened. 'No, ma'am, he isn't dead. There was a pretty bad smash-up up in Georgia about three days ago and he was unconscious till this morning. The report we got is he was on the critical list but they done took him off. He's in serious condition.'

'How serious is serious?' I asked.

'What?'

She was still nodding. 'You needn't worry. You can go if you wish—you've been very considerate.'

'Can I fetch you something? Is there anybody you want me to call? Lots of times the effect of distressing news don't sink in till later and it's kindly useful having somebody around.'

'Where did you say he was?'

He rustled the papers on his clipboard, happy to oblige. 'Georgia, ma'am, Valdosta—that's about two hundred mile north. This here isn't the official report but it says the accident happened about midnight last Wednesday smack in the middle of Valdosta. Mr Thee . . . Mr *Doe*, was alone in the car and they reckon he must have fell asleep. The car . . . well, there ain't much left of the car.'

'Did he hurt anyone else?'

'No, ma'am. Least it don't say so here.' He grinned. 'Looks like it was just him.'

She was angry.

'Why wasn't I notified earlier?' she asked.

'That's kindly irregular, ma'am. I don't know why.'

She nodded. She hadn't stopped nodding.

'We can call up to Valdosta and get you a place to stay. And we'll keep an eye on this place while you're gone. *Anything you want*, Mrs Doe, that's what I'm aimin' to say.'

She was silent for a long time as though she were going to say, *Would you repeat it please, I don't think I heard it right;* and there was even a smile on her face, not a happy one, a smile that says *life is long and many things happen that we can't control and can't change and can't bring back.* 'You've been very helpful. Please go.'

If my father were dead it meant we would move. Back to Canada perhaps. Or west to the mountains, north to cities. And if my father lived, that too would change our lives, somehow. My mother stayed in the living room after the officer left and I watched her from the crack of my door, drinking hot coffee and smoking more than she ever had before. A few minutes later came a knock on the front door and she hurried to open up. Two neighbour women whose children I knew but rarely played with stepped inside and poured themselves iced tea, then waited to learn what had brought the police to the Yankee lady's door.

My mother said there'd been an accident.

'I knowed it was that,' said Mrs Wade, 'and him such a fine-looking gentleman, too. I seen the po-lice settin' in your drive all evenin'-long and I said to my Grady that poor woman and her li'l boy is in for bad news when they get back from the pitchershow—or wherever you was at—so I called Miz Davis here and told her what I seen and wouldn't you know she said we best fix up a li'l basket of fruit—that's kindly like a custom with us here, since I knowed you was from outastate. What I brung ain't much just some navels and tangerines but I reckon it's somethin' to suck on when the times is bad.'

'I reckon,' said Mrs Davis, 'your mister was hurt pretty bad.'

'Yes.'

'They told you where he's at, I reckon.'

'Yes, they did.'

'Miz Davis and me, we thought if you was going to see him you'd need somebody to look after your li'l boy. I don't want you to go on worryin' your head over that at all. Her and her Billy got all the room he's fixin' to need.'

'That's very kind.'

I was out of bed now and back at the crack of my opened door. I'd never seen my mother talk to any neighbour women. I'd never been more aware of how different she looked and sounded. And of all the exciting possibilities opened up by my father's accident and possible death, staying back in an unpainted shanty full of loud kids was the least attractive. I began wishing my father wasn't hurt. And then I realized that the neighbour women with their sympathy and fruit had broken my mother's resistance. She would cry as soon as they left and I would have to pretend to be asleep, or else go out and comfort her, bring her tea and listen to her: be a salesman's son.

Audrey Davis was plump and straight-haired; Billy was gaunt, red-cheeked, and almost handsome. The children came in a phalanx of older girls who'd already run off, then a second wave ranging from the nearly pubescent down to infancy. At eight, I fell in the middle of the second pack whose leader was a ten-year-old named Carrie, with earrings and painted nails.

They ate their meals fried or boiled. Twenty years later I can still taste their warm, sweet tea, the fat chunks of pork, the chickpeas and okra. I can still smell the outhouse and hear the hiss of a million maggots flashing silver down the hole. The Davis crap was the fairest yellow. The food? Disease?

But what I really remember, and remember with such vividness that even now I wince, is this: sleeping one night on the living-room rug—it was red and worn down to its backing—I developed a cough. After some rustling in the back Miz Davis appeared at the door, clad in a robe tied once at the waist. One white tubular breast had worked free. The nipple was poised like an ornament at its tip. It was the first time I'd ever seen a breast.

Even as I was watching it, she set to work with a mixture for the cough. By the time I noticed the liquid and the spoon, she was adding sugar. I opened wide, anxious to impress, and she thrust in the spoon, far enough to make me gag, and pulled my head back by the hair. She kept the spoon inside until I felt I was drowning in the gritty mixture of sugar and kerosene. I knew if I was dying there was one thing I wanted to do; I brought my open hand against the palm-numbing softness of her breast, then, for an instant ran my fingertips over the hard, dry nipple and shafts of prickly hair. She acted as though nothing had happened and I looked innocent as though nothing had been intended. Then she took out the spoon.

After Audrey Davis's breast and kerosene my excreta turned a runny yellow. The night after the breast I was hiding in the sawgrass, bitten by mosquitoes and betrayed by fireflies, playing kick-the-can. The bladder-burning tension was excruciating for a slow, chubby boy in a running game, scurrying under the Davis jeep, under the pilings of the house, into the edges of the peat. My breath, cupped in the palm of my sweating hand, echoed like a deep-sea diver's as Carrie Davis beat the brush looking for me. Chigger bites, mosquito welts, burned and itched. I wanted to scream, to lift the house on my shoulders, to send the can in a spiraling arch sixty yards downfield, splitting imaginary goal posts and freeing Carrie's prisoners, but I knew—knew—that even if I snuck away undetected, even with a ten-foot lead on Carrie or anyone else, I'd lose the dash to the can. Even if I got there first I'd kick too early and catch it with my glancing heel and the can would lean and roll and be replaced before I could hide again. I knew finally that it would be my fate, if caught, to be searching for kids in a twenty-foot circle for the rest of the night, or until the Davis kids got tired of running and kicking the can from under me. Better, then, to huddle deep in the pilings, deeper even than the hounds would venture till I could smell the muck, the seepage from the outhouse, the undried spillage from the kitchen slops. No one would find me. I wouldn't be caught nor would I ever kick the goddam can. Time after time, game after game, after the kids were caught they'd have to call, 'Frankie, Frankie, come in free,' and it would be exasperation, not admiration, that tinted Carrie's voice.

My mother came back four days later and set about selling all the clothes and furniture that anyone wanted. There were brief discussions with the neighbour women who shook their heads as she spoke. Finally I drew the conclusion that my father was dead, though I didn't ask. I tried out this new profound distinction on Carrie Davis and was treated for a day or two with a deference, a near sympathy ('Don't you do that, Billy Joe, can't you see his daddy's dead?') that I'd been seeking all along and probably ever since.

But how was it, in the week or so that it took her to pack and sell off everything, that I never asked her what exactly had happened in Valdosta? Her mood had been grim and businesslike, the mood a salesman's son learns not to tamper with. I adjusted instead to the news that we were leaving Florida and would be returning to her family in Saskatchewan.

Saskatchewan! No neighbour had ever heard of it. 'Where in the world's that at?' my teacher asked when I requested the transfer slip. When I said Canada, she asked what state. The Davis kids had never heard of Canada.

One book that had always travelled with us was my mother's atlas. She had used it in school before the Great War—a phrase she still used—a comprehensive British edition that smeared the world in Imperial reds and pinks so that my vision of the earth had been distorted by Edwardian lenses. Safe pink swaths cut the rift of Africa, the belly of Asia, and lighted like a rash over Oceania and the Caribbean. And of course red dominated and overwhelmed poor North America. The raw, pink, bulging brow of the continent was Canada, the largest and reddest blob of Britishness in the flat projection of the world. Saskatchewan alone could hold half a dozen Texases and the undivided yellow of the desert southwest called the 'Indian Territories.'

It was the smell of the book that had attracted me and led me, even before I could read, to a tracing of the Ottoman Empire, Austro-Hungary, and a dozen princely states. That had been my mother's childhood world and it became mine too—cool, confident, and British—and now it seems to me, that all the disruptions in my life and in Mildred Blankenship's have merely been a settling of the old borders, an insurrection of the cool gazetteer with its sultanates, Boer lands, Pondichérys, and Port Arthurs. All in the frontispiece, with its two-tone map of the world in red and grey, emblazoned, WE HOLD A GREATER EMPIRE THAN HAS BEEN.

We rode for a week without a break. Too excited for sleep, I crouched against the railings behind the driver's seat with a road map in my hand, crossing off towns and county lines, then the borders of states. We'd left in April; we were closing in on winter again. The drivers urged me to talk, so they wouldn't fall asleep. 'Watch for a burnt-out gas station over the next rise,' they'd say, 'three men got killed there . . . down there a new Stucky's is going up . . . right at that guardrail is where eight people got killed in a head-on crash . . .' And on and on, identifying every town before it came, pacing themselves like milers, 'Must be 3:15,' they'd say, passing an all-night diner and tooting a horn, knowing every night clerk in every small-town hotel where the bundles of morning papers were thrown off. It had seemed miraculous, then, to master a five-state route as though it were an elevator ride in a three-story department store. Chattanooga to Indianapolis, four times a week. And on we went: Chicago, Rock Island, Ottumwa, Des Moines, Omaha, Sioux Falls, Pierre, and Butte, where my uncle John Blankenship was on hand to take us into Canada.

I watched my uncle for signs of foreignness. His clothes were shaggy, the car was English, and there were British flags in the corners of the windshield. But he looked like a fleshed-out Billy Davis from Oshacola County, Florida, with the same scraped cheeks, high colouring and sky-blue eyes, the reddened hands with flaking knuckles, stubby fingers with stiff, black hair. John's accent was as strange as the Davises'. The voice was deep, the patterns rapid, and each word emerged as hard and clear as cubes from a freezer.

The border town had broad dirt streets. A few of the cars parked along the elevated sidewalks were high, boxy, pre-war models I couldn't identify. The cigarette signs, the first thing a boy notices, were foreign.

'How does it feel, Franklin? The air any different?'

'It might be, sir.'

'You don't have to say 'sir' to me. Uncle John will do. You're in your own country now—just look at the land, will you? Look at the grain elevators—that's where our money is, in the land. Don't look for it in that chrome-plated junk. You can *see* the soil, can't you?'

The land was flat, about like Florida, the road straight and narrow and the next town's grain elevator already visible. It was late April and the snow had receded from the road-bed. Bald spots, black and glistening, were appearing in the fields under a cold bright sun. Three weeks ago, when my father was alive, the thermometer had hit ninety-five degrees.

'Of course you can. Grade A Saskatchewan hard, the finest in the world.'

The finest what? I wondered.

'Far as the eye can see. That's prosperity, Mildred. And we haven't touched anything yet—we're going to be a rich province, Mildred. We have the largest potash reserves in the world. You'll have no trouble getting work, believe me.'

'And how's Valerie?' my mother asked. 'And the children?'

Around such questions I slowly unwound. My uncle was no bus driver and Saskatchewan offered nothing for a map-primed child. I was a British subject with a Deep South accent, riding in a cold car with a strong new uncle. So many things to be ashamed of—my accent, my tan, my chubbiness. I spoke half as fast as my uncle and couldn't speed up.

'Ever been to a bonspiel, Franklin?'

'No, sir, I don't think so.'

'You'll come out tonight, then. Your Aunt Valerie is skip.'

I decided not to say another word. Not until I understood what the Canadians were talking about

Uncle John Blankenship, that tedious man, and his wife and three children made room for us in Saskatoon. A cold spring gave way, in May, to a dry, burning heat, the kind that blazed across my forehead and shrunk the skin under my eyes and over my nose. But I didn't sweat. It wasn't like Florida heat that reached up groggily from the ground as well as from above, steaming the trouser cuffs while threatening sunstroke. The Blankenships had a farm out of town and Jack, my oldest cousin, ran a trapline and kept a .22 rifle in the loft of the barn. During the summer I spent hot afternoons firing at gophers as they popped from their holes. Fat boy with a gun, squinting over the wheat through July and August, the combine harvesting the beaten rows, months after believing my father dead, and happy. As happy as I've ever been.

I looked for help from my cousins, for cousins are the unborn brothers and sisters of the only child. But they were slightly older, more capable, and spoke strangely. They were never alone, never drank Cokes which were bad for the teeth and stomach (demonstrated for me by leaving a piece of metal in a cup of Coke), never seemed to tire of work and fellowship. They were up at five, worked hard till seven, ate hot meaty-mushy breakfasts, then raced back to work and came to lunch red in the brow, basted in sweat, yet not smelling bad at all. They drank pasteurized milk with flecks of cream and even when they rested in the early afternoon they'd sit outside with a motor in their lap and a kerosene-soaked rag to clean it. I would join them, but with an ancient issue of *Collier's* or *National Geographic* taken from the pillars of bundled magazines in the attic, and all afternoon I'd sit in the shade with my busy cousins, reading about 'New Hope for Ancient Anatolia' or 'Brave Finland Carries On.' I was given an article from an old *Maclean's* about my grandfather, Morley Blankenship, a wheat pool president who had petitioned thirty thankless years for left-hand driving in Canada.

What about those cousins who'd never ceased working, who'd held night jobs through college, then married and gone to law school or whatever? *My* cousins, *my* unborn brothers with full Blankenship and McLeod blood and their medical or legal practices in Vancouver and Regina and their spiky, balding blond heads and their political organizing. Is that all their work and muscles and fresh air could bring them? Is that what I would have been if we'd stayed in Saskatoon, a bloody Blankenship with crinkles and crow's-feet at twenty-five?

And what if we'd stayed anywhere? If we'd never left Montreal, I'd have been educated in both my languages instead of Florida English. Or if we'd never left the South I'd have emerged a man of breeding, liberal in the traditions of Duke University with tastes for Augustan authors and breeding falcons, for quoting Tocqueville and Henry James, a wearer of three-piece suits, a user of straight razors. What calamity made me a reader of back issues, defunct atlases, and foreign grammars? The loss, the loss! To leave Montreal for places like Georgia and Florida; to leave Florida for Saskatchewan; to leave the prairies for places like Cincinnati and Pittsburgh and, finally, to stumble back to Montreal a middle-class American from a broken home, after years of pointless suffering had promised so much.

My son sleeps so soundly. Over his bed, five licence plates are hung, the last four from Quebec, the first from Wisconsin. Five years ago, when he was six months old, we left to take a bad job in Montreal, where I was born but had never visited. My parents had brought me to the US when I was six months old. Canada was at war, America was neutral. America meant opportunity, freedom; Montreal meant ghettos, and insults. And so, loving our children, we murder them. Following the sun, the dollars, the peace-of-mind, we blind ourselves. Better to be a professor's son than a salesman's son—better a thousand times, I think—better to ski than to feed the mordant hounds, better to swim at a summer cottage than debase yourself in the septic mud. But what do these licence plates mean? Endurance? Exile, cunning? Where will we all wind up, and how?

Because I couldn't master the five-cent nib that all the Saskatoon kids had to use in school, and because the teacher wouldn't accept my very neat Florida pencil writing, a compromise was reached that allowed me to write in ballpoint. I was now a third-grader.

The fanciest ballpoint pen on sale in Saskatoon featured the head and enormous black hat of Hopalong Cassidy. The face was baby-pink with blue spots for eyes and white ones for teeth and sideburns. It was, naturally, an unbalanced thing that hemorrhaged purplely on the page. The ink was viscous and slow-drying and tended to accumulate in the cross-roads of every loop. Nevertheless, it was a handsome pen and the envy of my classmates, all of whom scratched their way Scottishly across the page.

One day in early October I had been sucking lightly on Hoppy's hat as I thought of the sum I was trying to add. I didn't know, but my mouth was purpling with a stream of ink and the blue saliva was trickling on my shirt. My fingers had carried it to my cheeks and eyes, over my forehead and up my nostrils. I noticed nothing. But suddenly the teacher gasped and started running toward me, and two students leaped from their desk to grab me.

I was thrown to the floor and when I opened my mouth to shout, the surrounding girls screamed. Then the teacher was upon me, cramming her fingers down my throat, two fingers when the first didn't help, and she pumped my head from the back with her other hand. 'Stand back, give him air—can't you see he's choking? Somebody get the nurse!'

'Is he dying?'

'What's all that stuff?'

What was her name—that second woman who had crammed something down my throat? I could see her perfectly. For fifty years she had been pale and prim and ever so respectable but I remember her as a hairy-nostrilled and badly dentured banshee with fingers poisoned by furtive tobacco. I remember reaching out to paw her face to make her stop this impulsive assault on an innocent American, when suddenly I saw it: the blue rubble on my shirt, the bright sticky gobs of blue on the backs of my hands, the blue tint my eyes picked up off my cheeks. *I've been shot*, I thought. Blood is blue when you're really hurt. Then one of the boys let go of my arm and I was dropped to one elbow. 'That's *ink*, Miss Carstairs. That's not blood or anything—that's *ink*. He was sucking his pen.'

She finally looked closely at me, her eyes narrowing with reproach and disappointment. Her fingers fluttered in my throat. *Canadians!* I'd wanted to scream, *what do you want?* You throw me on the floor because of my accent and you pump your fingers in my throat fit to choke me then worst of all you start laughing when you find I'm not dying. *But I am.* Stop it. You stupid Yank with your stupid pen and the stupid cowboy hat on top and you sucking it like a baby. I rolled to my knees and coughed and retched out the clots of ink, then bulled my way through the rows of curious girls in their flannel jumpers who were making 'ugh' sounds, and, head down because I didn't want anyone else to catch me and administer first aid, I dashed the two blocks to the Blankenship house in what, coatless, seemed like zero cold.

I let myself in the kitchen, quietly, to wash before I was seen. In the living room, a voice was straining, almost shouting. It wasn't my mother and I thought for an instant it might be Miss Carstairs who somehow had beaten me home. I moved closer.

'John says you're a bloody fool and I couldn't agree more!'

Aunt Valerie held a letter and she was snapping the envelope in my mother's face. 'A bloody little fool, and that's not all—'

'I see I shouldn't have shown it to you.'

'He's not worth it—here,' she threw the letter in my mother's lap, 'don't tell me that was the first time. *She was there*— doesn't that mean anything to you? *That woman* was there the whole time. How much do you think he cares for your feelings? Does he know how you felt when you got there—'

'No one will ever know.'

'Well, someone better make *you* know. I don't think you're competent. I think he's got a spell on you if you want my opinion. It's like a poison—'

'I'm not minimizing it,' my mother broke in, and though she was sitting and didn't seem angry, her voice had risen and without straining it was blotting out my aunt's. 'I'm not minimizing it. I know she wasn't the first and she might not be the last—'

'That's even more—'

'Will you let me finish? I didn't marry a Blankenship. You can tell my brother that I remember very well all the advice he gave me and my answer to all of you is that it's my life and I'm responsible and you can all ...'

'Go ... to ... hell—is that it?'

'In so many words. Exactly. You can all go to hell.'

Go to hell: I remember the way she said it, for she never said it again, not in my presence. More permission than a command: *yes, you may go to hell*. But it lifted Aunt Valerie out of her shoes.

'Now I *know*!' she cried. 'I *see* it.'

'See what?'

'What he's turned you into. One letter from him saying he wants you and you're running back—like a ... like an I-don't-know-what! Only some things a woman can guess even when she doesn't want to. I don't deny he's a handsome devil. They all are. But to *degrade* yourself, really—'

Then my mother stood and looked at the door, straight at me, whom she must have seen. Her face was a jumble of frowns and smiles. I moved back toward the kitchen. 'This will be our address,' I heard her say. 'Mrs Mildred Thibidault.'

She didn't come to the kitchen. She went upstairs, and Aunt Valerie stayed in the living room. I pictured her crying or cursing, throwing the porcelain off the mantel. I felt sorry for her; I understood her better than my mother. But minutes later she turned on the vacuum cleaner. And I returned quietly to the kitchen then slammed the outside door loudly and shouted, 'I'm home, Aunt Valerie!' And then, knowing the role if not the words, I went upstairs to find out when we were leaving and where we would be going

*   *   *

This long afternoon and evening, I closed my eyes and heard sounds of my childhood: the skipping rope slaps a dusty street in a warm Southern twilight. The bats are out, the lightning bugs, the whippoorwills. I am the boy on yellow grass patting a hound, feeling him tremble under my touch. Slap, slap, a girl strains forward with her nose and shoulders, lets the rope slap, slap, slap, as she catches the rhythm before jumping in. The girls speed it up—*hot pepper* it's called—and they begin a song, something insulting about Negroes. The anonymous hound lays his head on my knee. Gnats encrust his eyes. *Poor dog*, I say. His breath is bad, his ears are frayed from fights, his eyes are moist and pink and tropical ...

All day the slap, slap. The rope in a dusty yard, a little pit between the girls who turn it. As I walked today in another climate, now a man, I heard boots skipping on a wet city pavement, a girl running with her lover, a girl in a maxi-coat on a Montreal street. *Tschip-tschip*: I'd been listening for it, boots on sand over a layer of ice. A taxi waited at the corner, its wipers thrashing as the engine throbbed. And tonight, over the shallow breathing of my son, an aluminum shovel strikes the concrete, under new snow.

What can I make of this, I ask myself, staring now at the licence plates on the wall. Five years ago in Wisconsin on a snowy evening like this, with our boy just a bundle in the middle of his crib, I looked out our bedroom window. Snow had been falling all that day, all evening too, and had just begun letting up. We were renting a corner house that year; my first teaching job. I was twenty-four and feeling important. I was political that year of the teach-in. I'd spoken out the day before and been abused by name on a local TV channel. A known agitator. Six inches of new snow had fallen. An hour later a policeman came to our door and issued a summons and twenty-dollar fine for keeping an uncleared walk.

America, I'd thought then. A friend called; he'd gotten a ticket too. Harassment—did I want to fight it? I said I'd think about it, but I knew suddenly that I didn't care.

Watching the police car stop at the corner and one policeman get out, kick his feet on our steps then hold his finger on the bell a full thirty seconds, I'd thought of other places we could be, of taking the option my parents had accidentally left me. Nothing principled, nothing heroic, nothing even defiant. And so my son is skiing and learning French and someday he'll ask me why I made him do it, and he'll exercise the option we've accidentally left him . . . *slap-slap*, the dusty rope. Patrolmen on our steps, the shovel scraping a snowy walk.

I'm still a young man, but many things have gone for good.

THE FABULOUS
EDDIE BREWSTER

ETIENNE was my father's only brother, old enough to have enlisted in the Canadian army in 1915 when my father was only six. After the war, Etienne had stayed in France as an interpreter for the Americans. Finally he married, fathered an intemperate New World brood of children, and in the thirties dropped from family correspondence, after notifying my aunt Gervaise that he had been elected mayor of his village. During those same years, my father drifted off the Broussard family farm, near Sorel, to a hardware store in Montreal. In 1938 he married my mother, *une Anglaise* from Regina. Eye trouble harboured him in Montreal when the new war broke out, and precipitated my arrival a few months after Dunkirk. When the war ended, my father took us into the States, where, he surmised, a fortune waited. He had relatives all over New England—Gervaise and Josephine were living with their husbands in Vermont—and none of them was breaking even, but my father easily explained their lack of success. 'They're afraid,' he said, 'afraid to leave Quebec.' Just *habitants* by his standards, whose children would be raised on beans and black bread for Sunday breakfast. My father wasn't afraid; he'd learned good English and sensed the future flow of money was southward, far southward. And so we ended in Hartley, a north-central Florida town of five thousand crackers, where he started selling jalousie windows and doors. We waited several months for a break while my father bronzed in God's own sun, caught his fill of bass, and cultivated a drawl around his *canadien* twang. Then we heard from Etienne.

Louis, mon cher, mon seul frère: Forgive me, my dear brother, for all these years of silence. All was well until the war took it away. Thinking of you all these years, believe me. I was the mayor and they put me in prison. My Verneuil-le-chétif is no more, just some buildings . . . everything is taken from me. My boys, fine boys Louis, only two left and they fight in Indochine. My girls gone from me, two in the Church, God keep them. Louis, help me, whatever you can send—I will not beg but as your only brother, I ask for help. The food is not so good in this camp, but with money I can buy little things on the black market. . . . Louis, if I could only see you now, my boy, my dear, dear boy. Bless you, Louis, your own brother Etienne.

Immediately, my father cabled two hundred dollars. A few weeks later came a second letter blessing us, thanking us, and asking if it were possible for him to return to America and maybe find work in the States? Could we perhaps sponsor him until he could get a start? He included a snap taken next to a prison shed. He wore prison greys and stood Chaplin-fashion, with hands at his side, feet out, a look both forlorn and astonished in his eyes. The picture did it; thirty years of estrangement instantly healed. My father condemned his own good health, his youth, our relative comfort, then decided to bring his brother over.

'Not to live here,' said my mother. 'Not with Frankie needing his own room—'

'He needs rest, Mildred. After a while, he gets fattened up, rested, I'll find him work.'

'What could he do, Lou? We don't know a soul who would hire an old refugee—no matter what he's been. He just wouldn't be happy.'

But Etienne's letters came more frequently: twice a week. He was in a DP camp outside Paris. 'Everyone but French here,' he wrote, 'with every day the Russians and the Germans and the British identifying refugees and taking them back—if they want to go or not. Good food costs money like hell. For myself I buy nothing, but there are others here, from Verneuil. Chocolate for the old women, tobacco for the old men, shoes for the kids. I am still their mayor, *non?*'

Finally my mother relented and the government granted permission for my father to bring Etienne over. Etienne in the DP camp had collected nearly five hundred dollars in three months, wiping out our first year's savings in the States. 'Either forget him, Lou, or bring him over,' said my mother. 'God knows it's a rotten choice.'

'Maybe we could afford a hundred a month. I could write him.'

'Send him a hundred and he'll squawk. But I don't like getting drained long distance. If he's taking our money, I want him under my nose.'

'Mildred—he's suffered. We can't imagine how he's suffered. Those Germans—they're not human.'

'Well, maybe suffering's made him hard,' said my mother. 'And how do we know what they imprisoned him for, eh?' Suspicion was instinctive with my mother, but that suspicion extended finally to herself. 'Oh, Lou, don't just listen to me. He's your brother, if you think you should bring him over, then bring him. One look at this place and he'll head back to Paris anyway, if he has any sense.'

'And I don't know him at all,' my father muttered. 'That's what makes it bad. Why did he come to me?'

But it was decided. My father wrote his sisters in Vermont, and somehow they persuaded their husbands to share Etienne's passage three ways. They all met their brother in New York, in February 1947. Down in Hartley, my mother transformed my toy- and map-strewn room into a study, suitable for a refugee mayor who had suffered but was accustomed to finer things. I slept the next year on the living-room sofa.

Hartley in 1947 was yet undiscovered by the prophesied boom. Inland towns in the north of Florida had no special interest in the tourist trade, being citrus regions intent on keeping the land in local, unreconstructed hands. It was small-town America with a Southern warp: proper and churchly, superstitious and segregated. As the only outsider in the school, I was a vulnerable freak and not allowed to forget it; as the only Yankees in town (the term outraged my mother—she remembered overturning Yankee cars in 1914 when the States had ignored their higher duties), we were treated cordially by the weekly *Citrus-Advocate* and Welcome Wagon lady, but suspiciously by the neighbours and businessmen. Once the Klan warned us to move after an interview with my mother had been aired on the radio ('. . . well, I think certain social changes are desirable and inevitable, yes . . .'). The night of the Watermelon Festival, the Klan had staged an unmasked parade down Dixie Highway with the unhooded mayor and sheriff leading the way.

Etienne was much heavier than the prison snap prepared us for. He had bought a sale-priced summer suit in New York, so all traces of his displacement had been left in port. He was silver-haired, very short, and classically fat, with the hard unencumbering fat of middle-aged Latins, even polar Canadian ones. Though he looked much older than my father, who was trim and dark-haired, the resemblance was arresting, and one was somehow certain they were brothers, not father and son.

'So—your lovely wife!' he cried, taking my mother in his bulging, tattooed arms. 'Louis tells me this was your idea, bringing an old man over. Bless you, bless you. You've saved my life!' He lifted her, pivoting her on his belly, then kissed her loudly as she settled down. She was three inches taller.

'This is Frankie,' said my father, urging me forward. I held out my hand.

'Kid,' he announced, taking my hand in both of his, 'it's good to see you. I'm your uncle Etienne and I've come around the world to see you.'

'You're home now, Etienne,' said my father.

'I feel it, Lou. I sure as hell feel it.' He carried in two belted suitcases—scuffed and greasy, plastered with stamps and permits—then showered while we met in the kitchen.

'Some DP!' said my mother. Her cheek was still red where Etienne had kissed her.

'He surprised me too, Mildred. But don't go by his English—he learned it all in the army, so it's pretty rough. But he's proud of it. He doesn't even want to speak French any more. Says he wants to be accepted by you and the town. He doesn't even want to hear it.'

'Why, for heaven's sake? He's the first Frenchman I've ever met ashamed of French.'

'Well, he's not a normal Frenchman.'

'I'm watching him,' said my mother. 'A special Frenchman doesn't have to be a typical American.'

'What do you want? He suffered *some*, but he wasn't tortured. I asked him that and he got offended. He asked me what kind of prisoner I thought he was. His family got scattered, but I don't think any got killed. His boys are fighting now in Indo-China. He was an important man and now he has nothing left.'

'And what about his wife? Or did he have one?'

'He didn't say anything. I guess she might have died, or maybe they're divorced.'

'Thank God for that,' said my mother. 'But what does he expect from us? He thinks it was me who brought him over.'

I'll tell him it was because we couldn't afford to keep him in France.'

My father traced a pattern on the oilcloth. 'That reminds me—he wants *you* to decide a proper allowance for him.'

'He what?'

'Mildred—he's a grown man. He doesn't want to beg, but he wants some freedom in town. Little things. He came over with nothing. He thinks I'm too generous, so you're supposed to decide.'

'Five dollars a week.'

'Don't be cheap, Mildred. Ten at least. Even so, he'll be running short. He needs shoes, shirts, a razor, a bathrobe—things to be respectable around the house.'

'You give him ten and all you're going to see for supper is this fatback and black-eyed peas, and that's a promise. Take your pick. Just settle it before you go back on the road again, because I want everything to go smoothly with Etienne. I don't want him begging.'

'It'll be settled,' my father promised.

Uncle Etienne at first spent his days inside in front of the fan, listening to the news reports and reading the morning paper from Tampa which he walked downtown to get. While my father was on the road selling the jalousie windows, Uncle Etienne would tell us tales of their childhood in Sorel: of inhuman poverty and his fatherliness towards Ti-Louis. God, he'd had some times, though, just after WWI, and it was clear to see why he had remained in Europe. His favourite story concerned the day the Americans, occupying a post next to the Canadians, had called for an interpreter. Young Broussard had scampered over, and for two weeks had been assigned to a young officer named Eisenhower. 'That s.o.b. couldn't make a move without me,' Etienne recalled. 'What a man he was! I could have sent him anywhere—imagine—me a twenty-year-old kid. And did we get along! We were buddies, Ike and me.

He wanted me with him when we hit Paris, believe me, but we got separated. Remind me to show you some letters from Ike. I always *knew* he was headed for the top. Always knew it. And the crazy joker couldn't even crap without word from me, and that's the God's own truth....'

While my father was away, it had been customary for my mother and me to eat lightly: a salad and iced tea with a dish of ice cream after—all if the icebox were working. But with Etienne at the table, such informality was disallowed. First, there had to be bread, crisped in the oven, then meat, gradually potatoes, and—due to his stomach ailments—they had to be baked. He would help with the shopping too, picking up steaks and chicken after scrupulous comparing. The apartment grew hotter with the oven on (Hartley ovens went unlighted from April to October), and my mother's patience grew shorter. She refused to cook to his specifications any more, and he astonished her by not complaining.

'Right!' he said. 'One hundred per cent right. Why should you cook when you've got a genuine French chef in the house? I'll cook. That's a bargain, eh, a real French chef for nothing?'

Small towns in central Florida, however, supply few of the staples of *haute cuisine*. Lamb was unheard of; similarly, all the more delicate vegetables. Hardiness was all a Florida cook demanded of her greens, that like paper towels they not disintegrate from oversubmersion. The new meals concocted by Etienne were no better-tasting, but the failures were more interesting: okra *parmesan*, a bouillabaisse of large-mouth bass, turnip-heart salad. I retired to Cokes and grilled-cheese sandwiches, and my mother tried bits of the main course, but concentrated on the salads. Etienne kept cooking for himself, undaunted by our disinterest and proud of his indispensability. When my father was home for the weekends, he ate enthusiastically in the steaming spicy kitchen.

Aside from the dinner hour, Etienne was now rarely home. It was a custom, he quickly discovered, for the town's older citizens to leave their respective dwellings very early, before the sun sucked the town to dust, and seek the public benches by the courthouse or under the commercial awnings along the Dixie Highway. By eight o'clock he would finish his tea and corn flakes at home and step out in his beige Panama with the tricolour *boutonnière*. If I happened to pass him during the day as I bicycled to the Lake Oshacola Park in search of shade and a Coke, or to the air-conditioned drugstore to check the new comics, I'd wave, but he rarely waved back. His circle of cronies was wide, no matter where he sat: the retired locals at the courthouse, or the wretched Yankees on Dixie Highway who had shunned St. Petersburg and Winter Park, or heard tales of Miami Beach, and had finally selected—at not much saving and very little comfort—the grove of cabins on swampy Lake Oshacola. He'd then return late in the afternoon with his bundle of vegetables, baked goods, and meats, shopped for in the Parisian fashion at separate stores. He arrived in time for the news, the ugly news of Communist riots, and he would curse in French. After iced tea, he'd calm down. The local news and Fred Peachum's hillbilly music came on, and we turned it off.

'How was your day, Etienne?' my mother would ask.

'Nice, nice day. Talked to friends. Nice town—you really should know more people, Mildred. I mean it. Very nice people.'

'Don't tell me about the people, Etienne. You had bad people in your village—we have them here. The majority.'

'Naw, Mildred. I mean it. You don't take an interest is your trouble. Louie's too. He won't get ahead working for other people.'

My mother agreed, but never said so. Though my father was making more selling the jalousie windows and doors in Florida than he had selling screws in Montreal, Florida had not been the gold mine he'd hoped for. I too missed the snow, hockey, French (which my mother barely spoke and Etienne refused to), and was uncomfortable in the heat. I'd forget to tap out my shoes for scorpions, I contracted foot worms, my allergies were stimulated, sand seeped in every place, and my mother's treasured Irish lace got mildewed. My father, however, was still hopeful. He greedily sought the sun, grew brown and striking, and felt at least that he had planted himself in fortune's path and had only to stay put and success would stumble across him.

But Etienne, we soon learned, had not been idle on those long afternoons. His cronies at the courthouse, or along the Dixie Highway, had a little power, a little influence, or at least helpful bits of information. One weekend, when my father had just returned from a lucrative venture into new territory—Mobile and New Orleans—Etienne mentioned that if *he'd* just made a thousand dollars, he'd know how to invest it.

'Property, Lou. Any town worth living in is worth buying up. Nobody advertises what's up for sale. If you got friends and if you're on the ball, you know what's up. Pay the taxes and it's yours. No one knows about it, so the mayor and his friends snap it right up. How do you think he owns this town? Smart man, the mayor.'

'What could I buy with a thousand dollars, assuming I wanted to invest it?' asked my father.

'Ah—that's the hitch, Lou. You couldn't buy. They wouldn't let you. It's exclusive, who they let buy. They don't know you.'

'They know you, eh?' asked my mother.

'That's right. I'm not up there for nothing. If I had the money, I'd form a partnership with you. Land or business.'

'What's to stop me going down tomorrow and buying up one of those places?' my father persisted. He was smiling, but dead serious, a gambler.

'They'd dump something on you that was half in the lake, Lou. The deedskeeper is the mayor's son-in-law. Fine boy named Stanley.'

'Typically American,' snapped my mother.

'You got to keep in touch,' said Etienne. 'Small town, after all. Naturally I'm telling you first, Lou, but I know you're not a rich man. Some of these others—the retired ones out along Dixie Highway waiting to die—they're rich. And they're dying to make a little more. There's a lot of them in town.'

'Watch out for your visa, Etienne,' said my mother. 'There's nothing in it about investing while you're here.'

'I'm not investing. I'm just advising. It's their money—or yours. I'd just have a job and maybe with a job they'd give me a visa. Maybe then old Ike would write them for me. I got to think of my future. My family—two boys getting shot at in Indo-China, that's no life for a boy, they get shot, crippled for life. Better I find them a place, maybe get them started. I got talents, Mildred, Lou, I may be bragging, but I got talents.' He took our plates to the sink, ran the water, and sprinkled some soap. 'Then my wife working like a slave in Paris,' he added.

'Your wife? What's this about a wife?' cried my mother.

'Sure I got a wife. Twenty-eight years married. What do you think? Her name's Arlette.'

Now my father joined in. 'How come you never told me about her?'

'Did you ever ask, Louie?'

'I thought maybe—the war.'

'Would I be here then?' he charged. 'Do I act like my wife is dead? She's working, that's all. A seamstress, like she was thirty years ago.'

'Well,' sighed my mother, 'you take the cake.'

'She was afraid you wouldn't bring us both over, or me alone if you knew I was leaving her back temporarily. She said, 'Go get well with your little brother in America and, maybe if you can, send me a little something back.' That's what I do with what you give me every week, send little things back she can't get in Paris. You think I spend it all on myself, maybe? I'm an old man, I don't need anything. Just a little safety, a little money so when I'm old they don't carry me off to the poorhouse. I've seen everything wiped out, Louie; I've got a few years left and I'm going to use them.'

'You still should have told us, Etienne,' said my father. 'We would have been happy to bring her over.'

'She's my responsibility,' Etienne insisted. 'Things will work out better this way. You think over what I said about your thousand dollars. In the morning, one way or another, I'm going into business.'

'Etienne—what an American you are,' my mother said.

My parents didn't invest with Etienne, and for several days the subject was dropped. The mention of Arlette had a softening effect on my mother, and the stories Etienne now told us of France included Arlette and were a little more suitable. Soon he received her letters at home instead of the post-office box he had been renting.

Then one night he asked, 'What do you think of my cooking?'

'It's fine,' said my mother. 'It reminds me of Montreal, when Lou and I used to eat out.'

This soured him; one thing he resented was those remote origins.

'Better than Montreal, Mildred. Etienne's really good,' said my father.

'What I meant was, would you pay for it?'

'We *are* paying for it,' my mother reminded.

'No—I mean at a restaurant, say. If I had all the right vegetables and the right meats, do you think people would pay for it?'

'I don't think so,' she said. 'There no money here, let alone taste. This is the worst food on the continent, why?'

'I know a man. Met him last week, comes from New Orleans, named Lamelin. Wife is dead and his boy died in the war—'

'How sad—'

'—and he had this restaurant in New Orleans, see, then he sold it when his boy was killed, and he came here when his wife up and died, so he's got money and he's itching to get back in the restaurant business. His wife was the cook, so he doesn't know much about that end. I do. He's the business type, see— has contacts all over, and lots of money.'

'What are you thinking about, Etienne?' asked my father.

'A French restaurant here,' he announced. 'Outside Hartley, a few miles, near the main highway. More like a night club, really, with drinks, good food, entertainment.'

'You're crazy,' my mother said. 'You know what they go for here? Hillbilly stuff.'

'I'll give them something better.'

'They don't want it. You could bring Chevalier and they wouldn't pay.'

'I'll educate them. We start with Cubans since they're cheap and maybe move up to French. Believe me, I know lots of kids would come over. That camp I was in—full of them. Singers, dancers, pretty girls, kids with talent—I saw them.'

'Lou—you tell him,' my mother pleaded. 'They don't *like* Cubans any better than they like Canadians. Look—all you can get on the radio is Havana; it even drowns out their hillbilly junk and they hate it. Etienne, as a businessman you'd fail utterly.'

'I'm not a businessman,' he reminded.

'But she's right, Etienne. You can't take any crazy chances here. Things are too expensive.'

Etienne slammed the table. 'So what do you know, eh? A window dresser? I don't see you making a big name for yourself. So, they want doors and windows and you supply them. Good, fine, the best of luck. But how bad does anyone want doors and windows? Not so bad they can't wait. Not so bad they got to have you and nobody else. But with me—I know what they need. Even if *they* don't know it yet, I know. French food, but not too French. Why waste it? Deluxe treatment. Beautiful girls—can you give them that? Maybe a chance to make a little money. I give them something just a little better than they got, but not so much better they feel bad they can't ever have it. And the entertainment—leave that to me. I'm not selling Havana music, I'm giving them Havana girls. So I'll ask you one more time—you want to back me up? Lou—what do you say?'

'Etienne, can't you see?' My father towered over him, speechless. 'Christ, it's just crazy.'

'I always thought the Germans were pigheaded, but you take the cake, Etienne, believe me,' added my mother.

'*Eh bien*,' he grumbled, 'no more—all right? No hard feelings, eh? You don't trust me with your money. That hurts me—once five hundred people trusted me with their lives—their lives, Louie—and I didn't let them down. No one was killed in my town. I can't wait now, Lou—I'm taking back everything I had and I'm taking it here. Let me stay here another month, that's all, and I'll move out. No more trouble from me.'

'Etienne, you stay with us. We insist,' said my father.

My uncle started to his room. 'No thanks, Lou—I wouldn't feel right any more. I'll be keeping late hours anyway. It's best like this.' He came out in a few minutes, dressed in the best he had.

'Just remember you had a chance,' he said. 'And now I'm off to the radio station. They're interviewing me, so you listen, eh?'

'Radio!' exclaimed my father.

'On the local news. The *Fred Peachum Show*. You be listening.'

Peachum was Hartley's own hillbilly, whose show cut into the network's *Swing Time from New York* each afternoon for two hours of jamboree music; the Clewiston Cowboys and some added talent from the pine flats of northern Florida. The local news was a reading of the police blotter including all traffic tickets, hospital records, court decisions, school awards, and crop reports, interspersed with tales, interviews, songs, weather, ads, and sports. We'd never listened to it in its entirety, except for the time my mother had irritated the Klan with her predictions. We waited that evening an agonizing hour for Etienne.

'Got a gentleman dropped in to say a few words here,' drawled Fred Peachum, 'and I reckon y'all gonna find him right interestin'. Come right in here and pull up a crate, Eddie. This here is ... ah ... Eddie Brewster I reckon is how you'd say it, and he come to Hartley out of Paris, France. Tell the folks listenin' in how long you been in town, Eddie.'

'Oh, jus' a mont',' said my uncle in a new accent, mellow as a *boulevardier*.

'Let's see here, accordin' to my information you got a brother in town permanent, don't you?'

'Yes, my brodder Louie. He sells door and window built special for Florida. He brought me over from France.'

'What's happenin' over there now, Eddie?'

'Ooh—terrible. So much is destroyed. Everything was beautiful before, now not so beautiful. I think sometimes there is nothing left. In my village, just the church.'

'Kindly like a miracle, ain't it?'

'Yes, many time I tell myself—a miracle.'

'That fake!' my mother cried. 'A miracle—'

'*Chut*,' hissed my father. 'He's a little nervous is all.'

'And how you makin' out in Hartley, Eddie? I reckon it's right peaceful, after the war and all....'

'Oh, this town is very nice. Very nice—nothing in the world I like more than to settle down right here. And this town is ready for big things, you believe me. There's gonna be smart people come down here, once everything gets back to normal. My brodder Louie—he's a smart boy—he come all the way down from Canada. There gonna be others, you see.'

'Like you say, Eddie, we got a nice li'l biddy town here. I'd kindly hate to see it change. But that's the reason you come by today, ain't it, Eddie, to tell the folks how you wanta change Hartley?'

'That is right. I want to give Hartley something for the way it has welcomed me. I think the best thing I can do is give the town something that is personal from me—a French restaurant, with entertainment. Everything cooked personal by me, and the entertainment is direct from Tampa, maybe even Cuba. My partner and me are looking for property now that is close to Hartley but near Gainesville too. It would be my little way of thanking Hartley and all the people.'

My mother was up now, and yelling above Fred Peachum's long reminiscence about Cajun soup in New Orleans. 'The humility of the man! Lou, he's crazy, he's out of his mind—he's going to show his undying gratitude by opening a restaurant, eh? He's already announced it. Do you realize we're responsible for him? What if he signs loans for ten thousand dollars? They can't touch him—they'll come to his sponsor, that's who. Lou—you've got to stop him. I thought he was sly, but I never realized he was incompetent. He's a sick old man, Lou, and we never realized it.' My father bowed his head, and nodded.

Etienne was talking again. 'We're just not free to give any more information now. My partner and me hope to announce everything next week. I appreciate letting me talk, Mr Peachum. You wait till you taste *my* turtle soup.'

'All right! Eddie Brewster, folks, come in to give you the dope on a gen-u-ine French restaurant right here in Hartley. You check your paper for the big news next week, hear?'

Our phone rang and rang in the hours we waited for his return. When he finally arrived, he brought with him Maurice Lamelin, lately of New Orleans, and a portfolio of documents. They had made a purchase and were business partners.

Lamelin looked as though he had suffered a double loss in the past year; he looked also, as Etienne had said, greedy to rebuild his fortune. He was a sallow little man, taller than Etienne, but in no way powerful. Technicalities were his specialty: he spoke with authority about vegetable distributorships, freezer consignments, licences, and fire laws. The building had been Etienne's contribution; through contacts at City Hall, he had heard of the old Sportsman's Club—a stucco structure with a tile roof, plazas, and a courtyard—going for back taxes and an unspecified transfer fee. The building was a local landmark, hastily erected in the twenties for a boom that never came. It stood a few miles outside Hartley on the main road to Gainesville. Landing the Sportsman's Club, my father agreed, was a shrewd move; it was the only possible site for a night club in all north-central Florida.

'We've got a new name for it, the Rustique,' said Etienne. 'I figured anyone can translate that. Come on out, we'll show it to you tonight.'

We drove out in Lamelin's new convertible. Cadillacs, the Cajun apologized, were back-ordered for months, so he had settled for a Chrysler at the same price.

At night, by flashlight and matches, the old structure with its faded mosaics, cracked beams, and resident lizards scurrying ahead, seemed like a Hollywood imitation of everything it, in fact was: Fitzgerald and Gloria Swanson, darkies mixing drinks, mannered but desperate poker games in the smaller rooms. Upstairs were rooms suitable for overnight accommodations. Lamelin planned to renovate them as soon as the kitchen equipment was installed. Already, we learned, the freezers and special gas ovens were on their way. Local merchants were providing furniture, thanks to the mayor's endorsement of Etienne's credit.

'How deep is the mayor's interest, Etienne?' asked my mother.

'He's nothing. Like a stockholder you might say. He has no power in this operation.'

'I'm the proprietor,' said Maurice Lamelin, 'and Broussard's my chef.'

'And impresario,' added my uncle.

'We'll be set up in two months,' continued Lamelin. 'We're gonna be the biggest thing between Jacksonville and Tampa.'

'Well, you'd better put some screens up,' said my mother. 'These mosquitoes are murder.'

The next day we returned, at Etienne's bidding, 'for a better picture.' Things had improved indeed; trucks unloaded in the marshy lot, neon experts measured the gables, power saws whined, and new timber was stacked outside for panelling the guest rooms and subdividing the ballroom. Lamelin prodded the workers: a tiny man, expertly profane. Etienne took us inside, showed us the kitchen area, the private dining rooms, the main room and stage, and the smaller rooms—for gambling.

'But you can't have gambling here!' said my father.

'How do you expect a place like this to make money, then, eh? You said yourself these people won't pay for food alone. So, let them try to win some money—what's the harm?'

'*Mon Dieu*—it's against the law, that's what!'

'Louie, Louie, what's the matter, you a kid? It's all clear with the law. All you need is a special licence so the county can collect some money too.'

'You know it's under the table, Etienne,' my mother charged. 'Don't try telling me it's legal.'

'All I'm saying is in Oshacola County it's as legal as selling doors and windows. It's called a Special Revenue Permit and we bought it and it's good till December 31.'

'Etienne—you listen to me,' my mother cried, 'so far as I'm concerned, it's illegal and what you plan is wrong, all wrong. I don't want you around the apartment, understand? If you need money for a hotel room, I'll give it to you personally. But don't come around, because I don't want to expose Frankie to any more of your double dealings.'

Etienne stepped back and held out his hands, palms up. 'Louie, what is she talking about? Tell her I'm doing this to bring Arlette over. You think I like taking chances at my age? You think I like the Cajun even? Mildred—you're my family. I feel like a grandpa to Frankie. Would I do anything to—to corrupt a kid? Louie, Louie, tell her, you can't just throw me out on the street like a dog, not after what I've been through, Lou?'

My father grabbed my mother's arm and pulled her to him. 'Why did you have to say such a thing, eh? Can't I have some peace as few times as I'm home?' Mother looked straight on, silent, her lips Scottishly tight. My father turned to his brother. 'Look, why didn't you tell me about the gambling, eh? Hell, if I had known *that* ... how do I know I'm not responsible for any bills you run up, maybe any crimes too? I sponsored you, but I sure as hell didn't think you'd start up a casino, not here. I'm trying to build something too, ever think of that? I'm new here too, I got a lot to lose too, only what I might lose is all in the future. So—'

'Lou, look at it like this. Let me stay till the restaurant's going good. After that I'll be working so hard I'll just stay in one of the rooms upstairs. Arlette will come over anyway. I don't want to sponge off you. Hey—where's she going?'

My mother yanked me with her to the car. We watched them argue awhile, and saw the screening go up; and the first tubes of neon. My father handed Etienne some money, then came back to the car, and without a word we drove home. 'Don't you ever butt into my personal business again,' he threatened as he let her out. 'Now I'm taking him into Tampa. Just don't wait up for me.'

That night we had salad and iced tea again, then we saw a movie: Margaret O'Brien. 'Your uncle Etienne is a bad man, Frankie, understand? I want you to try to forget him.'

The grand opening of the Rustique was publicized in all the area papers, and from most rural telephone poles in Oshacola County. For entertainment, Etienne had hired a flamenco guitarist and his troupe he'd found rolling cigar leaf in Tampa. Though Etienne rarely showed up in our apartment, my father often went out in the evenings before the opening to deliver mail or have a drink. He'd watch the floor show rehearse, and come back with tales.

'I saw girls, Mildred, nigger girls that bend over backwards so far that they go under a pole just *that* high off the ground.' He held his hand at shin level. 'Etienne was driving down to Orlando and he saw these niggers out in the celery field doing this crazy dance, see—'

'Don't call them niggers, please, Lou.'

'So he watched awhile, then he went over and offered them fifteen dollars to do it at the Rustique. They almost fell over him, they were so glad, being Bahamian and all. So he figures he's got the best entertainment in Florida outside of Miami Beach, and it cost him about fifty dollars total. After that, he found some Greek girls in Ybor City that belly dance—'

'Good Lord, Lou, they'll close him down. He can't run a place like that in the middle of nowhere. What'll people say? The Klan—they won't stand for that.'

'What do you mean? They know all about it.'

We were presented tickets for the opening night; Etienne figured a thousand tickets offering concessions on food and drinks had been won in contests or given away all over north-central Florida. Hard-drinking veterans now dominated the fraternities at the university, and they flocked up from Gainesville for the opening to sample all the attractions, especially Etienne's 'Normandy Knockout', a reported favourite of General Eisenhower's. Fred Peachum was the MC and many personalities (the mayor and Stanley the deedskeeper plus the sheriff) were interviewed by the table-hopping hillbilly. The whole operation was a huge success; even the guest rooms were rented by strung-out celebrators. My father came home high and happy but the next day cursed my mother for not letting him invest.

It wasn't long before the Rustique was returning an extravagant profit on weekends and breaking even most week nights. Etienne scoured the region for talent. The gambling—

and even sportier—activities in the rented rooms were the proud secrets of the town. When the next winter came the tourists took an inland route, thanks to enticing posters as far north as Augusta and Macon. They stopped in Hartley nearly as often as Daytona. The whole town prospered, as the *Citrus-Advocate* pointed out, and new motels were frantically erected. There was talk of a northern citrus processor coming to Hartley with a new scheme for freezing orange juice. The representative came, and after several conferences which Etienne joined, the processor was politely refused and advised to go further south. Oshacola County, it was felt, could make its money from Yankees without the mixed blessing of their industries.

After the winter season, the business slowed down somewhat, enabling Etienne to return to France for a visit to bring back Arlette. With Etienne gone, Lamelin closed the Rustique for two weeks to allow for some remodelling and general expansion. Already, rooms were being reserved for next winter by Yankees who would never get further south, and a golf course was contemplated, along with an improvement of the docks.

Etienne and Arlette had been back in Hartley a week before they visited us. Arlette was my mother's height and, like my mother, pale in her features. She was *alsacienne*, her hair blond-grey, and her eyes the palest blue. Had she been in Hartley, one felt, Etienne would never have started the Rustique. Her English, contrary to Etienne's report, was perfectly Gallic: proper in every respect, but barely understandable. In her presence Etienne sat quietly and humbly, while she answered my mother's questions. They were staying in the bridal suite at the club, but she would try to find a small home on the lake—maybe even on the ocean, thirty miles away.

'We cannot thank you enough, Etienne and I,' she said. 'Life was without hope for us in France. Etienne couldn't work, and I could only support myself—' she looked down at her fingers, those of an overworked, perhaps unpractised seamstress. 'It seems all that is behind us. Thank God.'

'Have you seen the town?' my mother asked.

'I have. It is very small, is it not? We lived in a village much smaller, of course, before the war, but very different, too. My husband was the mayor. But after the war things changed horribly. *They had no right,*' she cried suddenly, 'Etienne did nothing wrong. He saved many lives.'

'*Assez,*' he commanded. 'It's all forgotten.'

'How many would be killed? How many of our friends would they have killed if Etienne had not urged co-operation? One need not approve, in order to co-operate.'

'I saved many lives. I know it,' said Etienne. He stood, and placed his hands on Arlette's shoulders. She took his hands in hers, smiling, but not looking back. 'It's all in the past. I've proved I was right. One year in America and I'm one of the richest men in the county and they'll let me stay.' He looked over at us and said to my father, 'Who needs them, the little men who judge you after the danger's past? They're the bad ones— the little men who were not in sight but suddenly become the judges. France is full of them.'

Etienne and Arlette were silent, defensive, waiting for a response. Finally my mother said, 'I imagine you'll be very happy here, Madame. You'll find no one to judge you here.'

Ten years later, Etienne was elected mayor of Hartley. We were already North, predictably, a year before the authentic boom began. We sat out Etienne's salad days from dingy suburbs of Cleveland, Toronto, and Buffalo. We never heard from Etienne directly, but were sent clippings from the *Citrus-Advocate* (now a daily), third-hand from Gervaise. The winter my father introduced portable heaters for drive-in movies in Buffalo, his brother was able to bring over Gaspar and Gérard from Indo-China. A few months later, Gaspar married a local girl, a wealthy one, and at the moment he is sheriff of Oshacola

County. Arlette, a woman I barely remember but for her fingers, died before their beach home was completed. Etienne has retired alone to a sumptuous home by the golf course on Lake Oshacola—a course he invited Ike himself to open. My father goes down each winter for fishing and golf with his brother; everything again is cordial.

After their divorce several years ago, my mother went back to Canada and now teaches history in Regina.

AT THE LAKE

ALL THOSE LAKES up north with unsavoury names—Lac
Têtard, Lac Bibitte, Lac Sangsue (who would buy a cabin
to share with tadpoles, biting flies and leeches?)—take
their names from a surveyor's map and not from their pests.
Long ribbony Sangsue stretches out at the flanks of two steep
ridges six miles long and a quarter-mile wide. When I bought
the property on Lac Bibitte, Serge explained to me, 'Sure,
bibitte means bug. But look at the lake, round like a ball on top
and shaped like an egg down here. It's not Lac des Bibittes, you
know . . .' Têtard, on the other side of Mont Tremblant, has a
triangular head and a broad branching river that drains its tail
like larval legs. Anyway, the names might discourage some
people. Closer to the city the developers have been at work and
the homely names have gone through their initial manorial
transformations: Lac des Mulets, Lac Quenouille and Lac des
Castors into Lac Gagnon, Lac Ouellette and Lac Sauvé; thence
into their death agonies as 'Lac Paradis: 45-minutes-on-4-lane-
open-all-year fully winterized landscaped-in-your-choice-of
trees-ranchettes-from $10,000.' I have the diminishing satis-
faction that a place is worth twice as much after three years of
unimprovement and decided deterioration.

There are families on the lake who've blasted crannies into the soaring granite cliffs a hundred feet above the water: Germans who thread their way like mountain goats balancing a weekend's beer on their heads, who dive like Acapulco professionals from a board on their porch into its unsounded depth below. I have watched them in summers past from the wide porch of our cabin on the low, marshy shore across the way—fat men of fifty in bikini briefs walking to the board, their laughter and joking clear, if foreign, from a mile away. Beer can in hand, laughter clapping over the water, he raises his arms in a diving motion but releases his empty can instead and sends it spiralling to the water. Then he crumples from the board—it's serious and competent he is—straightening in time and cutting the water like a missile.

We used to go up for the middle of every week from early July when the black flies died until the end of September when autumn was well advanced. I'm an academic and like the blessed commuter who lives in the city and drives to a suburban job, I found myself always moving against the crowds. We abandoned the lake on weekends to the waterskiers and speedboaters, when gasoline generators and long horn blasts waked us from the dream of a northern retreat. I preferred Wednesdays on the lake. August Wednesdays when it might be eighty-five degrees in the city and bone-warming seventy at the lake after a swim, when the sun burned with a rare intensity through the clear, polished air. Erika and I would lie on towels on the dock, dangling our fingers for bluegills to nibble, peering down the pilings to the sandy bottom where the sluggish mountain carp sifted through the mosses clinging to the wood.

I spent those summers envying the Europeans and a few Canadians who've blasted the granite and erected the A-frame bunkers on girders sunk in into the bare rockface (their twin flag standards flying down at dock level, Red, Black, and Gold of the *Bundesrepublik,* and the adopted Maple Leaf), and I envied Serge, who hadn't missed a weekend at the cabin in fifteen years. Every weekend he has added cubits to his lands, his sewage, his dockery, his cabin, his soul; whereas I—a younger man more aware a thousand times of ravages, impurity and decay—have found the battle, or challenge, overwhelming. I ask myself what did I really want: electric blankets, pavement, a stove and fridge? And I say no, of course not; I wanted my son to grow up with nature. Skier, swimmer, fisherman, even hunter; I wanted him to grow up unflawed. I wanted the lake accessible yet remote, I wanted my cabin rustic but livable, I wanted a granite resolve to do on my marshy shore what old Germans had done on their cliffs; yet I wanted never to lose my immemorial torpor, my hours of dozing on a creaky dock peering at carp through the widening cracks. I wanted the end of black flies but no spraying, no lancing the swamps fed by fifteen feet of winter snows—relief from modest unfulfilments, exemption from levies I couldn't pay.

I was suckered into buying the place. Serge had advertised it in an English paper, and I'd called him at his hardware store in Lachute, gotten complicated directions, and then headed off one Sunday morning for the Laurentians, up past St-Jovite into Mont Tremblant Park. It was high summer, cool in the mountains (I drove with the window halfway up), the air was clear and the colours pure, as though I'd just awakened from a nap. The leaves were waxen, not yet dusty. The gravel road branched twice, snaked its way around the rim of Lac Sangsue, then sent off a single trail that rose steeply through an uncleared forest, like a logging road. I peered about for *gros gibier* prancing by the ravine at the edge of the trail. In the first mile there were two cabins, both of tarpaper studded with tin foil. I climbed one last long grade then came suddenly on the lake. There was an extensive marina and dozens of cars were parked over a sandy clearing. Most were foreign and expensive: Mercedes-Benzes, Renault 3000s, Volvos. I drove a VW van and had been feeling, until that moment, properly rustic and prepared. By prearrangement, I sent out three long *ooo-gahs* on the VW horn, and from far across the basin of the egg-shaped lake, a tall bearded man in tan shorts swung his arms over his head then got into his boat and speeded my way.

I said I was suckered. In the keel of the aluminum boat lay two large trout, and propped in the bow were two trolling rods with Daredevil spoons. Serge was about forty-five with stiff black hair and a well-trimmed beard, mostly grey over the chin. 'Just caught them twenty minutes ago—c'mon, you like to fish?'

We sped to his cabin and had a beer. There were two large rooms, one for cooking and eating with floor-to-ceiling windows looking out on the lake, and an elevated unwindowed room with a high-beamed ceiling containing a wood-burning fireplace, bunk beds covered with animal skins, a guncase and some mounted trophies. On the dining table I saw a freshly cut loaf of the round white bread they sell by the roadsides up north, a pot of still warm coffee, and Henri Troyat's *Tolstoi* in Livre de Poche. I'd always wanted to believe that somewhere not too far from where I would settle, *quincailliers* read the classics and fished (and academics worked with their hands and fell asleep sore and exhausted), that nature preserved as well as provided. That there was, in a part of the world I aspired to buy, a different heartbeat from the one that was dwarfing my manhood. Serge gutted the trout, fried the *filets* in garlic and butter, and I swabbed my plate with dabs of fresh bread, as I would after snails in a good French restaurant. We discussed manly things: dressing venison, tracking deer, baking corn and potatoes. I felt like a Boy Scout. We got back in the boat and Serge hauled up the minnow trap he kept at the end of his dock. He dumped a few minnows into a coffee can, threw out a tadpole that had slithered in and had already sucked the flesh from two minnows' bones, and then extracted a smallish fish that was three or four times longer than a minnow, and sleeker than a sunfish. *Trout,* I thought: *trout already! Lousy with trout! I'll buy!*

'Ah, just what we need.'

'A trout,' I said knowingly. Cannibalistic brutes.

'No, it's what you say in English?' He snapped its neck and laid it out in his hand. His hand was long, thick, pink-palmed, with old cuts etched in grease. 'Carp, no?'

I almost laughed. Carp, *here*? In this lovely lake? We were circling out beyond his dock, heading at high speed down the middle of a blue mountain lake. Water gurgled under my feet. *Carp are garbage fish.* Where I grew up we used to hunt carp with bows and arrows where the sewer pipes emptied into the river. If the water was clear enough, and the smell not too bad, we could see them below the surface. And where it was really bad we used to shoot at their fat black humps above the water line. Twenty-pound garbage bags. Suckers, we called them. Sewer carp. If we caught one, no torture was undeserved. We cut them, burned them, stuck them, kicked them. Then we nailed them head-down to a tree. Sometimes they'd still be flopping the next morning. I wanted to save my son from that kind of nature.

'Mountain carp,' he said. 'Keeps the lake clean. In Bibitte you got only carp, bluegill and trout. You get your perch in here on your *doré*, and—pfft—there goes your trout. They eat the little trout—see? And trout most of all goes for *this*.' He took my line, the heavy spoon and striped spinner, and then cut it off. He threaded catgut through the dead carp, through the mouth and out the anus, then reattached the cluster of hooks so they nestled at his tail.

'Lethal,' I said.

He winked. On his own spinner he simply attached a longish plastic ribbon, white on one side, with spots. We were under the high bluffs where Germans waved down. 'Your place is just across,' he said. 'That little cabin with the yellow door.' That was the first time I saw it. 'We'll go ashore after we catch your supper.' I was hooked.

There was still time that first summer, it being early July when we bought it, for a lot of indoor camping in the cabin.

There was, by communal agreement, no electricity. The cabin had been a fishing camp with a wood-burning stove, an ice-box, a pair of iron bunk frames and rusty springs with giant sodden mattresses that wouldn't burn, and a two-drawered dresser with a blistered top. We brought new things with us on every visit; a two-burner Coleman stove and a cold chest with twenty-five pounds of ice inside. We learned to live on cans of soft drinks, steak and fruit, cereal and powdered milk, and at night after the baby fell asleep, cups of instant coffee on the porch. We bought sleeping bags, a card table, a chemical toilet, lawn chairs and a pump. I threw away the springs and iron frames. I bought hoes, shovels, trowels, scythes and rakes; fishing rods, snorkels, grass seed and paint. Drapes, incinerator and asphalt tiles. An aluminum boat like Serge's, decidedly no motor. I liked to hear the water bubbling under me as I rowed. Each small repair revealed the bigger ones I couldn't yet handle. But that's why I bought the cabin, to gain skills, to become more competent. One summer I would devote to the dock; another to indoor plumbing. Eventually we would build on higher ground, where Serge had already sunk a foundation. That first August I scythed half an acre of virgin grass, picked a dozen quarts of delicious wild raspberries, dug out the little marshes, and lined the cutoffs with rock. Built a retaining wall. I dug out a substantial base for the incinerator, then built a fence around it from the iron poles and rusty springs of the old bunk beds, to keep the raccoons away at night.

After a month it was possible to sit under the naphtha lamp reading Painter's *Proust* at ten in the evening and step out onto the porch with a hot cup of coffee into a blackness primevally bright, stars spread like grains of sugar on a deep purple velvet. If I'd ever felt pride in something I'd done, and in a decision I'd made, it was this. Erika would come out too, sensing I'd left the cabin. If the mosquitoes had not been out, we could have shed our clothes and picked our way cautiously to the dock; we could have sat on the granite boulders and dangled our feet in black water in the dead of night when it seems less cold than daytime. I moved the baby out, bundled up safely, to let him sleep as we talked. But we stood instead on the porch wrapped only in the sounds of water slapping the aluminum boat, wind disturbing the trees, the sharp mosquito whines, and miles away, tunnelled over water and through the mountain ridges, the logging trucks changing gears just outside St-Jovite. That was the peak of my satisfaction.

On the first and last visits, in a summer, I would go alone. Too much work to do, no time for swimming and guarding a two-year-old from the rickety dock and water. I had come to see myself mirrored in my property; each summer I would try frantically to keep pace with nature, even to gain a little. We could live three days comfortably without help or supplies, and we could come and go with little more than a full, or empty, ice chest. We were still years away from Serge's standard, and more years away from my private dream of a hand-assembled cedar chalet (FOB Vancouver, $5,600), but at least we'd never lust for such German comforts as battery-powered television, twin 25-horsepower outboards, and kennels full of yapping lapdogs. I could see how sensible summers could stabilize a winter's excess and suggest humbler ambitions than the manipulation of knowledge.

I went up alone on a Sunday in late September. Few cars were there: Serge's Renault of course, and the Germans' Mercedes. Serge and the Europeans got along, especially in the winter when they staged snowmobile races on the lake. I rowed to the cabin, proud of my summer calluses, the tan, the rightness of owning something and trying to keep it the way it had always been. I beached the boat and pulled it under the porch, turned it over, then chained the prow to one of the pilings. First thing next summer, I told myself, clear out the scrap wood. Reinforce the steps. Paint the porch. I leaned the oars against the cabin, and unlocked the front door. At first I didn't believe what I saw. I sagged against the door and covered my eyes.

A large rock lay in the middle of the sleeping-room floor. The back-window drapes fluttered. Glass crunched and scraped underfoot. The sheets and blankets were chewed to fluffiness. Maybe some dishes were missing, I couldn't tell. My fishing rod still hung above the bed. Thank God, we'd taken home the sleeping bags the week before. The boxes of sugar and cereals were chewed open and littered everywhere. Raccoons, mice; the whole north woods had tramped through the cabin, except that 'coons don't throw rocks. I sat at my card table where the naphtha lamp lay leaking on its side. Hoping almost to hurt myself, I pounded the table. I'd never been invaded, never been stolen from before.

Later, of course, I swept up. After a long time I threw away the rock. The back window had always been shutterless. I had no yardstick to measure the frame; replacing glass would require a *vitrier* paid by the hour, driven in from St-Jovite and rowed to the cabin, sometime next spring in the middle of an academic week. I had only an ax and the old blistered dresser, antique or not. I knocked it down into planks in half a dozen blows. I nailed the drawer-bottoms to the sidings; they covered the hole but it looked like hell. Then I went on with my chores, letting water out of the pump, sealing the chimney flues, storing the oars, latching the other shutters, stripping down the beds, and burning the remains of sheets and blankets and rodent dung with all the splintered wood and cereal boxes. Erika would not have to know.

In the winter I have to think of other things: I dare not believe that Serge still drives to St-Jovite and parks his car for the weekend, then snowmobiles the rest of the way over back trails (chasing wolves, he told me once, finding a deer carcass steaming in a snowbank and circling out from it till he finds the pack); that the snow on the lake is as hard as concrete from the Ski-Doo rallies and the racket must be louder than a dozen sawmills at peak production. Our winter life doesn't allow for dreaming like that.

Spring is always an ugly season in the north; the snows melt slowly and with maximum inconvenience. Ours is not a landscape for unassertiveness; subtleties are easily lost. The stabbing summer green, the blood-red autumn, the pure white death of winter—but not the timid buds, the mud, the half-snow and week-long icy rains of spring. I begin in April to think of the damage up north, the puddles that must have formed under the tons of snow, the ravenous stirring-about of whatever animal spent the winter in my sleeping bag. Ice will float on the lake till the middle of May. Serge will take his ritual swim on the fifteenth of April. I will be marking final papers, delaying till the last possible Sunday the computing of my taxes. On my side of the lake the black flies are thick till the end of June. Erika can't take the flies, her face swells out, her eyes seal shut. Old bites will bleed for weeks. I go up alone on the first of July.

This time, I bring a yardstick. Window putty. All my sharpened tools. My swimming trunks and snorkel. I turn the boat over and haul it into the sun. Cautiously, I open the cabin. It is precisely as I left it: no famished bears, wolverines, caches of dynamite, mutilated corpses, no terrorists playing cards. Just the trapped coolness of winter inside a gloomy little camp with the shutters sealed, on a bright summer Monday with the temperature in the mid-seventies. I wanted to call out to Erika, as though she were with me—as though I had confided all my fears— *It's safe. We made it through another winter. I'll go out and catch our lunch!* And I'll say it next week, after I fix the window.

As the vision of liquor lures the drunkard off the wagon, so the lake called me on a hot summer day. I measured the window frame and lifted out the shards of glass, primed the pump, and repaired the broken lamp. I pumped up the Coleman stove and I put water on for coffee. The cabin had warmed up; I changed into my swimming trunks and dug out my snorkel.

As always the water stunned for a moment, one of those expanded moments I'd embraced as the essence of all I wanted from a place in the woods. Pain, astonishment and a swoon of well-being.

I paddled about for a timeless afternoon, snorkelling halfway across the lake, where only hands flashed white and puckered in my vision, then back along the shore near the dock, watching the bottom with its placid carp and bluegills rising to nibble my fingers. The deep exaggerated breathing through the snorkel was the sound of summers on Lac Bibitte. I was my own breath universalized; it was my collective body that drifted over the underwater swarms of tadpoles that rose from the mossy branches. *Cities of tadpoles!* I knew only that my back was burning, that the coffee water had boiled, and that I was ready for coffee on the dock and sun on my face and belly before locking up and heading back home. What finally happened to me that day is still happening. I remember pulling myself out of the water, drying myself with the towel I'd left on the dock. I felt myself restored. I was going to fish a bit, then maybe measure the loose planks on the dock. I went back inside where the valiant Coleman had boiled a large pan of water, and I stood barefoot on the asphalt tile aware of slivers of glass still about, but feeling too strong too care. Feeling reckless, swimsuit dripping heavily—*plop, plop*—almost thickly, on the floor. I spooned in the coffee, poured the water, snapped off the burner. My back was already registering the heat.

I must have turned about then, coffee in hand, taken a step or two toward the door. Barefoot, I felt something in the puddle of water at my feet. Water was still rolling down my legs. Thinking only of broken glass, I then glanced down at my feet.

In the puddle that had formed as I was making my coffee, three long brown leeches were rolling and twisting, one attached to the side of my foot and the other ones half on the tiles, slithering away. Another *plop* and a fourth dropped from my trunks, onto my foot, and into the wetness. I dropped the coffee, perhaps I deliberately poured it over my feet—I don't remember. I don't remember much of the next few minutes except that I screamed, ran, clawed at my trunks and pulled them off. And I could see the leeches, though I tried not to look, hanging from my waist like a cartridge belt. I swatted and they dropped in various corners of the cabin. I heard them dropping and I heard myself screaming, and I was also somewhere outside the man with leeches, screaming; I watched, I pitied, I screamed and cried.

Even later, when I was dressed and searching the cabin for the dark, shrivelled worms, scooping them up with a coffee spoon and dropping them in the flames of a roaring fire in the stove, my body was shaking with rage and disillusionment. I watched the man with the blistered back sit in his wretched little cabin, burning leeches. After an hour, losing interest, I turned away. I haven't been back since.

HOW I BECAME A JEW

CINCINNATI, SEPTEMBER 1950: 'I don't suppose you've attended classes with the coloured before, have you, Gerald?' the principal inquired. He was a jockey-sized man whose dark face collapsed around a greying moustache. His name was DiCiccio.

'No, sir.'

'You'll find quite a number in your classes here—' he gestured to the kids on the playground, and the Negroes among them seemed to multiply before my eyes. 'My advice is not to expect any trouble and they won't give you any.'

'We don't expect none from them,' my mother said with great reserve, the emphasis falling slightly on the last word.

DiCiccio's eyes wandered over us, calculating but discreet. He was taking in my porkiness, my brushed blond hair, white shirt and new gabardines. And my Georgia accent.

'My boy is no troublemaker.'

'I can see that, Mrs Gordon.'

'But I'm here to tell you—just let me hear of any trouble and I'm going straight off to the po-lice.'

And now DiCiccio's smile assessed her, as though to say *Are you finished?* 'That wouldn't be in Gerald's best interest,

Mrs Gordon. We have no serious discipline problems in the elementary school but even if we did, Mrs Gordon, outside authorities are never the answer. Your boy has to live with them. Police are never the solution.' He pronounced the word 'pleece' and I wanted to laugh. 'Even in the junior high,' he said, jerking his thumb towards the black, prison-like structure beyond the playground. 'There are problems.' His voice was still far-off and I was smiling.

DiCiccio's elementary school was new: bright, low and long, with greenboards and yellow chalk, aluminum frames and blond, unblemished desks. My old school in Georgia, near Moultrie, had had a room for each grade up through the sixth. Here in Cincinnati the sixth grade itself had ten sections.

'And Gerald, *please* don't call me "sir". Don't call anyone that,' the principal said with sudden urgency. 'That's just asking for it. The kids might think you're trying to flatter the teacher or something.'

'Well, I swan—' my mother began. 'He learned respect for his elders and nobody is taking that respect away. Never.'

'Look—' and now the principal leaned forward, growing smaller as he approached the desk. 'I know how Southern schools work. I know "sir" and "ma'm". I know they must have beaten it into you. But I'm trying to be honest, Mrs Gordon. Your son has a lot of things going against him and I'm trying to help. This intelligence of his can only hurt him unless he learns how to use it. He's white—enough said. And I assume Gordon isn't a Jewish name, is it? Which brings up another thing, Mrs Gordon. Take a look at those kids out there, the white ones. They look like little old men, don't they? Those are *Jews*, Gerald, and they're as different from the others as you are from the coloured. They were born in Europe and they're living here with their grandparents—don't ask me why, it's a long story. Let's just say they're a little hard to play with. A little hard to like, OK?' Then he settled back and caught his breath.

'They're the Israelites!' I whispered, as though the Bible had come to life. Then I was led to class.

But the sixth grade was not a home for long; not for the spelling champ and fastest reader in Colquitt County, Georgia. They gave me tests, sent me to a university psychologist who tested my memory and gave me some codes to crack. Then I was advanced.

Seventh grade was in the old building: Leonard Sachs Junior High. A greenish statue of Abraham Lincoln stood behind black iron bars, pointing a finger to the drugstore across the street. The outside steps were pitted and sagging. The hallways were tawny above the khaki lockers, and clusters of dull yellow globes were bracketed to the walls, like torches in the catacombs. By instinct I preferred the used to the new, sticky wood to cool steel, and I would have felt comfortable on that first walk down the hall to my new class, but for the stench of furtive, unventilated cigarette smoke. The secretary led me past rooms with open doors; all the teachers were men. Many were shouting while the classes turned to whistle at the ringing *tap-tap* of the secretary's heels. Then she stopped in front of a closed door and rapped. The noise inside partially abated and finally a tall bald man with furry ears opened the door.

'This is Gerald Gordon, Mr Terleski. He's a transfer from Georgia and they've skipped him up from sixth.'

'They have, eh?' A few students near the door laughed. They were already pointing at me. 'Georgia, you said?'

'Gerald Gordon *from* Georgia,' said the secretary.

'Georgia Gordon!' a Negro boy shouted. 'Georgia Gordon. Sweet Georgia Gordon.'

Terleski didn't turn. He took the folder from the girl and told me to find a seat. But the front boys in each row linked arms and wouldn't let me through. I walked to the window row and laid my books on the ledge. The door closed. Terleski sat at his desk and opened my file but didn't look up.

'Sweet Georgia,' crooned the smallish, fair-skinned Negro nearest me. He brushed my notebook to the floor. I bent over and got a judo chop on the inside of my knees.

'Sweet Georgia, you get off the floor, hear?' A very fat, coal-black girl in a pink sweater was helping herself to paper from my three-ring binder. 'Mr Tee, Sweet Georgia taking a nap,' she called.

He grumbled. I stood up. My white shirt and baggy gabardines were brown with dust.

'This boy is *not* named Sweet Georgia. He *is* named Gerald Gordon,' said Terleski with welcome authority. 'And I guess he's some kind of genius. They figured out he was too smart for the sixth grade. They gave him tests at the university and— listen to this—Gerald Gordon is a borderline genius.'

A few whistled. Terleski looked up. 'Isn't that *nice* for Gerald Gordon? What can we do to make you happy, Mr Gordon?'

'Nothing, sir,' I answered.

'Not a thing? Not an itsy-bitsy thing, sir?' I shook my head, lowered it.

'Might we expect you to at least look at the rest of us? We wouldn't want to presume, but—'

'Sweet Georgia crying, Mr Tee,' giggled Pink Sweater.

'And he all dirty,' added the frontseater. 'How come you all dirty, Sweet Georgia-man?' Pink Sweater was awarding my paper to all her friends.

'Come to the desk, Mr Gordon.'

I shuffled forward, holding my books over the dust smears.

'Face your classmates, sir. Look at them. Do you see any borderline types out there? Any friends?'

I sniffled loudly. My throat ached. There were some whites, half a dozen or so grinning in the middle of the room. I looked for girls and saw two white ones. Deep in the rear sat some enormous Negroes, their boots looming in the aisle. They looked at the ceiling and didn't even bother to whisper as they talked. They wore pastel T-shirts with cigarette packs twisted in the shoulder. And—God!—I thought, they had moustaches. Terleski repeated his question, and for the first time in my life I knew that whatever answer I gave would be wrong.

'*Mr Gordon's reading comprehension is equal to the average college freshman. Oh, Mr Gordon, just average? Surely there must be some mistake.*'

I started crying, tried to hold it back, couldn't, and bawled. I remembered the rows of gold stars beside my name back in Colquitt County, Georgia, and the times I had helped the teacher by grading my fellow students.

A few others picked up my crying: high-pitched blubbering from all corners. Terleski stood, scratched his ear, then screamed: 'Shut up!' A rumbling monotone persisted from the Negro rear. Terleski handed me his handkerchief and said, 'Wipe your face.' Then he said to the class: 'I'm going to let our borderline genius himself continue. Read this, sir, just like an average college freshman.' He passed me my file.

I put it down and knuckled my eyes violently. They watched me hungrily, laughing at everything. Terleski poked my ribs with the corner of the file. 'Read!'

I caught my breath with a long, loud shudder.

'*Gerald Gordon certainly possesses the necessary intellectual equipment to handle work on a seventh grade level, and long consultations with the boy indicate a commensurate emotional maturity. No problem anticipated in adjusting to a new environment.*'

'Beautiful,' Terleski announced. 'Beautiful. He's in the room five minutes and he's crying like a baby. Spends his first three minutes on the floor getting dirty, needs a hanky from the teacher to wipe his nose, and he has the whole class laughing at him and calling him names. Beautiful. That's what I call real maturity. Is that all the report says, sir?'

'Yes, sir.'

'You're lying, Mr Gordon. That's not very mature. Tell the class what else it says.'

'I don't want to, sir.'

'You don't want to. *I* want you to. *Read!*'

'It says: 'I doubt only the ability of the Cincinnati Public Schools to supply a worthy teacher.''

'*Well*—that's what we wanted to hear, Mr Gordon. Do you doubt it?'

'No, sir.'

'Am I worthy enough to teach you?'

'Yes, sir.'

'What do I teach?'

'I don't know, sir.'

'What have you learned already?'

'Nothing yet, sir.'

'What's the capital of the Virgin Islands?'

'Charlotte Amalie,' I said.

That surprised him, but he didn't show it for long. 'Then I can't teach you a thing, can I, Mr Gordon? You must know everything there is to know. You must have all your merit badges. So it looks like we're going to waste each other's time, doesn't it? Tell the class where Van Diemen's Land is.'

'That's the old name for Tasmania, sir. Australia, capital is Hobart.'

'If it's Australia that would make the capital Canberra, wouldn't it, Mr Gordon?'

'For the whole country, yes, sir.'

'So there's still something for you to learn, isn't there, Mr Gordon?'

The kids in the front started to boo. 'Make room for him back there,' the teacher said, pointing to the middle. 'And *now*, maybe the rest of you can tell me the states that border on Ohio. Does *anything* border on Ohio?'

No one answered while I waved my hand. I cared desperately that my classmates learn where Ohio was. And finally, ignoring me, Mr Terleski told them.

RECESS: on the sticky pavement in sight of Lincoln's statue. The windows of the first two floors were screened and softball was the sport. The white kids in the gym class wore institutional shorts; the other half—the Negroes—kept their jeans and T-shirts since they weren't allowed in the dressing room. I was still in my dusty new clothes. We all clustered around the gym teacher, who wore a Cincinnati Redlegs cap. He appointed two captains, both white. 'Keep track of the score, fellas. And tell me after how you do at the plate individually.' He blew his whistle and scampered off to supervise a basketball game around the corner.

The captains were Arno Kolko and Wilfrid Skurow, both fat and pale, with heavy eyebrows and thick hair climbing down their necks and up from their shirts. Hair like that—I couldn't believe it. I was twelve, and had been too ashamed to undress in the locker room. These must be Jews, I told myself. The other whites were shorter than the captains. They wore glasses and had bristly hair. Many of them shaved. Their arms were pale and veined. I moved towards them.

'Where *you* going, boy?' came a high-pitched but adult voice behind me. I turned and faced a six-foot Negro who was biting an unlit cigarette. He had a moustache and, up high on his yellow biceps, a flag tattoo. 'Ain't nobody picked you?'

'No,' I hesitated, not knowing whether I was agreeing or answering.

'Then stay where you're at. Hey—y'all want him?'

Skurow snickered. I had been accustomed to being a low-priority pick back in ball-playing Colquitt County, Georgia. I started to walk away.

'Come back here, boy. Squirrel picking you.'

'But you're not a captain.'

'Somebody *say* I ain't a captain?' The other Negroes had fanned out under small clouds of blue smoke and started basketball games on the painted courts. 'That leaves me and you,' said Squirrel. 'We standing them.'

'I want to be with them,' I protested.

'We don't want you,' said one of the Jews.

The kid who said it was holding the bat cross-handed as he took some practice swings. I had at least played a bit of softball back in Colquitt County, Georgia. The kids in my old neighbourhood had built a diamond near a housing development after a bulldozer operator had cleared the lot for us during his lunch hour. Some of the carpenters had given us timber scrap for a fence and *twice*—I remember the feeling precisely to this day—I had lofted fly balls tightly down the line and over the fence. No question, my superiority to the Arno Kolkos of this world.

'We get first ups,' said Squirrel. 'All *you* gotta do, boy, is get yourself on base and then move your ass fast enough to get home on anything I hit. And if I don't hit a home run, you gotta bring me home next.'

'Easy,' said I.

First three times up, it worked. I got on and Squirrel blasted on one hop to the farthest corner of the playground. But he ran the bases in a flash, five or six strides between the bases, and I was getting numb in the knees from staying ahead even with a two-base lead. Finally, I popped up for an out. Then Squirrel laid down a bunt and made it to third on some loose play. I popped out again and had to take his place on third, anticipating a stroll home on his next home run. But he bunted again, directly at Skurow the pitcher, who beat me home for a force-out to end the inning.

'Oh, you're a great one, Sweet Georgia,' Squirrel snarled from a position at deep short. He was still biting his unlit cigarette. 'You're a plenty heavy hitter, man. Where you learn to hit like that?'

'Georgia,' I said, slightly embarrassed for my state.

'Georgia? *Joe-ja?*' He lit his cigarette and tossed me the ball. 'Then I guess you're the worst baseball player in the whole state, Sweet Georgia. I *thought* you was different.'

'From what?'

'From them.' He pointed to our opponents. They were talking to themselves in a different language. I felt the power of a home-run swing lighten my arms, but it was too late.

'I play here,' said Squirrel. 'Pitch them slow then run to first. Ain't none of them can beat my peg or get it by me.'

A kid named Izzie, first up, bounced to me and I tagged him. Then a scrawny kid lifted a goodly fly to left—the kind I had hit for doubles—but Squirrel was waiting for it. Then Wilfred Skurow lumbered up: the most menacing kid I'd ever seen. Hair in swirls on his neck and throat, sprouting wildly from his chest and shoulders. Sideburns, but getting bald. Glasses so thick his eyeballs looked screwed in. But no form. He lunged a chopper to Squirrel, who scooped it and waited for me to cover first. Skurow was halfway down the line, then quit. Squirrel stood straight, tossed his cigarette away, reared back, and fired the ball with everything he had. I heard it leave his hand, then didn't move till it struck my hand and deflected to my skull, over the left eye. I was knocked backwards, and couldn't get up. Skurow circled the bases; Squirrel sat at third and laughed. Then the Jews walked off together and I could feel my forehead tightening into a lump. I tried to stand, but instead grew dizzy and suddenly remembered Colquitt County. I sat alone until the bells rang and the grounds were empty.

Every Saturday near Moultrie, I had gone to the movies. In the balcony they let the coloured kids in just for Saturday. Old ones came Wednesday night for Jim Crow melodramas with coloured actors. But we came especially equipped for those Saturday mornings when the coloured kids sat in the dark up in the balcony, making noise whenever we did. We waited for too much noise, or a popcorn box that might be dropped on us. Then we reached into our pockets and pulled out our broken yo-yos. We always kept our broken ones around. Half a yo-yo is great for sailing since it curves and doesn't lose speed. And it's very hard. So we stood, aimed for the projection beam, and fired the yo-yos upstairs. They loomed on the screen like bats, filled the air like bombs. Some hit metal, others the floor, but some struck home judging from the yelps of the coloured kids and their howling. Minutes later the lights went on upstairs and we heard the ushers ordering them out.

A second bell rang.

'That burr-head nigger son-of-a-bitch,' I cried. 'That god-damn nigger.' I picked myself up and ran inside.

I was late for geometry but my transfer card excused me. When I opened the door two Negro girls dashed out pursued by two boys about twice my size. One of the girls was Pink Sweater, who ducked inside a girls' room. The boys waited outside. The windows in the geometry room were open, and a few boys were sailing paper planes over the street and side-walk. The teacher was addressing himself to a small group of students who sat in a semicircle around his desk. He was thin and red-cheeked with a stiff pelt of curly hair.

'I say, do come in, won't you? That's a nasty lump you've got there. Has it been seen to?'

'Sir?'

'Over your eye. Surely you're aware of it. It's really quite unsightly.'

'I'm supposed to give you this—' I presented the slip for his signing.

'Gerald Gordon, is it? Spiro here.'

'Where?'

'Here—I'm Spiro. Geoffrey Spiro, on exchange. And you?'

'Me what?'

'Where are you from?'

'Colquitt County, Georgia.'

He smiled as though he knew the place well and liked it. 'That's South, aye? Ex-cellent. Let us say for tomorrow you'll prepare a talk on Georgia—brief topical remarks, race, standard of living, labour unrest and whatnot. Hit the high points, won't you, old man? Now then, class'—he raised his voice only slightly, not enough to disturb the coloured boys making *ack-ack* sounds at pedestrians below—'I should like to introduce to you Mr Gerald Gordon. You have your choice, sir, of joining these students in the front and earning an 'A' grade, or going back there and getting a 'B', provided of course you don't leave the room.'

'I guess I'll stay up here, sir,' I said.

'Ex-cellent. Your fellow students, then, from left to right are: Mr Lefkowitz, our old friends Liesl and Magda, Mr Willie Goldberg, Mr Irwin Roth, and Mr Harry Frazier. In the back, Mr Morris Gordon (no relative, I trust), Miss Etta Bluestone, Mr Orville Goldberg (he's Willie's twin), and Mr Henry Moore. Please be seated.'

Henry Moore was coloured, as were the Goldberg twins, Orville and Wilbur. The girls, Liesl, Magda, and Etta, were pretty and astonishingly mature, as ripe in their way as Wilfrid Skurow in his. Harry Frazier was a straw-haired athletic sort, eating a sandwich. The lone chair was next to Henry Moore, who was fat and smiled and had no moustache or tattoo. I took the geometry book from my scuffed, zippered notebook.

'The truth is,' Mr Spiro began, 'that both Neville Chamberlain and Mr Roosevelt were fascist, and quite in sympathy with Hitler's anticommunist ends, if they quibbled on his means. His evil was mere overzealousness. Public opinion in the so-called democracies could never have mustered against *any* anticommunist, whatever his program—short of invasion, of course. *Klar?*' He stopped in order to fish out a book of matches for Liesl, who was tapping a cigarette on her desk.

'*Stimmt?*' he asked, and the class nodded. Harry Frazier wadded his waxed paper and threw it back to one of his classmates by the window, shouting, 'Russian MIG!' I paged through the text, looking for diagrams. No one else had a book out and my activity seemed to annoy them.

'So in conclusion, Hitler was merely the tool of a larger fascist conspiracy, encouraged by England and the United States. What *is* it, Gerald?'

'Sir—what are we talking about?' I was getting a headache, and the egg on my brow seemed ready to burst. The inner semicircle stared back at me, except for Harry Frazier.

'Sh!' whispered Morris Gordon.

'At *shul* they don't teach it like that,' said Irwin Roth, who had a bald spot from where I sat. 'In *shul* they say it happened because God was punishing us for falling away. He was testing us. They don't say nothing from the English and the Americans. They don't even say nothing from the Germans.'

'Because we didn't learn our letters good,' said Morris Gordon. The matches were passed from the girls to all the boys who needed them.

'*What* happened?' I whispered to Henry Moore, who was smiling and nodding as though he knew.

'Them *Jews*, man. Ain't it great?'

'Then the rabbi is handing you the same bloody bullshit they've been handing out since I went to *shul*—ever since the bloody Diaspora,' Spiro said. 'God, how I detest it.'

'What's *shul*, Henry? What's the Diaspora?'

'Look,' Spiro continued, now a little more calmly, 'there's only one place in the world where they're building socialism, really honestly *building* it'—his hands formed a rigid rectangle over the desk—'and that's Israel. I've seen children your age who've never handled money. I've played football on turf that was desert a year before. The desert blooms, and the children sing and dance and shoot—yes, shoot—superbly. They're all brothers and sisters, and they belong equally to every parent in the *kibbutz*. They'd die for one another. No fighting, no name calling, no sickness. They're big, straight and strong and tall, and handsome, like the Israelites. I've seen it for myself.

Why any Jew would come to America is beyond me, unless he wants to be spat on and corrupted.'

'*Gott*, if the rabbi knew what goes on here,' said Roth, slapping his forehead.

'What's a rabbi, Henry? *Tell me what a rabbi is!*'

'What*ever* is your problem, Gerald?' Spiro cut in.

'Sir—I've lost the place. I just skipped the sixth grade and maybe that's where we learned it all. I don't understand what you-all are saying.'

'I must say I speak a rather good English,' said Spiro. The class laughed. 'Perhaps you'd be happier with the others by the window. All that *rat-tat-tat* seems like jolly good fun, quite a lift, I imagine. It's all perfectly straightforward here. It's *your* country we're talking about, after all. Not mine. Not theirs.'

'It's not the same thing up North,' I said.

'No, I daresay . . . look, why don't you toddle down to the nurse's office and get something for your head? That's a good lad, and you show up tomorrow if you're feeling better and tell us all about Georgia. Then I'll explain the things you don't know. You just think over what I've said, OK?'

I was feeling dizzy—the bump, the smoke—my head throbbed, and my new school clothes were filthy. I brushed myself hard and went into the boys' room to comb my hair, but two large Negroes sitting on the window ledge, stripped to their shorts and smoking cigars, chased me out.

Downstairs, the nurse bawled me out for coming in dirty, then put an ice pack over my eye.

'Can I go home?' I asked.

The nurse was old and fat, and wore hexagonal Ben Franklin glasses. After half an hour she put an adhesive patch on and since only twenty minutes were left, she let me go.

I stopped for a Coke at the drugstore across from Lincoln's statue. Surprising, I thought, the number of school kids already out, smoking and having Cokes. I waited in the drugstore until the sidewalk was jammed with the legitimately dismissed, afraid that some truant officer might question my early release. I panicked as I passed the cigar counter on my way out, for Mr Terleski was buying cigarettes and a paper. I was embarrassed for him, catching him smoking, but he saw me, smiled, and walked over.

'Hello, son,' he said, 'what happened to the head?'

'Nothing,' I said, 'sir.'

'About this morning—I want you to know there was nothing personal in anything I said. Do you believe me?'

'Yes, sir.'

'If I didn't do it in *my* way first, they'd do it in their way and it wouldn't be pretty. And Gerald—don't raise your hand again, OK?'

'All right,' I said. 'Goodbye.'

'*Very* good,' said Mr Terleski. 'Nothing else? No *sir*?'

'I don't think so,' I said.

The street to our apartment was lined with shops: tailors with dirty windows, cigar stores piled with magazines, some reading rooms where bearded old men were talking, and a tiny branch of a supermarket chain. Everywhere there were school kids: Jews, I could tell from their heads. Two blocks away, just a few feet before our apartment block, about a dozen kids turned into the dingy yard of the synagogue. An old man shut the gates in a hurry just as I stopped to look in, and another old man opened the main door to let them inside. The tall spiked fence was painted a glossy black. I could see the kids grabbing black silk caps from a cardboard box, then going downstairs. The old gatekeeper, a man with bad breath and puffy skin, ordered me to go.

At home, my mother was preparing dinner for a guest and she was in no mood to question how I got the bump on the head. The guest was Grady, also from Moultrie, a whip-thin red-faced man in his forties who had been the first of my father's friends to go North. He had convinced my father. His wife and kids were back in Georgia selling their house, so he was eating Georgia food with us till she came back. Grady was the man we had to thank, my father always said. 'Me and the missus is moving again soon's she gets back,' he announced at dinner. 'Had enough of it here.'

'Back to Georgia?' my father asked.

'Naw, Billy, out of Cincinnati. Gonna find me a place somewhere in Kentucky. Come in to work every day and go back at night and live like a white man. A man can forget he's white in Cincinnati.'

'Ain't that the truth,' said my mother.

'How many niggers you got in your room at school, Jerry?' Grady asked me.

'That depends on the class,' I said. 'In geometry there aren't any hardly.'

'See?' said Grady. 'You know five years ago there wasn't hardly no more than ten per cent in that school? Now it's sixty and still going up. By the time your'n gets through he's gonna be the onliest white boy in the school.'

'He'll be gone before *that*,' my father promised. 'I been thinking of moving to Kentucky myself.'

'Really?' said my mother.

'I ain't even been to a baseball game since they got that nigger,' Grady boasted, 'and I ain't ever going. I used to love it.'

'You're telling me,' said my father.

'If they just paid me half in Georgia what they paid me here, I'd be on the first train back,' said Grady. 'Sometimes I reckon it's the devil himself just tempting me.'

'I heard of kids today that live real good and don't even see any money,' I said. 'Learned it in school.'

'That where you learned to stand in front of a softball bat?' my mother retorted, and my parents laughed. Grady coughed.

'And let me tell you,' he began, 'them kids that goes to them mixed schools gets plenty loony ideas. That thing he just said sounded comminist to me. Yes, sir, that was a Comminist Party member told him that. I don't think no kids of mine could get away with a lie like that in my house. No, sir, they got to learn the truth sometime, and after they do, the rest is lies.'

Then Father slapped the fork from my hands. 'Get back to your room,' he shouted. 'You don't get no more dinner till I see your homework done!' He stood behind me, with his hand digging into my shoulder. 'Now say good night to Grady.'

'Good night,' I mumbled.

'Good night *what*?' my mother demanded. 'Good night *what*?'

'Sir,' I cried, 'sir, sir, sir! Good night, sir!' the last word almost screamed from the hall in front of my bedroom. I slammed the door and fell on the bed in the darkened room. Outside, I could hear the threats and my mother's apologies. 'Don't hit him too hard, Billy, he done got that knot on the head already.' But no one came.

They started talking of Georgia, and they forgot the hours. I thought of my first school day up North—then planned the second, the third—and I thought of Leonard Sachs Junior High, Squirrel, and the Jews. The Moultrie my parents and Grady were talking about seemed less real, then finally, terrifying. I pictured myself in the darkened balcony under a rain of yo-yos, thrown by a crowd of Squirrels.

I concentrated on the place I wanted to live. There was an enormous baseball stadium where I could hit home runs down the line; Liesl was in the stands and Mr Terleski was a coach. We wore little black caps, even Squirrel, and there were black bars outside the park where old men were turning people away. Grady was refused, and Spiro and millions of others, even my parents—though I begged their admission. *No, stimmt?* We were building socialism and we had no parents and we did a lot of singing and dancing (even Henry

Moore, even the chocolatey Goldberg twins, Orville and Wilbur) and Liesl without her cigarettes asked me the capitals of obscure countries. 'Is-real,' I said aloud, letting it buzz; 'Is-real,' and it replaced Mozambique as my favourite word; *Is-rael, Is-rael, Is-rael,* and the dread of the days to come lifted, the days I would learn once and for all if Israel could be really real.

SOUTH

IT WAS THE SOUTH. My father had been in an accident in Valdosta, and the word they used was *crushed*: his legs, his back, his ribs, his hip. His arms were merely broken. We had no insurance. Until the accident we had been surviving in town. I was in the second grade. My mother stayed in the three rooms that weren't quite an apartment but served the landlady as one. They were three equal-sized rooms, all of them with long, screened windows, all of them wallpapered and carpeted. In the corner of one room she'd installed a refrigerator and a two-burner electric range; in another there was a shower stall and a chemical toilet, and in the third there was a dresser and a bed. I slept on a pallet in the kitchen.

A few months after the accident, my father was allowed to go home. He was still in the body cast for the broken back. He lay in his BarcaLounger, nearly straight out. He'd been selling BarcaLoungers before the accident, and he always believed fervidly in the products he represented. Later on, when he went back to selling, he would treat the BarcaLounger mystically, saying, 'This li'l honey saved my life,' and he could make his voice quaver like a Southern politician on Confederate Memorial Day. He wasn't even American. What he meant to say was that even a man crippled by pain and rendered immobile could master his convalescence, could still feel he had something useful to do with himself by going up and down in his BarcaLounger. In 1946, it was a whirlpool bath and physiotherapist in one moulded slab of aluminum. He needed that little mechanism. He couldn't read, and this was before television, and the only radio station, from Ocala, was hard to get and even harder to understand. He and my mother I don't ever remember talking.

They had no money, of course. And then they exhausted the resources of eventual recovery—the donations of friends up north, my mother's relations in Canada, her bonds provided by a provident father.

So we left the three rooms. Things got sold that I'd never even seen unpacked. My mother's family was well-to-do, and my mother was a woman of taste. She'd been a decorator, and she'd accumulated things in Europe and in England and then in Montreal, where she'd met my father. Those things—Meissen things, Dresden things, Prague things, sketches she'd done in German and British museums, watercolour renderings she'd done for clients in Montreal, heavy silverware in a rich, burgundy-velvet-lined case, candlesticks, cut-glass bowls, little framed paintings and etchings and cameos done on porcelain or ivory—they meant nothing at all to me. She unwrapped them and cried; she tried to tell me the stories of their acquisition, the smuggling out. They meant nothing at all, to my shame. A BarcaLounger now—that was a valuable thing. When all my mother's boxes were empty, I carried them to the trash. All that I liked, and saved for a while, were the yellowed sheets of newspaper she'd packed them in, a dozen years before. I liked foreign-looking things. Some of the newspapers were in Gothic face. Some of them were in French.

So 'a coloured man' was paid a dollar or two to move us from the three rooms into something we could afford. For the move someone donated a wheelchair, and so we walked across town—my mother, the coloured man and me, each carrying suitcases and boxes—and my father trailed behind, pushed indifferently by another part of the coloured man's family, called a coloured boy. He nudged my father down the main street (there were no sidewalks) with bursts of energy the way a boy might kick a stone for a few blocks until it careens under a car or somewhere out of reach. The first time my father's chair began to tip, causing him to wrench his back in an insane balancing act, the boy was canned, and I was appointed to finish the task. He made room on his lap for a suitcase and a lamp. His legs were pink, withered and scaly and would remain that way for years, until the rest of him started to shrink.

The new place was actually larger than the three rooms. It might have been called a house—it was detached but set back from the street, as a garage or a laundry house might have been. It gave us an address with an 'A' at the end—something new in all our travels, 'a sign' my mother said. Its virtue was that it was very, very cheap. The figure of ten dollars a month sticks in my mind. The facilities were outdoors, in an overgrown garden heavy with many other scents. Florida to me is always a collection of odours; it's the only thing I miss, and it's the first thing I notice about any new place I'm set down in. The outdoor commode—as my mother termed it—hadn't been used in a very long time; it was, like our small house, tilting and in need of paint. The virtue of an unused toilet cannot be exaggerated. It was quiet, neutral, and hygienic as nature itself. We soon took care of that, but rankness and a need for lime didn't set in for a few weeks. I don't know how my father used it, or even if he did; I suspect now my mother had arranged something with boards and a bucket and newspaper-linings in the house that she slopped outside every morning.

School was going on. I hadn't missed a day. I had started kindergarten outside of Atlanta and had put in a chunk of first grade in Gadsden, Alabama, and we had come to Leesburg,

Florida, at the end of the first grade, before my father's accident, so that I was remembered by a few kids when second grade started. I usually didn't have that advantage. Most of the moves in our life were timed for summer, so that each September I began a new school. In Leesburg, Florida, in 1946, I had a small history.

I was more sociable in the days before my father's accident and the move across town. I remember, in those warm twilight evenings under the bare bulb of streetlights, the endless circling of bicycles in the fine dust of our lane; the weekend work-up games of baseball. I remember the first time I caught a pass thrown by an older boy and the buoyant worn pigskin, the fine black bubble of inner tube bursting between the laces. I had a curious side-arm throwing motion with a baseball that older boys watched and tried to imitate, without my control. Let's just say it was a Southern town in post-war America, and so far as I knew anything about myself, I fitted in. I was accepted. Kick-the-can, fishing with doughballs, endless summers of bicycling, football and baseball; a subtropical life led out of doors, with rings of dust tamped down by sweat, scabs on the knees and elbows still forming or just falling off, a dingy, uneven tan, dingy, uneven blondness in all hair.

Things of course were working.

I was sociable. In the first grade, and in the summer, kids had come home with me; I went home with them. My mother baked, served, poured. Her exaggerated notion of Florida heat led her to elaborate formations of Jell-O and gallons of iced tea and lemonade and—universally rejected by everyone but me—buttermilk. She disapproved of Coke, that Southern elixir, and wouldn't stock it. No one seemed to notice those three strange, papered rooms in the widow's house, or that my father was never home, or that my mother had an accent no one understood. She had no friends. My parents went nowhere, even on the five or six days a month when my father was home.

He lived entirely for himself. My mother lived entirely for me. I found this a satisfactory arrangement. I lived entirely for the release from school.

After our move, Grady was my only friend. I remember walking over to his house after school. It was a small town in those days, and a child revealed everything about himself from the direction he nosed his bicycle in from the stands outside of school. Each cardinal compass point indicated who and what you were, what your father did and what your prospects in life were going to be. I was an exception because our little laundry shed of a house was the last white-occupied structure on that side of town. The county, I learned many years later, was 70 per cent black. All street services—pavement, lights, water, sewage—ended half a block from our address, although houses like ours, unpainted and tilting on stilts, with old cars and refrigerators in the ungrassed yards, teeming with children and with sullen young men and women and old black women in straw hats with flowers on the brims, continued for many undemarcated blocks. My mother would embarrass me horribly by walking into Niggertown and running her hands over the heads of little girls and then standing in the yards calling up to women of her age, 'I'm your new neighbour. We live just on the other side of the streetlight there. I hope you'll come over for tea some afternoon.'

As I say, I was an exception, going east from school, down the Dixie Highway, and cutting through the alleys behind the stores where the Jim Crow serving windows were. Grady Stanridge went the other way, where the better families lived. They were the new people in town, people with businesses, people like us only younger and not from so far away. It's hard to understand, even now, that the parents were just starting out in life—they were in their twenties, the men navy and army veterans with tattoos and a hunger to repossess their lives;

and that there were also a number of kids in my class who had never seen (and would never see) their fathers; and that the remarriage of young widows and subsequent moving to larger towns was a favourite topic in our first and second grades.

Grady and I strolled down the Dixie Highway. His father had the Western Auto store. Grady could take anything he wanted from the store—games, baseball gloves, fishing equipment. He was generous and I was greedy. I took a yo-yo—one of those deluxe Duncans at thirty-five cents—and a wooden vial of fish-hooks. Grady also took a yo-yo, and we were back on the shaded sidewalk, 'walkin' our babies' and 'loopin' the loop', when I saw my mother across the street, making her way from the cool, deep shade of the west side of town.

I prayed she wouldn't cross over. She had the Canadian custom of smothering me with 'dears' and 'darlings' and even 'preciouses' in every conversation, and she even extended the custom to my little friends, as she called them. The one acceptable term of endearment—honey—she never used.

She was carrying a small package from the butcher's, and from the colour of stain on the outside I knew it to be liver, her—and my—favourite. We got it for ten cents a pound, since it wasn't considered fit for white consumption. It was assumed, whenever I was sent out to buy it, that we were getting it for our cleaning lady. I tried to keep my mother from going for it, since I knew she wouldn't go along with my lie. She didn't see me. By the time we got to Grady's house I had mastered 'cat in the cradle' and my middle finger was cold and white and nearly asphyxiated.

His house was Florida Moorish, with a tile roof, Mexican grille work and rows of tall, narrow windows, curved on top. The outside was stucco; the grounds were well-tended, with oranges in the back, hibiscus and bougainvillea along the trellises and a tightly tufted, low-pile lawn. The walkway was crushed limestone, rendered white in the Florida sun.

Mrs Stanridge was smoking in the living room, taking her afternoon break, it seemed, with a tall drink in a frosted, narrow glass. The house was very neat; even with all the windows—which were clean—the glass tables and the various ledges showed no dust. There was a large portrait hung over a small fireplace; the woman was stout and grey-haired. Her black dress and the rows of pearls and the wavy hair reminded me of a movie matron, the kind of stuffy lady Groucho Marx would spill something on.

Grady led me to the kitchen for iced tea, made in the Southern fashion with no lemon and lots of sugar. Our house always featured lemons, and raw, tart foods were prized over all others. I used to chew rhubarb like celery, pop cranberries like cherries, suck lemons and chew limes. I didn't mind the way Southerners cooked their food, with pots of vegetables boiling all day till they were soggy brown messes, but I realized my friends couldn't eat at my place at all because they found everything, from meat to vegetables to dessert, raw. Of course, with my father laid out in his BarcaLounger, and with my living on the edge of Niggertown, I understood I couldn't bring anyone home at all.

We heard Mrs Stanridge out in the living room suddenly cursing and then shouting, 'Grady, get in here!' She seemed to be frantic; all the order that had been apparent a few minutes earlier had been overturned. She'd opened the breakfront drawers and had silverware out on the dining table. She had stacks of newspapers scattered on the rug.

'Where is it?' she demanded. 'Have you hidden it?'

'Hidden what, ma'am?'

'Hidden my purple flower pot. I have people coming over, and I went out to cut some flowers, and now I don't have my flower pot to put them in!'

'I don't even remember no purple flower pot!'

'It was purple. It was antique. It was right on the ledge under Big Mama's picture.'

Grady looked at the ledge. Not even a dust ring; the ledge thinly underscored the painting, nothing else.

'It's the onliest thing I care about. I had that flower pot before I even met Mr Stanridge.' Mrs Stanridge was almost whining.

'Well, don't look at me—I just got here,' said Grady.

'I'm upset.'

'I'll look for it.'

'I think I know what happened.'

'Maybe you took it to the kitchen.'

'I should have put two and two together,' she said. 'It was the lady done it.'

'What lady?'

'The cleaning lady.'

'May-Lou?'

'You know May-Lou quit on me. The cleaning lady that answered the ad.'

'Why would she want an old flower pot?'

'I seen her lifting it, even.'

I could see a purple flower pot nestled nicely in the upper shelf of the breakfront. 'Excuse me, ma'am,' I said.

Grady was in the kitchen. He shouted out, 'It ain't back here.'

'She stole it, that's what. May-Lou might have broke it and not told me. But this one was too careful. She stole it.'

'Ma'am?' I asked again.

'And her acting so superior. Like she was too good to clean a white lady's house. I even let her eat on my good plates.'

'Is that it, there?' I pointed, and Grady's mother reluctantly followed its direction. She hugged the pot like a rescued child, then set it back on the ledge and stepped away from it, just to admire it all over again.

'Thank God,' she said. 'And I promise you,' she said, as though she were speaking directly to the pot or maybe someone's ashes inside it and not to Grady and me, who were walking our yo-yos just above carpet level, 'I promise I ain't never hiring a white woman to do coloured work again!'

How easy it is for a boy, and then a young man, to write praises to his father. He sat there through my childhood and through my high-school years, and then he left, married two more times, and died. Never did we talk, never did he explain to me the passions (here I am again, calling them *passions* when I know for sure they were nothing but blind lusts) that drove him. And I have so deliberately mythologized him, the manly force in my life, the dark, romantic, French, medieval, libidinous force in my life, the foreign element in my life, believing somehow that his eighteen siblings, his six wives, his boxing career, his violence and his drinking and his police record, his infidelities, in some way ennoble *me*, tell me I'm not just the timid academic son of my mother's rectitude.

And she, who cleaned other people's houses while I attended school and my father reclined on his BarcaLounger, and finally returned to schoolteaching herself in Winnipeg after she finally left him, and who now lives alone in an apartment in Winnipeg, forgetting if she's eaten, forgetting to cook the things she's bought and keeps shoving into the refrigerator (the final smell in my catalogue of odours is the aroma of age, the rotting in the cold of orange-juice cans and Chinese dinners)—how easy it is for a boy and for a young man and even for a man now embarked on middle age to see his mother as nothing exceptional in the universe, nothing at all, an embarrassment in fact, against the extravagance of his father.

Mother, why couldn't we love you enough?

IDENTITY

Porter, Reg and Hennie. My parents for several years. Mysteries to me, to each other. Gone now, even in name.

My earliest memory is of falling off an armchair when I was three and breaking my arm. A bad break, poorly mended. Even now the extended arm, with the elbow resting, barely grazes the tabletop. For the wrist and hand to conspire with gravity is an act of will. Think of the forearm as I do, a slow hypotenuse connecting that original fracture to a slightly skewed grand disclosure. Needless to say, I'm still waiting for it.

I'd been watching my father reading and writing in a Queen Anne chair. For years that memory stood as evidence that we'd been a normal, happy family. Father reading, son at his side, a little spill, nothing too serious. Despite the small imperfection it left me, it is a pleasant memory. It occurred to me since, however, that we never owned Queen Anne furniture, especially not in 1943, and that I cannot remember my father ever reading or writing. When I was thirteen and having to learn to read and write all over again, I discovered something else I'd always suspected: my father couldn't read or write at all.

That same year, 1943, I remember sitting on my tricycle at the top of a steep hill. This part of the memory is a moment, even now, of rather intense pleasure. And then I flung my legs out straight and rode like the breeze to the bottom of the little hill. Unfortunately, the hill was our driveway and the bottom of it was our garage door, and the door was down. From that episode, I received a bent nose, a broken collarbone and a skull fracture. After the fracture I became an epileptic. It was bad as a child, not so severe now. From internal evidence, you will conclude that I'm writing this as a man of forty-three.

Such are the sheltering memories of childhood. Or the preferred fictions of adulthood. I once overheard my mother, talking to a friend long after I'd grown up, relate a more intriguing version of those same injuries. There'd never been a chair or a tricycle and garage door. There'd only been New Year's Eve, 1943, and a scrounged-up baby-sitter recommended by someone down at Sears, where my father worked. And she had a soldier husband who'd wangled a holiday pass, only to find her apartment empty. He saw our address on a piece of paper. He confronted her there, in our second-floor apartment on Reading Road, stabbed her and shot her visiting boyfriend, and then went to work on me, his only witness. So I was killed, at least to his satisfaction. I have never, consciously, been able to replay a single frame of that incident. So much for the theories of Freud or the plots of Ross Macdonald. I think of the armchair and the tricycle constantly.

Let more bones break, more moves be made. Those early memories are from Cincinnati—a freak appearance in our lives, a town that did not claim us—from deep in America, a country, as it turned out, that did not claim me either.

Turned out, not in the passive sense of a plot that runs its course, but in the active sense of total reversal, like a pocket being turned out, like deadbeats being turned out of a bar. There are millions like me on this continent (I know, I meet them everywhere) who constitute no bloc, and who, for all their numbers, have no champion. The implications radiate like angles from a protractor, like tracks from a roundhouse, though I'm unable to pursue them all. Think rather of Reg and Hennie Porter and me, lying just a degree or two off plumb, or the prime horizontal axis. Think of life led slightly off balance.

In Pittsburgh in 1952 I was standing on the roof of an apartment building, with matches, a knife and rabbit ears under opaque plastic. With matches I burned off an inch or so, stripped it with the knife, then spliced the copper onto the frail set of rabbit ears that had come with our first television set. Then I lashed the whole contraption to the giant brick apartment-house chimney and crawled to the edge of the roof and called down, 'How about it now?'

Staring down six floors to our opened window on the second floor was the closest thing I knew to an epileptic aura. The sidewalk yo-yoed, close enough to step out on.

Peter Humphries, my only friend, was in our apartment. He was from the third floor. My parents both worked, so did his mother. His father did not seem to exist, even in memory.

He shouted up, 'It's just a test pattern!'

He couldn't know that that was the whole point. I'd succeeded. It meant to me—though it was only channel 9 in Steubenville, Ohio, or 7 in Wheeling, West Virginia—that features were materializing from outer space. New test patterns, new readers of local news, new advertisers, new street names, different phrasing of the same Tri-State weather, different politics: the mark of sophistication was access to all the channels. I'd exhausted KDKA, and the only NBC outlet before we got our own WIIC on channel 11 was channel 6 in Johnstown. Farther out in the mountains there was rumoured to be a channel 10 in Altoona and a channel 3 downriver in Huntington, West Virginia. Pittsburgh, in other words, was an exciting place, if you had the right connections. Pittsburgh eventually got more than enough channels, but not in 1952. We were always deprived, last in everything, at least in the years I lived there. But with ingenuity and agility and rabbit ears lashed to a chimney, hope existed for more than snow on channels 2, 3,

6, 7, 9 and 13, which was educational. On exceptional nights with my antenna pointing in the right direction I'd gotten Cleveland, and Chambersburg, almost in Maryland. A collector with luck could get a picture, however furry, and enough voice to make a positive identification, on every VHF channel, and he could pull in signals from four states, not counting freaks, which once, with the help of clouds, sunspots and a low-flying airplane, brought in Detroit and Buffalo.

The point is, I was king of the airwaves. I might not have known much about my parents or myself, or about Peter Humphries for that matter, but those questions never arose. I knew the important things, like call letters and the names of news readers and where to shop for Mercurys and Fords in Steubenville. It was the essence of my new-found teenagerliness to know everything about strangers and occult signals materializing from snow, and to know nothing at all about the forces that had made me, the scars and handicaps that were about to reclaim me.

All of this happened nearly thirty year ago. I haven't seen Pittsburgh in a quarter of a century, and probably all those familiar faces have scattered or died, although I still catch KDKA on the car radio, deep in the night. The magic is gone, but I'll stick with it till it fades completely to hear again those little neighbouring town names: Belle Vernon, Castle Shannon, Blawnox, Sewickley—names that were ushering in life to me, holding promises of jobs and adventure. Those were all threshold names, places I couldn't have located on an Allegheny County map, but that nevertheless were part of my private empire, my homeland, the back of my hand, whose borders were marked by the snowy extremities of Wheeling, Altoona, Chambersburg and Cleveland.

Peter Humphries is about to leave this story, but not before he leaves his mark, freshly, on me again. His mother was divorced—*divorcée* was one of those words, probably the only one, that a 1952 Pittsburgh kid pronounced in a self-consciously French way, to imbue it with its full freight of accompanying *negligées* and *lingerie* and *brassières* and of other things that came off in the night and suggested a rich inner life—she had dates, and Peter often slept over with us on nights when she planned to stay away. Or didn't plan, but stayed away anyway. As a cocktail waitress, then hostess, she didn't come home till three or four in the morning anyway, then slept till noon.

He might have been the gateway to my adolescence, but as it turned out—that phrase again—he was merely the last of my childhood friends. In a life of sharp and inexplicable and unmendable breaks, I have a special feeling for these friends of a special time and place. They seem to me, all of them, including my parents, prisoners of peculiar moments, waving at me from ice floes as dark waters widen between us. I remember all of them sharply, for they never were given a chance to grow out and modify; they were forever the last way I saw them, just as Pittsburgh is, which is to say they are essences of themselves and of my own poor perception of them. Even so, they give a surer sense of my own continuity than anything I can conjure in myself.

Peter was predictably avid for sex. He was riveted on the female body, every part of it, in ways that only a deeply troubled boy can be: hating it, fearing it, desiring it. He found my ignorance of it and my indifference to learning about it from him something of an affront. It marked me as being just a kid, which I was.

Being with Peter, the only friend I had, was like standing at the tip of an enormous funnel; all the sexual knowledge available to pubescent, provincial Americans in 1952 was swirling past me, and not a precious drop was wasted, not with Peter and his mother nearby. I wasn't in their apartment that often—they had the cheaper, one-bedroom model—but every time I entered it I was struck by the fumes of something lurid. Peter's mother wasn't much older than thirty, her hair was black and ringleted, her body lean and firm, her habits and language loose and leering. She'd strung clotheslines across the living room, and her entire stock of lingerie and negligees was usually on display. Her job demanded a lot of buttressing and tressing, as well as display and ornamentation. The apartment was always dark, always a den, in deference to her strange professional hours. I'd never seen so many bottles and lotions; things to drink, to spray, to paint, to rub in, to rub off; it shocked me, the absence of normal food, the exclusion of anything not related to her body, skin and hair. The sofa was draped in suggestive dresses still in dry-cleaner's plastic, and the kitchen had hosiery soaking in the sink and a slab of meat defrosting on the counter. Peter slept in the dining room, on a foldaway cot that he had to dispose of in a closet every morning. They had a large television set, a 'deal' she'd gotten from a motel close-out, but it didn't work.

What I responded to, of course, was the implicit savagery of that mother-son situation. She had nothing of the mother in her. She was a cruel woman who got by on lies about her youth, supported by candlelight and booze. A thirteen-year-old at home—who, as luck would have it, looked much older, with a jockey-like ropy body and tight, lined face of a child who wouldn't be growing much taller or broader—was the last thing in the world she would acknowledge as her own. They treated each other like husband and wife; he drank with her, gave her massages and sometimes crawled into bed with her.

There wasn't a time I visited when his mother was up and moving that I didn't leave that apartment without something shocking to me, some hunk of flesh observed or knowledge that would stimulate me like a laboratory rat in an uncontrolled experiment. She would excite a centre of consciousness, but leave me without completion or comprehension. A moment caught in the kitchen, with Mrs Humphries talking casually of 'ragging it' and needing some peace and quiet; of a man's voice muffled by the door to her bedroom shouting out, 'Hey, what the—?'

The most frightening moment didn't concern her at all. It was with Peter alone. 'Hey, want to see something? Look in here.' And before I could stop him, he was into his mother's clothes, underwear first, then the dresses and finally the make-up, all very professionally applied. We avoided each other for a few weeks after that. He'd let something drop.

My mother called her 'the slut'. Peter called her 'her' and 'she'. To have been the son of such a woman, to have absorbed the full blast without any shield (even grown men could take her only one night at a time) was a formula for disaster more potent than even my own. I envied him the nakedness of things in his life. His mother was to me, thanks to the luxury of deflection, like a pair of 3-D glasses on the world; things I couldn't have noticed in my mother or in my secretive parents stood in sharp relief thanks to her. And thanks to Peter, on those nights he'd shared my bed, I learned how women were built, what Kotexes were for, where 'it' went and how it got there. Thanks to Peter, I became a statistically normal American pre-teen, as judged by the Kinsey Foundation.

In most areas of development, I was keeping pace. Peter was the sexual guide, his mother the sexual quarry and my parents, the ultimately mysterious Reg and Hennie, were receding nicely from me as peers took over. A career based on my odd little passion for resolving distant images, for pulling in signals, was suggesting itself. It would be consistent with all this data to say that I grew up to become an astronomer, monitoring deep-dish radio telescope on a thin-aired mountaintop far from the murk of Pittsburgh. But even as children we are scouts; more daring and treacherous than the troops we lead, than the adults we become.

I have spoken of all the things I knew in 1952. What I didn't know was about to kill me. I died in 1952, not from my epilepsy or a fall from a sixth floor or an electric jolt or anything else from that world of Pittsburgh or Peter Humphries. These fragments stand out to me now, against a black background, and that seems to be the nature of childhood as it bleeds into adolescence: that we see faces without the lies and sympathies of self-protection, we can live events without antecedent or consequence. They appear tantalizingly sharp, but in a veil of snow and static: we can make them out, but then they fade and are no more.

My parents: Reg and Hennie Porter. My name is Philip. Phil Porter. Reg was working in a department store called Rosenbaum's in downtown Pittsburgh. It's been gone a quarter of a century now, so I'll not disguise any of these names. Names are treacherous anyway.

Reg was a good-looking man, about fifty, with dense white chest hair and forearms thick as Popeye's, hairy and with 'Amor Vincit' tattooed on one in a thin, unfurled banner under a starlet's face, neck and bare shoulders down to what promised to be indecent cleavage. He'd been married twice before, so far as I knew, and I'd found that out only when I overheard it. It didn't seem safe to ask if he had other children, though they'd hardly be kids. He might have married at twenty or less, so conceivably there were other Porters around, somewhere in New England, where he came from. He usually had the accent to prove it. But those kids could be thirty. My parents had been married eighteen years—I knew that from their number of anniversaries. I loved every aspect of that man.

If I could stop time, or stop narration, I would linger on the lean, graceful, grey-haired buxom figure of my mother (as she suddenly stands out to me) in the late summer of 1952. She was a woman softened by the grey in her hair, made younger by it (I don't remember her dark-haired, but I suspect she had looked almost masculine, the kind of young woman who must have a very handsome brother somewhere; a face that seems to find its resolution in the opposite sex). She hadn't married till thirty-two. Grey hair had finally focused her face, the way a beard might define an otherwise unspectacular set of features.

I've said enough. You will know already that the story is beginning to turn inside out. I had Oedipal longings—still do, doubtless, since I've never consciously considered them or worked them out—and my hours of staring into snowy screens, rejoicing with any faint signal, offers to me now a portrait of sublimation. There is sexual energy sparking over the gaps. And all my attempts at refining the images are doomed because the interference is built in: in my brain where blood vessels and nerve endings just don't quite reach, where some blunt or sharp object—in my case, a shard of bone—sliced through. And of the other connections to family and to place and even to language, I cannot speak at all. Those were things out on the street, outside of me entirely, about to knock on our door.

All right. People wonder what it's like to die, and since I've done it several hundred little-bad times and a few great convulsive big-bad times, and have died in other ways, too, I'll start small and build.

Dying is like this. You are twelve, coming back to the apartment after school. Picture it September, those scratchy days when the heat is up and school's not serious yet and the summer pursuits are still operative. I came home with a cherry sno-cone, about four o'clock. The front door was half open. Inside were half-packed boxes, all over the place, where selections of our things had been thrown in. My mother dashed from the kitchen to another opened box, a stack of china against her bosom, and eased them into the box and scrunched some pages of the *Post-Gazette* around them. She was a careful packer, and this was not careful packing. And because of my unexpected entrance, my shocked silence, her concentration, she did not see me. I caught her in expressions

I'd never seen before; she was smaller, younger, sexier than she'd ever appeared before, all the more so for her obvious distress, or distraction, or anger—whatever indefinable thing it was. We'd moved many times before, and usually under bad conditions—to towns we didn't know and where we had no address. Those moves were chance things: pack up the car, flee a city and travel to a place where a job might be waiting. Then find an apartment after a few days in a squalid hotel, unpack, put the boy in school. We'd sometimes moved when rent was due; my father was so calm about it he could meet a landlord at the door, listen politely to his demand, reach in his pocket for the chequebook, saying all the time, 'Sure, sure', and then slap his forehead, 'God, forgot it!'

'That's okay, what about tomorrow?' the landlord would say.

'Right you are,' my father would say, 'first thing in the morning.' And two hours later we'd be at the outskirts of town, heading deeper into America.

My death was standing at the open door of my apartment, seeing my mother run from the kitchen clutching a stack of plates against her blouse and dropping them into a box, and thinking:

1. We're moving.
2. We're skipping.
3. Something terrible is happening.
4. Christ, my mother is a *sexy* woman.
   a) On reflection, this last insight is tempered by the further insight that nearly any woman, when viewed unannounced, in the privacy of her living room, is sexy. That is, the act of observing is sexy.
   b) She legitimately was sexy. Her hair was up, but falling down, the grey and the black, and she was in slacks and one of my father's shirts, and she was looking good.

c) Sexiness, if I am now to lift it from any immediate context or application to any particular woman, is (for me) an appearance that borders on slovenliness. Sex will never embrace me in tennis shorts, in a bikini, or in any fetishistic combination of high heels and low neckline. Sex is the look that says, 'Help me out of these clothes', or shows that things she's wearing are a constriction, not an attraction.

On that late summer day in 1952, standing quietly and excitedly in the door of our apartment that was soon not to be our apartment, I had a seizure. When I woke up a few minutes later, my mother was holding the wooden spoon she used to keep me from biting my own tongue (what abuse that spoon had taken, over the years!). My mind was absolutely clean: I woke up remembering only that I knew something about my mother. And I knew something else: that this move was different from the others. In this one, the furniture was staying, but papers I'd never seen before were littering the floor. Papers in old leather folders with the crushed ribbons of official documents that had not been untied in a generation. When I could walk, she helped me back to the bedroom. She indicated that I should fall over my parents' double bed, but I ritually opened my own bedroom door.

Sitting on my bed was my father. I saw him in bright colour, the way only an epileptic can see the world, after an attack. I saw every pore, every hair, intensely sharp. I would not have recognized him on the street. He was crying, and it looked to me that he had been crying for hours and that he had nothing left to cry with. His shirt buttons were torn open, but his tie was still knotted, red silk over chest hair. His sleeves were rolled back, those massive arms lay helpless at his side and the cuff links were still stuck in the cuffs, and I worried that they'd fall out. My mother pushed me hard, out of my room and into theirs, and I was still groggy two hours later when she put two suitcases in my hands and told me to march quickly and quietly to the car, which was parked in the alley.

We headed north towards Buffalo and slipped through the middle of New York State all night long. He knew where he was going, though he didn't tell me. Around two o'clock in the morning he pulled into a large motel between Syracuse and Utica, waking me again, almost shaking me to make sure I was awake.

'Philip,' he said, all the time shaking me. 'Philip, until I tell you it's okay to talk, I don't want you to say a word. Not one word. Not even if someone talks to you, understand?'

'Even if things seem wrong,' my mother said. 'Even if you don't understand a thing.'

At three in the morning my father and I went prowling through the parking lot of that large motel while my mother slept in the car. I was scouting for a licence plate and a dollar bounty offered by my father. Finally I found one, on a black, pre-war Ford. My father stripped it of its plate—like Pennsylvania, they had only a rear plate—and put it on our car. Our plate was creased until it snapped, then buried. At five o'clock we were on the road again, over the Adirondacks, with my mother driving. They were talking now of 'the border', and the motels were flying two sets of flags, the American and a red British one, and ads were appearing for duty-free items. When the customs houses were in view, she pulled off to the side. My father took over. 'Tell him,' he told my mother and she turned around to face me.

'In a minute we'll be going to Canada. Canada is where your father and I come from.' She flashed some of those documents in front of me. 'We're going to Montreal. We have relatives in Montreal.'

I still had not spoken, could not speak.

'Our name will change when we go over the border. Forget all you ever knew about Porter. Our real name is Carry-A. Like this—see?' She showed me a plastic-coated green-framed card with an old picture of my father on it. I couldn't pronounce the name, but the letters bit into my brain. Réjean Carrier.

'What's my name?' I asked.

'I thought I told you to shut up,' said my father.

There were two cars in front of us. My father found a radio station playing strange music in a foreign language.

'You can be anything you want to be,' said my mother.

DUNKELBLAU

WILLI NADEAU has lain abed since birth, dumb and apparently unreachable, his bones as fragile as rods of hollow glass. He sleeps on pillows, his crib is padded. He is four. His mother is forty-two and has lost her only family. The boy, the lump, is all she lives for. Two succeeding pregnancies have ended in the seventh month. She remembers a burning, the heavy settling, and knows she is carrying another death. A brother is stillborn and a sister, lumpish as Willi, survives three months. Willi lives—if that's the word—because he is the first, before she developed antibodies to his father. His parents are profoundly incompatible.

In 1944, Army research synthesizes a thyroid extract. The pills are tiny, mottled brown. Two weeks after giving him the medicine, his mother feels his neck twitch as she sponges him in the kitchen sink. A week later, he kicks, and in a moment as dramatic in his family as Helen Keller at the water pump, he starts singing the words and music of 'Don't Fence Me In'. He justifies all her faith in keeping him at home, in reading the medical journals and pestering doctors, the four years of talking to him in both her languages, reading to him, hanging maps and showing pictures.

Like many a genius before him, though he is nearly five, he speaks in complete sentences before taking his first step. He demands his dozen glasses of cold milk a day be served in a heated bunny mug. He is a wilful, confident child, his mother's image. He likes the feel of heat on his lips, the icy cold going down. Each glass has to have a spoonful of molasses or of Horlick's Malted Milk, unstirred, at the bottom. No flecks of cream can show. The nightly slabs of liver or other organ meats, purchased on special rations, are shaped into states or countries, pre-determined by Willi and his mother from prior consultation. She starts taking him to Carnegie Library and Museum as soon as he can walk.

He memorizes the Pittsburgh trolley-numbering system. The Holy Roman Emperors, the Popes, the Kings of England. He memorizes everything, his brain is ruthlessly absorptive, a sponge, like his bones and muscles. Toy-sized yellow and red trolleys pass across a forested valley outside his bedroom window. He is still unsteady on his feet in the winter of 1945 when they take their number 10 trolley down to Liberty Avenue and then one of the 70s out to Oakland to the Library and Museum.

His first memories are of the Library, the smell of old books, the low chairs and tables of the children's room, and of staring into the adult reading room—no children allowed— while his mother checks the carts of new arrivals. The adult room is a cave of wonders, where steam rises from the piled-up coats and scarves. The six-story ceiling, the polished wood and the corridors of books overhead absorb the coughs and page-shufflings of the white-haired men and women who sit around the tables. That is the world that awaits him— admission to the adult room, permission to sit under those long-necked lamps that hang from the rafters six floors up to nearly graze the tabletops, flooding the tables with a rich yellow light under bright green shades. It is a world worth waiting for, like the dark blue volumes of *My Book House* which his mother reads from every night and which are laid out above his bed, mint green to marine blue, a band of promise to take him from infancy to adolescence.

The main hall that connects the Library with the Museum is lined with paintings that his mother holds him up to see. Murky oils, Pittsburgh scenes from the Gilded Age, operagoers alighting from horse-drawn cabs in the gaslit snows of Grant Street, children riding their high-wheeled bicycles down Center Avenue. He feels the stab of every passing, irretrievable image. He can look in those faces of 1870, at the girls with their hands in fur muffs and their collars up, their eyes glittering and cheeks round and pink and full of life, and know exactly what his mother is thinking, because she is always thinking it: even these happy children are all gone, as dead as the snows and horses and all but the finest buildings, gone forever.

And there are darker Pittsburgh landscapes, with the orange glow of hellish pits fanning through the falling snow, the play of fires lighting the genteel ridges high above. Pittsburgh, with its blackened skies and acrid fumes, its intimate verticality of heaven and hell, forces allegory on all who live there. 'So simplistic,' she says, drawing his finger so close to the canvas that the guards stand and snap their fingers. Columned mansions on gaslit streets, perched above the unbanked fires, the bright pouring of molten streams of steel by sooty, sweating men far below. Heaven and Hell on the Monongahela. On their trolley rides, high on the sides of smoke-blackened buildings, he sees faded signs in lettering he can't read but knows is old. That the signs have accidentally survived but mean nothing fills him with dread and wonder, and he asks if the companies are still there, *Isidor Ash, Iron-Monger*. Those three and four-digit telephone numbers, do they still work, who do you get if you call, an imprisoned voice? Where do they all go?

He thinks of Hans von Kaltenborn and Gabriel Heatter and all the singers as being inside the radio. He presses his forehead against the back of the radio, inhaling the hot electric thrill of music from faraway cities, watching for miniature Jack Bennys and Edgar Bergens. 'Be very quiet, and quick, they'll run if they see you,' his mother says. In 1945, his father calls all the men on the street over to study the first sketches of the 1946 Ford, with headlights in the fenders and no running boards. When the war is finally over he promises to junk their '38 Packard for one of these streamlined babies.

Nineteen forty-five means the children gather at the top of the dead-end street to intercept their fathers as they turn in, to be swept to their driveways like young footmen standing on the running boards and clinging to the mirrors and spotlights. The loudest kids live across the street. They're the three sons of the football coach at Duquesne. In the winter, he sleds with his father, held tight in his lap while two of the coach's sons stand on a toboggan and pass them, arguing about the war. We'll win because the Russians are on our side and Russians are eight feet tall.

In the winter, his mother piles up old papers and boards around the edge of their five-by-five porch off the kitchen and floods it in order to teach him ice-skating. She ties a pillow around him and lets him walk around the edges of the porch. His feet and ankles are undefined, like pillows. Coming down hard on an ankle, a hip, an arm, can crack a bone. But his father is Canadian and his parents met there and they skated and skied together before he was born. Knowing how to skate makes him a better son. It is important to his father and to his doctor for him to pass for normal as soon as possible.

They live on a crowded street at the edge of a heavily wooded valley that surrounds a tributary of the Allegheny River. In the winter, his father and the football coach ski down a path they have cleared to the rocks and boulders that mark the stream-bed. He's older than the coach, but a better skier and skater. 'What a beautiful animal your father is,' his mother says, watching him from the porch. On clear winter days, a rarity in Pittsburgh in those years, he can see through the blackened branches to the top of the Gulf Building and red lights on Mt. Washington. Willi transplants all his mother's night-time readings of Robin Hood into those woods. It is Sherwood Forest. Pittsburgh is Nottingham. The deer and bear and Merry Men are all out there, somewhere.

In the spring, when the ice is a morning's whitened blister over the concrete, the porch becomes his mother's studio. The buds have not yet opened, yet she arranges her paints and papers on the card table and carries out a chair to do her watercolours. She puts Mozart records on to play and keeps the kitchen door open so she can hear.

She brought her paints and bundles of drawings from Europe. Everything else is lost. Her brushes burst with colours that never drip. It reminds the boy of Disney cartoons, when a full paintbrush washes over the screen, creating the world as it touches down. That's how her paintings grow. Her colours seem especially intense, and have German names which never have satisfactory equivalents in English. He doesn't know they're enemy words; he thinks of them as irreplaceable tablets of pure colour. He laughs at *dunkelblau*, a funny word that becomes a code between them. Sometimes a fat man is Herr Dunkelblau. The last volumes of *My Book House* where the stories require too much explaining, are deep blue, dunkelblau. Other times she lies in bed behind closed window shades, holding her head with a dunkelblau. The opposite of dark, *dunkel*, he knows is *hell*, light.

'Watercolour must come down like rain,' she says. 'It should come quick like a shower and make everything shine, like rain. But it should not touch everything, not like oils.' Oils sound old and dutiful, like the museum.

'A paintstorm,' he says.

She sets him up with his paper and brushes and Woolworth's paints though he sometimes sneaks a swipe of her colours, thick and gripping as mud on his brush. Every few minutes she has to blow soot off her paper. When her German paints are gone, she'll quit painting.

She's a woman of Old World habits. Mondays and Fridays she does the wash. Because of the soot she has to take down all the white curtains, beat the rugs and bedspreads, take off the slipcovers and scrub the white shirts whose collars come back each day so black they look dipped in ink. Tuesdays are dyeing days, mixing the boxes of Rit that line the window ledge over the washtubs, to bring lime green to a Pittsburgh winter, or dunkelblau to a hot summer. Thursdays she makes the soap. Antiseptic odours fill the house, making his eyes run. Orange cakes of fresh soap are cut into shapes of states and countries. The shirts and sheets sink into the hot tub where she adds broken cakes of soap, and he adds the drops of blueing, and loses himself in the smoky trail of its dispersion. Such excitement for a child, catching the world in one of its paradoxes: adding stains to make clothes whiter. He can watch it spread forever, like watching cigarette smoke rise from his mother's ashtray or from the stubs his father burns down to nothingness, the smoke going straight up then suddenly hitting an invisible barrier and spreading out. On cleaning days, he's allowed to play in the coal bin, reading the old marks and dates of deliveries from before he was born, and throw his clothes in at the last minute, standing against the cold enamel of the washing tub as the islands of his shirt and pants and underwear resist, then drown.

Wednesdays she does the shopping, which means an afternoon of baking bread and an evening of stirring the bright orange colour tabs into the margarine. It's another low-grade art experience, like the blueing, with the added pleasure of being able to eat some of the results, melted over a bowl of Puffed Rice.

In the late summer of 1945, the war in Europe is over and the spirit on the radio is always upbeat. The arrival of troop ships is announced and train schedules from New York or Los Angeles tell Pittsburghers where to meet their boys. His mother listens for news of Europe, but there's never enough. Nineteen forty-five is a year to gladden everyone but her. 'Just because you're German and you lost?' he asks her once, remembering the taunt of the coach's sons, and she runs from the room. He asks her who the best singer is—Bing Crosby, she says—and the funniest person—Bob Hope, she guesses, though they both prefer Jack Benny—and the prettiest woman—she couldn't say, ladies don't know who's pretty that way, but maybe he could ask his father—so, okay, the handsomest man—Van Johnson, they say—but the men she thinks are handsomer aren't around any more.

Nineteen forty-five is the happiest year in his father's life and in the lives of the men on their street, whose jobs will all be getting bigger. There'll be houses to buy and new businesses to open and of course new cars, especially new cars. They're all thinking of leaving Pittsburgh. The Depression mentality is over, they've won the war, they're Number One in the world. But everything about 1945 makes his mother sadder, especially everyone's happiness. She shows him pictures of old men and women and children in striped pyjamas. 'So now we know that men are hideous beasts,' she says. 'What kind of world is this?' Nineteen forty-five is the saddest year in existence. His father says it's like a sickness, her questions. You're crazy, he says. We'll all be rich if she'll just shut up and give him a chance.

She's busier than ever on the afternoons when the housework and shopping are done, painting the full, dark green summer of August, 1945. The atom bomb ends the war with Japan. He watches the woods and asks her if that isn't a bit of smoke rising through the trees, coming from the bottom of the woods, along the riverbank.

His father's winter ski-run offers a sightline through the woods if he goes between their house and Hutchisons' and stretches out on his stomach and peers down it as far as he can. He sees nothing at first, just the collapse of the vanishing point into a thicket of trees, but then he sees something: men, and maybe a horse. Horses in the woods! The woods are uninhabited, vast and practically virgin timber. When he shouts 'Men!' and 'Horses!' his mother says, 'Oh, God!' and puts her brush in a glass of clean water.

They go out the front of the house, to the top of the street. They walk down a block, turn and come to another dead-end street much like theirs, but poorer. The houses are low and wooden, more like sheds or garages. Their house is brick. Dogs and chickens run over the yards. Where the street abuts on a different part of the woods, a rutted path eases down into the dark. From there, they can see what the forest has given birth to: many men and some children, and two horses pulling a wagon.

'Gypsies!' she whispers.

Already the women on the street are chasing down their dogs and loose chickens. They stand at the top of the trail and shout at the wagoners in words he can't understand. 'It's Polish,' his mother says. 'They're warning them not to come too close.' Children come out of the houses, carrying utensils and beating them with spoons.

'Stay close,' she says.

They wait for the wagon to mount the hill. The wagon is fat, ready to split, decked out in bells and leather straps with metal pots hanging from the corners. The men wear black hats with silver discs around the brims. There are no women. There are boys with long curly hair under their hats and men with open shirts and blackened arms beating spoons against the pots making a kind of chant. Street dogs are howling. The gypsies stop the noise just in front of the line of Polish women, and the boys lower the cart's back gate to expose a stone wheel operated by an old, white-haired man. The man wears an earring, something the boy has never seen, and it frightens him.

She wants him to watch. She holds him up, as she does in front of the paintings at the Library. And then she walks the length of the wagon with him, peering inside. 'You should see and not be frightened,' she says. The gypsies don't seem to care. The gypsy children follow them, laughing, and pull at his mother's skirt.

'Stop it!' she commands. 'You're very ill-behaved.'

They pull again.

'Brats! *Bengeln!*'

They giggle louder. '*Unverschämt!*'

When she speaks harshly like that, she's usually very angry and usually the person she's angry with, his father, does not understand. Bad behaviour is the only thing that gets her angry. Other things make her sad. Finally one of the men inside the wagon barks out a command and the children back off.

'Come to my street when you finish,' she says, pointing over the row of low, unpainted houses. 'I have some things.' The Polish women are now lined up with knives and scissors and some large cooking pots.

In one of the dark blue *Book Houses* there's a picture of a gypsy man holding a white horse in the moonlight, calling under a girl's window. For Willi, gypsies are a people out of the dream world of pictures and legends, and this is the first time he's seen something from his books come alive. In his light green world of *Book House* the pictures are all of talking animals. Later on they become magicians in tall caps decorated with stars and moons, then knights on horseback, Crusaders and explorers. He's not given up the notion that their woods contain Robin Hood and his men, and now that it's given birth to gypsies, he takes heart again.

They hurry back to their house and his mother empties all the kitchen drawers and takes out the pots and pans and cake dishes, everything metal that is scratched or dented or has grown dull. She bundles them in a sheet and lays them on the front lawn. Then she grabs her drawing pad and some pencils and starts sketching from the front of the house. It's the first time she's sketched the street and not the woods. The beauty, she says, is all in the back.

In the front are houses just like theirs, and an open lot across the street where the larger boys play football and fathers play catch with their sons. He can't play—any shock can still shatter his bones. The opposite side of the street is much higher than theirs, even the empty lot is higher than the roof of their house. He can stand on the grass and see over his house and over the woods all the way to the Gulf Building. In other summers the sons of the football coach batted tennis balls and scuffed-up golf balls into high arcs over his house and the Hutchisons' into the trees and valley beyond.

Before the gypsies turn the corner, with the distant banging of the pots and clanging of the bells, and then the sharp cracking of the horsewhip, his mother has sketched in the roof lines, the trees and the open lot. She's gotten the big tricycles in the driveways and one parked car.

'Gypsies! Lock your houses, take in your children, mind your dogs!' women on the street yell out, but soon enough they stand in their driveways clutching their knives and cooking pots. His mother pulls the covering sheet off her pile of metal utensils and tells a man everything needs polishing and sharpening and smoothing out, and she doesn't care how long it takes. By the time they're finished, she's gotten their picture, every detail in place with her pencils and charcoal: the horses, the children in their hats chasing dogs, all the clutter the wagon contains. She keeps sharpening her pencils against a block of sandpaper. She ignores the children who watch over her shoulder. Normally she stops anything she's drawing in order to demonstrate. When they leave, her arms are shaking, her hair is sticking to her forehead.

Later, when she sprays fixative, she says she hasn't worked so hard since her days at art school. She adds the drawing to her oldest sketches, those of German cathedral doors and Egyptian pottery and Nefertiti's head from the Berlin Museum, and country scenes of cows and horses and farmers bundling hay.

'A drawing should show everything,' she says, and that's what she likes about the gypsies; they are art, frightening and fascinating, their wagons are beautiful because they totally express the lives they lead.

'The war was fought over people like them,' she says. 'And people like us.'

But the gypsies don't go away. Smoke from their encampment drifts up from the riverside, settles in a blue haze with the rest of Pittsburgh's smog. Through the early fall they're a familiar sight on the streets, and gradually the girls and women appear too, dressed in bandannas and wide colourful skirts. They come to the front doors, bold as you please, the neighbours say, offering to do housework and tell fortunes, selling eggs and strange-smelling flowers so strong they can drug you in the night. His mother draws the line at letting gypsies in the house. She doubts the wide skirts are purely a fashion statement.

As the leaves turn and drop they can see through to the encampment. There are four wagons and several cooking fires. His mother sketches it all, the ghostly outlines of the wagons through the tracery of branches, the horses, the pen for animals rumoured but unseen—bears, panthers, half-tamed wolves. It's a curious relationship she has with gypsies, to admire but not to trust, to adore as subjects while wishing they'd leave. The boy wants them gone. They excite his mother and make her strange. The gypsies are closer than he'd thought possible. He can hear them at night.

The assault begins with the coach's sons. They throw crushed limestones from the open lot across the street. They bat stones and golf balls, they use slingshots and their well-trained arms. They sneak down the slope and throw from the

Nadeaus' side of the street, even from the corridor between their house and the Hutchisons', until his mother chases them off. From the sharp whinny of the horses, the barking and the occasional echo of stones on wood or metal, he knows the stones are striking home.

In early November the gypsies leave. 'West Virginia,' people say, a proper place for gypsies. Winter comes and the snows. His father and the coach are back on their ski run and the boy is strong enough to skate across the flooded porch. His father's plans are to leave Sears and go south, now that the country is back to normal. No more Carnegie Library, no more streetcar numbers to memorize, and maybe he'll never get a card for the adult reading room. When his father mentions the word 'south' his mother shudders and leaves the room.

Being European, she doesn't believe in baby-sitters. She doesn't leave him until he is strong enough to walk on his own and be careful with appliances. On New Year's Eve they're invited to a party next door at Hutch and Marge's, friends of his father, a gregarious man. It's a cold, snowless night and he's allowed to sleep in the living room on the sofa with the radio on to see if he can stay awake for 1946. His mother promises she'll come over and wake him.

The Christmas tree is up, the electric train circles the wrinkled sheet city of snowy hills. When he wakes up with only the tree lights on, the radio is humming but not playing music and he thinks he must have slept through everything. Nineteen forty-five is the first year of his consciousness, the year of his true birth, and now it is over. It has died, and he is born. The worst year in history, his mother says. The best, his father counters. He gets up and looks next door to Hutch and Marge's where a light is on and it looks close enough to run to, barefoot in his pyjamas.

The door is open and the vestibule is jammed with fur coats. The air inside is hot and thick with smoke and forced, loud laughter. His father and the coach are the oldest men in the room, and the loudest and happiest. Theirs is a young street of mainly childless couples ready now to start their families. The women are getting pregnant, there's a sharp bite of sexuality in the air, lives are going places but still on hold, the country is going places, big places, but hasn't quite gotten over its wartime gloom and pinchpenny habits. Those are the attitudes he hears and takes as truth. He sides with his father in the arguments because his father's a great one for looking ahead, on the bright side, to the future. The aluminum Train of Tomorrow is barrelling down the tracks, taking them all to a chrome-plated, streamlined, lightweight future and cities like Pittsburgh with their dirty bricks and labour problems are in the way of progress. If you're in the way, better clear out. A damned shame some people just can't get in the spirit.

149

'And you think the south is progress?' his mother demands.

His father is singing, with his back to the fireplace. Not French songs, the way they usually ask him to at parties, but Bing Crosby songs. Around the mirror over the mantel, Hutch and Marge have pasted all their Christmas cards. Their tree is bigger than the Nadeaus', and the lights blink and some other candles bubble. Everyone is outlined in blue and red and faint ghostly yellow. All the women except his mother are blonds, with big round coral earrings and bright lipstick that stains their cigarettes. Some still wear little hats with their veils half pulled down.

He stands in the hallway, leaning against a fur coat, peering around the edge. They're singing the New Year's Song his mother taught him, and they're blowing on paper trumpets and strapping on little cone-shaped hats. His mother stands at the far end of the living room, by the kitchen door where the light is strongest. *I don't feel like celebrating,* she declared earlier and his father had left on his own, shouting, *You can't ruin it for me,* but she went anyway, a few minutes later. He peels off his pyjamas and wraps himself in her fur coat. No one notices him. Her head is down and her hands hold the sides of her face, pressing down her veil. She seems to be rocking back and forth. Someone has set a lime-green party hat on top of her black pillbox with the single pheasant feather.

They're counting backwards. When the numbers get smaller, the noise increases and he's shouting with everyone, trailing the heavy coat, 'It's 1946! It's 1946!' running naked into the living room like the Baby New Year with the sash. A few women hug him and squeeze him tight in their unsteadiness. His father looks around to see how he's gotten there—he has Marge and another woman on his arms—and all the men are going around collecting kisses.

'For God's sake, Liesl—' his father calls and she drops to her knees with her arms open as he pushes his way to her through a jitterbugging dance floor. It seems to take hours. She rolls up her veil to touch her eyes with a paper napkin.

Her fur coat falls from his shoulders as she lifts him. He rubs his cheek against the rough and the fine mesh of her veil, feels her cool satin dress against his naked body, and they dance. It seems the whirling will go on forever, even as the music dies out, then the laughter, and he and his mother dance their way out the door, shivering, across the icy grass to home.

GRIDS AND DOGLEGS

WHEN I WAS SIXTEEN I could spend whole evenings with a straight-edge, a pencil, and a few sheets of unlined construction paper, and with those tools I would lay out imaginary cities along twisting rivers or ragged coastlines. Centuries of expansion and division, terrors of fire and renewal, recorded in the primitive fiction of gaps and clusters, grids and doglegs. My cities were tangles; inevitably, like Pittsburgh. And as I built my cities, I'd keep the Pirates game on (in another notebook I kept running accounts of my team's declining fortunes—'Well, Tony Bartirome, that knocks you down to .188'—the pre-game averages were never exact enough for me), and during the summers I excavated for the Department of Man, Carnegie Museum. Twice a week during the winter I visited the Casino Burlesque (this a winter pleasure, to counter the loss of baseball). I was a painter too, of sweeping subjects: my paleobotanical murals for the Devonian Fishes Hall are still a model for younger painter-excavators. (Are there others, still, like me, in Pittsburgh? This story is for them.) On Saturdays I lectured to the Junior Amateur Archaeologists and Anthropologists of Western Pennsylvania. I was a high school junior, my parents worked at their

new store, and I was, obviously, mostly alone. In the afternoons, winter and summer, I picked up dirty clothes for my
father's laundry.

I had—obviously, again—very few friends; there were not
many boys like me. Fat, but without real bulk, arrogant but
ridiculously shy. Certifiably brilliant but hopelessly unstudi-
ous, I felt unallied to even the conventionally bright honour-
rollers in my suburban high school. Keith Godwin was my
closest friend; I took three meals a week at his house, and usually slept over on Friday night.

Keith's father was a chemist with Alcoa; his mother a pillar
of the local United Presbyterian Church, the Women's Club,
and the University Women's chapter. The four children (all but
Keith, the oldest), were models of charm, ambition and beauty.
Keith was a moon-faced redhead with freckles and dimples—
one would never suspect the depth of his cynicism—with just
two real passions: the organ and competitive chess. I have
seen him win five simultaneous blindfold games, ten-second
moves—against tournament competition. We used to play
at the dinner table without the board, calling out our moves
while shovelling in the food. Years later, high-school atheism
behind him, he enrolled in a Presbyterian seminary of Cal-
vinist persuasions and is now a minister somewhere in California. He leads a number of extremist campaigns (crackpot
drives, to be exact), against education, books, movies, minori-
ties, pacifists—this, too, was a part of our rebellion, though
I've turned the opposite way. But this isn't a story about Keith.
He had a sister, Cyndy, one year younger.

She was tall, like her father, about five eight, an inch taller
than I. Hers was the beauty of contrasts: fair skin, dark hair,
grey eyes and the sharpness of features so common in girls
who take after their fathers. Progressively I was to desire her
as a sister, then wife and finally as lover; but by then, of course,
it was too late. I took a fix on her, and she guided me through

high school; no matter how far out I veered, the hope of eventually pleasing Cyndy drove me back.

In the summer of my junior year I put away the spade and my collection of pots and flints, and took up astronomy. There's a romance to astronomy, an almost courtly type of pain and fascination, felt by all who study it. The excitement: that like a character in the childhood comics, I could shrink myself and dismiss the petty frustrations of school, the indifference of Cyndy and my parents; that I could submit to points of light long burned out and be rewarded with their cosmic tolerance of my obesity; that I could submit to the ridicule I suffered from the athletes in the lunch line, and to the Pirates' latest losing streak. I memorized all I could from the basic texts at Carnegie Library, and shifted my allegiance from Carnegie Museum to Buhl Planetarium. There was a workshop in the basement just getting going, started for teenage telescope-builders, and I became a charter member.

Each week I ground out my lens; glass over glass through gritty water, one night a week for a least a year. Fine precise work, never my style, but I stuck with it while most of the charter enthusiasts fell away. The abrasive carborundum grew finer, month by month, from sand, to talc, to rouge—a single fleck of a coarser grade in those final months would have ploughed my mirror like a meteorite. Considering the winter nights on which I sacrificed movies and TV for that lens, the long streetcar rides, the aching arches, the insults from the German shop foreman, the meticulous scrubbing-down after each Wednesday session, the temptation to sneak upstairs for the 'Skyshow' with one of the chubby compliant girls— my alter egos—from the Jewish high school: *considering all that*, plus the all-important exclusiveness and recognition it granted, that superb instrument was a heavy investment to sell, finally, for a mere three hundred dollars. But I did, in the fine-polishing stage, because, I felt, I owed it to Cyndy. Three hundred dollars, for a new investment in myself.

Astronomy is the moral heavyweight of the physical sciences; it is a humiliating science, a destroyer of pride in human achievements, or shame in human failings. Compared to the vacant dimensions of space—of time, distance and temperature—what could be felt for Eisenhower's heart attack, Grecian urns, six million Jews, my waddle and shiny gabardines? My parents were nearing separation, their store beginning to falter—what could I care for their silence, their fights, the begging for bigger and bigger loans? The diameter of Antares, the Messier system, the swelling of space into uncreated nothingness—these things mattered because they were large, remote and perpetual. The Tammany Ring and follies of Hitler, Shakespeare and the Constitution were dust; the Andromeda galaxy was *worlds*. I took my meals out or with the Godwins, and I thought of these things as I struggled at chess with Keith and caught glimpses of Cyndy as she dried the dishes—if only I'd had dishes to dry!

The arrogance of astronomy, archaeology, chess, burlesque, baseball, science-fiction, everything I care for: humility and arrogance are often so close (the men I'm writing this for—who once painted murals and played in high school bands just to feel a part of something—they know); it's all the same feeling, isn't it? Nothing matters, except, perhaps, the proper irony. I had that irony once (I wish, in fact, I had it now), and it was something like this:

In the days of the fifties, each home room of each suburban high school started the day with a Bible reading and the pledge of allegiance to the flag. Thirty mumbling souls, one fervent old woman and me. It had taken me one night, five years earlier, to learn the Lord's Prayer backwards. I had looked up, as well, the Russian pledge and gotten it translated into English:

this did for my daily morning ablutions. The lone difficulty had to do with Bible week, which descended without warning on a Monday morning with the demand that we, in turn, quote a snatch from the Bible. This is fine if your name is Zymurgy and you've had a chance to memorize everyone else's favourite, or the shortest verse. But I am a Dyer, and preceded often by Cohens and Bernsteins (more on that later): Bible week often caught me unprepared. So it happened in the winter of my senior year that Marvin Bernstein was excused ('We won't ask Marvin, class, for he is of a different faith. Aren't you, Marvin?') And then a ruffian named Callahan rattled off a quick, 'For God so loved the world that he gave his only begotten Son . . .' so fast that I couldn't catch it. A Sheila Cohen, whose white bra straps I'd stared at for one hour a day, five days a week, for three years—Sheila Cohen was excused. And Norman Dyer, I, stood. 'Remember, Norman,' said the teacher, 'I won't have the Lord's Prayer and the Twenty-second Psalm.' She didn't like Callahan's rendition either, and knew she'd get thirty more. From me she expected originality. I didn't disappoint.

'Om,' I said, and quickly sat. I'd learned it from the Vedanta, something an astronomer studies.

Her smile had frozen. It was her habit, after a recitation, to smile and nod and congratulate us with, 'Ah, yes, Revelations, a lovely choice, Nancy . . .' But gathering her pluckiness she demanded, 'Just what is that supposed to mean, Norman?'

'Everything,' I said, with an astronomer's shrug. I was preparing a justification, something to do with more people in the world praying 'Om' than anything else, but I had never caused trouble before, and she decided to drop it. She called on my alphabetical shadow (a boy who'd stared for three years at my dandruff and flaring ears?), another Catholic, Dykes was his name, and Dykes this time, instead of following Callahan, twisted the knife a little deeper, and boomed out, 'Om . . . amen!' Our teacher shut the Bible, caressed the marker, the white leather binding, and then read us a long passage having to do, as I recall, with nothing we had said.

That was the only victory of my high school years.

*   *   *

I imagined a hundred disasters a day that would wash Cyndy Godwin into my arms, grateful and bedraggled. Keith never suspected. My passion had a single outlet—the telephone. Alone in my parents' duplex, the television on, the Pirates game on, I would phone. No need to check the dial, the fingering was instinctive. Two rings at the Godwins'; if anyone but Cyndy answered, I'd hang up immediately. But with Cyndy I'd hold, through her perplexed 'Hellos?' till she queried, 'Susie, is that you?' 'Brenda?' 'Who is it, please?' and I would hold until her voice betrayed fear beyond the irritation. Oh, the pleasure of her slightly hysterical voice, 'Daddy, it's that *man* again,' and I would sniffle menacingly into the mouthpiece. Then I'd hang up and it was over; like a Pirates loss, nothing to do but wait for tomorrow. Cyndy would answer the phone perhaps twice a week. Added to the three meals a week I took with them, I convinced myself that five sightings or soundings a week would eventually cinch a marriage if I but waited for a sign she'd surely give me. She was of course dating a bright, good-looking boy a year ahead of me (already at Princeton), a conventional sort of doctor-to-be, active in Scouts, choir, sports and Junior Achievement, attending Princeton on the annual Kiwanis Fellowship. A very common type in our school and suburb, easily tolerated and easily dismissed. Clearly, a girl of Cyndy's sensitivity could not long endure his ministerial humour, his mere ignorance disguised as modesty. Everything about him—good looks, activities, athletics, piety, manners—spoke against him. In those years the only competition for Cyndy that I might have feared would have come from someone of my own circle. And that was impossible, for none of us had ever had a date.

And I knew her like a brother! Hours spent with her playing Scrabble, driving her to the doctor's for curious flaws I was never to learn about ... and, in the summers, accompanying the family to their cabin and at night hearing her breathing beyond a burlap wall ... Like a brother? Not even that, for as I write I remember Keith grabbing her on the stairs, slamming his open hands against her breasts, and Cyndy responding, while I ached to save her, 'Keith! What will Normie think?' And this went on for three years, from the first evening I ate with the Godwins when I was in tenth grade, till the spring semester of my senior year; Cyndy was a junior. There was no drama, no falling action, merely a sweet and painful stasis that I aggrandized with a dozen readings of *Cyrano de Bergerac*, and a customizing of his soliloquies ... 'This butt that follows me by half an hour ... An ass, you say? Say rather a caboose, a dessert ...' All of this was bound to end, only when I could break the balance.

We are back to the telescope, the three hundred well-earned dollars. Some kids I knew, Keith not included this time, took over the school printing press and ran off one thousand dramatic broadsheets, condemning a dozen teachers for incompetence and Lesbianism (a word that we knew meant more than 'an inhabitant of Lesbos,' the definition in our highschool dictionary). We were caught, we proudly confessed (astronomy again: I sent a copy to *Mad* magazine and they wrote back, *'Funny but don't get caught. You might end up working for a joint like this'*). The school wrote letters to every college that had so greedily accepted us a few weeks earlier, calling on them to retract their acceptance until we publicly apologized. Most of us did, for what good it did; I didn't—it made very little difference anyway, since my parents no longer could have afforded Yale. It would be Penn State in September.

I awoke one morning in April—a gorgeous morning—and decided to diet. A doctor in Squirrel Hill made his living prescribing amphetamines by the carload to suburban matrons. I lost thirty pounds in a month and a half, which dropped me into the ranks of the flabby underweights (funny, I'd always believed there was a *hard* me, under the fat, waiting to be sculpted out—there wasn't). And the pills (as a whole new generation is finding out) were marvellous: the uplift, the energy, the ideas they gave me! As though I'd been secretly rewired for a late but normal adolescence.

Tight new khakis and my first sweaters were now a part of the new-look Norman Dyer, which I capped one evening by calling the Arthur Murray Studios. I earned a free dance analysis by answering correctly a condescending question from their television quiz the night before. Then, with the three hundred dollars, I enrolled.

I went to three studio parties, each time with the enormous kid sister of my voluptuous instructress. That gigantic adolescent with a baby face couldn't dance a step (and had been brought along for me, I was certain), and her slimmed-down but still ample sister took on only her fellow teachers and some older, lonelier types, much to my relief. I wanted to dance, but not to be noticed. The poor big-little sister, whose name was Almajean, was dropping out of a mill-town high school in a year to become … what? I can't guess, and she didn't know, even then. We drank a lot of punch, shuffled together when we had to, and I told her about delivering clothes, something she could respect me for, never admitting that my father owned the store.

But I knew what I had to do. For my friends there was a single event in our high school careers that *had*, above all, to be missed. We had avoided every athletic contest, every dance, pep rally, party—everything voluntary and everything mildly compulsory; we had our private insurrections against the flag and God, but all that good work, all that conscientious effort, would be wasted if we attended the flurry of dances in our last two weeks. The Senior Prom was no problem—I'd been barred because of the newspaper caper. But a week later came the Women's Club College Prom, for everyone going on to higher study (92 per cent always did). The pressure for a 100 per cent turnout was stifling. Even the teachers wore WC buttons so we wouldn't forget. Home room teachers managed to find out who was still uninvited (no one to give Sheila Cohen's bra a snap?). The College Prom combined the necessary exclusiveness and sophistication—smoking was permitted on the balcony—to have become the very essence of graduation night. And there was a special feature that we high schoolers had heard about ever since the eighth grade: the sifting of seniors into a few dozen booths, right on the dance floor, to meet local alums of their college-to-be, picking up a few fraternity bids, athletic money, while the band played a medley of privileged school songs. I recalled the pain I had felt a year before, as I watched Cyndy leave with her then-senior boyfriend, and I was still there, playing chess, when they returned around 2 a.m. for punch.

It took three weeks of aborted phone calls before I asked Cyndy to the College Prom. She of course accepted. Her steady boyfriend was already at Princeton and ineligible. According to Keith, he'd left instructions: nothing serious. What did *he* know of seriousness, I thought, making my move. I bought a dinner jacket, dancing shoes, shirt, links, studs, cummerbund; and I got ten dollars' spending money from my astonished father. I was seventeen, and this was my first date.

Cyndy was a beautiful *woman* that night; it was the first time I'd seen her consciously glamorous. The year before she'd been a girl, well turned-out, but a trifle thin and shaky. But not tonight! Despite the glistening car and my flashy clothes, my new near-mesomorphy, I felt like a worm as I slipped the white orchid corsage around her wrist. (I could have had a bosom corsage; when the florist suggested it, I nearly ran from the shop. What if I jabbed her, right *there*?) And I could have cried at the trouble she'd gone to, for *me*: her hair was up, she wore glittering earrings and a pale sophisticated lipstick that made her lips look chapped. And, mercifully, flat heels. The Godwin family turned out for our departure, so happy that I had asked her, so respectful of my sudden self-assurance. Her father told me to stay out as long as we wished. Keith and the rest of my friends were supposedly at the movies, but had long been planning, I knew, for the milkman's matinee at the Casino Burlesque. I appreciated not having to face him—wondering, in fact, how I ever would again. My best-kept secret was out (oh, the ways they have of getting us kinky people straightened out!); but she was mine tonight, the purest, most beautiful, the *kindest* girl I'd ever met. And for the first time, for the briefest instant, I connected her to those familiar bodies of the strippers I knew so well, and suddenly I felt that I knew what this dating business was all about and why it excited everyone so. I understood how thrilling it must be actually to touch, and kiss, and look at naked, a beautiful woman whom you loved, and who might touch you back.

The ballroom of the Women's Club was fussily decorated; dozens of volunteers had worked all week. Clusters of spotlights strained through the sagging roof of crepe (the lights blue-filtered, something like the Casino), and the couples in formal gowns and dinner jackets seemed suddenly worthy of college and the professional lives they were destined to enter. A few people stared at Cyndy and smirked at me, and I began to feel a commingling of pride and shame, mostly the latter.

We danced a little—rumbas were my best—but mainly talked, drinking punch and nibbling the rich sugar cookies that her mother, among so many others, had helped to bake. We talked soberly, of my enforced retreat from the Ivy League (not even the car stealers and petty criminals on the fringe of our suburban society had been treated as harshly as I), of Keith's preparation for Princeton. Her grey eyes never left me. I talked of other friends, two who were leaving for a summer in Paris, to polish their French before entering Yale. Cyndy listened to it all, with her cool hand on my wrist. 'How I wish Keith had taken someone tonight!' she exclaimed.

Then at last came the finale of the dance: everyone to the centre of the floor, everyone once by the reviewing stand, while the orchestra struck up a medley of collegiate tunes. 'Hail to Pitt!' cried the president of the Women's Club, and Pitt's incoming freshmen, after whirling past the bandstand, stopped at an adjoining booth, signed a book and collected their name tags. The rousing music blared on, the fight songs of Yale and Harvard, Duquesne and Carnegie Tech, Penn State, Wash and Jeff, Denison and Wesleyan ...

'Come on, Normie, we can go outside,' she suggested. We had just passed under the reviewing stand, where the three judges were standing impassively. Something about the King and Queen; nothing I'd been let in on. The dance floor was thinning as the booths filled. I broke the dance-stride and began walking her out, only to be reminded by the W.C. president, straining above 'Going Back to Old Nassau', to keep on dancing, please. The panel of judges—two teachers selected by the students, and Mr Hartman, husband of the club's president—were already on the dance floor, smiling at the couples and poking their heads into the clogged booths. Cyndy and I were approaching the doors, near the bruisers in my Penn State booth. One of the algebra teachers was racing toward us, a wide grin on his florid face, and Cyndy gave my hand a tug. 'Normie,' she whispered, 'I think something wonderful is about to happen.'

The teacher was with us, a man much shorter than Cyndy, who panted, 'Congratulations! You're my choice.' He held a wreath of roses above her head, and she lowered her head to receive it. 'Ah—what is your name?'

'Cyndy Godwin,' she said. 'Mr Esposito.'

'Keith Godwin's sister?'

'Yes.'

'And how are you, Norman—or should I ask?' Mr Wheeler, my history teacher, shouldered his way over to us; he held out a bouquet of yellow mums. 'Two out of three,' he grinned, 'that should just about do it.'

'Do what?' I asked. I wanted to run, but felt too sick. Cyndy squeezed my cold hand; the orchid nuzzled me like a healthy dog. My knees were numb, face burning.

'Cinch it,' said Wheeler. 'King Dyer.'

'If Hartman comes up with someone else, then there'll be a vote,' Esposito explained. 'If he hasn't been bribed, then he'll choose this girl too and that'll be it.'

I have never prayed harder. Wheeler led us around the main dance floor, by the rows of chairs that were now empty. The musicians suspended the Cornell evening hymn to enable the WC president to announce dramatically, in her most practised voice, 'The Queen approaches.'

There was light applause from the far end of the floor. Couples strained from the college booths as we passed, and I could hear the undertone, '. . . he's a brain in my biology class, Norman something-or-other, but I don't know her . . .' I don't *have* to be here, I reminded myself. No one made me bring her. I could have asked one of the girls from the Planetarium who respected me for my wit and memory alone—or I could be home like any other self-respecting intellectual, in a cold sweat over *I Led Three Lives*. The Pirates were playing a twinighter and I could have been out there at Forbes Field in my favourite right-field upperdeck, where I'm an expert . . . why didn't I ask her out to a baseball game? Or I could have been where I truly belonged, with my friends down at the Casino Burlesque. . . .

'You'll lead the next dance, of course,' Wheeler whispered. Cyndy was ahead of us, with Esposito.

'Couldn't someone else?' I said. 'Maybe you—why not you?' Then I said with sudden inspiration, 'She's not a senior. I don't think she's eligible, do you?'

'Don't worry, don't worry, Norman.' I had been one of his favourite pupils. 'Her class hasn't a thing to do with it, just her looks. And Norman'—he smiled confidentially—'she's an extraordinarily beautiful girl.'

'Yeah,' I agreed, had to. I drifted to the stairs by the bandstand. 'I'm going to check anyway,' I said. I ran to Mrs Hartman herself. 'Juniors aren't eligible to be Queen, are they? I mean, she'll get her own chance next year when she's going to college, right?'

Her smile melted as she finally looked at me; she had been staring into the lights, planning her speech. 'Is her escort a senior?'

'Yes,' I admitted, 'but *he* wasn't chosen. Anyway, he's one of those guys who were kept from the Prom. By rights I don't think he should even be here.'

'I don't think this has ever come up before.' She squinted into the footlights, a well-preserved woman showing strain. 'I presume you're a class officer.'

'No, I'm her escort.'

'Her *escort?* I'm afraid I don't understand. Do I know the girl?'

'Cyndy Godwin?'

'You don't mean Betsy Godwin's girl? Surely I'm not to take the prize away from that lovely girl, just because—well, just because *why* for heaven's sake?'

The bandleader leaned over and asked if he should start the 'Miss America' theme. Mrs Hartman fluttered her hand. And then from the other side of the stand, the third judge, Mr Hartman, hissed to his wife. 'Here she is,' he beamed.

'Oh, dear me,' began Mrs Hartman.

'A vote?' I suggested. 'It has to be democratic.'

The second choice, a peppy redhead named Paula, innocently followed Mr Hartman up the stairs and was already smiling like a winner. She was a popular senior, co-vice-president of nearly everything. Oh, poise! Glorious confidence! Already the front rows were applauding the apparent Queen, though she had only Mr Hartman's slender cluster of roses to certify her. Now the band started up, the applause grew heavy, and a few enthusiasts even whistled. Her escort, a union leader's son, took his place behind her, and I cheerfully backed off the bandstand, joining Cyndy and the teachers at the foot of the steps. Cyndy had returned her flowers, and Mr Wheeler was standing dejectedly behind her, holding the bouquet. The wreath dangled from his wrist.

'I feel like a damn fool,' he said.

'That was very sweet of you, Normie,' Cyndy said, and kissed me hard on the cheek.

'I just can't get over it,' Wheeler went on. 'If anyone here deserves that damn thing, it's you. At least take the flowers.'

I took them for her. 'Would you like to go?' I asked. She took my arm and we walked out. I left the flowers on an empty chair.

I felt more at ease as we left the school and headed across the street to the car. It was a cool night, and Cyndy was warm at my side, holding my arm tightly. 'Let's have something to eat,' I suggested, having practised the line a hundred times, though it still sounded badly acted. I had planned the dinner as well; *filet mignon* on toast at a classy restaurant out on the highway. I hadn't planned it for quite so early in the night, but even so, I was confident. A girl like Cyndy ate out perhaps once or twice a year, and had probably never ordered *filet*. I was more at home in a fancy restaurant than at a family table.

'I think I'd like that,' she said.

'What happened in there was silly—just try to forget all about it,' I said. 'It's some crazy rule or something.'

We walked up a side street, past a dozen cars strewn with crepe.

'It's not winning so much,' she said. 'It's just an embarrassing thing walking up there like that and then being left holding the flowers.'

'There's always next year.'

'Oh, I won't get it again. There are lots of prettier girls than me in my class.'

An opening, I thought. So easy to tell her that she was a queen, deservedly, any place. But I couldn't even slip my arm around her waist, or take her hand that rested on my sleeve.

'Well, I think you're really pretty.' And I winced.

'Thank you, Norman.'

'Prettier than anyone I've ever—'

'I understand,' she said. Then she took my hand and pointed 165 it above the streetlights.

'I'll bet you know all those stars, don't you, Normie?'

'Sure.'

'You and Keith—you're going to be really something someday.'

We came to the car; I opened Cyndy's door and she got in. 'Normie?' she said, as she smoothed her skirt before I closed the door, 'could we hurry? I've got to use the bathroom.'

I held the door open a second. *How dare she*, I thought, that's not what she's supposed to say. This is a date; you're a queen, my own queen. I looked at the sidewalk, a few feet ahead of us, then said suddenly, bitterly, 'There's a hydrant up there. Why don't you use it?'

I slapped the headlights as I walked to my side, hoping they would shatter and I could bleed to death.

'That wasn't a very nice thing to say, Norman,' she said as I sat down.

'I know.'

'A girl who didn't know you better might have gotten offended.'

I drove carefully, afraid now on this night of calamity that I might be especially accident-prone. It was all too clear now, why she had gone with me. Lord, protect me from a too-easy forgiveness. In the restaurant parking lot, I told her how sorry I was for everything, without specifying how broad an everything I was sorry for.

'You were a perfect date,' she said. 'Come on, let's forget about everything, OK?'

Once inside, she went immediately to the powder room. The hostess, who knew me, guided me to a table at the far end of the main dining room. She would bring Cyndy to me. My dinner jacket attracted some attention; people were already turning to look for my date. I sat down; water was poured for two, a salad bowl appeared. When no one was looking, I pounded the table. *Years of this*, I thought: slapping headlights, kicking tables, wanting to scream a memory out of existence, wanting to shrink back into the stars, the quarries, the right-field stands—things that could no longer contain me. A smiling older man from the table across the aisle snapped his fingers and pointed to his cheek, then to mine, and winked. 'Lipstick!' he finally whispered, no longer smiling. I had begun to wet the napkin when I saw Cyndy and the hostess approaching—and the excitement that followed in Cyndy's wake. I stood to meet her. She was the Queen, freshly beautiful, and as I walked to her she took a hanky from her purse and pressed it to her lips. Then in front of everyone, she touched the moistened hanky to my cheek, and we turned to take our places.

NORTH

IN THE BEGINNING, my mother would meet me at the '*Gar-çons*' side of Papineau School. She might have been the tallest woman in the east end of Montreal in the early fifties. I was walking with my friend Mick. I was thirteen, and he was older but smaller. From the neck up he looked twenty. He was in my cousin Dollard's class. He had discovered me on the first day of school, standing by the iron gate looking puzzled. 'Take the garkons,' he had advised, under his breath. *Garkons* was an early word in my private vocabulary. In the beginning, I had to trust strangers' pronunciations, or worse, my own.

'You're not one of them, are you, eh?' I liked that; *them*—it sounded science-fiction. How could he tell? Getting no answer, he went on, 'My old lady, she ups and marries this Frog. What's your story?'

My story? Same old story, too preposterous. Until the week before, I'd been Phil Porter, content but lonely, riding the airwaves of Pittsburgh, attaching rabbit-ears to our apartmenthouse chimney, pulling in seven channels from adjacent states. All I said to Mick that first day was, 'My name's Carrier, but I'm not French.'

'Me too. Bloody Fortin. All the Fortins in my family are English and all the Sweeneys are French. Funny, eh? Where you from—the States? Vermont?'

Pittsburgh rang no bells for Mick Fortin. He only knew the cities that sent us tourists—Burlington, Plattsburgh, and half of Harlem, plus the cosy loop of the old NHL. 'Do you have a job yet?' he asked me, and I feared for a minute that a job was required in this new world of the French eighth grade, like my pens and tie and white shirt for school. Mick was too ignorant, too solicitous, too eager with his confessions to be trusted. He promised me a job in the spring, down along St. Catherine Street, passing out peep-show leaflets to the Yanks. 'You've heard of Lili St. Cyr, eh?' I hadn't, but nodded. 'All you gotta do is say, "C'mon'n see her! Lili St. Cyr's younger and sexier sister!" All the girls down there call themselves St. Cyr something, Mimi or Fifi. The Yanks, they eat it up.' In the beginning, I welcomed my mother's intervention.

We'd left Pittsburgh in the middle of the night. My father had assaulted a man at work. He'd found him seated at his desk, feet on an opened drawer, packing up my father's pictures and souvenirs. A younger man, brought in from the outside. He got his first three words in—'You're out, Porter'—and then my father grabbed his ankles and spilled him backwards out of the chair. Then he picked him off the floor and shoved him only once, and the new manager found himself bursting through fresh drywall and skidding to a halt by the water cooler. And my father caught the first elevator to Canada, convinced that no one knew his secret name and true identity. Some time in the middle of that night, somewhere in the middle of upstate New York, my father Reg Porter reverted to Réjean Carrier, and I was allowed to retain my name of Phil, but Porter was taken from me forever. 'You weren't born in Cincinnati like we always said,' my mother explained. 'I'm sorry, but we had to tell you that. You were born in Montreal.'

We moved into the apartment of his older brother, Théophile. I bumped Dollard from his room, and my parents took the living-room sofa. Théophile's six daughters were married, or in the church. In a pantry-sized bedroom off the kitchen lived Aunt Louise who'd married an American in Woonsocket and seen all three of her sons go down with the *Dorchester* in 1942. She didn't speak, she only lit candles, and the smell of wax permeated the apartment. My mother would have the sheets and pillows stored away each morning by seven o'clock, and I don't think they went out during the day. I don't know what they and my aunt Béatrice, who spoke no English, did all day.

The first big fight had been over my schooling. School had been in session nearly a month when we arrived on Théophile's doorstep. I hadn't known a word of French, though I began collecting words from Dollard that first day. From him, everything began with '*maudit...*' and ended with '*... de Christ sanglant.*' In a week I knew some nouns and adjectives; no verbs, no sentences. French neutralized my mother's education; she was like a silent actress. I learned to read her eyes, her lips, and to listen to her breathing, and her feelings came through like captions. She would nod her head and say, 'wee-wee', which made the simplest French words come out like baby-talk. She was one of those western Canadians of profound good will and solid background, educated and sophisticated and acutely alert to conditions in every part of the world, who could not utter a syllable of French without a painful contortion of head, neck, eyes and lips. She was convinced that the French language was a deliberate debauchery of logic, and that people who persisted in speaking it did so to cloak the particulars of a nefarious design, behind which could be detected the gnarled, bejewelled claws of the Papacy. She was, of course, too well-bred to breathe a word of this suspicion to anyone but me. All evening, then, as she stood next to Béatrice at the sink, peeling, washing, baking and frying our food, it was Béatrice's steady stream of incomprehensible opinions and my mother's head-jerking wee-wees, the smell of wax and Dollard's obscene mutterings that initiated me into a world that would be, for all I knew, mine forever.

My mother had wanted to send me to an English school, although the nearest one was at the end of two trolley rides. I was silent about it. English would obviously be easier, but not necessarily preferable. I wanted to belong, and no one I knew in Montreal spoke English, except my mother. Canadian schools, my mother said, were light-years ahead of American, and English was the only language for an intelligent boy who didn't want to become a priest. French school was so fundamentally *wrong,* it was alluring to contemplate. For the first time in my life no one could possibly expect anything from me. Théophile settled it. He was a member of the St-Jean-Baptiste Society. No one living under his roof would even study English, let alone go to school in it. Anyway, it wasn't safe. There was no way to get to an English school that didn't cut through the middle of the Jewish ghetto, where French boys were routinely butchered. He had this on good authority, though they didn't dare print it in the communist press. Dozens of French boys had disappeared—altar boys—they only used the purest blood. My mother retired to the bathroom. My father chimed in, 'They'd kill him on this street, for sure. They'd kill any kid on this street if he went to an English school.'

Tricks of the mind. Even in my memories of those three strange years, nuns and classmates seem to be speaking to me in English—a clear violation of the natural universe—and I seem to be writing papers and speaking up in class, always in English. This is clearly not so, for there's a band of three years in my life when I discovered nature where even now I'm still learning the English names. Fish, trees, flowers, weeds, food, drinks can all send me to the dictionary. And the discovery of myself as a sexual creature—slightly different from the discovery of sex itself—that too is a function of French.

For the first time in my life I felt that school was a punishment. Nuns were wardens, the cracking of the cane was arbitrary and malicious. We were prisoners serving time for a crime whose nature would presently be revealed. I assumed my guilt; it was my ignorance of the charge, not my innocence, that made the confusion so painful. I was caned in the second week. The impossible had happened *to me*. I was made to mumble an act of contrition. I wasn't even Catholic. *'Pourquoiça?'* I kept demanding as the cane kept whizzing down, day after day for a week. Even harder, for my question suggested arrogance. There would be no explanation. He was a Brother of the Order of Mary, who otherwise smiled at me when he passed me in the halls. In the second week, Soeur Timothée let it out: my cousin Dollard had been cutting classes and acting unrepentant to the brothers. *'Hôtage!'* she hissed at me, taking over the caning. *'Tu sais hôtage?'* I learned quickly enough. Finally my mother noticed the backs of my hands, the welts and bruises. She raged, with only my father and me to understand her.

'Discipline!' he exclaimed. 'That's what they give, and he has to learn to take it!' I hadn't told them about Dollard. I hadn't even told Dollard about the punishment I was taking on his behalf, but I hoped word would drift back to him before my fingers fell off. My father was defending them, in his way. Compared to *his* years with the brothers, when he'd been given to them at the age of five for eventual priesthood, my life had been one of silken pillows. If my hands hadn't been as soft as a girl's there wouldn't even be bruises. 'Look at Dollard's hands—they're like hockey gloves,' he shouted. My father wasn't defending the church—he hated it from the depths of his bowels—but he revered its implacable authority. Whatever they did to you, you should be grateful; it made you tough enough in later life to keep telling them to go to hell.

'Discipline!' my mother raged. 'You fools. You bloody fools—is that what discipline is to you? Treating children like animals? Beating them into submission? It's medieval, it's madness. You're crazy, can't you see? You're twisted, and I won't have you twisting your son the same way.' She grabbed my hands and clutched my fists to her chest. 'Discipline isn't just learning how to take pain. Discipline doesn't mean you have to be stupid. God, if the bloody church told you tomorrow the earth was flat, you'd start telling yourselves you knew it was flat all along, right? Wouldn't you? Wouldn't you?'

I felt guilty, terribly guilty, bringing on such an argument. There was injustice here, on every side. My father—that unemployed, wrecked shell of a man—was standing in for Théophile and Dollard, whose stupidities were unassailable, and for the brothers at school whose cruelties, given the system, were unremarkable and fairly even-handed. My father hadn't been inside a church in forty years, not since he'd fled the barbarities of a harsher time and place and taken those memories, that rage, into the streets of Montreal and beyond. But against my mother, his words and logic were pathetic.

Now his voice was weary. 'Okay,' he admitted. His fists were heavy in front of his face; he kept balling them up and flinging them open. 'You don't know how they think. How they work . . . It's . . .' and he shrugged his shoulders, empty of words. I wanted to complete it for him; I understood more about it than he ever would. What the brothers were doing to me to get to Dollard would have worked in any family in Papineau School—we were the freaks. I was suffering a complicated shame. Then my father came up with a new inspiration. 'You think the Sistine Chapel was painted without discipline?' There was a series of pictures taped to the dining-room wallpaper, cut from the pages of *Life* magazine, celebrating Vatican art. The Sistine Chapel won many arguments in the Hochelaga district of Montreal in the early fifties.

In memory, Pittsburgh came bursting through like a freak radio signal. In my junior-high classes, the sexes had mingled, the girls had steamed and giggled in a heavy-breasted, painted-up pool of pubescent sexuality. They wore whatever they could get away with. They stuffed lewd and graphic promises through the ventilation slats of our lockers and raced for the girls' rooms between classes to smoke like little hellions. They were utterly available, begging to be touched.

But in Papineau we entered and left by the '*Garçons*' and '*Filles*' sides of the building, as though joint entombment for eight hours a day was concession enough to sordid physiology; the nuns and brothers even positioned themselves like Holy Crossing Guards two and three blocks away, to prolong the segregation. Coeducation was a sad fact of life, but withering disapproval could safeguard our innocence at least till high school. The girls wore black jumpers and no make-up, and their hair was cut uniformly straight and short. Not a ponytail, not a bleach job in the lot. I'd been too young in Pittsburgh to act on my impulses, to inhale those lusty vapours rising from the breeding pens of an American junior high school. Now, I felt, I could. Just turn me loose, anywhere in America. I burned in hell, remembering it.

And then, miraculously, the nuns gave me a girl. At four o'clock after another gruelling day of faint comprehension, Soeur Timothée told me to stay after class—not for discipline—but to meet my own, private, ninth-grade tutor, Thérèse Aulérie. Tutor and general *ange gardien* in everything from penmanship (we were on the continental system, with crossed sevens, ones like giant carat marks; whenever I require assurance that indeed these things happened to me I have it still, in my handwriting) to the foundations of all advanced knowledge: Latin, French and the Catholic religion. Thérèse was Papineau's outstanding student in classics, French, apologetics and even natural science.

Ninth-grade girls back in Pittsburgh simply had more going for them than Thérèse Aulérie, despite her brilliance. There was first of all the question of make-up, that bright impasto of sexual longing, so innovatively applied by American teenagers. They had Hollywood and television to guide them, not to mention the Terry Moore sweaters stretched over the mountain-building process we runty seventh- and eighth-graders could measure by the week, if not the hour (just as I scrutinized my chin for each new black whisker, cherished each new fissure in my cracking vocal chords and checked every inch of my body for other rampant endocrinal signposts worth flaunting).

In Papineau, everything was hidden. Girls in jumpers, no make-up, no hair-styles; they took their cue from Soeur Timothée. But Thérèse Aulérie was a slight improvement. She had the palest skin and the greenest eyes I had ever seen (it was the first time I'd been forced to focus on such adult, literary features as fine skin and expressive eyes), and lips that were natural and pink to a sheen of edibility. She wore clear nail polish—a vanity, she later confessed—and the only other exposed acreage of flesh, her cheeks, was delicately flushed, and dimpled. Her voice was low and throaty, a woman's voice coming from the face of Margaret O'Brien. She looked so *nearly* familiar it seemed impossible that she didn't speak a word of English and even regarded hearing it as a low-grade, unclassifiable sin.

We began with apologetics. We had a small handbook of Nuns and Monks and Teaching Orders, and my first job was to learn how to identify the various orders by their special dress, their expertise, their place and date of founding. I'd thought of them as exotic wildlife anyway: tracking them with an imprimatured bestiary seemed a natural way of pinning them down. I started rattling off their dates and countries of origin with an ease that astonished her, leaving Thérèse to fill in the substantive issues—for her at least: were they known best for their piety or their charity? Their compassion or courage? Their humility or brilliance? Most of our brothers were Marists, with a Sacred Heart in the chapel. The nuns were mainly our local Greys and Ursulines, but a sharp eye could spot a Blessed Virgin on special assignment. This part was easy, like learning the makes and models of new cars. Thérèse, once she dropped the ninth-grade condescension, was full of unofficial data about every order. *Les laides, les bêtes, les gueules, les graisses.* Soeur Timothée, I learned, was called Soeur La Morse. 'What's a *morse?*' I asked, and Thérèse tapped imaginary tusks and made deep seal-like grunts. 'Walrus!' I laughed, and she repeated, in a voice suddenly high and girlish, 'wal-rus.' In fact, Thérèse Aulérie, for all her grades and piety and possible calling as a Sister of Charity, was a sharp little cookie who began confiding to me of her visits to the States, a Chinese restaurant she'd been taken to in Manchester, New Hampshire, the weekends at Old Orchard Beach and the television she'd stared at for a solid, slothful weekend in a Burlington motel. She'd even gone to New York City when she was six, and she still had all the postcards. In her America, everyone spoke French except the people on television.

'Did you really go to school in America?' she asked in French. My French wasn't good enough to answer more than an authentic, Dollardish *'ouai'.* No way to describe its wonders.

'Comme Hartchie?' she asked. *'Et Véronique?'*

It took me a few seconds to catch on. *'Et Juggie aussi,'* I laughed.

'Ah, Juggie,' she nodded gravely. *'Juggie j'aime beaucoup.'*

We sighed; I for the multiplicity of stories I couldn't build upon, the impossibility of representing myself in a language I didn't know, or to a girl who didn't know mine.

'Et ton nom, était-il toujours Carrier là-bas?'

It didn't seem strange to her that people changed names when they crossed the border. In America, I tried to explain, we'd sailed under a flag of translation. *'Porter,'* she tried, in her curious, high-pitched English. *'Non, c'est laid, ce nom-là. Carrier, c'est un bon nom canadien.'*

I answered, with sad conviction sealing the linguistic gaps, 'Anyway, names *ne fait rien.'*

She drew her desk closer. '*Épeles mon nom de famille. Divines.* Go ahead. Try!'

'A-U—' I began. And she giggled, shaking her head.

'*Mon vrai nom. Commences avec "o"*, like dis, eh?' I loved it when she tried her English. It came out like Dollard's, but without the threat. '*C'est le vrai français, mon nom, de la France, pas d'ici.*' She wrote, 'O'L—'

'O'Leery?' I spelled.

'O'Leary,' she corrected. '*Ça c'est le nom de mon grandpère.*' She turned the paper as though admiring a work of art. 'Nice,' she said.

I felt I'd been handed a powerful interpretive tool, but I didn't yet know how to wield it. Here I was, a Carrier who spoke no French, and she was an O'Leary who read 'Archie' comic books but knew no English, and we were together in a darkening classroom in Montreal under a cross, flanked by the photos of the Cardinal of Montreal and the Holy Father. We were linked beyond simple assignments. My guardian angel, according to Sister Walrus, who would lead me from ignorance to power, just as the sisters and brothers would lead me from hellfire to righteousness.

Thérèse closed her book after the quiz on habits and orders and asked me, slowly and with grand gestures, can girls (she pointed to herself) in the ninth grade in America really wear lipstick (she ran her pinkie over her lips) and dress the way they want? She formed a gentle, wavy outline with her hands, passing over an imaginary female form just outside her square-cut jumper with all the lewdness (I fantasized) of a sailor describing his last night's conquest. Can they really go out on dates? She clawed my wrist at the word '*rendez-vous*'. Those new words burned themselves in my brain: *maquillage . . . s'habiller comme l'on veut . . . rendez-vous.* Do they all have cars? How late can they stay out? She was suddenly like a little girl, and somewhere in the late fall gloom, and then under the yellow globes of a four-thirty northern autumn night, I started imagining a Thérèse O'Leary in make-up, and I noticed how her jumper flared out modestly in front and filled out gently in the rear, and how a nice wide belt would have pinched it together, just right. And how her voice, that deep French purr, would have driven American boys wild.

It must have been in those weeks in our daily hour after school and in our walks away from school for two low, mean, icy, glorious unsupervised blocks to her trolley stop that the current in our little relationship shifted direction. By the end of our first month, her English improved to the level of fairly detailed conversation. I rummaged through my mother's suitcase and found a proper belt. Once on a Saturday I passed her with her parents at Dupuis Frères department store, and she was in a sweater and skirt, wearing lipstick and pearl earrings.

I came to think of my five hours a week with Thérèse as my parole from solitary. I came to understand my mother's use of the word 'drab' to describe the interiors and the streets, the minds and souls and conversations of East End Montreal. One big icy puddle of frozen gutter water, devoid of joy, colour, laughter, pleasure, intellect or art. School and home and church and the narrow East End streets that connect them are the same colour even now in my memory, linked in a language that I didn't understand except through its rhythms. Recitations in class took on a dirge-like quality, like the repeated Hail Marys on Sunday radio. Eventually even I, who knew neither Latin nor French nor the lists of martyrs to the Iroquois, could stand and repeat the proper syllables. The name of our school, Papineau, figured in Quebec history as a great patriot who had tried to rid the province of English and American influences, and his name was repeated on the street outside and on panel trucks and signboards of plumbers and plasterers and in the *épicerie* where Aunt Béatrice did her shopping. It seemed slightly blasphemous, like Latin ballplayers carrying the name of Jesus. The same few names popped up everywhere, with six

Tremblays in my class and over half of us clustered alphabetically at 'La—' and nearly all of us ending in '—ier'. Our names were as predictable as Americans', as unmistakable as Chinese, and mine was one of the commonest. We were common, and we learned to feel comfortable only in the presence of other *bons noms canadiens*. 'Ignorance!' my mother had cried one night, fleeing the dinner table. She had bought red table napkins, something to brighten the winter gloom, and my uncle had slammed his to the floor, saying it would *'causer l'acide'*.

And so, my mother began meeting me after school, a block from where I parted from Thérèse. Sometimes we would ride the trolley downtown and go into Eaton's or Ogilvy's—places that felt off-limits to the rest of the family. And there I would glow in the mystical power of speaking English, a power that wasn't furtive or dirty, as it felt in the apartment. The power of not having to scratch for words and not biting back the urge to comment, or even attack.

On the furniture floor of Eaton's she said. 'I worked here, you know. I was even the head of this whole department.' We walked through the model home, the half-dozen bedrooms and dining rooms featuring different styles of decoration. 'Your father was one of the salesmen. Until I saw him, I never even bothered learning their names. I knew he was wrong for me. Knew from the beginning.' No one recognized her now, though it had been only thirteen years. She'd gone to the States, been lost to history. 'I was a very different woman in those days. I want you to understand that. It wasn't easy, back then, in this city. Women couldn't even vote. And they don't accept women here, not English women, not Protestant women. They'll never do that.' I could read her eyes and breath; I wanted to avoid the tears that I knew were coming. 'I deserve it all, don't I? Sleeping on a floor in Hochelaga. No wonder they don't want to remember me—I must look a sight.' She trailed her fingers in the dust of the dining-room tables and nightstands, then took me up to the cafeteria on the top floor. We would have our tea and scones, sometimes served with a little lemon curd. She perked up, over tea. 'I don't want you to despise them. They are what they are. Deep down, they're good people. They've taken us in when we could have ended up ... I don't want to think how we could have ended up, and they've shared what they have. But I *do* resent them, I can't help it. I resent their tight little ways, not with money—darling, do you understand what I'm saying? Their fist-like little souls, always ready to fight you or slink away like a beaten dog—does that make sense? I don't want you growing up like them.'

It was always harder, going back to Hochelaga after scones and lemon curd and a few hours of uninterrupted English. The urge to speak our language seemed to die when the trolley crossed St. Lawrence. In a few weeks I would reach a linguistic equilibrium, and I probably could have been happy enough— given endless lemon curd or access to Thérèse O'Leary—existing like a child in either world. But I was being forced, subtly at first, every day, to make moral decisions. French or English were the terms, but they were merely covers for personalities inside and out that I wanted to keep hidden.

One Friday in early December my mother held me back from school. Quietly, she motioned me to put on my coat. We took the trolley downtown not quite to Eaton's, then walked up to Sherbrooke past the clean grey limestone and green copper roofs of McGill University, that Gibraltar of Englishness. 'Some day you'll go here,' she said. 'I don't care what it takes or if you graduate from French school or American schools— they'll have to let you in.' I welcomed her authority. We stood on Milton Street just outside the iron railings; I wanted to reach inside. I could understand the shouts of the students, their quiet conversations as young couples passed us on the sidewalk. 'Who are those men in black robes?' I asked. 'Judges?'

'Professors,' she said. 'This is the greatest university in the world.' She so rarely allowed herself the luxury of an uncontested assertion—'too American' was her feeling about any claim to undisputed superiority—that I knew I'd been handed an indisputable fact. I trusted my mother more than any nun, even more than any Jesuit. 'Come,' she said, and we turned down Prince Arthur, through a maze of small half-streets that curled between Pine and St. Urbain. We stopped in front of a tall apartment block of dull cherry brick, where long icicles hung over the door. 'I want you to meet an important person in my life,' she said. 'And in yours, I hope.'

'Who?' And I swear, had she asked me, *Who do you think?* I would have answered, *My father. My real father.* There was something monumental inside, the clarity behind all the confusions. Her gloved finger ran down the row of buzzers. At 'Perleman, E.' she stopped.

We were buzzed inside. My mother's hands were shaking. 'Ella is a brilliant woman. A professor at McGill.' In the tiny elevator she whispered, 'I used to live right here, in this building. When I came back from England and got that job at Eaton's.'

'With her?'

'I called her last week. I haven't seen her in thirteen years. She sounded—' and her voice was stumbling now, 'grand. She's a grand girl.'

'You used to get letters from her,' I remembered. Back in Pittsburgh I saved the high-denomination Canadian stamps that came to us on those thick envelopes from Montreal.

'She's my dearest friend. The times we had! Oh, Lord, the times …'

Ella was standing by the elevator, a gnome-like woman of my mother's age, wrapped in a stiff green skirt and a man's sweater that smothered her body like a duffel bag. My mother had to stoop to hug her, and she was already losing control, while Ella merely patted her back and shoulders and mur-

mured. 'There, there, Hennie,' in what seemed to be a lilting accent. Her dark brown eyes were wide and sad, and her skin was a fine, translucent pink. Her hair was entirely grey and nearly as short as mine. She looked, I thought, like Albert Einstein. She pulled us down the hall to her opened apartment door. I could easily see over her head into a living room dingy with smoke and oppressive with apartment heat. It must have been eighty-five degrees inside, and I started clawing desperately at my scarf and *tuque,* as she picked up a lavender shawl and draped it over her shoulders.

'Dolly,' she called out, and a gaunt woman, slightly younger, shuffled out from the bedroom. 'This is Henny, whom I've spoken so much about. And her boy, Philip.' I nodded, regretting the day of school I was missing. 'This is Dolly. Dolly works in the accounts office at McGill. So.' Dolly took that as a sign to go to the kitchen and prepare some tea.

If McGill was the world's finest university and Ella one of its professors, I reasoned that she must be the smartest woman in the world. That went a long way to forgiving her appearance and her strange habits. She picked up a pipe from the nearest coffee table, and as she sucked on it, drawing in the flame, I could swear it *was* Einstein peering at me over the flame and bowl of the pipe. My mother was bearing up. She too was watching me, and I was behaving myself; nothing strange about a woman smoking a pipe. It was impossible to think of Ella ever crying, ever getting too personal and sentimental, and for that I was grateful.

'So. You must forgive two old women who haven't seen each other …'

Ella and my mother were seated across from me on the sofa, and Ella was patting my mother's hand. 'I must say you look well, Hennie, everything considered. Some of us got old rather quickly.'

'You look just the same, Ella.' My mother was staring down at her lap, at Ella's hand.

'Well, nothing ever happens in Montreal, so who can tell? The city hasn't changed one bit. The things we fought for have gradually come to pass—we can vote now, Hennie—isn't that grand? But the workers are still oppressed and the church still runs things and the police behave like Tartars and the corruption is still a public joke and our candidates still lose their deposits every election. Remember our election parties?' My mother smiled, and Ella let out a sharp bark of a laugh. 'We'd all come back here to this apartment'—she was looking at me again—'the finest candidates who ever ran for public office in this country, and we'd sit around sipping sherry waiting for a call. And outside the police were waiting. If we'd actually won we'd have gone directly to jail. Oh, Lord, such innocent hopes! I might as well be just off the boat for all that's changed in twenty years!'

'Ella came from Austria, dear,' my mother explained. 'She studied with Freud.'

Ella was quick to jump in. 'No, no, dear. Never studied. *Was analysed* by one of his pupils. Which means only I *was discussed* over *kaffee* and *küchen*. The Perleman complex,' she giggled. 'No, I'm afraid I was too normal. I never made it into Freudian literature. You have heard perhaps of Freud, Philip?'

'Is it like a Freudian slip?'

'If you are not referring to a ladies' undergarment, yes, there is such a thing as a Freudian slip. You of course understand what this is—this Freudian slip as you call it?'

My mother was nodding fiercely, urging me on. What was it, a test? 'Usually when you're talking and something dirty slips out accidentally. Or something embarrassing, like those radio bloopers. There's a nun in school I keep being afraid I'm going to call a *morse*, because that's her nickname.'

'People always think Freud has to be dirty. Ah, well.'

'You never told me about this nun, darling.'

'What exactly is a *morse*, Philip?'

'You know, that big seal-like thing, with tusks.'

'You mean a walrus, dear?' My mother's face looked stricken with pain, and she turned to Ella. 'He's . . . you see?'

'Now, now. Mothers *worry,* don't they, Philip? It's perfectly all right to learn a second language. I've done it, many have done it.'

'You were forced to,' said my mother. 'It's not like having your mother tongue taken from you. They won't let him speak English. I'm the only person he can speak English with.'

Dolly came in from the kitchen, bearing a teapot on a silver tray, four fine china cups and a plate of biscuits around a jar of lemon curd. She lifted a lavender shawl off the teapot and Ella asked me, 'Do you know what this is called, Philip?'

'A cover?'

'A cosy. A tea-cosy. Very strange word, I always thought.'

'I like lemon curd,' I said, emphasizing those last two words. 'I don't see why it's called lemon curd. It's more like lemon pudding. I mean, milk gets curds. Curds and whey. Maybe because it's sour, but then why don't we have rhubarb curd and apple curd? Or do we? In French—' but I stopped myself.

'Dear,' said my mother, 'I'm sorry.'

'English is not an especially logical language, Philip. As you have discovered. But tell me—are you enjoying yourself in Montreal? At school?'

'It's all right.'

'Your mother tells me it's sometimes . . . a little primitive.'

'They *beat* you, darling.'

'They apologized. That's a big thing, getting them to apologize. La Morse herself, showed remorse.' They didn't appreciate my rhyme. 'It wasn't easy at the beginning even understanding things. Basic words, basic anything.'

'What do you study?'

'It seems all he studies is Catholicism,' said my mother.

The truth was, apologetics was the easiest subject, since it required no thought, just memorization. It was also the quickest way to get good grades. The math was easier than Pittsburgh math, once I learned the number system. In Latin, though the text was in French, I was starting from the same place as other students. Given an even chance, I would always excel. 'That's not true,' I said. The truth, I realized, was unspeakable. The truth was, I *liked* apologetics. I spooned deeply in the curd pot and smeared it over a biscuit.

'So. A difference of perception, maybe?'

My mother took this as a rebuke. Her head sank. I wanted to console her, but instead helped Dolly drag over a dining-room chair.

Ella looked at my mother; she looked at Dolly; I helped myself to more lemon curd. Finally Ella asked, in a softer voice, 'Do they make you go to Mass? Do they try to convert you?'

'I don't think so. I mean, everyone's Catholic, so they just assume I am too. I mean with a name like Carrier—' But I could see that, too, hurt my mother. 'I mumble the prayers, but I don't go to Mass.'

'You can go, dear. I don't want you to feel ... different.'

'I don't feel different,' I said.

'Would you like to go to an English school?'

'I can't. My uncle—'

'Never mind about your uncle. Would you *like* to go to a good English school? The *best* English school? A private school?'

'I don't know.'

'Philip, your mother and I and Dolly have discussed a plan. If you say yes, your mother will discuss it with your father. Dolly and I, we have no children. Probably there's a limit to the amount of charitable contributions I can make. You can live with us, and we will send you. I know professors, I know musicians, writers, artists. We go out every night, or we have people here who are the leaders not just of this city, not just this country—'

'—the *world,* darling. Ella is known all over the world.'

'That's not the point. The point is, we want to share this—what should I call it? Power? Connection? Good fortune? You could stay here in your own room and go home on the weekends, of course. You would be prepared for McGill. I don't know what else there is to say.'

'Say you will think about it, dear.'

'I don't think my mother really wants me to leave,' I said.

'She is the one who brought it up. She is deeply worried, what is happening to you.'

'Nothing is happening to me.'

'She wants what is best. French schools in this city are, well, substandard.'

Inwardly, I panicked. There seemed to be no way of saving myself from everyone's good intentions.

'Before it's *too late,* darling. Before you lose everything you've got. They'll take it from you, believe me,' and her voice suddenly cracked and her head fell to Ella's lap and I could hear the words torn from her chest. 'Like ... they've ... taken ... it ... from ... me!'

185

Ella took little note of the distraction; she placed her hand in my mother's hair and said to me, coldly and evenly, 'Guess, please, Philip, how many products of classic French-Canadian education we have on the McGill faculty. Go ahead.'

I knew that any answer would be humiliating. 'Obviously,' she said, 'you've guessed correctly. How many French-Canadian *students* do you think I have?' She waited. 'Let me tell you a little parable about the power of education. On this continent at the present time there are approximately six million French Canadians—am I right?'

'Yes,' I admitted. It depended on how you counted our lost brothers and sisters in the West, New England and Louisiana. I'd just been reading about them, grieving for them, in my history class. My palms were sweating, my neck hairs rising.

'And there are approximately five million Jews on this continent,' she said. She smiled briefly. 'End of parable. Do you understand what I am saying about education? Do they teach you *that* in French school? Do you know how the minds of those people have been *wasted*? How they continue to be wasted? Have they taught you anything about Freud?'

'No,' I whispered.'

'Einstein?'

'Back in Pittsburgh.'

'Karl Marx?'

I felt a terrible pressure in my chest. It was the name that seemed to be hovering in the air all afternoon. All that talk of *the workers* and *the people* and the candidates who never got elected. There had been a cartoon circulated in school on the eve of the latest election: Karl Marx in a Santa suit, with 'Parti Libéral' stencilled on his sack of toys.

'No!' I retorted.

'They're doing a splendid job of educating you, aren't they? You should be spending your time learning about science, politics, history, literature—'

'—and how to get electrocuted for being Russian spies?' I demanded.

My mother raised her head, and Ella stared back at me, hard, for several seconds. 'Ella, I'm sorry—' my mother began, but Ella raised her hand, and my mother was silent. Dolly carried the tray back to the kitchen.

'I can't say I'm surprised,' said Ella.

'I'm going back to school,' I said. My mother reached out for me, imploring me to wait, we would all go to Murray's for lunch, but I thanked her, and the other women, for the lemon curd and tea, and wished them a pleasant lunch and a good afternoon.

There's a special light that strikes Montreal in April; a light so strong, so angled, that it bores through windows and the glass panels of apartment doors with the intensity of a projection beam. It acts like a magnifying lens, picking out cobwebs and dust motes, adding dimensions to the grain of wood, nubbiness to the sleekest fabric, seams and crannies to the tightest skin. The sidewalks resemble tidal basins with their residues of sand, and the snow is shrunk to black tongues of gritty ice, seeking shade. The walk home from school took a little longer, as I crushed little ice bridges over the swirling melt, and stood on rims of rounded ice till they snapped with a hollow thud and I could kick the chunks away. The days were longer, and even my tutorials with Thérèse ended in plenty of daylight. My grades were better than average, and the nuns' comments were even flattering. Nevertheless, Thérèse and I agreed that the tutoring should continue. Her English was far from perfect.

I think my mother found the courage, some time that winter, to keep calling Ella and to make their lunches a regular event. I was going downtown on my own, now that the weather had improved. Mick had come through with a job on St Catherine Street, just as he'd promised. I took over an old stand of his just up from the train station, handing out mimeographed leaflets of naked girls behind strings of balloons, naked girls with one leg up in a bathtub, naked girls doing just about anything, plus the offer of a free drink or free admission. It was cold work and a little seedy; Mick, as a trusted long-time employee, had been promoted to inside work with the props, nearer the girls. My job next year, if I proved reliable.

'Where's this place at, kid?' and it was a pleasure to direct the tourists in their language, to hear them mutter to their buddies just off the train, 'Smart kid, you hear him?' and 'Ask him if he has a sister.' I learned to put on a touch of a Dollardish accent, to guarantee full credit for my linguistic accomplishment, and sometimes a little tip. I earned a quarter for every two hundred leaflets I passed, and a nickel for every one redeemed at the Club Lido.

Dollard had dropped out of school and gotten a job at Steinberg's, loading and delivering. Two of Théophile's sons-in-law got big jobs in the States, drywalling for a motel chain, and suddenly our little apartment was filled with new appliances. Béatrice stored an automatic washing machine on the back gallery so that the hot soapy water could gush over the cars below. We got a television set, the first anyone had seen, even though Canadian television was barely launched, rudimentary. That didn't stop me from buying the wires and rigging some rabbit-ears and tying them to our chimney in an attempt to coax something, anything, from the air. Burlington, Plattsburgh—those towns that provided night-time English radio in my room—where were you when it really counted? Even KDKA in Pittsburgh came in, most nights.

There was talk of our moving out. My mother's old teaching licence was approved by the Protestant school board, but she didn't dare mention it in Théophile's house. Béatrice crossed herself whenever the word 'Jew' entered the conversation, as it frequently did these days with Dollard's new employment; she might have thrown herself over the gallery at the mention of Protestants. My father looked for work, but he had to lie about previous employment—or find someone to lie for him. The future would always be insecure. I would hold up my hand against the glass of the front door, and April light passed through it like X-rays. The tangle over where to live and where to send me would flare again in the summer, and the fall could be another disaster. I studied my skeleton on the door while the grunts and curses and cleaning sounds passed in the air around me.

Everyone had a few hours to themselves on Sunday afternoon, after the Mass and big meal. We dressed for the meal, and even Dollard managed some pleasantness for the few hours it took. I kept him supplied with free-drink passes at the Club Lido. Thanks to Mick, I even got in a few hours' work backstage, drew close to undressed women, heard and understood all their complaints. I told my mother those nights I was at the Forum, standing for hockey.

Those warming Sunday afternoons Thérèse and I would meet at the trolley stop nearest her apartment, and if the weather was nice we'd walk to Parc LaFontaine. We had a bet: she'd read two English books for every French book I read. It wasn't fair; she'd discovered Nancy Drew and the Hardy Boys while I slogged through Claudel and St-Denys-Garneau. She was doing well, she had wonderful discipline. And on Sundays she wore her churchgoing, dinner-eating dress and earrings, and she was a marvellous sight. Once, a priest walked by; she stiffened, but he smiled down at us and chuckled, '*Ah, jeune Montréal!*' She made me ashamed of the money I earned working the train station; I spent all of it I could on her.

By May we could walk all the way downtown if we wanted. May in Montreal is like April in Paris; the light is more forgiving, the haze of green is everywhere and the schoolwork, despite nuns' warnings, starts to relent. I remember a Sunday in May as though it is borne to me now on the laser beams of April light, imprinted and never to be forgotten. Walking down St. Catherine Street with Thérèse O'Leary. We went to Murray's, and she'd taken my hand as we walked out. I'd ordered and paid in English, and she'd been terribly impressed. She'd promised me she'd do it, but had gotten too embarrassed at the last moment. We were walking behind a group of old ladies in white gloves and wide-brimmed hats, the tea-drinking ladies of Westmount, and Thérèse had been frightened of them, afraid of what they might be saying about her. Just gossip, I said, mindless things, and I translated some of it, to reassure her. She shook her head and acted ashamed. '*Sh'peux pas!*' she declared, pounding the side of her head with her fists, '*Idiote!*' then giggled. '*Mais tu peux, non?* You hunnerstan' every word, non? Smart guy!' She took my hand in both of hers and swung my arm like the clapper of the biggest bell in the world.

EXTRACTIONS
AND CONTRACTIONS

Student Power

L EAVING my office on the twelfth floor and boarding the elevator with ten students, I have this winter's first seizure of claustrophobia. Eleven of us in heavy overcoats, crammed shoulder to shoulder in an overlit stainless steel box, burning up. The elevator opens on eleven and two students turn away, seeing that it's full. We stop on ten but no one is waiting. We are trapped by the buttons other people press before they take the stairs. We will stop on every floor, it is one of those days, though we can take no one in and all of us, obviously, are dressed for the street. On eight as the doors open and no one presses 'C' to close them quickly, I have a sense of how we must appear to any onlooker—like a squad of Gothic statuary, eyes averted upward, silent, prayerful. On seven I sense there will be a student waiting as the door opens. He looks in, smiles, and we smile back. The doors do not close and we wait. He opens his briefcase and assembles a machine gun. We cannot move; we are somehow humiliated by overcrowding. No one presses 'C'. A burst of fire catches us all, economically gunned down by a grinning student. The doors close and do not open again until we tumble out in the main lobby.

The Street

Early November is colder this year than last. Twelve floors up, without windows, I forget about the cold. I have been reading Faulkner for five hours and haven't thought once of winter. I have been thinking, in fact, that with my citizenship papers I can now apply for government support in the summer. I could have before, but it didn't seem right.

It is cruel to confront the streets now: snowless but windy and in the lower twenties. Such mildness will not return until late March. November and March, deadly months. Depressing to think the dentist, like winter, is waiting. The cold wind on a bad tooth anticipates so much. I try to remember these streets as they were in June; a sidewalk café, the devastating girls in the briefest skirts and bra-less sweaters. These streets had so many tourists in the summer, forever asking directions and making me feel at home. At the end of the block parked in a taxi space, I spot a modest car with snow on the trunk and Maryland plates. On the left edge of the back bumper is a tattered *McCarthy for President* sticker and on the right, as I kick off a little snow, is the red-framed bilingual testament: *I'm Proud to Be a Canadian/Je suis fier d'être canadien.*

The Dentist

My teeth, my body, my child, my wife and the baby she is carrying are all in the hands of immigrants. All Jews. I do not know how this develops; because I am an immigrant too, perhaps. Our friends warned us against the indigenous dentists. Between hockey pucks and Pepsi caps, they said, Quebec teeth are only replaced, never filled.

This dentist's office is in a large, formerly brick office building that was stripped to its girders over the summer and then refaced with concrete panels and oblong windows. Inside, however, not a change. The corridors are still reminiscent of older high schools, missing only the rows of olive-drab lockers. The doors are still darkly varnished and gummy from handling. The doctors and accountants still have their names in black on stippled glass. All this, according to Dr Abramovitch, pains a dentist, whose restorative work is from the inside out. 'Rotten inside,' he snorts, poking my tooth but meaning the building. He is a man of inner peace, rumoured to be a socialist. The rest of our doctors are socialists. His degrees are in Hebrew but for one that puzzles me more, in Latin. I am in the chair waiting for the freeze to take effect before I realize that *Monte Regis* means Montreal. I then remember a novel I have just read, a French-Canadian one, in which the narrator, a vendor of hot dogs, must decide on a name for his hot dog stand. The purists suggest *Au roi du chien chaud*. He chooses *Au roi du hot dog*. The author, I am told, is a separatist. I wonder if he cares that at least one outsider has read him. Poor Montreal, I now think, puts up with so much.

There is a battle this afternoon to save a tooth. The pulp is lost but the enamel is good. It is cheaper, he explains, to pull the tooth. But after pulling there must be a bridge and years later, another one. But pulling only the nerve (his brow smooths out) and packing the canal, though the work is tedious and expensive, is lavishly recommended. 'I get forty-five for a nerve job, ten for a straight extraction,' he says. *Pulling a nerve* is a sinister phrase, smacking of an advanced, experimental technique. But he is appealing, I can see, to all that is aesthetic in dentistry. No McTeague, this man, though his wrists bulge with competence. His extractions have been praised. I debate denying him any nerve, for with a numb jaw I can play the hero. *Lace the boot tighter, Doc. I gotta lead my men* . . . finally, though, no John Wayne stuff for me. I consent, and he rams a platinum wire up the holes he has drilled, plunges it up and down then pulls it out, yellow with nerve scum. This is not how I pictured my nerve, though I had never hoped to look at a nerve, surely not my own, surely not this afternoon when I left my office. Brain surgery, too, I am told, is painless after the skull is cut through. I can hear the platinum probe grinding in my cheekbone nearly under my eye and I think of those pharmaceutical ads that used to appear in the *National Geographic* of Incas performing brain surgery, spitting cocaine juice into the open skull as they cut.

'Success,' he pronounces. He is happy, the tooth will drain, in a week he'll pack it. Leaving, I have my doubts. No John Wayne, certainly, I'm beginning to feel like Norman Mailer. A nerve ripped from my body at thirty. I am a young man, haven't deteriorated much since twenty-one, expect to remain the same at least till thirty-five. But somehow, some day, some *minute,* the next long decline begins to set in. At forty I will be middle-aged. At forty-five, twenty-five years from my grave. When does it start—with a chipped tooth? A broken nose? A broken leg even? Oh, no. It begins in choices. The road downhill is slick with fat and fallen hair and little pills. Bad styles and bad convictions. Painkillers, contraceptives, tranquillizers and weak erections. Pulled nerves.

St. Catherine Street

From the dentist's, east on St. Catherine is an urban paradise. No finer street exists in my experience, even in November. St. Catherine should be filmed without dialogue or actors, just by letting the crowds swarm around a mounted camera and allowing a random soundtrack to pick up the talk, Dopplering in and fading out, from every language in the world.

But west on St. Catherine, especially in November, is something else. Blocks of low buildings after Guy Street, loan offices on top and business failures down below. Auto salesrooms forever changing franchises, drugstores offering two-hour pregnancy tests, news and tobacco stands, basement restaurants changing nationalities. But if it can be afforded, or if one lives only with a wife, a convenient location. Someday Montreal will have its Greenwich Village and these short streets between St. Catherine and Dorchester will be the centre.

I stop at an unlighted tobacconist's for the papers. One window bin is full of pipes and tins of tobacco, the other of dusty sex magazines from every corner of the Western world. The owner stands all day at the door and opens it only if you show an interest. Otherwise, it's locked, without lights. I stop in daily for my *Star* and *Devoir*. I always have two dimes because he keeps no observable change. He always responds, '*Merci.*' His face implies that he has suffered; also that he survives now in his darkened store by selling far more than the *Star, La Presse* and all the Greek and German stag magazines. I have seen men enter the store and say things I couldn't understand and the owner present them with Hungarian, with Yiddish, with Ukrainian, with Latvian papers. Then they chat. Perhaps he speaks no English and just a word or two of French. Like my dentist, a man, ultimately, of mystery.

My Wife

Is it most significant that I say first she is a Ph.D. teaching at McGill and making more than I; or that she is the mother of our five-year-old boy, and is now eight months pregnant and still teaching? Or that she is Indian and is one of those small radiant women one sees on larger campuses, their red or purple *sari-ends* billowing under Western overcoats? I'm home early to let the frozen jaw thaw and to see if the nerveless tooth will keep me from lecturing tonight. My wife should be in her office and our son at the sitter's.

The apartment seems emptier than usual; there's been some attempt at tidying, the lights are off and the afternoon gloom through the fibreglass curtains is doubly desolate. I drop the briefcase, turn on the lights in the front room, then put coffee water on to boil in the dark narrow kitchen. Roaches scurry as I hit the light. I realize, on touching the cups, that the heat is low—maybe off. We have only five rooms but a very long hall; it curves twice and divides the apartment sharply. It costs us a great deal.

There is nothing distinctive about our place: given our double income, our alleged good taste, our backgrounds, this becomes distinctive. Other Indian, or semi-Indian, couples we know keep a virtual bazaar of silks and brasses and hempen rugs and eat off the floor at least once a week. Burn fresh incense every day. And though I do not like them, I sometimes envy them. There are days in November even without aching teeth that I realize how little I've done to improve our lives, how thwarted my sense of style has become.

I am sipping coffee when I hear the toilet flush in the rear of the apartment. I hurry back and find my wife rearranging the covers over her belly. She smiles and tells me to sit and keep time while she rests.

Contractions

Starting three hours earlier she's been having regular contractions of a mild variety; so mild that she hasn't bothered to call me. The cycle is steady but speeding up. 'I'm sorry I haven't done the shopping,' she says, smiling like a Hemingway heroine whose pain would crush a man. She assures me the contractions are light—almost delicious. Indians like massages, have special names for pressures and positions; it is something I have learned, something I can administer. 'It's a false alarm,' she insists. Nevertheless I decide to call Dr Lapp. He seems ignorant of the case until I remind him that my wife is the Indian lady. 'Ah, yes,' he says, 'don't panic.' I am to take her in only if they get severe and come every two minutes.

'This is silly,' she protests when they begin coming every two minutes. 'I'm actually looking forward to them.' She wants me to leave her at home and go back to school to eat and prepare my lecture. But I stand by my duty: pack her bag, call the sitters and tell them I'll pick up our boy around ten-thirty. They offer to have him spend the night, but I refuse. I want him with me.

The Hospital

We live just off St. Catherine, just where we want to be, but the hospital is suburban, in the deadly western sections, because all of Dr Lapp's patients live there. We do not have a French doctor because, I suppose, of the rumoured Catholic position on the primacy of the fetus. Dr Lapp is from Boston but interned at McGill and, for some reason, stayed. One doesn't trust a people until one trusts their doctors. This suburban hospital is reached by a three-dollar taxi ride. It fits into the neighbourhood like a new church or modern school; low, long, red-brick, like every duplex on every street in the far western sections of Montreal. This is where my colleagues live; this is all they know of Montreal if, like me, they came here late: a bus line, a transfer point, the Metro stops, and school. Some shopping, some bookstore browsing, a downtown bank, a movie or two a month. None of them speaks a dozen words of French.

The doors of this hospital are marked: TIREZ/PULL, POUSSEZ/PUSH, and beyond the CAISSE/RECEPTION-IST, I see a sign: ASCENSEUR/ELEVATOR. For some reason I am thinking of a little test I once administered to some friends of mine in the English department, and not of my wife, who is being admitted. It was a recognition test. All of the men had either been born or had lived at least five years in Montreal. I supplied some everyday words and asked if they could give equivalents in English, and some of the words, I recall, were *tirez, poussez* and *défense de stationner,* and *arrêtez.* A man who owned a car identified both *arrêtez* and *sortie.* The others felt embarrassed and a little defensive. They told me that I should give such a test to some of the others, those who were harder to know and not quite so friendly, who lived in converted stables and in lofts down in the Old City, whose second wives were French-Canadian and whose children went to rugged little lycées in Outremont. Those men were, admittedly, a little frightening. Also a little foolish. Is there nothing in between? I wonder now what I was trying to prove my first year here with my evening courses in conversational French, my subscriptions to French magazines, my pride in reserving English for school and home, no place else. The depth of my commitment—to trivia.

Mongolism

Secretly I have been worrying that this second child will be mongoloid. It seems that the papers and all the polite journals that flood our house have recently featured technical articles for the common reader on mongolism. I know the statistics and I know what to look for even in a newborn infant. Position of the ears, size of tongue, bridge of nose, shape of feet, length of fingers. Blood, heart, lungs. The options: to commit him on sight to a home that will clean him, feed him, and let him die from the simplest illness; or to take him home and try to make him comfortable, all the time hoping that his weakened organs will overcome our love, our guilt, and fail him. Strangely, I do not fear anything physical. Because I am a professor and tend to minimize the physical? Because I seek punishment for the way we live, what we're doing to our boy who deserves better, with too many sitters and too much unlicensed television while we read and prepare? I support, in a bloodless and abstract way, euthanasia. Youth in Asia. I fear for the child because I refuse to doubt myself? I fear for the child because I fear even more my intentions toward him?

I remember the night he must have been conceived. My wife had been off her pills, for they make her sick too many mornings. She would vomit and teach, vomit and teach. I was sick with migraine. We had been quiet in bed. I gave her a kiss and turned away. A few minutes later, as I turned back in the dark, my lips brushed her nose. She had turned toward me, not away, and suddenly it was like discovering a beautiful stranger in my bed; there was nothing tender that night, nothing to become this child like his begetting. The only good sign. As for the rest, no health can come from something so unplanned, from parents so slovenly, an apartment so pest-infested and uninviting.

Evening Lecture

Another three-dollar ride home, quick change from possible paternity clothes, no supper or preparations, heat definitely gone, then a brisk walk down St. Catherine to school. Even in winter, when the weather can be the most unpleasant on the continent, I've found myself surfacing from the Metro and gawking at the buildings and people rather than moving on, out of the cold. Tonight, maybe a father for the second time, I walk slowly, smiling. I'll never be quite at home here, though now even a citizen; I'm as much a stranger in my way as the others that I know. Colleagues in the suburbs, legendary swingers down in the stables near the docks—this city makes fools of us all.

Then I think that living here is perhaps a low-grade art experience. I feel the life of the sidewalk, feel content for inexplicable reasons, simply for being here. Where else in the world is *Englais* spoken? I read in the paper of a French-Canadian student leader explaining in English why he demonstrated: *We are not complotting,* he said. *We are manifesting for more subventions.* And I understood every word. I shouldn't complain of those western suburbs and of the isolation of the housewives that I teach, nor should I worry about my tolerant, scholarly friends who see so little around them. Perhaps they see beyond the obvious, beyond the neutralizing bilingualism that surrounds them. Perhaps I'm only stuck on the obvious.

There are hundreds, thousands of evening students milling along the boulevard and side streets in front the school. The boulevard is five lanes wide but pinched to a trickle while parents, boyfriends, and taxis drop off students. I am caught in a crowd moving slowly toward the revolving doors, and I am thinking now only of the lecture, wondering how I'll pick up my boy after the lecture and get him fed and dressed for school in the morning and finally—Lord—what we'll do if this is the real baby, tonight, six weeks before the Christmas holidays when he was providentially due. Must everything we do be so tightly budgeted? In *Buddenbrooks* the hero dies prematurely after a dental visit, without a nerve even being discussed. I could die tonight of a dozen things, all deserved.

An Indian

From the hundreds in front of the school, I am grabbed by an Indian man in high Tashkent fur cap and lambswool coat. He seizes an elbow as though in anger, his gloved fingers press painfully through my coat and sports jacket.

'This is not the Krishna Temple?'

I give him directions.

He frowns, presses me harder, for this does not please him. Crowds of students swirl around us. Why seize me, I want to cry, the scent of a martyred wife is that strong? He can tell? But his grip is serene, impersonal, and painful.

'Nevertheless, I will enter,' he says, 'this place.'

'Fine.'

'I must present documents.' Again, he is asking. I tell him he mustn't.

'What this place is?'

'A university.' I know this will confuse him. This is the largest academic building in the Commonwealth, I am told, but it looks nothing like a school. He presses harder.

'It is very late.'

The lobby is packed like a department store, which it already resembles with its escalators and high ceilings. We push through a door, two by two, and his grip loosens until I begin to pull away. 'You are not a student,' he says, or asks, 'you are,' and he strains as though making a difficult judgement, 'another thing.' And then suddenly he drops my arm and takes off through the crowd. No chance to catch him, *shake him* and demand how he found me, of all people, tonight of all nights. A brown angel, not of death but perhaps of impairment? My wife in pain? Dying? The baby? Me? I push to the escalator then turn quickly in order to find him in the lobby and it is not difficult; he cuts through the crowd as though somehow charmed, just as I had feared. Students part to let him pass, even those who do not see him.

I call my wife during the intermission. The contractions have stopped, she's had a pill and will spend the night. Home after breakfast. A little fatigued, they said. She is preparing her Wednesday lecture.

The Night

From school I take a taxi to the baby-sitter's—two dollars—and gather my son in his blanket and carry him back to the waiting cab. Another two-fifty. I get home to find it much colder, the first heat failure of the winter. What does this mean? I put him in our bed, look for extra blankets but can't find them, call the landlord's answering service, then crawl in with my boy, fully dressed in the clothes I lectured in.

Sometime deep and cold in the night he pulls the cover from me and tugs my hand until I waken. He is crying, standing on the rug with his pyjama bottoms down and pointing toward the bathroom. I follow his hand and see—in several peaks—the movement he'd run to the bathroom to prevent. The largest mounds are on the rug; several more, including what he's stepped on and carried far down the hall and all over the bathroom floor, is on the hardwood overlap around the rug.

It is three in the morning. The time of the crack-up. I stoop, shivering, over piles of gelatinous shit on our only decent possession, an Irish wool rug. My boy, guilty and frightened, steps up his crying. *Back to bed,* I snap, weary but forgiving, and he counters, 'Where's Mommy?' but there is not time to explain. 'You're bad!' he cries, and hits me, screams louder, and I'm close to tears. Can I just leave it, I wonder, not so much wanting to as not knowing where to start. Then I carry him to the bathroom, clean his feet, his bottom, and return him to bed. I have never been so awake; I can see perfectly with no lights on. I mop the hall and bathroom floor. In the half-dark kitchen I grab a knife and cereal bowl, then the rug shampoo and brush from an undisturbed plastic tub under the sink. I scrape the rug with the knife, try to pick up everything I can see with the help of the bathroom light, then dip the brush in hot soapy water and begin to scrub.

For a minute or two it goes well, then I notice glistening shapes staggering from the milky foam; the harder I press, the more appear. *My child has roaches,* his belly is teeming, full of bugs, a plague of long brown roaches is living inside him, thriving on our neglect. The roaches creep and dart in every direction, I whack them with the wooden brush but more are boiling from the foam and now they appear on my hand and arm. I see two on the shoulder of my white shirt. I shout but my throat is closed after an evening lecture—I sputter phlegm. These are not my son's; they are the rug's. The other side of this fine Irish rug that we bought for a house in the suburbs that we later decided against, this rug that we haven't turned in months and haven't sent out to be cleaned, is a sea of roaches. I drop the brush and look underneath. Hairpins and tufts of tissue: an angry wave of roaches walking the top of the brush and glistening in the fibres like wet leaves beginning to stir. *My brush,* I want to cry: the brush was my friend. I pick it up and run with it down the hall, the filthiest thing I've ever held. I hear the roaches dropping to safety on the floor. It occurs to me as I open the apartment door and then the double doors of the foyer, and as I fling the brush over one curb of parked cars, that a drop of soapy water anywhere in this apartment would anger the roaches: the drawers, the mattresses, the good china, the silverware at night. First brushes, then rugs, and anything fine we might possibly buy or try to preserve; everything will yield to roaches. All those golden children of our joint income, infested.

Morning Dawns

After the rug I do the floors again, even the kitchen and hall and living room. I rewash every dish, spray ammonia where I can't reach. Then I throw away the mops and sponges, as the pharaohs killed their slaves, then killed the slaves that had dug the graves, killed the slaves that killed the slaves ... not a sponge, a rag, a bucket, a mop, a scrap of newspaper or length of paper-towelling left. At six o'clock in a freezing apartment, with an aching former nerve, I open the windows and clean the outside, wiping with my handkerchief, then throwing it away. By six o'clock near-light, by street and alley lamp, the place looks clean and ready for people. Ready for more than our basic used Danish. *Ready for youth,* I let myself think: for sitars in the corner, fishnets on the wall, posters, teakwood chests. In with pillows and garish cottons, out with sofas, tables and doors. Sitting on the Danish sofa, wrapped in my overcoat, I can almost hear the guests arriving, smell the incense, sway to Ravi Shankar records ...

But I'm not young, any more.

I part the fibreglass curtains. It is snowing heavily now, with tiny flakes. The cars will be stuck—thank God we walk. The brush I threw is white, straddled by the tracks of an early car. After such roaches, what improvement? A loft, a farm-house, a duplex five miles out? Five years in this very place living for the city, the city our prize. For what we've caught, stopped, saved, we could have camped along St. Catherine Street. Holding on to nothing, because we were young and didn't need it. Always thinking: there is nowhere else we'd rather be. Nowhere else we can be, now. Old passports, pulled nerves, resting in offices. I think of my friends, the records they cry over, silly poems set to music, and I could cry as well. For them, for us. At the window I watch the men brush off their windshields, hear the engines trying to start. My son will soon be waking. I drop the curtains and go to put on water.

EYES

YOU JUMP into this business of a new country cautiously. First you choose a place where English is spoken, with doctors and bus lines at hand, and a supermarket in a *centre d'achats* not too far away. You ease yourself into the city, approaching by car or bus down a single artery, aiming yourself along the boulevard that begins small and tree-lined in your suburb but broadens into the canyoned aorta of the city five miles beyond. And by that first winter when you know the routes and bridges, the standard congestions reported from the helicopter on your favourite radio station, you start to think of moving. What's the good of a place like this when two of your neighbours have come from Texas and the French paper you've dutifully subscribed to arrives by mail two days late? These French are all around you, behind the counters at the shopping centre, in a house or two on your block, why isn't your little boy learning French at least? Where's the nearest *maternelle*? Four miles away.

In the spring you move. You find an apartment on a small side street where dogs outnumber children and the row houses resemble London's, divided equally between the rundown and remodelled. Your neighbours are the young personalities of

French television who live on delivered chicken, or the old pensioners who shuffle down the summer sidewalks in pyjamas and slippers in a state of endless recuperation. Your neighbours pay sixty a month for rent, or three hundred; you pay two-fifty for a two-bedroom flat where the walls have been replastered and new fixtures hung. The bugs *d'antan* remain, as well as the hulks of cars abandoned in the fire alley behind, where downtown drunks sleep in the summer night.

Then comes the night in early October when your child is coughing badly, and you sit with him in the darkened nursery, calm in the bubbling of a cold-steam vaporizer while your wife mends a dress in the room next door. And from the dark, silently, as you peer into the ill-lit fire alley, he comes. You cannot believe it at first, that a rheumy, pasty-faced Irishman in slate-grey jacket and rubber-soled shoes has come purposely to *your* small parking space, that he has been here before and he is not drunk (not now, at least, but you know him as a panhandler on the main boulevard a block away), that he brings with him a crate that he sets on end under your bedroom window and raises himself to your window ledge and hangs there nose-high at a pencil of light from the ill-fitting blinds. And there you are, straining with him from the uncurtained nursery, watching the man watching your wife, praying silently that she is sleeping under the blanket. The man is almost smiling, a leprechaun's face that sees what you cannot. You are about to lift the window and shout, but your wheezing child lies just under you; and what of your wife in the room next door? You could, perhaps, throw open the window and leap to the ground, tackle the man before he runs and smash his face into the bricks, beat him senseless then call the cops . . . Or better, find the camera, affix the flash, rap once at the window and shoot when he turns. Do nothing and let him suffer. *He is at your mercy,* no one will ever again be so helpless—but what can you do? You know, somehow, he'll escape. If you hurt him, he can hurt you worse, later, viciously.

He's been a regular at your window, he's watched the two of you when you prided yourselves on being young and alone and masters of the city. He knows your child and the park he plays in, your wife and where she shops. He's a native of the place, a man who knows the city and maybe a dozen such windows, who knows the fire escapes and alleys and roofs, knows the habits of the city's heedless young.

And briefly you remember yourself, an adolescent in another country slithering through the mosquito-ridden grassy fields behind a housing development, peering into those houses where newlyweds had not yet put up drapes, how you could spend five hours in a motionless crouch for a myopic glimpse of a slender arm reaching from the dark to douse a light. Then you hear what the man cannot; the creaking of your bed in the far bedroom, the steps of your wife on her way to the bathroom, and you see her as you never have before: blond and tall and rangily built, a north-Europe princess from a constitutional monarchy, sensuous mouth and prominent teeth, pale, tennis-ball breasts cupped in her hands as she stands in the bathroom's light.

'How's Kit?' she asks. 'I'd give him a kiss except that there's no blind in there,' and she dashes back to bed, nude, and the man bounces twice on the window ledge.

'You coming?'

You find yourself creeping from the nursery, turning left at the hall and then running to the kitchen telephone; you dial the police, then hang up. How will you prepare your wife, not for what is happening, but for what has already taken place?

'It's stuffy in here,' you shout back. 'I think I'll open the window a bit.' You take your time, you stand before the blind blocking his view if he's still looking, then bravely you part the curtains. He is gone, the crate remains upright. 'Do we have any masking tape?' you ask, lifting the window a crack.

And now you know the city a little better. A place where millions come each summer to take pictures and walk around must have its voyeurs too. And that place in all great cities where rich and poor co-exist is especially hard on the people in-between. It's health you've been seeking, not just beauty; a tough urban health that will save you money in the bargain, and when you hear of a place twice as large at half the rent, in a part of town free of Texans, English and French, free of young actors and stewardesses who deposit their garbage in pizza boxes, you move again.

It is, for you, a city of Greeks. In the summer you move you attend a movie at the corner cinema. The posters advertise a war movie, in Greek, but the uniforms are unfamiliar. Both sides wear moustaches, both sides handle machine guns, both leave older women behind dressed in black. From the posters outside there is a promise of sex; blond women in slips, dark-eyed peasant girls. There will be rubble, executions against a wall. You can follow the story from the stills alone: moustached boy goes to war, embraces dark-eyed village girl. Black-draped mother and admiring young brother stand behind. Young soldier, moustache fuller, embraces blond prostitute on a tangled bed. Enter soldiers, boy hides under sheets. Final shot, back in village. Mother in black; dark-eyed village girl in black. Young brother marching to the front.

You go in, pay your ninety cents, pay a nickel in the lobby for a wedge of *halvah*-like sweets. You understand nothing, you resent their laughter and you even resent the picture they're running. Now you know the Greek for 'Coming Attractions', for this is a gangster movie at least thirty years old. The eternal Mediterranean gangster movie set in Athens instead of Naples or Marseilles, with smaller cars and narrower roads, uglier women and more sinister killers. After an hour the movie flatters you. No one knows you're not a Greek, that you don't belong in this theatre, or even this city. That, like the Greeks, you're hanging on.

Outside the theatre the evening is warm and the wide sidewalks are clogged with Greeks who nod as you come out. Like the Ramblas in Barcelona, with children out past midnight and families walking back and forth for a long city block, the men filling the coffeehouses, the women left outside, chatting. Not a blond head on the sidewalk, not a blond head for miles. Greek music pours from the coffeehouses, flies stumble on the pastry, whole families munch their *torsades molles* as they walk. Dry goods are sold at midnight from the sidewalk, like New York fifty years ago. You're wandering happily, glad that you moved, you've rediscovered the innocence of starting over.

Then you come upon a scene directly from Spain. A slim blond girl in a floral top and white pleated skirt, tinted glasses, smoking, with bad skin, ignores a persistent young Greek in a shiny Salonika suit. 'Whatsamatta?' he demands, slapping a ten-dollar bill on his open palm. And without looking back at him she drifts closer to the curb and a car makes a sudden squealing turn and lurches to a stop on the cross street. Three men are inside, the back door opens and not a word is exchanged as she steps inside. How? What refinement of gesture did we immigrants miss? You turn to the Greek boy in sympathy, you know just how he feels, but he's already heading across the street, shouting something to his friends outside a barbecue stand. You have a pocketful of bills and a Mediterranean soul, and money this evening means a woman, and blond means whore and you would spend it all on another blond with open pores; all this a block from your wife and tenement. And you hurry home.

Months later you know the place. You trust the Greeks in their stores, you fear their tempers at home. Eight bathrooms adjoin a central shaft, you hear the beatings of your son's friends, the thud of fist on bone after the slaps. Your child knows no French, but he plays cricket with Greeks and Jamaicans out in the alley behind Pascal's hardware. He brings home the oily tires from the Esso station, plays in the boxes behind the appliance store. You watch from a greasy back window, at last satisfied. None of his friends is like him, like you. He is becoming Greek, becoming Jamaican, becoming a part of this strange new land. His hair is nearly white; you can spot him a block away.

On Wednesday the butcher quarters his meat. Calves arrive by refrigerator truck, still intact but for their split-open bellies and sawed-off hooves. The older of the three brothers skins the carcass with a small thin knife that seems all blade. A knife he could shave with. The hide rolls back in a continuous flap, the knife never pops the membrane over the fat.

Another brother serves. Like yours, his French is adequate. '*Twa lif d'hamburger*,' you request, still watching the operation on the rickety sawhorse. Who could resist? It's a Levantine treat, the calf's stumpy legs high in the air, the hide draped over the edge and now in the sawdust, growing longer by the second.

The store is filling. The ladies shop on Wednesday, especially the old widows in black overcoats and scarves, shoes and stockings. Yellow, mangled fingernails. Wednesdays attract them with boxes in the window, and they call to the butcher as they enter, the brother answers, and the women dip their fingers in the boxes. The radio is loud overhead, music from the Greek station.

'*Une et soixante, m'sieur. Du bacon, jambon?*'

And you think, taking a few lamb chops but not their salt-less bacon, how pleased you are to manage so well. It is a Byzantine moment with blood and widows and sides of dripping beef, contentment in a snowy slum at five below.

The older brother, having finished the skinning, straightens, curses, and puts away the tiny knife. A brother comes forward to pull the hide away, a perfect beginning for a gameroom rug. Then, bending low at the rear of the glistening carcass, the legs spread high and stubby, the butcher digs in his hands, ripping hard where the scrotum is, and pulls on what seems to be a strand of rubber, until it snaps. He puts a single glistening prize in his mouth, pulls again and offers the other to his brother, and they suck.

The butcher is singing now, drying his lips and wiping his chin, and still he's chewing. The old black-draped widows with the parchment faces are also chewing. On leaving, you check the boxes in the window. Staring out are the heads of pigs and lambs, some with the eyes lifted out and a red socket exposed. A few are loose and the box is slowly dissolving from the blood, and the ice beneath.

The women have gathered around the body; little pieces are offered to them from the head and entrails. The pigs' heads are pink, perhaps they've been boiled, and hairless. The eyes are strangely blue. You remove your gloves and touch the skin, you brush against the grainy ear. How the eye attracts you! How you would like to lift one out, press its smoothness against your tongue, then crush it in your mouth. And you cannot. Already your finger is numb and the head, it seems, has shifted under you. And the eye, in panic, grows white as your finger approaches. You would take that last half inch but for the certainty, in this world you have made for yourself, that the eye would blink and your neighbours would turn upon you.

I'M DREAMING OF
ROCKET RICHARD

W E WERE NEVER quite the poorest people on the block,
simply because I was, inexplicably, an only child. So
there was more to go around. It was a strange kind of
poverty, streaked with gentility (the kind that chopped you
down when you least expected it); my mother would spend
too much for long-range goals—Christmas clubs, reference
books, even a burial society—and my father would drink it
up or gamble it away as soon as he got it. I grew up thinking
that being an only child, like poverty, was a blight you talked
about only in secret. 'Too long in the convent,' my father
would shout—a charge that could explain my mother's way
with money or her favours—'there's ice up your cunt.' An only
child was scarcer than twins, maybe triplets, in Montreal just
after the war. And so because I was an only child, things happened to me more vividly, without those warnings that older
brothers carry as scars. I always had the sense of being the first
in my family—which was to say the first of my people—to
think my thoughts, to explore the parts of Montreal that we
called foreign, even to question in an innocent way the multitudes of unmovable people and things.

When I went to the Forum to watch the Canadiens play hockey, I wore a Boston Bruins sweatshirt. That was way back, when poor people could get into the Forum, and when Rocket Richard scored fifty goals in fifty games. Despite the letters on the sweatshirt, I loved the Rocket. I loved the Canadiens fiercely. It had to do with the intimacy of old-time hockey, how close you were to the gods on the ice; you could read their lips and hear them grunt as they slammed the boards. So there I stood in my Boston Bruins shirt loving the Rocket. There was always that spot of perversity in the things I loved. In school the nuns called me 'Curette'—'Little Priest'.

I was always industrious. That's how it is with janitors' sons. I had to pull out the garbage sacks, put away tools, handle simple repairs, answer complaints about heat and water when my father was gone or too drunk to move. He used to sleep near the heating pipes on an inch-thick, rust-stained mattress under a Sally Ann blanket. He loved his tools; when he finally sold them I knew we'd hit the bottom.

Industriously, I built an ice surface, enclosed it with old doors from a demolished tenement. The goal mouth was a topless clothes-hamper I fished from the garbage. I battered it to splinters, playing. Luck of the only child: if I'd had an older brother, I'd have been put in goal. Luckily there was a younger kid on the third floor who knew his place and was given hockey pads one Christmas; his older brother and I would bruise him after school until darkness made it dangerous for him. I'd be in my Bruins jersey, dreaming of Rocket Richard.

Little priest that I was, I did more than build ice surfaces. In the mornings I would rise at a quarter to five and pick up a bundle of *Montréal Matins* on the corner of Van Horne and Querbes. Seventy papers I had, and I could run with the last thirty-five, firing them up on second- and third-floor balconies, stuffing them into convenient grilles, and marking with hate all those buildings where the Greeks were moving in or the Jews had already settled and my papers weren't good enough to wrap their garbage in. There was another kid who delivered the morning *Gazette*s to part of my street—ten or twelve places that had no use for me. We were the only people yet awake, crisscrossing each other's paths, still in the dark and way below zero, me with a *Matin* sack and him with his *Gazette*. Once, we even talked. We were waiting for our bundles under a street lamp in front of the closed tobacco store on the corner. It was about ten below and the sidewalks were uncleared from an all-night snow. He smoked one of my cigarettes and I smoked one of his and we found out we didn't have anything to say to each other except *merci*. After half an hour I said, 'Paper no come,' and he agreed, so we walked away.

Later on more and more Greeks moved in; every time a vacancy popped up, some Greek would take it—they even made sure by putting only Greek signs in the windows—and my route was shrinking all the time. *Montréal Matin* fixed me up with a route much further east, off Rachel near St-André, and so I became the only ten-year-old in Montreal who'd wait at four-thirty in the morning for the first bus out of the garage to take him to his paper route. After a few days I didn't have to pay a fare. I'd take coffee from the driver's thermos, his cigarettes, and we'd discuss hockey from the night before. In return I'd give him a paper when he let me off. They didn't call me Curette for nothing.

The hockey, the hockey! I like all the major sports, and the setting of each one has its special beauty—even old De Lorimier Downs had something of Yankee Stadium about it, and old Rocky Nelson banging out home runs from his rocking-chair stance made me think of Babe Ruth, and who could compare to Jackie Robinson and Roberto Clemente when they were playing for us? Sundays in August with the Red Wings in town, you could always get in free after a couple of innings and see two great games. But the ice of big-time hockey, the old Forum, that went beyond landscape! Something about the ghostly white of the ice under those powerful lights, something about the hiss of the skates if you were standing close enough, the solid *pock-pock* of the rubber on a stick, and the low menacing whiz of a Rocket wrist shot hugging the ice—there was nothing in any other sport to compare with the *spell* of hockey. Inside the Forum in the early fifties, those games against Boston (with the Rocket flying and a hated Boston goalie named Jack Gelineux in the nets) were evangelical, for truly we were *dans le cénacle* where everyone breathed as one.

The Bruins sweatshirt came from a cousin of mine in Manchester, New Hampshire, who brought it as a joke or maybe a present on one of his trips up to see us. I started wearing it in all my backyard practices and whenever I got standing room tickets at the Forum. Crazy, I think now; what was going on in me? Crying on those few nights each winter when the Canadiens lost, quite literally throwing whatever I was holding high in the air whenever the Rocket scored—yet always wearing that hornet-coloured jersey? Anyone could see I was a good local kid; maybe I wanted someone to think I'd come all the way from Boston just to see the game, maybe I liked the good-natured kidding from my fellow standees ("ey, you Boston,' they'd shout, 'oo's winning, eh?' and I'd snarl back after a period or two of silence, *'Mange la bâton, sac de marde . . .'*). I even used to wear that jersey when I delivered papers and I remember the pain of watching it slowly unravel in the cuffs and shoulders, hoping the cousin would come again. They were Schmitzes, my mother's sister had met him just after the war. *Tante* Lise and Uncle Howie.

I started to pick up English by reading a *Gazette* on my paper route, and I remember vividly one spring morning—with the sun coming up—studying a name that I took to be typically English. It began *Sch,* an odd combination, like my uncle's; then I suddenly thought of my mother's name—not mine—Deschênes, and I wondered: could it be? Hidden in the middle of my mother's name were those same English letters, and I began to think that we (tempting horror) were

English too, that I had a right, a *sch,* to that Bruins jersey, to the world in the *Gazette* and on the other side of Atwater from the Forum. How I fantasized!

Every now and then the Schmitzes would drive up in a new car (I think now they came up whenever they bought a new car; I don't remember ever sitting in one of their cars without noticing a shred of plastic around the window-cranks and a smell of newness), and I would marvel at my cousins who were younger than me and taller ('They don't smoke,' my mother would point out), and who whined a lot because they always wanted things (I never understood what) they couldn't get with us. My mother could carry on with them in English. I wanted to like them—an only child feels that way about his relatives, not having seen his genetic speculations exhausted, and tends to see himself refracted even into second and third cousins several times removed. Now I saw a devious link with that American world in the strange clot of letters common to my name and theirs, and that pleased me.

We even enjoyed a bout of prosperity at about that time. I was thirteen or so, and we had moved from Hutchison (where a Greek janitor was finally hired) to a place off St-Denis where my father took charge of a sixteen-apartment building; they paid him well and gave us a three-room place out of the basement damps. That was *bonheur* in my father's mind—moving up to the ground floor where the front door buzzer kept waking you up. It was reasonably new; he didn't start to have trouble with bugs and paint for almost a year. He even saved a little money.

At just about the same time, in the more spacious way of the Schmitzes, they packed up everything in Manchester (where Uncle Howie owned three dry-cleaning shops) and moved to North Hollywood, Florida. That's a fair proportion: Hutchison is to St-Denis what Manchester is to Florida. He started with one dry-cleaning shop and had three others within a year. If he'd really been one of us, we'd have been suspicious of his tactics and motives, we would have called him lucky and undeserving. But he was American, he had his *sch,* so whatever he did seemed blessed by a different branch of fate, and we wondered only how we could share.

It was the winter of 1952. It was a cold sunny time on St-Denis. I still delivered my papers (practically in the neighbourhood), my father wasn't drinking that much, and my mother was staying out of church except on Sunday—and we had just bought a car. It was a used Plymouth, the first car we'd ever owned. The idea was that we should visit the Schmitzes this time in their Florida home for Christmas. It was even their idea, arranged through the sisters. My father packed his tools in the rear ('You never know, Mance; I'd like to show him what I can do ...'). He moved his brother Réal and family into our place—Réal was handy enough, more affable, but an even bigger drinker. We left Montreal on December 18 and took a cheap and slow drive down, the pace imposed by my father, who underestimated the strain of driving, and by my mother, who'd read of speedtraps and tourists languishing twenty years in Southern dungeons for running a stop sign. The drive was cheap because we were dependent on my mother for expense money as soon as we entered the States, since she was the one who could go into the motel office and find out the prices. It would be three or four in the afternoon and my father would be a nervous wreck; just as we were unloading the trunk and my father was checking the level of whiskey in the glove compartment bottle, she'd come out announcing it was highway robbery, we couldn't stay here. My father would groan, curse and slam the trunk. Things would be dark by the time we found a vacancy in one of those rows of one-room cabins, arranged like stepping stones or in a semicircle (the kind you still see nowadays out on the Gaspésie with boards on the windows and a faded billboard out front advertising 'investment property'). My mother put a limit of three dollars a night on accommodations; we shopped in supermarkets for cold meat, bread, mustard and Pepsis. My father rejoiced in the cheaper gas; my mother reminded him it was a smaller gallon. Quietly, I calculated the difference. Remember, no drinking after Savannah, my mother said. It was clear: he expected to become the manager of a Schmitz Dry Kleenery.

The Schmitzes had rented a spacious cottage about a mile from the beach in North Hollywood. The outside stucco was green, the roof tiles orange, and the flowers violently pink and purple. The shrubs looked decorated with little red Christmas bulbs; I picked one—gift of my cousin—bit, and screamed in surprise. Red chilies. The front windows were sprayed with Santa's sleigh and a snowy 'Merry Christmas'. Only in English, no *'Joyeux Noël'* like our greeting back home. That was what I'd noticed most all the way down, the incompleteness of all the signs, the satisfaction that their version said it all. I'd kept looking on the other side of things—my side—and I'd kept twirling the radio dial, for an equivalence that never came.

It was Christmas week and the Schmitzes were wearing Bermuda shorts and T-shirts with sailfish on the front. *Tante* Lise wore coral earrings and a red halter, and all her pale flesh had freckled. The night we arrived, my father got up on a stepladder, anxious to impress, and strung coloured lights along the gutter while my uncle shouted directions and watered the lawn. Christmas—and drinking Kool-Aid in the yard! We picked chili peppers and sold them to every West Indian cook who answered the back doorbell. At night I licked my fingers and hummed with the air-conditioning. My tongue burned for hours. That was the extraordinary part for me: that things as hot as chilies could grow in your yard, that I could bake in December heat, and that other natural laws remained the same. My father was still shorter than my mother, and his face turned red and blotchy here too (just as it did in August back home) instead of an even schmitzean brown, and when he took off his shirt, only a tattoo, scars and angry red welts were revealed. Small and sickly he seemed; worse, mutilated.

My cousins rode their chrome-plated bicycles to the beach, but I'd never owned a two-wheeler and this didn't seem the time to reveal another weakness. Give me ice, I thought, my stick and a puck and an open net. Some men were never meant for vacations in shirtless countries: small hairy men with dirty winter boils and red swellings that never became anything lanceable, and tattoos of celebrities in their brief season of fame, now forgotten. My father's tattoo was as long as my twelve-year-old hand, done in a waterfront parlour in Montreal the day he'd thought of enlisting. My mother had been horrified, more at the tattoo than the thought of his shipping out. The tattoo pictured a front-faced Rocket, staring at an imaginary goalie and slapping a rising shot through a cloud of ice chips. Even though I loved the Canadiens and the Rocket mightily, I would have preferred my father to walk shirtless down the middle of the street with a naked woman on his back than for him to strip for the Schmitzes and my enormous cousins, who pointed and laughed, while I could almost understand what they were laughing about. They thought his tattoo was a kind of tribal marking, like kinky hair, thin moustaches, and slanty eyes— that if I took off my shirt I'd have one too, only smaller. *Lacroix,* I said to myself: how could he and I have the same name? It was foreign. I was a Deschênes, a Schmitz in the making.

On Christmas Eve we trimmed a silvered little tree and my uncle played Bing Crosby records on the console hi-fi-short-wave-bookcase (the biggest thing going in Manchester, New Hampshire, before the days of television). It would have been longer than our living room in Montreal; even here it filled one wall. They tried to teach me to imitate Crosby's 'White Christmas', but my English was hopeless. My mother and aunt sang in harmony; my father kept spilling his iced tea while trying to clap. It was painful. I waited impatiently to get to bed in order to cut the night as short as possible.

The murkiness of those memories! How intense, how foreign; it all happened like a dream in which everything follows logically from some incredible premise—that we should go to Florida, that it should be so hot in December, that my father should be on his best behaviour for nearly a month . . . that we could hope that a little initiative and optimism would carry us anywhere but deeper into debt and darkest despair . . .

I see myself as in a dream, walking the beach alone, watching the coarse brown sand fall over my soft white feet. I hear my mother and *Tante* Lise whispering together, yet they're five hundred feet ahead ('Yes,' my mother is saying, 'what life is there for him back there? You can see how this would suit him. To a T! To a T!' I'm wondering is it me, or my father, who has no future back there, and *Tante* Lise begins, 'Of course, I'm only a wife. I don't know what his thinking is—'), but worse is the silent image of my father in his winter trousers rolled up to his skinny knees and gathered in folds by a borrowed belt (at home he'd always worn braces), shirtless, shrunken, almost running to keep up with my uncle who walks closer to the water, in Bermuda shorts. I can tell from the beaten smile on my father's lips and from the way Uncle Howie is talking (while looking over my father's head at the ships on the horizon), that what the women have arranged ('It would be good to have you close, Mance . . . I get these moods sometimes, you know? And five shops are too much for Howie . . .') the men have made impossible. I know that when my father was smiling and his head was bobbing in agreement and he was running to keep up with someone, he was being told off, turned down, laughed at. And the next stage was for him to go off alone, then come back to us with a story that embarrassed us all by its transparency, and that would be the last of him, sober, for three, four or five days . . . I can see all this and hear it, though I am utterly alone near the crashing surf and it seems to be night and a forgotten short-wave receiver still blasts forth on a beach blanket somewhere; I go to it hoping to catch something I can understand, a hockey game, the scores, but all I get wrenching the dial until it snaps is Bing Crosby dreaming of a white Christmas and Cuban music and indecipherable commentary from Havana, the dog races from Miami, *jai alai*.

That drive back to Montreal lasted almost a month. Our money ran out in Georgia and we had to wait two weeks in a shack in the Negro part of Savannah, where a family like ours—with a mother who liked to talk, and a father who drank and showed up only to collect our rent, and a kid my age who spent his time caddying and getting up before the sun to hunt golf balls—found space for us in a large room behind the kitchen, recently vacated by a dead grandparent. There were irregularities, the used-car dealer kept saying, various legal expenses involved with international commerce between Canadian Plymouths and innocent Georgia dealers, and we knew not to act too anxious (or even give our address) for fear of losing whatever bit of money we stood to gain. Finally he gave us $75, and that was when my father took his tools out of the back and sold them at a gas station for $50. We went down to the bus station, bought three tickets to Montreal, and my father swept the change into my mother's pocketbook. We were dressed for the January weather we'd be having when we got off, and the boy from the house we'd been staying in, shaking his head as he watched us board, muttered, 'Man, you sure is crazy.' It became a phrase of my mother's for all the next hard years. 'Man, you sure is crazy.' I mastered it and wore it like a Bruins sweater, till it too wore out. I remember those nights on the bus, my mother counting the bills and coins in her purse, like beads on a rosary, the numbers a silent prayer.

Back on St-Denis we found Réal and family very happily installed. The same egregiously gregarious streak that sputtered in my father flowed broadly in his brother. He'd all but brought fresh fruit baskets to the sixteen residents, carried newspapers to their doors, repaired buzzers that had never worked, shovelled insanely wide swaths down the front steps, replaced lights in the basement lockers, oiled, painted, polished ... even laid off the booze for the whole month we were gone (which to my father was the unforgivable treachery); in short, while we'd sunk all our savings and hocked all our valuables to launch ourselves in the dry-cleaning business, Réal had simply moved his family three blocks into lifelong comfort and security. My father took it all very quietly; we thought he'd blow sky-high. But he was finished. He'd put up the best, and the longest, show of his life and he'd seen himself squashed like a worm underfoot. Maybe he'd had one of those hellish moments when he'd seen himself in his brother-in-law's sunglasses, running at his side, knowing that those sunglasses were turned to the horizon and not to him.

A CLASS OF
NEW CANADIANS

ORMAN DYER hurried down Sherbrooke Street, collar
turned against the snow. 'Superb!' he muttered, passing
a basement gallery next to a French bookstore. Bleached
and tanned women in furs dashed from hotel lobbies into
waiting cabs. Even the neon clutter of the side streets and the
honks of slithering taxis seemed remote tonight through the
peaceful snow. *Superb,* he thought again, waiting for a light and
backing from a slushy curb: a word reserved for wines, cigars
and delicate sauces; he was feeling superb this evening. After
eighteen months in Montreal, he still found himself freshly
impressed by everything he saw. He was proud of himself for
having steered his life north, even for jobs that were menial by
standards he could have demanded. Great just being here no
matter what they paid, looking at these buildings, these faces,
and hearing all the languages. He was learning to be insulted
by simple bad taste, wherever he encountered it.

Since leaving graduate school and coming to Montreal,
he had sampled every ethnic restaurant downtown and in the
Old City, plus a few Levantine places out in Outremont. He
had worked on conversational French and mastered much
of the local dialect, done reviews for local papers, translated

French-Canadian poets for Toronto quarterlies, and tweaked his colleagues for not sympathizing enough with Quebec separatism. He attended French performances of plays he had ignored in English, and kept a small but elegant apartment near a colony of *émigré* Russians just off Park Avenue. Since coming to Montreal he'd witnessed a hold-up, watched a murder and seen several riots. When stopped on the street for directions, he would answer in French or accented English. To live this well and travel each long academic summer, he held two jobs. He had no intention of returning to the States. In fact, he had begun to think of himself as a semi-permanent, semi-political exile.

Now, stopped again a few blocks farther, he studied the window of Holt Renfrew's exclusive men's shop. Incredible, he thought, the authority of simple good taste. Double-breasted chalk-striped suits he would never dare to buy. Knitted sweaters, and fifty-dollar shoes. One tanned mannequin was decked out in a brash chequered sportscoat with a burgundy vest and dashing ascot. Not a price tag under three hundred dollars. Unlike food, drink, cinema and literature, clothing had never really involved him. Someday, he now realized, it would. Dyer's clothes, thus far, had all been bought in a chain department store. He was a walking violation of American law, clad shoes to scarf in Egyptian cottons, Polish leathers, and woollens from the People's Republic of China.

He had no time for dinner tonight; this was Wednesday, a day of lectures at one university, and then an evening course in English as a Second Language at McGill, beginning at six. He would eat afterwards.

Besides the money, he had kept this second job because it flattered him. There was to Dyer something fiercely elemental, almost existential, about teaching both his language and his literature in a foreign country—like Joyce in Trieste, Isherwood and Nabokov in Berlin, Beckett in Paris. Also it was necessary for his students. It was the first time in his life that he had done something socially useful. What difference did it make that the job was beneath him, a recent Ph.D., while most of his colleagues in the evening school at McGill were idle housewives and bachelor civil servants? It didn't matter, even, that this job was a perversion of all the sentiments he held as a progressive young teacher. He was a god two evenings a week, sometimes suffering and fatigued, but nevertheless an omniscient, benevolent god. His students were silent, ignorant and dedicated to learning English. No discussions, no demonstrations, no dialogue.

I love them, he thought. They need me.

He entered the room, pocketed his cap and earmuffs, and dropped his briefcase on the podium. Two girls smiled good evening.

They love me, he thought, taking off his boots and hanging up his coat; I'm not their English-speaking bosses.

I love myself, he thought with amazement even while conducting a drill on word order. I love myself for tramping down Sherbrooke Street in zero weather just to help them with noun clauses. I love myself standing behind this podium and showing Gilles Carrier and Claude Veilleux the difference between the past continuous and the simple past; or the sultry Armenian girl with the bewitching half-glasses that 'put on' is not the same as 'take on'; or telling the dashing Mr Miguel Mayor, late of Madrid, that simple futurity can be expressed in four different ways, at least.

This is what mastery is like, he thought. Being superb in one's chosen field, not merely in one's mother tongue. A respected performer in the lecture halls of the major universities, equipped by twenty years' research in the remotest libraries, and slowly giving it back to those who must have it. Dishing it out suavely, even wittily. Being a legend. Being loved and a little feared.

'Yes, Mrs David?'

A *sabra:* freckled, reddish hair, looking like a British model, speaks with a nifty British accent, and loves me.

'No,' he said, smiling. *'I were* is not correct except in the present subjunctive, which you haven't studied yet.'

The first hour's bell rang. The students closed their books for the intermission. Dyer put his away, then noticed a page of his Faulkner lecture from the afternoon class. *Absalom, Absalom!* his favourite.

'Can anyone here tell me what the *impregnable citadel of his passive rectitude* means?'

'What, sir?' asked Mr Vassilopoulos, ready to copy.

'What about *the presbyterian and lugubrious effluvium of his passive vindictiveness?'* A few girls giggled. 'OK,' said Dyer, 'take your break.'

In the halls of McGill they broke into the usual groups. French Canadians and South Americans into two large circles, then the Greeks, Germans, Spanish and French into smaller groups. The patterns interested Dyer. Madrid Spaniards and Parisian French always spoke English with their New World co-linguals. The Middle Europeans spoke German together, not Russian, preferring one occupier to the other. Two Israeli men went off alone. Dyer decided to join them for the break.

Not *sabras,* Dyer decided, not like Mrs David. The shorter one, dark and wavy-haired, held his cigarette like a violin bow. The other, Mr Weinrot, was tall and pot-bellied, with a ruddy face and thick stubby fingers. Something about him suggested truck-driving, perhaps of beer, maybe in Germany. Neither one, he decided, could supply the name of a good Israeli restaurant.

'This is really hard, you know?' said Weinrot.

'Why?'

'I think it's because I'm not speaking much of English at my job.'

'French?' asked Dyer.

'French? Pah! All the time Hebrew, sometimes German, sometimes little Polish. Crazy thing, eh? How long you think they let me speak Hebrew if I'm working in America?'

'Depends on where you're working,' he said.

'Hell, I'm working for the Canadian government, what you think? Plant I work in—I'm engineer, see—makes boilers for the turbines going up North. Look. When I'm leaving Israel I go first to Italy. Right away—bamm I'm working in Italy I'm speaking Italian like a native. Passing for a native.'

'A native Jew,' said his dark-haired friend.

'Listen to him. So in Rome they think I'm from Tyrol—that's still native, eh? So I speak Russian and German and Ital ian like a Jew. My Hebrew is bad, I admit it, but it's a lousy language anyway. Nobody likes it. French I understand but English I'm talking like a bum. Arabic I know five dialects. Danish fluent. So what's the matter I can't learn English?'

'It'll come, don't worry.' Dyer smiled. *Don't worry, my son;* he wanted to pat him on the arm. 'Anyway, that's what makes Canada so appealing. Here they don't force you.'

'What's this *appealing*? Means nice? Look, my friend, keep it, eh? Two years in a country I don't learn the language means it isn't a country.'

'Come on,' said Dyer. 'Neither does forcing you.'

'Let me tell you a story why I come to Canada. Then you tell me if I was wrong, OK?'

'Certainly,' said Dyer, flattered.

In Italy, Weinrot told him, he had lost his job to a Communist union. He left Italy for Denmark and opened up an Israeli restaurant with five other friends. Then the six Israelis decided to rent a bigger apartment downtown near the restaurant. They found a perfect nine-room place for two thousand kroner a month, not bad shared six ways. Next day the landlord told them the deal was off. 'You tell me why,' Weinrot demanded.

No Jews? Dyer wondered. 'He wanted more rent,' he finally said.

'More—you kidding? More we expected. *Less* we didn't expect. A couple with eight kids is showing up after we're gone and the law in Denmark says a man has a right to a room for each kid plus a hundred kroner knocked off the rent for each kid. What you think of that? So a guy who comes in *after* us gets a nine-room place for a thousand kroner *less*. Law says no way a bachelor can get a place ahead of a family, and bachelors pay twice as much.'

Dyer waited, then asked, 'So?'

'So, I make up my mind the world is full of communismus, just like Israel. So I take out applications next day for Australia, South Africa, USA, and Canada. Canada says come right away, so I go. Should have waited for South Africa.'

'How could you?' Dyer cried. 'What's wrong with you anyway? South Africa is fascist. Australia is racist.'

The bell rang, and the Israelis, with Dyer, began walking to the room.

'What I was wondering, then,' said Mr Weinrot, ignoring Dyer's outburst, 'was if my English is good enough to be working in the United States. You're American, aren't you?'

It was a question Dyer had often avoided in Europe, but had rarely been asked in Montreal. 'Yes,' he admitted, 'your English is probably good enough for the States or South Africa, whichever one wants you first.'

He hurried ahead to the room, feeling that he had let Montreal down. He wanted to turn and shout to Weinrot and to all the others that Montreal was the greatest city on the continent, if only they knew it as well as he did. If they'd just break out of their little ghettos.

At the door, the Armenian girl with the half-glasses caught his arm. She was standing with Mrs David and Miss Parizeau, a jolly French-Canadian girl that Dyer had been thinking of asking out.

'Please, sir,' she said, looking at him over the tops of her tiny glasses, 'what I was asking earlier—*put on*—I heard on the television. A man said *You are putting me on* and everybody laughed. I think it was supposed to be funny but put on we learned means get dressed, no?'

'Ah—*don't put me on*,' Dyer laughed.

'I yaven't 'erd it neither,' said Miss Parizeau.

'To put some*body* on means to make a fool of him. To put some*thing* on is to wear it. Okay?' He gave examples.

'Ah, now I know,' said Miss Parizeau. 'Like bullshitting somebody. Is it the same?'

'Ah, yes,' he said, smiling. French Canadians were like children learning the language. 'Your example isn't considered polite. "Put on" is very common now in the States.'

'Then maybe,' said Miss Parizeau, 'we'll 'ave it 'ere in twenty years.' The Armenian giggled.

'No—I've heard it here just as often,' Dyer protested, but the girls had already entered the room.

He began the second hour with a smile that slowly soured as he thought of the Israelis. America's anti-communism was bad enough, but it was worse hearing it echoed by immigrants, by Jews, here in Montreal. Wasn't there a psychological type who chose Canada over South Africa? Or was it just a matter of visas and slow adjustment? Did Johannesburg lose its Greeks, and Melbourne its Italians, the way Dyer's students were always leaving Montreal?

And after class when Dyer was again feeling content and thinking of approaching one of the Israelis for a restaurant tip, there came the flood of small requests: should Mrs Papadopoulos go into a more advanced course; could Mr Perez miss a week for an interview in Toronto; could Mr Giguère, who spoke English perfectly, have a harder book; Mr Côté an easier one?

Then as Dyer packed his briefcase in the empty room, Miguel Mayor, the vain and impeccable Spaniard, came forward from the hallway.

'Sir,' he began, walking stiffly, ready to bow or salute. He wore a loud grey chequered sportscoat this evening, blue shirt and matching ascot-handkerchief, slightly mauve. He must have shaved just before class, Dyer noticed, for two fresh daubs of antiseptic cream stood out on his jaw, just under his earlobe.

'I have been waiting to ask *you* something, as a matter of fact,' said Dyer. 'Do you know any good Spanish restaurants I might try tonight?'

'There are not any good Spanish restaurants in Montreal,' he said. He stepped closer. 'Sir?'

'What's on your mind, then?'

'Please—have you the time to look on a letter for me?'

He laid the letter on the podium.

'Look *over* a letter,' said Dyer. 'What is it for?'

'I have applied,' he began, stopping to emphasize the present perfect construction, 'for a job in Cleveland, Ohio, and I want to know if my letter will be good. Will an American, I mean—'

'Why are you going there?'

'It is a good job.'

'But Cleveland—'

'They have a blackman mayor, I have read. But the job is not in Cleveland.'

Most honourable Sir: I humbly beg consideration for a position in your grand company . . .

'Who are you writing this to?'

'The president,' said Miguel Mayor.

I am once a student of Dr Ramiro Gutierrez of the Hydraulic Institute of Sevilla, Spain . . .

'Does the president know this Ramiro Gutierrez?'

'Oh, everybody is knowing him,' Miguel Mayor assured. 'He is the most famous expert in all Spain.'

'Did he recommend this company to you?'

'No—I have said in my letter, if you look—'

*An ancient student of Dr Gutierrez, Salvador del Este, is
actually a boiler expert who is being employed like supervisor is
formerly a friend of mine* ...
'Is he still your friend?'
*Whenever you say come to my city Miguel Mayor for talking
I will be coming. I am working in Montreal since two years and
am now wanting more money than I am getting here now* ...
'Well ...' Dyer sighed.
'Sir—what I want from you is knowing in good English
how to interview me by this man. The letters in Spanish are
not the same to English ones, you know?'
I remain humbly at your orders ...
'Why do you want to leave Montreal?'
'It's time for a change.'
'Have you ever been to Cleveland?'
'I am one summer in California. Very beautiful there and
hot like my country. Montreal is big port like Barcelona.
Everybody mixed together and having no money. It is just a
place to land, no?'
'Montreal? Don't be silly.'
'I thought I come here and learn good English but where
I work I get by in Spanish and French. It's hard, you know?'
he smiled. Then he took a few steps back and gave his cuffs a
gentle tug, exposing a set of jade cufflinks.
   Dyer looked at the letter again and calculated how long he
would be correcting it, then up at his student. How old is he?
My age? Thirty? Is he married? Where do the Spanish live in
Montreal? He looks so prosperous, so confident, like a male
model off a page of *Playboy*. For an instant Dyer felt that his
student was mocking him, somehow pitting his astounding
confidence and wardrobe, sharp chin and matador's bearing
against Dyer's command of English and mastery of the side
streets, bistros and ethnic restaurants. Mayor's letter was painful, yet he remained somehow competent. He would pass his
interview, if he got one. What would he care about America,

and the odiousness he'd soon be supporting? It was as though a superstructure of exploitation had been revealed, and Dyer felt himself abused by the very people he wanted so much to help. It had to end someplace.

He scratched out the second 'humbly' from the letter, then folded the sheet of foolscap. 'Get it typed right away,' he said. 'Good luck.'

'Thank you, sir,' said his student, with a bow. Dyer watched the letter disappear in the inner pocket of the chequered sportscoat. Then the folding of the cashmere scarf, the draping of the camel's hair coat about the shoulders, the easing of the fur hat down to the rims of his ears. The meticulous filling of the pigskin gloves. Mayor's patent leather galoshes glistened.

'Good evening, sir,' he said.

'*Buenas noches,*' Dyer replied.

He hurried now, back down Sherbrooke Street to his day-time office where he could deposit his books. Montreal on a winter night was still mysterious, still magical. Snow blurred the arc lights. The wind was dying. Every second car was now a taxi, crowned with an orange crescent. Slushy curbs had hardened. The window of Holt Renfrew was still attractive. The legless dummies invited a final stare. He stood longer than he had earlier, in front of the sporty mannequin with a burgundy waistcoat, the mauve and blue ensemble, the jade cufflinks.

Good evening, sir, he could almost hear. The ascot, the shirt, the complete outfit, had leaped off the back of Miguel Mayor. He pictured how he must have entered the store with three hundred dollars and a prepared speech, and walked out again with everything off the torso's back.

I want that.

What, sir?

That.

The coat, sir?

Yes.

Very well, sir.

And *that.*

Which, sir?

All that.

'Absurd man!' Dyer whispered. There had been a moment of fear, as though the naked body would leap from the window, and legless, chase him down Sherbrooke Street. But the moment was passing. Dyer realized now that it was comic, even touching. Miguel Mayor had simply tried too hard, too fast, and it would be good for him to stay in Montreal until he deserved those clothes, that touching vanity and confidence. With one last look at the window, he turned sharply, before the clothes could speak again.

WORDS FOR
THE WINTER

SEPTEMBER, month of the winding down. For a month we've lived the charade of ruddy good health up in the mountains north of Montreal. Swimming, rowing, tramping up the mountain just behind our cabin, baking trout over the coals at night. Drinking from the last pure-water lake in the Laurentians, reading by sunlight on the dock, sleeping in the cool mountain air from dark till the sunrise at 5 a.m. This is how I dreamed it would be: water, trout and mountains. And in this small way, I have succeeded.

Serge rows over around seven o'clock with two large trout, cleans them in our sink, and Erika spices them for baking. It was Serge who built our cabin and half the others on the lake after his family opened it up for exploitation. He's a Peugeot dealer in St-Jovite with a beard and a sordid past, and in the compulsive way of people who have painfully come through, he tells us about his failures, his vices, his present contentment. Like most reformed sinners and drinkers I've met, he is a mystic. 'This lake, you know,' he tells us in English, for emphasis, 'he save my life. Every weekend now for ten year I am coming to him by myself. Without him, I am a dead man. Three time already, I am a dead man.'

I have seen the scars. A knifing from his *voyou* days in Montreal. A cancerous lung. His heart. But he's a fit man now. He makes me feel that I'm only a teacher too young to have suffered and deserved the lake, but too old to ever learn the proper physical skills. To buy this cabin I simply answered a newspaper ad, got into his boat and saw those trout he'd caught that morning. As we talk, he cuts little wedges of pine to shore up our cabin and make the door fit tighter. He cuts cardboard to make the pump airtight. Unobtrusive skills I'll never master. Lurid stories I can only hope to copy, of gamblers in Acapulco, jail terms, a bankruptcy, an oath in an oxygen tent to be reborn.

The city lies an hour and a half to the south. We drop six hundred feet and gain two weeks of summer. A stagnant dome of dust and fumes squats over the city. September is still hot, street smells penetrate closed windows. It is a street of tenement, some of greystone, some of dark brick, some with porches, and some with the traditional winding outside staircases of old Montreal. The neighbourhood has been French, then Jewish, then Italian and now Greek, with Chinese and West Indians waiting their turn. A Ukrainian Church, a *yeshiva*, an Esso station, and a Greek grocery store bracket the street. We rent a nine-room flat in the three-story tenement. The flat across the hall has been subdivided; a large and violent family of Greeks in the back four rooms, two students and a Jamaican night watchman in the front three rooms, with one kept as a dining room, equipped with a stove and fridge. Above us a commune of hippies; above them, a nameless horde of student-age workers, French-Canadian, who often fight. In the single basement flat lives an extended family of Jamaicans with uncountable children all roughly the same age. Our four-year-old son plays with two of theirs; rugged, gentle boys of five and seven.

The winters are an agony. In January our broad summer street narrows to a one-lane rut, an icy *piste de luge* banked by walls of unmovable cars. I stand with the Greeks and West Indians at the bus stop, wrapped in double gloves, double socks, and a scarf under my stocking cap, stamping my feet under a fog of human warmth. We stand like cattle in a blizzard, edging closer than we would in summer, smoke and vapour rising through the wool, each of us dreaming of heat and coffee. The Greeks and West Indians must want to die.

You survive by subtraction. Pick a date: March 15, say. The coldest days bring wind and an arctic sun, much suffering, but one day less. Warmer days, those above zero, inevitably bring snow—and one day less. Some time in January we enter the trough, two weeks of winter torpor when pipes burst and cars give out and the wind cuts viciously through the flat, rattling under the doors and around the windows—your tongue could stick to those icy windows—and water could boil on the ancient radiators. The sky is a pitiless, cloudless blue, and tons of sulphur are pushed into the shrunken air. The day is reached when the city voluntarily closes down. You cancel classes like everyone else, you eat whatever you find in the fridge, your child has a nosebleed every few minutes. It's then you think of your landlord in Florida, of your own days before coming here, when winter was short and bracing, a good time for steady work. Your students hobble to classes on their *après-ski* plaster casts—proud souvenirs of the climate they love. You think of the rings of winter that surround Montreal: caribou foraging north of the mountains, men in the mining camps, timber wolves riding the flatcars into the city, holing up in the cemeteries and living on suburban strays. We are in the dentist's chair for another forty days. Even Erika sleeps late, turns in early, and admits to constant headaches. Christopher suffers his nosebleeds and hasn't been out in twenty days. The mice have left us alone. The Jamaican children come up to play, riding tricycles through our endless flat.

Only the mailman still makes it through. By the time one of us dresses warmly enough to step out to the mail-slots, our

letters have already been fished out of the mutilated slot—
years of theft have left the brass doors buckled—and have been
ripped into tiny pieces and dropped like an offering outside our
door. Letters from Germany, computerized cheques and bills. I
know who does this: the Greek girl across the hall. She will go to
stores for you. She will play with your boy when she finds him
alone. And she will steal his toys and kick the smaller Jamaican girls when she finds them alone. Last summer her father
beat her in the hall, in front of me and the Laflamme kids
who live next door; a slim scar-faced tyrant whose wife stood
behind him, looking at her fingers. Laflamme's kids howled
with pleasure, '*Ooo, Irène va pleurer!*' but she didn't, not for
the moments that I could bear to watch. I wanted to protect
her, for whatever she'd done, that bruised furtive little thing
with the Anne Frank face. That cheat, that thief, that cunning
wretched child.

I buy the traps six at a time and throw the whole thing out,
when successful, in a single grand gesture, wasting a garbage
sack but feeling cleaner. Laflamme's kids pick up all the sacks
on garbage nights, and I've watched them, in their curiosity,
untie the empty ones and dump out the mouse and trap, lift
the spring and kick the mouse aside; thus saving a trap and
garbage sack to take back home.

There are worse things than mice. The lake has taught us
to live with black flies and leeches. Now the mice have lost
their power to offend. Kit is fascinated, leaves peanuts for
them in old jar lids. At night we hear the dragging of the lids,
the busy tapping of tiny claws on the ancient linoleum. One
got trapped with a peanut half-expelled. Their fur bloodless,
eyes unclotted, they seem merely frozen in gesture. I'm almost
afraid to lift that clamp from their neck, for fear if I did they'd
rise to bite me, or slide unconscious up my sleeve.

This evening I was reading in the living room, the large
front double room that looks out over the street. There came a
tapping so low and rhythmic that I absorbed it into my read-

ing. I hadn't wanted to leave the chair. But the tapping persisted and I knew it came from closer than I wanted to admit, from the parlour behind the sliding doors, where we keep the summer tires and suitcases. I could see the leather lid of Erika's suitcase panting from inside, as though it had an embolism. It was her old belted bag from Germany, the one she kept her secrets in, everything portable and priceless from her first twenty years. I could picture the inside of that bag as though I had X-ray vision, the mouse-nests of shredded paper. For a moment I allowed myself to think exactly what it meant about us, about me. I have stained her with the froth of mice, their birth and death, in all my dreams and failures.

I bent to touch the suitcase and a single mouse leaped out, squeezing between the lid and clasp where she'd forgotten to re-cinch the belts. A small black one. Without opening the lid, expecting to hear the chirping of a dozen more inside, I cradled the suitcase like a baby in my arms and carried it down the hall past Erika who was reading in the bedroom. I placed it flat in the dry bathtub. She followed me in, standing at the door.

'Did you kill it?'

'There may be more inside,' I said.

The flat is long and cheap and full of pests. Four usable bedrooms and a dining room, a double living room, kitchen, and two studies. It costs us ninety dollars a month, plus heat. We took it at my insistence, after Erika decided to quit her job and return to school. I wanted to sink into the city, to challenge it like any other immigrant and go straight to its core. We painted everything when we moved, put down rugs and tried to grow plants. At night, by muted lamp, with our leather chairs, white tables, colourful paintings, the front room looks beautiful. But the rest of the flat has defeated us.

I return to the parlour. No squeals from the closet, but I open it anyway, knocking the old shoes with a tube of Christmas wrapping paper, and the black little thing scurries out, under the door to the hall and down the hall past the bathroom, with me in pursuit. 'Mouse in the hall,' Erika calls out in an even voice, still on her knees and lifting papers out of the tub to give them a shake and a repacking. The mouse darts into the dining room, under the radiator where the linoleum has lifted and there must be a hole. I've spoken to Laflamme about it—he refused to act without the landlord's directive, and gave me a box of steel wool instead. 'Stuff it under there,' he said, 'it's mouseproof.' And the landlord stays in Florida until the first of April.

I can hear the mouse under the radiator. I can see the old lids they've dragged underneath.

'No mice,' she announces from the bathroom. 'But *do* something.'

She snaps the locks, tightens the belts. I poke twice with the cardboard tube, but it's too thick to reach all the way.

'If there'd been mice in there I would have left you.'

I'll have to force him out. The pipes are scalding hot.

'There are some things that would kill me,' she says.

We have DDT in the back, an old aerosol can for roaches, and I fetch it. She wouldn't leave, not literally. But she would retreat a little further, which is worse. Some things would kill me, too. There are old droppings on the pantry shelves where we store only hardware. Cold drafts along the wood—there's a hole somewhere, Monsieur Laflamme. *Il y a un trou dans la . . . dans le . . . pantry?* Moving here was going to perfect my French, which remains what it always was: a nicely polished vintage car poking along a new expressway. A danger to myself and others. A tall can of Raid, cold to the touch, might do the trick. I lay down a cover of spray, until my eyes smart and the coughing begins.

'What are you spraying?' she calls.

'Guess.'

'Is that you coughing—or it?'

Best not to speak. Better indeed to kill, with my shoe if necessary. First come the roaches, staggering up the walls and falling back. I hear activity under the coils, I see a shadow slinking along the moulding, around the clumps of steel wool, in the shadow of the drapes and television. A slow shadow I prod once with the cardboard to knock into the open. He can barely walk, his front paws splay, his back legs drag. I douse him again from six inches out till his black coat glistens and he stops for good. His eyes are shining, his motion arrested, and he could kill a city of bugs by walking among them. I spray again, idly, and he doesn't move. I get a garbage sack and spread its top; then, the other tube of wrapping paper and chopstick the mouse into the sack. There is a puddle of Raid beneath him, reflecting light like a lake of gasoline. If I had the man's Florida address, I'd send him this. I will move Erika's bag, then wash.

In the spring of this year, a tragedy. Nikos, a quiet boy of six who often played with the Jamaicans in our building, fell to his death from the second-floor balcony next door. I'd seen him sitting on the rail eating his lunch, and I'd waved. A second later he flashed silently across my vision, a white shirt striking the muddy yard with a whip-sharp crack. I was the only witness. I was afraid to touch him; his body heaved in agonies that seemed adult, one leg kicking in and out. I was screaming on the silent street, 'Ambulance! Police! *Au secours!*' and the street slowly bristled to life. Women who never came out opened their doors and ran toward me, those squat Greek women with their hands flat on their cheeks as they ran, and I was still over the body screaming, 'Did you call for help? Did you call the police?' but they fought to get to the boy. A single word was passed, *Nikos, Nikos,* and wailing began from the steps to the sidewalk as I pushed an older woman back. 'Are you the mama? *Nikos's mama?*' but I didn't think she was and I pushed her till she fell. 'Listen to me. Understand. His neck is broken. He cannot be touched—' But they were like the insane, their faces twisted around their open mouths and accusing eyes. *Oh, God, I had dreamed of loving the Greeks,* and now I wished to annihilate them. One of theirs lay injured and I stood accused—a man, a foreigner, tall and blond—and they attacked. From below my shoulders they leaped to hurl their spittle, to scratch my face, to rip my shirt and trenchcoat. I was consumed with hatred for them all, a desire to use my size and innocence, my strength and good intentions, to trample them, to will them back to Greece and their piggish lives in the dark. They pecked like a flock of avenging sparrows, and one finally broke through to throw herself on the child and roll his body over.

Her scream was the purest cry of agony and sorrow I have ever heard. In the distance, a siren. The women let me go; all they had wanted was to scream. I gained the sidewalk and started walking. I felt a pity for us all that I had never felt before. Next to me stood Irene, the mail thief from across the hall.

'Who was it that fell—Nickie?' she asked.

She kept up with me. I was almost running.

'He was a dumb kid anyway,' she said.

'Try to think better of him now, Irene.'

'He's my cousin. You should see the toys he's got up there. And he's a crybaby.'

'He didn't cry this time, Irene, so cut it out.'

'Those old women—wow, they really gave it to you, eh? I heard them talking and they thought you did it. They thought you're the devil or something—really crazy, eh?'

We were walking up the steps to our building, a father and daughter to anyone passing. 'Irene—who's going to tell his mother?'

'I don't know. My ma is her sister. His pa went back to Greece a long time ago. That was pretty stupid of him playing up on the balcony like that, eh?'

For a moment, in my hatred, I thought she'd done it; shades of *The Bad Seed,* she'd been up there all along taking his toys and making his morning miserable. But no one had left the building. Accidents were still possible, even here. We were standing by the mail-slots. Our letters, as usual, lay shredded on the steps.

'Irene—tell me one thing. Why do you tear up our mail?'

'Who says I do that? It was Nikos did it.'

'Don't lie. I'm not going to hit you. I want to know *why.*'

Her voice was a woman's; her face, Anne Frank's. 'Okay. I'll tell you. But I won't say it again. Nikos said we should do it. I told him about the way you waited for the mail all the time. So he thought that would really get you mad. It was him that did it. See if it happens again.'

'Listen: Nikos was an innocent little kid. You're the one that knows how to hurt. And you know I wouldn't go to your father because of what he'd do to you. You know I disapprove of that even more than stealing.'

'Boy, you sure must think I know a lot,' she said. 'I don't even know what you're talking about.' And with that she extracted a key from her purse and disappeared, singing softly, behind the outer door of her apartment.

Late April rain, the snow is down on the west-facing slopes. Our mail has been left alone. I am learning to appreciate small favours: mail, mouselessness, the stirrings of spring. I enter the apartment carrying two bags of groceries, and walk directly to the kitchen to begin unloading. I'd kicked the door shut, but left the key ring dangling outside. Then I went out again to fetch Kit from downstairs and drive down to McGill to pick up Erika from the library—and I discovered that the keys were gone. Stolen. No car keys, no way now of getting back inside. Even Laflamme was useless since we'd never trusted him with a spare key. I went downstairs and found Kit drawing on cardboard boxes that he and his friends had hauled in from the alley. The basement apartment is the worst I've seen, with a ceiling that drips, broken plaster, linoleum worn through to the mossy boards and children everywhere, holding sandwiches as they play. They have no furniture, only beds and a table to eat from. I ask the mother and the eldest daughter if I can leave him there while I take a bus to find my wife, to get a key.

'Daddy—I want to go with you,' he calls, running to the door and dropping his peanut butter sandwich.

'You can't, dear. It's still cold and you don't have a coat.'

'Get my coat.'

'That is something I cannot do. You'll have to stay. Now let me go.' He's clutching my trenchcoat, suddenly aware that I'm leaving him behind and not just letting him play.

'Kit—let go.'

He gives a jerk just as I try to break free; I feel the seam of my trenchcoat opening up, tearing like a zipper as Kit and his friends giggle. 'Goddammit!' I scream and before I know it I've freed my coat and seized him by the shoulders and begun to shake him violently. 'I told you to let go, I told you twice. Why can't you listen! What do I have to do to make you listen?' His face is inches from mine and white with terror. In his eyes I can read his hope that I'm only playing, and I want to stamp that out too. '*Understand?*' I give him a final shake. Limp in my arms he belches, and part of his sandwich comes heaving out.

I run from the basement, from Kit's screaming, the twin halves of my trenchcoat flapping on my back like the pattern for an immensely fat man's pair of pants. *My keys, my keys.* Car, house, office and cabin. The locker in the basement, the trunks in the locker. The cabin is elaborately locked; I will have to smash a window. The car is locked, rolled up tight. Again a window. The front of my shirt is stained, the Greeks at the bus stop are staring at me.

At this moment, Irene must be in the flat. There is much to steal that we will never miss. Something infinitely small but infinitely complicated has happened to our lives, and I don't know how to present it—in its smallness, in its complication—without breaking down. I who live in dreams have suffered something real, and reality hurts like nothing in this world.

GOING TO INDIA

1.

A MONTH before we left I read a horror story in the papers. A boy had stepped on a raft, the raft had drifted into the river. The river was the Niagara. Screaming, with rescuers not daring to follow, pursued only by an amateur photographer on shore, he was carried over the falls.

It isn't death, I thought, it's watching it arrive, this terrible omniscience that makes it not just death, but an execution. The next day, as they must, they carried the photos. Six panels of a boy waving ashore, the waters eddying, then boiling, around his raft. The boy wore a T-shirt and cut-off khakis. He fell off several feet before the falls. Who would leave a raft, what kind of madman builds a raft in Niagara country? Children in Niagara country must have nightmares of the falls, must feel the earth rumbling beneath them, their pillows turning to water.

I was raised in Florida. Tidal waves frightened me as a child. So did 'Silver Springs', those underground rivers that converge to feed it. Blind white catfish. I could hear them as a child, giant turtles snorting and grinding under my pillow.

My son is three years old, almost four. He will be four in India. Born in Indiana, raised in Montreal—what possible fears could he have? He finds the paper, the six pictures of the boy on a raft. He inspects the pictures and I grieve for him. I am death-driven. I feel compassion, grief, regret, only in the face of death. I was slow, fat and asthmatic, prone to sunburn, hookworms and chronic nosebleeds. My son is lean and handsome, a tennis star of the future, and I've tried to keep things from him.

'What is that boy doing, Daddy?'

'I think he's riding a raft.'

'But how come he's waving like that?'

'He's frightened, I think.'

'Look—he felled off it, Daddy.'

'I know, darling.'

'And there's a water hill there, Daddy. Everything went over the hill.'

'Yes, dear. The boy went over the water hill.'

'And now he knows one thing, doesn't he, Daddy?'

'What does he know?'

'Now he knows what being dead is like.'

2.

A month from now we'll be in India. I've begun to feel it, I've been floating for a week now, afraid to start anything new. Friends say to me, 'You still here?' not just in disappointment, more in amazement. They've already discarded the Old Me. 'Weren't you going to India? What happened—chicken out?' They expect transmutation. 'I *said* June,' I tell them, but they'd heard April. 'I'd be afraid to go,' one friend, an artist, tells me. 'There are some things a man can't take. Some changes are too great.' I tell him I *am* afraid, but that I have to go.

I never cared for India. My only interest in the woman I married was sexual; that she was Indian did not excite me, nor was I frightened. Convent-trained, Brahmanical, well-to-do, Orthodox and Westernized at once, Calcutta-born, speaker of eight languages, she had simply overwhelmed me. We met in graduate school at Indiana. Both of us were in comparative literature, and she was returning to Calcutta to marry a forty-year-old research chemist selected by her father. Will you marry him? I asked. Yes, she said. Will you be happy? Who can say, she said. Probably not. Can you refuse? I asked. It would be bad for my father, she said. Will you marry me? I asked, and she said, 'Yes, of course.'

It was Europe that drove me mad.

Five years ago I threw myself at Europe. For two summers I did things I'll never do again, living without money enough for trolley fare, waking beside new women, wondering where I'd be spending the next night, with whom, how I'd get there, who would take me, and finally not caring. Coming close, those short Swedish nights, those fetid Roman nights, those long Paris nights when the *auberge* closed before I got back and I would walk through the rain dodging the Arabs and queers and drunken soldiers who would take me for an Arab, coming close to saying that life was passionate and palpable and worth the pain and effort and whoever I was and whatever I was destined to be didn't matter. Only living for the moment mattered and even the hunger and the insults and the occasional jab in the kidneys didn't matter. It all reminded me that I was young and alive, a hitchhiker over borders, heedless of languages, speaking just enough of everything to cover my needs, and feeling responsible to no one but myself for any jam I got into.

I would have given anything to stay and I planned my life so that I could come back.

Not once did I think of India. Missionary ladies from Wichita, Kansas, went to India. Retired buyers for Montgomery Ward took around-the-world flights and got heart attacks in Delhi bazaars. I was only interested in Europe.

At graduate school in Indiana I was doing well, a Fulbright was in the works, my languages were improving, and a lifetime in Europe was drawing closer. Then I met the most lushly sexual woman I had ever seen. Reserved and intelligent, she confirmed in all ways my belief that perfection could not be found in anything American.

But even then India failed to interest me. I married Anjali Chatterjee, not a culture, not a subcontinent.

3.

When we married, the Indian community of Indiana disowned her. Indian girls were considered too innocent to meet or marry Western boys although hip Indian boys always married American girls. Anjali was dropped from the Indian Society, and only one Indian, a Christian dietician from Goa, attended our wedding. So the break was clean, my obligations minimal. I had her to myself.

Her parents were hesitant, but cordial. Also helpless. They had my horoscope cast after the marriage, but never told us the result. They asked about my family, and we lied. To say the least, I come from uncertain stock. My parents had been twice divorced before divorcing each other. Four of the five languages I speak are rooted in my family, each grandparent speaking something different, and the fifth, Russian, reflects a secret sympathy that would destroy her parents if they knew. I have scores of half brothers and sisters, cousins-in-law, aunts and uncles known by the cars they drive, or by the rackets they operate. My family is broad and fluid and, though corrupt, fabulously unsuccessful. Like gypsies they cover the continent, elevating a son or two into law (a sensible precaution), some into the civil service, others into the army and only one into the university. My instructions for this trip are simple: do not mention divorce. My parents are retired, somewhat infirm, and comfortably off. After a while we can let one die (when we need the sympathy), and a few months later the second can die of grief. They will leave their fortune to charity.

4.

E. M. Forster, you ruined everything. Why must every visitor to India, every well-read tourist, expect a sudden transformation? I, too, feel that if nothing amazing happens, the trip will be a waste. I've done nothing these past two months. I'm afraid to start anything new in case I'll be a different person when I return. And what if this lassitude continues? Two fallow months before the flight, three months of visiting, then what? What the hell is India like anyway?

I remember my Florida childhood and the trips to Nassau and Havana, the bugs and heat and the quiver of joy in a simple cold Coca-Cola, and the pastel, rusted, rotting concrete, the stench of purple muck too rank to grow a thing, too well to ever be charmed by the posters of palms and white sand beaches. 253 Jellyfish, sting rays, sand sharks and tidal waves. Roaches as long as my finger, scorpions in my shoe, worms in my feet. Still, it wasn't India. Country of my wife, heredity of my son.

Will *his* children speak of their lone white grandfather as they settle back to brownness, or will it be their legendary Hindu grandmother, as staggering to them as Pushkin's grandfather must have been to him? Appalling, that I, a comparatist who needs five languages, should be mute and illiterate in my wife's own tongue! And worse, not to care, not for Bengali or Hindi or even Sanskrit.

I thought you were going to India—
I am, I am.
But—
Next week. Next week.
And don't forget those pills, man. Take those little pills.

5.

We are going by charter, which still sets us back two thousand dollars. Two thousand dollars just on kerosene! Another two thousand for a three-month stay; hundreds more in preparation, in drip-dry shirts, in bras and lipsticks for the flocks of cousins; bottles of aftershave and Samsonite briefcases for their husbands. A complete set of the novels of William Faulkner for a cousin writing her dissertation. Oh, weird, weird, what kind of country am I visiting? To prepare myself I read. *Nothing could prepare me for Calcutta,* writes a well-travelled Indian on his return. City of squalor, city of dreadful night, of riots and stabbings, bombings added to pestilence and corruption. Somewhere in Calcutta, squatting or dying, two aged grandmothers are waiting to see my wife, to meet her *mlechha* husband, to peer and poke at her outcaste child. In Calcutta I can meet my death quite by accident, swept into a corridor of history for which I have no feeling. I can believe that for being white and American and somewhat pudgy I deserve to die—somewhere, at least—but not in Calcutta. Receptacle of the world's grief, Calcutta. *Indians, even the richest, are corrupted by poverty;* Americans, even the poorest (I add), are corrupted by wealth. How will I react to beggars? To servants? Worse: how will my wife?

6.

I know from experience that when Anjali dabs the red *teep* on her forehead, when the gold earrings are brought out, when the miniskirts are put away and the gold necklace and bracelets are fastened to her neck and arms (how beautiful, how inevitable, gold against Indian skin), when the good silk saris with the golden threads are unfolded from the suitcases, that I have lost my wife to India. Usually it's just for an evening, in the homes of McGill colleagues in hydraulics or genetics, or visitors to our home from Calcutta, who stay with us for a night or two. And I fade away those evenings, along with English and other familiar references. Nothing to tell me that the beautiful woman in the pink sari is my wife except the odd wink during the evening, a gratuitous reference to my few accomplishments. The familiar mixture of shame and gratitude; that she was born and nurtured for someone better than I, richer, at least, who would wrap her in servants, a house of her own, a life of privilege that only an impoverished country can provide. One evening I can take. But three months?

7.

Our plane will leave from New York. We go down two days early to visit our friends, the Gangulis. To spend some money, buy the last-minute gifts, another suitcase, enjoy the air-conditioning, and eat our last rare steaks. I've just turned twenty-seven; at that age, one can say of one's friends that none are accidental, they all fulfill a need. In New York three circles of friends almost coincide; the writers I know, the friends I've taught with or gone to various schools with, and the third, the special ones, the Indo-Americans, the American girls and their Indian husbands.

Deepak is an architect; Susan was a nurse. Deepak, years before in India, was matched to marry my wife. She was still in Calcutta, he was at Yale, and he approved of her picture sent by his father. One formality remained—the matching of their horoscopes. And they clashed. Marriage would invite disaster, deformed children most likely. He didn't meet her until his next trip to India when he'd gone to look over some new selections. Alas, none were beautiful enough and he returned to New York to marry the American girl he'd been living with all along.

Deepak's life is ruled by his profound good taste, his perfect, daring taste. Like a prodigy in chess or music he is disciplined by a Platonic conception of a yet-higher order, one that he alone can bring into existence. Their apartment in the East Seventies was once used as a movie set. It is subtly Indian, yet nothing specifically Indian strikes the eye. One must sit a moment, sipping a gin, before the underlying Eastern-ness erupts from the steel and glass and leather. The rug is Kashmiri, the tables teak, the walls are hung with Saurashtrian tapestries—what's so Western about it? The lamps are stone-based, chromium-necked, arching halfway across the room, the chairs are stainless steel and white leather, adorned with Indian pillows. It is a room in perfect balance, like Deepak; like his marriage, perhaps. So unlike ours, so unlike us. Our apartment in Montreal is furnished in Universal Academic, with Danish sofas and farm antiques, everything sacrificed to hold more books. The Who's-Afraid-of-Virginia-Woolf style.

But he didn't marry Anjali. I did. He married Susan, and Susan, though uncomplaining and competent, is also plain and somewhat stupid. Very pale, a near-natural blond, but prone to varicosed chubbiness. An Indian's dream of the American girl. And so lacking in Deepak's exquisite taste that I can walk into their place and in thirty seconds *feel* where she had been sitting, where she'd walked from, everything she'd rearranged or brushed against. Where she's messed up the Platonic harmony even while keeping it clean. Still, Deepak doesn't mind. He cooks the fancy meals, does the gourmet shopping: knows where to find mangoes in the dead of winter, where the firmest cauliflower, the freshest *al dente* shrimp, the rarest spices, are sold. When Deepak shops he returns with twenty small packages individually wrapped and nothing frozen. When Susan returns it's with an A&P bag, wet at the bottom.

When the four of us are dining out, the spectators (for we are always on view) try to rearrange us: Deepak and Anjali, Susan and me. Deepak is tall for a Bengali—six-two perhaps—and impressively bearded now that it's the style. He could be an actor. A friend once described him as the perfect extra for a Monte Carlo scene, the Indian prince throwing away his millions, missing only a turban with a jewel in the centre.

How could he and Anjali have a deformed child?

I'm being unfair. He is rich and generous, and there is
another Deepak behind the man of perfect taste. He told me
once, when our wives were out shopping, that he'd tried to
commit suicide, back in India. The Central Bank had refused
him foreign exchange, even after he'd been accepted at Yale.
He'd had to wait a year while an uncle arranged the necessary
bribes, spending the time working on the uncle's tea estate in
Assam. The uncle tried to keep him on a second year, claiming he had to wait until a certain bureaucrat retired; Deepak
threw himself into a river. A villager lost his life in saving him,
the uncle relented, a larger bribe was successful and Deepak
the architect was sprung on the West. He despises India, even
while sending fifty dollars a month to the family of his rescuer.

But his natural gift, so resonant in itself, extends exactly
nowhere. He rarely reads, and when he does he confines himself to English murder mysteries. He is a man trapped in certain talents, incapable of growth, yet I envy him. They eat well,
live well, and save thousands every year. They have no children, despite Susan's pleading, and they will have none until
the child's full tuition from kindergarten through university
is in the bank. While we empty our savings to make this trip
to India. We'll hunt through bazaars and come up with nothing for our house. There is malevolence in our friendship; he
enjoys showing me his New York, making the city bend to his
wishes, extracting from it its most delicate juices. We discuss
India this last night in America; aside from the trips to land a
wife, he's never been back. And he won't go back, despite more
pleading from Susan, until his parents die.

8.

None of Deepak's restaurants tonight: it is steak, broiled at
home. Thick steaks, bought and cut and aged especially, but
revered mainly for wet red beefiness. 'Your meat *chagla*,' he
calls out from the kitchen, spearing it on his fork and holding

it in the doorway, while Anjali, Susan and I drink our gin and our son sips his Coke. A *chagla* is a side of beef. 'Normally I use an onion, mushroom and wine sauce, but don't worry—not tonight. Onions you will be having—bloody American steak you won't.'

The time is near; two hours to lift-off. Then Deepak drives us to the airport because he says he enjoys the International Lounge, especially the Air-India lounge where any time, any season, he can find a friend or two whose names he's forgotten, either going back or seeing off, and he, Deepak, can have a drink and reflect on his own good fortune, namely not having to fly twenty-four hours in a plane full of squalling infants, to arrive in Bombay at four in the morning.

And so now we are sitting upstairs sipping more gin with Susan and Deepak, and of course two young men run over to shake his hand and to be introduced, leaving their wives, who are chatting and who don't look up....

'Summer ritual,' he explains. 'Packing the wife and kids off to India. That way they can get a vacation and the parents are satisfied and the wives can boss the servants around. No wonder they're smiling. . . .' Looking around the waiting room he squints with disgust. 'You'll have a full plane.'

No Americans tonight, the lounge is dark with Indians. We're still in New York, but we've already left. 'At least be glad of one thing,' Deepak says. 'What's that?' I ask. He looks around the lounge and winks at us. 'No cows,' he says.

No, please, I want to say, don't laugh at India. This trip is serious, for me at least. 'Don't ruin it for me, Deepak,' I finally say. 'I may never go over again.' 'You might never come back either,' he says. We are filing out of the lounge, down a corridor, and up a flight of stairs. Anjali and Deepak are in good spirits. Susan is holding our son, who wants another Coke.

'. . . and the beggars,' Deepak is saying. '*Memsahib,* take my fans, my toys, my flowers, my youngest daughter—'

'—then suddenly a leprous stump, stuck in the middle of the flowers and fans,' says Anjali.

'Maybe that's India,' I say, 'in an image, I mean.'

Deepak and Anjali both smile, as if to say, *yes, perhaps it is. Then again, perhaps it isn't. Maybe you should keep your eyes open and your mouth shut.* And then we are saying goodbye, *namaste*-ing to the hostess, and taking our three adjoining seats. India is still a day away.

9.

'Listen for the captain's name,' says Anjali. Need I ask why? Anjali's erstwhile intendeds staff the banks, the hospitals, the courts, the airlines, the tea estates of Assam and West Bengal. They are all well-placed, middle-aged, fair-complected, and well-educated Brahmins.

'D'Souza,' we hear. An Anglo-Indian, not a chance.

'I heard that Captain Mukherjee is flying for Air-India now,' she tells me. 'He was very dashing at Darjeeling in '58, flying for the air force.' Another ruptured arrangement.

There are times when I look at her and think: She, who had no men before me will have many, and I, who had those girls here and there and everywhere even up to the day I married but none after, will have no more, ever. All of this is somehow ordained, our orbits are conflicting, hers ever wider, mine ever tighter.

This will be a short night, the shortest night of my life. Leaving New York at nine o'clock, to arrive six hours later in London's bright morning light, the sunrise will catch us east of Newfoundland around midnight New York time. During the brief, east-running night two businessmen behind me debate the coming British elections. Both, as Indians, feel sentimental toward Labour. As businessmen, they feel compromised. They've never been treated badly. Both, in fact, agree that too many bloody Muslims have been admitted, and that parts of England are stinking worse than the slums of Karachi or Bombay. Both will be voting Tory.

In the absurd morning light of 3 a.m. while the plane sleeps and the four surly sari-clad hostesses smoke their cigarettes in the rear, I think of my writing. Flights are a time of summary, an occasion for sweating palms. If I should die, what would I make of my life? Was it whole, or just beginning? I used to write miniature novels, vividly imagined, set anywhere my imagination moved me. Then something slipped. I started writing only of myself and these vivid moments in a confusing flux. That visionary gleam: India may restore it, or destroy it completely. We will set down an hour in London, in Paris, in Frankfurt and even Kuwait—what does this do to the old perspectives? Europe is just a stop-over, Cokes in a transit room on the way to something bigger and darker than I'd ever imagined. Paris, where I survived two months without a job; Frankfurt where six years ago I learned my first German—*wo kann man hier pissen?* How will I ever return to Europe and feel that I've even left home? India has already ruined Europe for me.

10.

From London we have a new crew and a new captain: His name is Mukherjee. Anjali scribbles a note to a steward who carries it forward. Minutes later he returns, inviting Anjali to follow him through the tiny door and down the gangway to the cockpit. Jealous Indians stare at her, then at me. And I, a jealous American, try to picture our dashing little captain, moustached and heavy-lidded, courting my wife when he should be attending to other things.

She stays up front until we land in Paris. My son and I file into the transit room of Orly, and there in a corner I spot

Anjali and the captain, a small, dark, sleepy-looking fellow with chevroned sleeves a mite too long for his delicate hands.

'Hello, sir,' he says, not reaching for my hand. He holds a Coke in one, a cigarette in the other. 'Your wife's note was a very pleasant distraction.'

'Nice landing,' I say, not knowing the etiquette.

'Considering I couldn't find the bloody runway, I thought it was. They switched numbers on us.'

'So,' I say. 'You're the fam—'

'No, no—I was just telling your wife: you think that I am Captain *Govind* Mukherjee formerly Group Captain Mukherjee of the IAF. But I am Sujit Mukherjee—regrettably a distant cousin—or else I would have met this charming lady years ago. I was just telling your wife that Govind is married now with three children and he flies out of Calcutta to Tokyo. I *knew* she was not referring to me in the chit she sent forward and I confess to a small deception, sir—I hope I am forgiven—'

'Of course, of course. It must have been exciting for her—'

'Oh, exciting I do not know. But disappointing, *yes*, decidedly. You should have seen the face she pulled spotting Sujit Mukherjee and not Govind—' Then suddenly he breaks into loud, heavy-lidded laughter, joined by Anjali and a grey-haired crew member standing to one side.

'This is my navigator, Mr Misra,' says the captain. 'Blame him if we go astray.'

'And this is our son, Ananda,' I say.

'*Very* nice name, Ananda. Ananda means happiness.'

'Are you the driver?' Ananda asks.

'Yes, yes, I am the *driver*,' the captain bursts into laughter, 'and Misra here is my wiper,' and Misra breaks into high-pitched giggles. 'Tell me, Ananda, would you like to sit with us up front and help drive the plane?'

'Would I have to go through that little door?'

261

'Yes,'

'No,' he says decisively. He holds my hand tightly, the captain and navigator bow and depart, and then we go for a Coke.

Somewhere out there, I remind myself, is Paris.

11.

Back in the plane the purser invites me forward; Captain Mukherjee points to the seat behind him, the rest of the crew introduce themselves, a steward brings me lemonade, and the plane is cleared for leaving the terminal. Then an Indian woman clutching a baby bursts from the building, dashes across the runway waving frantically.

'Air-India 112—you have a passenger—'

'Stupid bloody woman,' the captain says under his breath. 'Air-India 112 returning for boarding,' he says, then turns to me: 'Can you imagine when we're flying the jumbo? Indians weren't meant for the jumbo jets.'

Then the steward comes forward, explaining that the woman doesn't speak Hindi, English or Tamil and that she doesn't have a ticket and refuses to take a seat. The only word they can understand is 'husband'. The captain nods, heavy-lidded, smiling faintly. 'I think I should like a glass of cold water,' he says, 'and one for our passenger.' He takes off his headphone, lights a cigarette. Turning fully around he says to me: 'We have dietary problems. We have religious problems and we have linguistic problems. All of these things we prepare for. But these village women, they marry and their husband goes off to Europe and a few years later he sends for them. But they can't read their tickets and they won't eat what we give them and they sit strapped in their seats, terrified, for the whole trip. Then they fall asleep and we can't wake them. When they wake up themselves they think they're on a tram and they've missed their stop, so they tell us to turn around. London, Paris, Rome—these are just words to them. The husband says he will meet her in Paris—how is she to know she must go through customs? She can't even read her own language let alone *douane*. So she goes to the transit room and sits down and the husband she's probably forgotten except for one old photograph is tapping madly on the glass and when the flight reboards she dutifully follows all the people—'

'Captain, someone is talking to her.'

'Fine, fine.'

'She is to meet her husband in Paris.'

'Did you tell her this is Paris?'

'She won't believe *me*, Captain. She wants you to tell her.'

'Misra—take my coat and go back and tell her.' To me he adds, 'She wouldn't believe I'm the captain. Misra makes a very good captain with his grey hair. Where is my bloody ice water?'

'Yes, Captain. Right away, Captain.'

Moments later we are taxiing down the runway, gathering speed and lifting steeply over Paris. The Seine, Eiffel Tower, Notre Dame, all clear from the wraparound windows. And, for the first time, my palms aren't sweating. Competence in the cockpit, the delicate fingers of Captain Mukherjee, the mathematical genius of Navigator Misra, the radar below, the gauges above. I settle back and relax. Below, the radar stations check in: Metz, Luxembourg, Rüdesheim, Mainz. I recognize the Rhine, see the towns I once hitchhiked through, and bask in the strangeness of it all, the orbits of India and my early manhood intersecting.

We descend, we slow, and Frankfurt appears. We turn, we drop still lower, slower, two hundred miles per hour as we touch down. Everything perfect, my palms are dry again. It's been years since I felt such confidence in another person. The silence in the cockpit is almost worshipful.

The ground-crew chief, a grey-bearded Sikh, comes aboard and gives the captain his instructions for take-off, which the captain already knows. The weather conditions in Kuwait: 120° with sandstorms. Mukherjee nods, smiles. I ease out silently; *namaste*-ing to the captain and crew, thanking them all as they go about their chores.

12.

Within an hour we are farther East than I've ever been. Down the coast of Yugoslavia, then over the Greek islands, across the Holy Land. What if the Israelis open fire? Those SAM missile sites, Iraqi MIGs scrambling to bring us down. Trials in Baghdad, hanging of the Jewish passengers. India is officially pro-Arab, an embarrassment which might prove useful.

This was the shortest day of my life. The east is darkening, though it's only noon by New York time. An hour later the stars are out; we eat our second lunch, or is it dinner? Wiener schnitzel or lamb curry. Ananda sleeps; Anjali eats her curry, I my Wiener schnitzel.

'After Kuwait things will deteriorate,' she says. 'The food, the service, the girls—they always do.'

We've been descending and suddenly the seat-belt sign is on. Kuwait: richest country in the world. City lights in the middle of the desert, and an airfield marked by permanent fires. Corridors of flames flapping in a sandstorm and Captain Mukherjee eases his way between them. Sand stings the window, pings off the wings like Montreal ice.

'*The ground temperature is forty-five degrees centigrade*' the hostess announces, and I busily translate: 113° F.

'*The local time is 10:00 p.m.*'

I whisper to Anjali, '"I will show you fear in a handful of dust . . ."'

'*Through passengers ticketed on Air-India to Bombay and New Delhi will kindly remain in the aircraft. We shall be on the ground for approximately forty-five minutes.*'

I can feel the heat through the plastic windows. Such heat, such inhuman heat and dryness. I turn to Anjali and quote again:

'Here is no water but only rock
Rock and no water and the sandy road ...'

A ground crew comes aboard. Arab faces, one-eyed, hunched, followed by a proud lieutenant in the Kuwaiti uniform. These are my first Muslims, first Arabs. They vacuum around our feet, pick up the chocolate wrappers, clear the tattered London papers from the seats. It's all too fast, this 'voyage out', as they used to call it. We need a month on a steamer, shopping in Italy, in Cairo, bargaining in the bazaars, passing serenely from the Catholic south to the Muslim heartland, thence to holy, Hindu India. The way they did it in the old novels. In Forster, where friendship and tolerance were still possible. No impressions of the Waste Land in a Forster novel. No one-eyed, menacing Arabs. But Forster is almost ninety, and wisely, he remains silent. The price we pay for the convenience of a single day's flight is the simple diminishment of all that's human. Just as Europe is changed because of India, so India is lessened because of the charter flight. I'm bringing a hard heart to India, dread and fear and suspicion.

13.

We are in the final hours over the Persian Gulf and the Arabian Sea, skimming the coast of Iran then aiming south and east to Bombay. Kuwait gave us children who play games in the aisles, who spill their Cokes on my sleeve. Captain Mukherjee, Misra and the crack London crew ride with us as passengers; the new stewardess is older, heavier, and a recent blonde. No one sleeps, though we've set our watches on Bombay time and it is suddenly three o'clock in the morning.

'Daddy will be leaving for the airport now,' says Anjali.

I've never met her parents. They've flown 1,500 miles to meet us tonight, to see us rest a day or two before joining us on the flight back to Calcutta.

'The airport will be a shock,' she says. 'It always is.'

'Anything to get off this plane.'

Three-thirty.

Ananda has taken the window seat; he sits on his knees with his face cupped to the glass. He's been to India before, three summers before. He's forgotten his illness, remembers only an elephant ride and a trip to the mountains where he chased butterflies up the slopes.

Twenty minutes to India. I can feel the descent. Business-men behind me agree on the merits of military rule.

'*Ladies and gentlemen—*'

The lights go on, a hundred seat belts buckle on cue. Lights suddenly appear beneath us. There are streets, street lamps, cars, bungalows, palm trees. My first palms since Florida—maybe I'll like it here—and we glide to a landing, our fifth perfect landing of the day.

Everyone is standing, pulling down their coats and bag-gage. I'd forgotten how much we carried aboard (three days ago, by the calendar): a flight bag of clothes for Ananda, cam-era equipment, liquor and cigars for my father-in-law, my rain hat and jacket, our three raincoats and two umbrellas. We put on everything we can and then line up, facing first the rear and then the front, clutching our passports.

'*Ladies and gentlemen, we have landed at Santa Cruz Air-port in Bombay. The local time is 4:00 a.m. and the temperature is 33° centigrade...*'

'Over ninety,' I whisper.

'It's been raining,' she says.

As we file to the front and the open door, I can feel the heat. My arms are sweating before I reach the ladder. An open bus is waiting to take us to the terminal. No breeze, SRO. The duty-free bag begins to tear.

I follow our beam of light across the tarmac. A man is sleep-ing on the edge of the cement, others have built a fire in the mud nearby.

'Tea,' Anjali explains.

Other thoughts are coming to me now: not the howling sand of Kuwait—*mud*. Not the empty desert—*people*. Not the wind—*rain*. I want to scream: *'It's four in the bloody morning and I'm soaking with sweat. Somebody do something!'* Even in the open bus as we zip down the runway there's no breeze, no relief. Anjali's hair, cut and set just before we left, has turned dead and stringy, her sari is crushed in a thousand folds. This is how the world will end.

We are dropped in front of the terminal. Families are sleeping on the steps. Children converge on our bus, holding out their hands, making pathetic gestures to their mouth. I have a pocket full of *centimes* and *pfennigs* from this morning's stops, but Anjali frowns as I open my hand. 'They're professionals,' she says. 'If you must give to beggars wait at least till you get to Calcutta.' They pull my sleeve, grab Ananda by the collar of his raincoat, until a man behind us raises his hand. 'Wretched little scum,' he mutters. They scatter and I find myself half-agreeing.

We have come inside. Harsh lights, overhead fans. Rows of barriers, men in khaki uniforms behind each desk, desks laden with forms and rubber stamps. The bureaucracy. Behind them the baggage, the porters squatting, the customs, more men, more forms. Then the glass, the waiting crowd, the parents, the embraces, the right words, the corridors. *I'm not ready,* I want to scream, *turn this plane around.* I've stopped walking, the passports are heavy in my hand, I've never been so lost.

'Darling, what's the matter?' she asks, but she has already taken my hand, taken the passports, the declarations, and given me the flight bag in their place. Ananda stands before me, the beautiful child in his yellow slicker, black hair plastered to his forehead. I take his hand, he takes Anjali's, and I think again: *I'm not prepared,* not even for the answer which comes immediately: and if you're not, it says, who is?

TRANSLATION

1.

A<small>T FORTY-THREE</small>, Porter, *né* Carrier, feared he was sick again. The warning came at night with a vision and an odour just as it always had. Debbie suspected nothing. She was mincing tuna for a week's supply of sandwiches. He loved the sound of a long silver spoon knocking the sides of an empty mayonnaise jar.

He said, 'For the first time in my life, I really know that I'm going to die. It's a profound awareness.'

She didn't look up. 'Am I disagreeing?' She'd been spending most weekends with him for the past two years. She would soon be thirty.

'It's the way you're looking in that bowl.'

'Philip, how do you *want* me to look into a bowl of tuna fish? Let me translate what you're saying. You're saying that you read in a paper today that someone who meant the world to you when you were fourteen years old just died.' She looked up, smiling wickedly for confirmation. 'You're the proverbial ear in the forest, don't you know? The one that actually hears every tree that falls? It's okay, Porter, it's okay to die.'

'You'll find more mayonnaise in the pantry.'

'If every man's death diminished me the way it does you—
God, I'd disappear!' She licked mayonnaise off her knuckles.
'But you don't actually diminish, do you? You're no anorexic.
I'm sure you grieve in your way, but it keeps you going.'

Much as Porter loved her most days, he knew the relationship was ending. Not because of her reaction, which was
appropriate. It was ending because of the vision.

Dying had been a spectacle, something older people did
for his pity or instruction. Death had been mowing down the
radio greats of his childhood and the holdover politicians of
the New Deal, then the actors his parents had thrilled to and
the boys of his happiest summers when he'd been a child and
they'd been in their prime. And now there was no gap left.
He'd sung their songs, thrilled to their debuts, made love to
them in his dreams. He'd been standing at the end of a long
queue, bored by how slowly it moved, but now the soft shuffle
of the quotidian had taken him to the ticket stand and the
open doors of a darkened theatre.

'People I've loved are dying,' he said.

'Porter, dear, you have many lovable traits. But please don't
tell me you know what it is to love.' She smeared two Ry-Krisps
with tuna salad. 'Not that it matters.'

He'd heard it often enough. Until Amy, his first wife, left,
Porter had thought himself a deprived, embittered man
capable of great tenderness. She taught him he was a sophisticated lover from a privileged background, lacking none of the
graces except a core of essential decency.

2.

His childhood dream had been of a glacier, or at least of something cold, mountainous and inexorable bearing down on him.
He could hear and even see through its gelatinous distortions
the grinding of boulders and forests, and he could smell the
scorched, catastrophic swath of natural pavement in its path.

He would wake, often screaming. It moved a foot a year, and he couldn't outrun it. He always woke when the ice touched him with its scalding cold. When flesh met glacier they were fused, like a tongue to an ice tray.

His mother would be holding him and by then extracting the wooden spoon she kept at his bedside. He would bury his aching head in her breast, and she would hold him, swaying.

'The glacier again?' and he would nod. 'See, there's nothing out there.' He wouldn't open his eyes. After those attacks colours were too bright to bear, and the odours of the world all bordered on rottenness. It was as though life were offering a putrefied version of itself for his eyes and nose only.

Those were the attacks at night in sleep. In the day his nose would fill with a sweet, burnt odour, and colours would turn red like ageing film and kids would say, 'Hey, Porter, I'm talking to you!' Sometimes he'd find himself on the floor or on the ground, his muscles numb from supreme exhaustion.

But all of that ended thirty years before.

Why now should life suddenly turn perilous? He went to his doctor for the first time in three years. Since his last visit he'd cut down his drinking to a few beers a week, had gum surgery and three crowns put in and lost thirty pounds. He jogged twenty miles a week and in the winter lifted weights and swayed to calisthenics. The doctor declared him 100 per cent fit, a model of 1980s self-reclamation. America was seeing a generation of potential centagenarians.

'By the way,' he asked, 'what are you guys pushing for epilepsy?'

'Doing another story, Porter?' Porter had not been totally honest with his doctor. He'd never been honest with anyone. When he was forced into magazine writing between novels, he found the doctor an enthusiastic collaborator. He'd helped him with 'Mid-Life to Mod-Life', 'Toward a More Perfect Carcinogen', and his steroids piece, 'Higher, Faster, Stronger . . . Dumber?'

'I'd heard that epileptic medicine can slow you right down to idiocy. If they'd treated Dostoevsky—no *Crime and Punishment.*'

'No way,' said the doctor. 'Any new medicine comes on stronger at the beginning than it needs to be—look at the first birth-control pills, the Salk vaccine, the tranquillizers. The first generation anti-convulsants might have turned him into a zombie for a few weeks, but we'd have had him driving a car inside a month.'

'That's very reassuring. And now?'

'Designer doses, Porter. Tegratol, Dilantin, some phenobarb at night. We'd have nailed it. What are you writing?'

'I was thinking of giving a character a very heavy curse.'

'Diabetes is good,' the doctor mused. 'Mainstream, too, with lots of paraphernalia. Or what about Huntington's chorea? That can *really* ruin your day.' Porter's doctor conferred imaginary disorders with greater enthusiasm than ever went into their healing.

'Let me get back to you,' he said.

3.

One day Debbie was making tuna salad and inviting him to parties, and a few weeks later she was busy in Manhattan with her children. A month after that she announced she wanted to go to Europe for spring break, alone.

He wasn't even disappointed. In marriage most men are tempted early and often by other women. Porter loved women, but his great temptation was solitude. Amy had called him a libertine monk. Debbie left him in February. Snow was deep; he doubled his calisthenics and bench-presses and set August as the date for the delivery of his novel. After five earlier books of stories and two novels with child and adolescent characters, this was to be his wet-winged emergence into the adult world of marriage and poisonous self-knowledge. He was not unhappy, in his bitter, private way, that no one would be interfering with his ridiculous little schedules.

He lived in a cottage in Duchess County. Amy had kept their old house in Binghamton, their kids were on scholarship, and with a pasta diet, a garden and few vices, he could just about live on his writing. The nearest town was Poughkeepsie, where Debbie taught. He went into New York when he had good reasons.

According to many who knew him, Porter wasn't altogether sane. He'd been a professor, then had changed jobs, surrendered tenure, taken pay cuts and finally come to the conclusion—logical under the circumstances—that the remaining obligations were too strenuous, underpaid and insecure to keep at all. He taught for a while as an adjunct in metropolitan campuses with 'at' in their titles. The self-destruction had cost him a marriage.

During the February thaw, the dripping icicles and the hiss of wet tires on the exposed blacktop outside the cottage lured him into three days of bonus running. He valued the accretion of small details and the web of images that clung to him as he ran. He loved the things of this world, passionately. He loved activities like running that stimulated a disinterested scrutiny. Running was like writing a short story, a familiar habit begun in pain but ending breathless and exultant. Weight-lifting, so dramatically exerting, so ambitious, was like writing novels.

As he ran that first day looking at the early buds on the trees and hedgetips, he realized he couldn't name a single tree in English. He'd probably never known them in French—there hadn't been many trees in his life as a Carrier. They all existed in some abstraction of treeness. He was a writer, after all, and to name was to know. All he knew for certain was childhood in Pittsburgh and adolescence in Montreal, plus some articles aided by a doctor's vocabulary.

He smelled it again, a putrescence in the world, as though a winter's worth of carcasses had been shovelled to the roadside.

He took three days off for a trip to the city, uncharacteristically, to check out the movies and bookstores. When he got back to his typewriter, the novel was cold.

4.

Thirty years before when he'd been X-rayed at Pittsburgh General, the neurologist had termed his epilepsy 'trauma-induced', meaning that a childhood injury—a skull fracture at the age of three—was the probable cause. And with adolescence the skull might achieve adult contour, and he could be free of seizures for the rest of his life.

It had returned a day or two after the thaw. He'd been writing in bed—still his position for serious work—when he'd noticed a puddle of coffee on his sheets and the mug overturned in the blanket. The coffee was almost cold.

He'd known many people like himself—arrested cancer victims, one-time cardiac patient, recovered alcoholics—who'd mastered the etiquette of daily gratitude. They never planned, they never deferred. Gratitude had never been Porter's style, but he heard himself praying over the coffee stains, *Please, God, don't let it come back. Let me finish this one last book, that's all I ask.*

In response, God pinged him lightly a second time. Like mice and returned cheques, seizures came in clusters.

The medicine he'd taken all his childhood had made him slow. It hadn't been until his rebirth as Philippe Carrier in Montreal that the curse had disappeared. His high school had classified epileptics with the insane and retarded. There'd been a girl, Marie Bolduc, nicknamed *la tordue*, who'd been taken around to classes strapped in her wheelchair where she sometimes slumped and stiffened ten times an hour. Her neck was one enormous muscle. The sisters never caned her, despite her blatant disruptiveness and frequent inattention, though they were not above using her as an example of God's wrath, or His mercy.

She'd been the first death in his life, the first of his generation to go under. Laid out to her full length in the open casket, neck cushioned against the satin, she'd been a tall, pretty girl. Some of his classmates had snickered, half-expecting the coffin to give a sympathetic lurch. He'd snickered louder than any of them.

When he returned to his novel after that seizure and the memory of a distant funeral Mass (having epilepsy, he'd once written of a character, was like writing with a ballpoint pen that occasionally skipped), his arm was numb, his fingers cold and tingling, and he found it immensely hard to catch up with his thoughts. He remembered perfectly the gelatinous, unresponsive, mental fatigue of epilepsy. He remembered feeling like a human glacier, an obstruction, slow and brutish. In the depths of his brain he could smell fresh ironing, and he caught a glimpse of a woman in a bathrobe who disappeared before he could recognize her.

When he next looked at his novel, it was dead. He didn't recognize the writing, he couldn't even imitate it. He turned a page and wrote three sentences that had nothing to do with anything he'd ever written:

The sons of suicides bear a graceless burden. She let go of my hand as the bus approached. 'There's something I must do,' she said, and pulled away.

5.

And so it was not to be the novel that made Porter relatively rich and famous; it was *Head Waters*, an autobiography. During his years as a professor he'd often lectured on autobiography, calling it a maligned and poorly described art form that attracted more than its share of hacks. 'The self-biographers,' he'd termed them, those who saw their own lives as miniature histories, who began their books with the fatal words, 'I was born . . .' as though life had not existed before them, and the glory and pain of self-consciousness—the true subject of all autobiography—were not finding the niche where one fit, but clearing a site for the shopping-mall of the self. Porter called autobiography the democracy of bafflement. Every success reinvented the form.

He refused all medication while he wrote. He was forced to spread pillows under his chair. He glued a strip of foam rubber to the metal rim of his typewriter, and he gave up trying to drive.

Because he even feared walking into the village for food (twice he'd fallen, spilling his groceries, and once he'd wakened to see tire tracks across his loaf of bread), he took in a woman. Her name was Petra, a Middle European who assisted in Vassar's Russian program. She was forty and had never married. Sex between them was infrequent and barely satisfying. Porter felt himself diminishing as a man, disappearing into his infirmities and literary graces. He made love like an old man seeking comfort. From one of those early encounters, Petra got pregnant. Porter counselled abortion (half-heartedly; his soul was deeply Catholic), and in their second year Petra and his daughter stayed weekends and came over twice a week.

Hannah was an old-fashioned little girl: wide-eyed, well behaved, Old World. Even as a pre-toddler she sat on the breakfast table while her mother cooked, playing with silverware and paper plates, never dropping them on the floor, never straying over the edge. Her isolation and intensity frightened him. He thought, 'Hanno Buddenbrooks,' and felt she was doomed, a dead end, the last Carrier, the last Simonovska. She had taken her mother's name. He'd resigned his role in this second family. He doubted he'd live much beyond her early schooling.

Petra never intended marriage or motherhood. Yet in some strange and uncharacteristic way, he had *courted* her. She had arrived as a companion, a cook, a driver; he had forced the issue. She mentioned that her previous experiences with men were less frequent than those with women, but her deepest drives were, like his, private, studious, uncommunicative.

He wondered if Hannah would grow up to reflect on the absurdity of her birth, that in a normal world she would never have been. She owed her life to his epilepsy. Would it shock her? Amuse her? She was a child of accident and calculation; she never cried, never whined, took delight in spoons and glasses and started violin and piano lessons before she was three. She stared at the world like an intent Anne Frank, with a face perfectly composed and adult. Even if he was forced to leave her early he could see exactly how she'd look twenty years down the line.

6.

Some time in his forty-fifth year Porter asked his body, 'Okay, what do you want? What are you trying to tell me?'

He'd been studying his face in the bathroom mirror. Of course he'd aged, lost weight, and his hair and whiskers were greying. But it was the cuts, the scabs, the myriad nicks and tiny bruises he suddenly noticed; like a drunk's. The dozens of small stumblings, the sprains and burns and confused looks from everyone but Petra that indicated to him he was having more episodes than he'd even suspected. The ballpoint pen was running out of ink.

An interviewer came over from Boston, and Porter must have blanked out in the middle of a question. When he'd come out of it the interviewer was saying to his sound man, 'We'll go back to where I ask, "Why did you leave Montreal and return to the United States?"' And to Porter he'd said matter-of-factly, 'Would you like a glass of water?'

Porter, still confused, had mumbled, 'Montreal can break your heart.'

But now his body was giving no answers, 'My head's shrinking, is that it?' The skull was closing in ever so slightly. There had to be a message in it. In rational, pain-free moments he caught glimpses of his disease like a shadow leaving the room the second he snapped on a light. He could almost catch it, almost smell it (the smell of ironed clothes turned sour), and once or twice alone in his cottage he heard himself shouting. 'Stop, you!' and his mind tried to lock on the shadow. It was *possession*, wasn't it, just as the ancients and the conjurers had always said—a devil to be cast out. At least that was one alternative.

Once in his teen years in Montreal, an orphan living with whores and working in a strip joint, young Carrier had dragged himself to a free clinic, complaining of fatigue, weight loss, stomach pains, bleeding and worst of all, *a sense of evil*. The nun had taken down the symptoms, pausing a while on *malaise globale*, but otherwise moved by his distress and orphaned state.

'Where do you live?' the doctor had asked.

'Around,' he'd answered, not wishing to compromise the janitors who let him sleep in basements and the girls who gave him food and a bed in their off-hour mornings. Those had been his *célinesque* years in Montreal, when the city had finally made sense to him.

The doctor was listening to his stomach. 'What are you eating?'

'Whatever I can get,' he'd answered. Waitresses would sneak it out. He was only seventeen.

The doctor seemed to be addressing the nun. 'I would say this young man is harbouring a serpent in his bowels.' Then he turned to Carrier. 'A worm, understand, young man? You may well have thirty feet of tapeworm swimming around down there—no wonder you're weak and bleeding. Its head is chewing into your stomach, and by now it's taking four-fifths of everything you eat. And it's *still* not satisfied. So we'll feed it a little something extra.'

Carrier's complaint was not uncommon in the slum clinics of Montreal in the mid-fifties. The doctor had free samples in his drawer, and the effects, he warned, would be dramatic. 'If you are in the habit of gazing fondly at your stool, I would strongly advise against it for the next three weeks,' he said.

Porter, remembering the chunks of the beast as they passed through him, thought again of purgation, and something in his deeply Catholic soul responded. *I've got you, you bastard.* He tapped his temple. *You can run, but you can't hide.* He put away his razor blade—no use taking chances—he'd let his beard grow out, white or not. He looked into his eyes so closely he could almost see the beast behind them.

Hiding, are you?

I'm taking you home, baby.

7.

Porter dreaded the Canadian border. The simplest questions of an immigration officer were the imponderables of his life: What is your name? Where were you born? What is your nationality? If Porter had a demon in his brain, taking it to Montreal was like poking a stick in its cage. He didn't have a passport and couldn't get one. Canada was the world for Porter; America was all there was for Carrier.

Head Waters had been a success in several languages. Philippe Carrier's *Les Sources de mémoire* had been a local best-seller for Éditions d'aujourd'hui. They'd wanted him to go on the talk shows in Montreal, but he'd refused. 'Ah, we understand, M'sieur Carrier,' the publisher had said. 'We're very small, and we can't afford to pay you well.' It wasn't that, but better they thought it was. The simple truth was that he was an illegal alien, just as his father had been, and sooner or later, given publicity, questions would be asked.

Often he'd had to rehearse his border crossings. He'd work on his accent, seeking to match it to his New York plates and licence. In his bus-riding years, he would go up to Montreal as fun-loving Phil Porter, and return to the States as humble Carrier, down to visit a cousin. He was always afraid the officer would ask him first, 'Where were you born?' instead of 'Where do you live?'

Phil Porter, in reality, did not exist. No such person had ever been born. 'Porter' had been his father's fiction, easily dropped when cornered (*coincé*, in fact, was his father's favourite word), but Porter had been trapped in it. Like any threatened faith, it now seemed all the more precious. He held an American social insurance card under one name, and a Canadian social insurance card under another. It was a complicated little drama, but one that suited him. For this trip in the summer of his forty-sixth year he'd flown in as Phil Porter, Expos fan, for a week of baseball.

This isn't my city, he told himself in the airport bus. *It was Carrier's city. It's all an accident.* Let it go. False intimacies can kill. Acknowledged attachments bring only bills and sentimental cards on Father's Day. Bills he willingly paid for the privacy they bought.

The infinite perversity of life—as the nuns would say— was that the sincere involvements undertaken with a dream of permanence, marriage and fatherhood, had deserted him. Only the coldest and most brutal, Petra and Hannah, showed any sign of lasting. And one other. One other chunk of flesh that inhabited his body and possessed his mind *still*. Porter, a man of few attachments, was haunted by unbearable intimacies. Even a French rock station listened to by a Haitian taxi-driver lit cells in Porter that were floodlights in Carrier's cave.

8.

He met Florence Lachance, the publicist for his publisher, in a small Lebanese restaurant in a remodelled area behind the Main. It was a hot day, and she wore a T-shirt and jeans, with the publisher's logo over her modest bosom. Across her back was a picture of his book. It didn't concern him.

'They've loved it,' she said, riffling through a packet of reviews. He was called, in a casual translation, not quite a cultural chameleon, more a ... what? Newt? Mud-puppy? Thanks a lot.

'They're calling you a new Kerouac,' she went on. 'There's a word they use at the university—*porterisme*—for a kind of special Quebec tragedy.'

He read a long review more closely. To its author he was an intermediate cultural life-form, not slimy by intention like Monsieur Trudeau, not a cultural chameleon like the Ottawa mandarins, but a permanent, arrested cultural larva with lungs for land and gills for water.

She watched him frown and reached across to tap his hand. 'Oh! Not *you*, M'sieur Carrier. It's the *situation* you describe. Ten years ago people would have said it's what happens when you're just a colony. They would have called you *vendu*. Now they see we're all like ... those things. I can't say the word.'

'Axolotls,' he said. He thought: I *am* my condition.

She giggled. She looked so chagrined he wanted to hold her. The role of publicist for a Quebec publishing house seemed so cosy and absurd, so *sincere* and guileless, that he felt light-headed with remorse.

Les fils des suicides supportent un fardeau sans grâce.

'Who's this Madeleine Choquette?'

Florence squinted and asked, 'Seriously? Madeleine Choquette?' As though he'd asked, Who's this Wayne Gretzky character?

'She begged us to let her do you. You'll meet her.'

'A writer, then?'

'One of the important writers. She's also very well known in France. People compare your book with hers all the time—maybe you don't like that? Do they ask you that—why you don't come back? Why you don't write in French?'

'All the time,' he said, lying graciously. No one in the States knew or cared that he'd had a double life. Most Americans couldn't really conceive of it, and most of those who did couldn't conceive of its being French-Canadian. They were talking in French, but his French, he wanted to say, wasn't good enough. It had once been a thin, elastic membrane, transparent and stuffed with words. Now it was a loose sack of familiar phrases, a duffel bag to drag along on trips to Montreal. *Fardeau* or *charge*? *Supporter* or *appuyer*? What's wrong with good old *porter,* 'to carry'? Hell would be having to make a conscious choice, like a translator, between dozens of perfectly serviceable likenesses for every phrase of every sentence.

He could tell, looking at her in her blue-tinted glasses, at her confused little frown and her nervous way with a cigarette, that she'd asked another question while he'd ducked under his unspeakable little cloud.

'Can I get you anything?' she whispered.

'Now you know something else about me. Not just an axolotl, but an axolotl with epilepsy.'

A familiar path doubling over. He wondered if he was doomed to enter a violent convulsive stage, as he had when he was eleven and twelve back in Pittsburgh. Would he be driven all the way back to the battering when he was three, was he doomed to repeat it all?

She recovered graciously. 'We have an interview with Corinne Carrier at Radio-Canada. You'll like her, and she knows Madame Choquette. She'll introduce you, M'sieur Carrier.'

Carriers and Smiths, thought Porter. Everything in Quebec was sooner or later connected, everyone eventually related. So much so that the names were interchangeable, like Changs. Only a fool or a foreigner would assume an actual, blood connection.

9.

In the buried years that Carrier had lived in his uncle Théophile's flat, his cousin Dollard, two years older, had been his window on an intolerable future. Dollard had dropped out of school at fourteen and worked at a series of manual jobs, digging and filling, until Théophile's political and church connections had gotten him on the city payroll. He was sent to work as a *fossoyeur* at Côte-des-Neiges Cemetery, the Vatican City of digging and filling. By that time, Carrier and his parents had left Théophile's flat and found a smaller one of their own a few miles west on Snowden. His father sold kitchen equipment in a restaurant-supply house on the Main. His mother had started substitute teaching in the Protestant schools all over the western parts of the island.

And then his father disappeared. Not exactly vanished— he first got in practice by making himself scarce. He would come home to sleep in the middle of the week, but wouldn't show up on weekends. Fishing, he said, or hunting, knowing that his wife didn't approve of either, or the men he did it with. Then he disappeared altogether.

Carrier and his mother moved into two rooms near McGill. She wanted him to transfer to a Protestant English school before his French Catholic allegiance cost him his soul, and her job. 'Before it's too late,' she always put it, but he fought her. He was sixteen; the brothers wanted him to go to Laval.

One day after school young Carrier took a trolley over to the restaurant-supply store. It was a Jewish place, but the men inside spoke every language on the Main. His father spoke a pretty fair Yiddish, perfect Italian and adequate Greek and Portuguese. He could even make Armenians and Lebanese feel at home. Carrier *fils* had won a Latin prize at school, and he wanted to show it to his father. But Mr Samelowitz said Carrier *père* hadn't been working there for months. Something unpleasant, but he wouldn't go into it. For as long back as Carrier could remember, people had spoken of his father in hushed, embarrassed tones. Where he had gone, no one knew, or would tell. That's how it remained.

He tried to remain faithful to both families, as much as Montreal etiquette permitted. They were now living on the English side of town—which Théophile equated with wealth and perfidy—though no one around them spoke a word of English or had a dime to their name. If his father was in touch with them, they never mentioned it. Nevertheless, he had attended Dollard's wedding three years later, in Longueuil. The wife, Paulette, he remembered as another small, squat, beetle-browed addition to a family already overrun with cultural clichés. At the time, she was three months pregnant. And there *had* been a daughter, he recalled, born the following spring, twenty-five years ago. And he remembered her name as Corinne.

Quebec might be twice the size of Texas, but its people were all one family. In a family of five million there are bound to be thousands of Corinne Carriers; hundreds, perhaps, with parents by the name of Dollard and Paulette. Still, it was possible. It was a culture made for coincidence.

*   *   *

One look at Corinne Carrier seemed to confirm an utter lack of common ancestry, for which Porter, ever on the lookout for new love, gave silent thanks. She was the right age for cousinhood—twenty-five—but too tall, too beautiful, with long, greying hair, a rectangular face with large green eyes and a generous mouth. The classic Carrier face was just the opposite: small features pulled chinward like a cod's. He associated her kind of charm with ageing stars of the French cinema—not quite beautiful, but so animated they turned nearby men into unwitting cameras. She wore a thirsty satin blouse and faded jeans with beaded moccasins. She moved and spoke with expensive, inherited grace. Her French was Radio-Canada International, without the pouting, asphyxiating gutturals of Paris. Her show was called *Quelques paroles pour l'après-midi,* or more familiarly, *Corinne t'en parle.* Bright tapestries from Asia or Africa were hung on her dressing-room walls. Interspersed were dozens of framed black-and-white stills taken from movies. *Her* movies. She took him on a tour of her walls.

'We were shooting in Cuba last year,' she explained. 'Those are from a documentary we made on child care in Cuba, Nicaragua and China.'

There she stood with Castro, same height, her arm on his shoulder, looking chic and committed. She was a serious woman—another blow against consanguinity. Quebec had a long history of turning out flirts and strippers and kit teny bundles of winter delight, but something on the scale of Corinne? He'd have to go to Scandinavia to find her equivalent. A Quebec girl going to China? To Cuba! The girls he'd known had been lucky to get to Plattsburgh.

Porter asked if she had children—he was old enough now for avuncular questions—and she tossed off an amused shrug that told him her interests were feminist and political, not personal. 'I'm only twenty-five, *please,* m'sieur!' In his Quebec, the only twenty-five-year-old un-married women he'd known had been whores or nuns. One, in fact, Jeannine Jolicoeur, La Soeur Dure et Mure, had scandalized the eastern townships, stripping down to rosary beads from a nun's starched habit.

She took him into the radio studio, introduced him to Reeshar, her sound man, a Gauloise-addicted, permed, tanned, but still pudgy man Porter's age, then sat him across from her behind a mike. They had a few minutes, but she was already in her interviewing mode, elbows on thighs, slumped forward, cleavage from the satin blouse as daunting as a *Cosmo* cover girl's. There was nothing on American television to touch her.

'I read your book last year as soon as it came out, of course, because of our connection. I thought it utterly remarkable. Frankly, I wasn't ready for those reviews, though! What did you think of them?'

What do I think of being a newt, an axolotl? He asked instead, 'What connection?'

'Oh, don't tell me!—you don't know? I didn't think I had to tell you—'

'Not Dollard's daughter?'

'Of course. I've been hearing about you all my life. My father's brilliant cousin in America! When I started publishing my novels I even thought of sending them to you, but I figured you'd think it presumptuous. What if you hated them? What if you didn't want to hear from anyone up here? After all, you called yourself Porter.'

'How could I think it presumptuous? If I'd known, it might have saved me.' Her *novels*? Her films? Dollard's little girl? 'I mean, I'm terribly out of touch.'

'Who wouldn't be? It doesn't matter, you're out of the woodwork now, and *I'll* introduce you, starting tonight.'

An old word leaped to mind, bringing a smile to his lips; *cousine de fesse gauche*. A kissing cousin. 'So, frog begets princess,' he said. How had any of this happened in just a generation? Mutations without a missing link.

'He wants to see you, by the way. He's alone—my mother's dead.'

'We'll see.'

'Where men still outlive women—that's backward,' she said. 'We've still got a long way to go. As you remind us, m'sieur.' That seemed to be her cue to begin.

'I have just one request,' he said. He tapped the glass, alerting Richard. 'Put this show on a two-minute delay, okay?' Corinne frowned; she was all spontaneity.

'In case my French is rusty,' he explained.

10.

Corinne lived off St. Denis near Carré St-Louis. When he'd last inhabited the area it had been a low, squalid slum, dismal and tubercular. Post-war immigration and the diaspora from the old Jewish ghetto had made the area an attractive no man's land of suspect ethnicity between the once-solid halves of a bilingual city. And now, with the rest of the English nearly gone, the fulcrum had shifted further east, and the area was young, upscale, arty and French. Soho *de chez nous,* thought Porter. If he were ever to return to Montreal, as he sometimes fantasized, he too would settle near St. Louis Square.

On a steamy night in July, Corinne and Richard threw a cocktail party in his honour. Alas, the pudgy little sound man in the tight polo shirt, jeans and gold chain was more than a sound man, and Porter had been slow in picking up the inflections.

Porter had been sipping beer in the kitchen, a lone, bushy-bearded, middle-aged man in shirtsleeves among men in abused leathers, cropped beards and baggy corduroys. Quebec was both chic and Third World at the same time; unlike New York, everyone smoked. The uncirculated summer air was dense and blue. It was like being in a Bogart movie, or something terribly earnest and existential.

He was the oldest male, but for two white-maned eminences from the upper levels of publishing. Richard came close, but worked at looking younger in his leather jacket, tight jeans, frizzy grey hair and tightly trimmed black beard. Culture matters, thought Porter; four hundred miles south of here and he'd look decked out for Fire Island or a cruise down Christopher Street.

He wondered why he'd let himself in for all this. Corinne was the only obvious reason, but Richard, if not older prohibitions, had blocked that possibility even before it arose. To meet his translator, perhaps. Or something older and more characteristic of him: to prove that even in a Montreal so utterly transformed he still had force, continuity. He didn't recognize any of the locally famous names, he'd read none of their books, he didn't know their films or plays or songs or the names of their publishing houses. He wanted to know if any of that really mattered. He wanted to prove to himself that he still had currency.

Richard had followed him to a small porch off the remodelled kitchen. They didn't seem to have much in common, beyond an obvious interest in Corinne.

'I listened very carefully to your interview this afternoon,' Richard said, in the French they had been using together, then looked up slyly and added in English, 'Right on, man!'

'Which part was right on?'

'Oh, the part about the perils of collective thinking. Or feeling a double loyalty and catching shit for not being loyal enough for either side. And not being able to explain *why* you feel so goddamned intense about your French-Canadianness when there's at least six million just like you in New England who don't give a damn.'

The man's English, at the very least, was remarkable. Not that it was unaccented, more or less like Corinne's, but that it was *noticeably* accented.

'And do you know what really broke me up? It was when Coco asked you such a simple little question as—'

'—*where was I born*? But that's not such a simple little question. I didn't know till I was thirteen, and it still gets me in trouble.'

'Man, you turned white! It made my own hands sweat. I know *exactly* what you mean.'

'Just where were you born, Richard?'

He snorted. 'Shit, can't you tell? I didn't speak a word of *French* till I was twenty-three years old—that beats you by ten years. Look, do I sound *strange* or something?'

'You sound,' said Porter, 'like you learned your English in New York City.'

'Well? You think *you* got identity problems? I grew up as Dick Goldstein in the Bronx. Came up here to dodge the draft, got a degree at McGill, got involved in anti-war stuff, then in PQ stuff, the independence thing, got married, had kids. Everybody's story.'

'Except that now you're Ree-shar and you live with Corinne Carrier. I'd call that life after death.'

'And I've got two Jewish kids who went to French schools because that was the right thing to do, and now one's a folk-singer in France and the other's a lumberjack on the North Shore and they both refuse to speak a word of English except when they sing. Try explaining *that* to their *zeyde* and *bubbe*. I did my six months for amnesty so I can at least go back and visit them.'

'Have they met Corinne?'

'Sure. She freaks them out.'

Porter could tell they'd gathered a small crowd behind him; he could smell the smoke of discovery. He could even detect the fragrance of his left-cheek cousin just at his elbow.

Richard winked and slipped back into French. 'The Expos get back in town tomorrow, and I'm on the television crew. If you want to go, just get word to Coco.'

That seemed to be her cue; she turned Porter with a touch on his shoulder. 'M'sieur Carrier, there's someone here who's been waiting to meet you.' An older woman in a pastel dress stepped forward. 'May I present to you Madeleine Choquette, your translator? Madame Choquette, my cousin, Philippe Carrier.'

11.

Earlier in the evening he had noticed her, a stocky, grey-haired woman with youthful skin, and he'd assumed she was a publisher's wife. She had the assurance and the accessories that would have led anyone looking at her and Corinne together to think, 'Of course!': mother and daughter. They made sense together. Maybe there hadn't been a mass mutation of the provincial gene-pool; parts of the Montreal generations really did fit together.

A flashbulb went off. Corinne moved automatically to the middle; the party had suddenly found its focus. He felt his translator's arm tighten around him, and he knew she had come alone. A young man wanted to know what he'd thought of the translation. He had to admit that he hadn't yet read it.

She said to him later, 'Don't apologize, Mr Porter. Please, don't even bother reading it. In fact, you're the *last* person who should read it.' Just as Florence Lachance had said, her English was perfect.

'You're the first person in Montreal to call me Porter.'

'That's how I know you,' she laughed. 'And because you're no Carrier.' She held out two fingers and pinched them just under his nose. 'We're *this* close, you and me. But I'm on one side and you're on the other, and no one but you or me could tell us apart.'

'So what does that make me?'

'An American. A Franco-American. Like the spaghetti.'

Just when he was getting used to being a newt, an axolotl.

It was a warm night, still early. Corinne's apartment opened on a pedestrian mall lined with restaurants and bistros. Somewhere on these streets that were now closed to traffic, young

Carrier had lived with whores, had slept on their sofas, gotten up at noon and made his way to the backs of unsanitary restaurants where part-time hookers, the sisters of strippers, the girlfriends of various petty gangsters and enforcers on the block, served him food. By afternoon he'd show up on Dorchester Street where he had a job sweeping and mopping at the Club Lido. Fifi Laflamme, *née* Jeanne Gobeil, had been a headliner, and there was Kitty Coulombe who worked with doves and Soeur Cerise, too outrageous even for Montreal. And every night there'd been a circle of men around the horseshoe stage slurping drinks and reaching up for a feel, whom Carrier zapped with imaginary death rays as he worked the reds and purples. He could remember it all perfectly tonight, the girls, the smells and the twisted alleys off rue de Bullion, the steamy nights of unscreened windows and the ice-etched glass of winter with pans of water on the rads, the girls waiting in front of the *casses-croûtes* for Americans dropped off by taxi-drivers.

He was seventeen and dreaming of purity, living in the midst of sin and disease. The girls had TB, they had social diseases ('Honey, I'd let you climb on 'cause I really like you, but I'm doing you a favour, see?'), they had little kids that Carrier would take to the park on nice days while their mothers slept.

Why *can't* I forget all this?

He'd written about those years. He'd squeezed it all out, but he was still tortured.

It was all so Catholic, so medieval, he was a four-hundred-year-old man. He remembered trying to sleep on a torn sofa as Félice Gagnon stood under sixty punishing watts, not his forgiving reds and blues, ironing a dress. She'd stand there for hours half-dressed in a pair of black undies as he buried himself in the crooks of her sofa.

Tonight with his translator in Montreal he felt as though he'd been reduced to a burst of static and flung into space for thirty years, and only now, with this woman, finally captured.

He wanted to trust her, this woman so close to him in fate but from the other side of the world. They had a small second dinner at a Greek seafood restaurant, fried squid, salad, retsina.

He'd often wondered, back in his married days, and in his years with Debbie, what it would take to make a healthy, vigorous, attractive man ever grow interested in an older woman. Even if he *ought* to. Even if it was the best thing for him, not to mention the right political thing to do? It just seemed unnatural. And now he knew that unblemished young women were merely the least complicated form of a polymorphous attraction.

Of course, he was no longer healthy, young or vigorous.

'I want to hold you,' he said.

'Of course you do,' said his translator. 'And you will.'

12.

These were dangerous streets for Porter, the steep downtown slopes between MacGregor and Sherbrooke—Peel, Stanley, Drummond, Mountain—for it was in a tourist room between Burnside and St. Catherine on Peel that young Carrier had last lived with his mother. After seeing Madeleine home (a woman of a certain age leads a complicated life, she reminded him; he could not visit her *that* night, but was welcome the next morning), Porter had walked back down Park from Outremont to the complex around Pine, then down the rest of the mountain to Sherbrooke.

It had been Peel Street in 1956, before Montreal joined the twentieth century. No Métro, no autoroutes, no democracy, no self-expression outside of stripping and skating. Carrier and his mother had two rooms. She still went by the name of Hennie Porter; otherwise questions would arise. In the winter, she would leave before dawn for her teaching assignment. He would take off in his coat and tie for the *collège* on Côte-Ste-Catherine across from the Oratory. And when he got back his mother would still be gone, and he'd change clothes and walk down to the Club Lido. His mother thought he was selling programs at the Forum. He remembered that year, even now, as a happy time.

She was fifty-two, an attractive woman with dark hair and bold, non-Carrier features. She surprised people by her age. Education and travel kept her young, she said—she didn't know what people did in this life without memories of better times. She'd studied and worked in Europe and held responsible decorating jobs in Montreal before getting married. She should never have married, she said, though she didn't regret motherhood. That was her matrimonial refrain.

The schizophrenic twenties and thirties had formed her. She doodled flappers on the backs of envelopes, sketched Art Deco interiors, hung pictures of Shaw and Huxley. But she'd been in Germany for the rise of Hitler, been forced from the Bauhaus to Prague, from Prague to Warsaw, Warsaw to London and London finally to Montreal. Thanks to his mother, Carrier learned—long before he could ever use it in dead, repressive Montreal—that once upon a time there had been a human place of sublime achievement against which the accomplishments of North America were to be held accountable and owing.

She was also a gloomy reactionary, cynical and suspicious. She attracted men without much effort—Carrier was an expert, reading lust in the eyes of strangers—but her only friends were mannish couples of unmarried women. She had married in her early thirties and suffered his father's instability and constant infidelities.

In 1956, Carrier was living in three discrete worlds: that of his mother and a cultured, English-speaking world focused on McGill University; that of a scholarship boy at an elite French *collège,* and that of a janitor in a bilingual shrine to venereal veneration. He was choking on female intimacy. The celibate world of the *collège* was his island of relief from a sea of powders, creams and endless costuming. He led a life of pure disguise; if the brothers had discovered his job, he would have been dropped from school. If the Protestant school board knew he attended a French Catholic school, his mother would have been fired. If his mother ever found out where he worked, she would have died. If he'd acted on any of his passions, he would have been arrested.

He and his mother had evolved an elaborate sexual etiquette. In matters of modesty, she was not of this century. They neither spoke of sex, nor alluded to any of its forms. They kept all doors locked even during the mildest states of disarray.

Then one day he'd come home from school and found his mother in the bathroom with the door open. She was preparing for her bath. She stood before the mirror in her dressing-gown and was busy brushing out her hair. He made as much noise as he could, and she turned to face him. 'Hello, dear, did you have a good day?' she asked, perkier than usual, then unknotted the bow and spread her arms, and the robe fell open. He'd expected a joke to save him at the last minute, like the girls at the Lido, a slip at least, but her body had engulfed him, white, close, utterly, utterly nude. His legs went rubbery. 'I'll go—' he said, and she answered him, stepping out of the bathroom and moving towards him, 'No, it's quite all right. We're two adults here, aren't we? Why don't you put some tea water on?' and he ran for the kitchen cubicle while the rings of the shower curtain scraped against the rusty pole.

He stood in the kitchen watching the gas rings, hands moist and shaking, eyes burning from the vision. It was as though the gas had sucked all the air out of the room and the pounding of the water and the echoes off the bathroom tiles were in the kitchen with him. He could hear it all again tonight, nearly thirty years later, and his breath still came short.

When he had dared to turn, holding out the cup of tea, she was unwrapping herself from the towel in order to dry her hair. An alien being had occupied her body. 'Just put it down, dear,' she said, as she took a chair and finished drying her legs and thighs.

13.

One day in the winter of his sixteenth year, Philippe Carrier had been a scholarship student at Jean-de-Brébeuf with a bright future before him in law or the classics, and the next day he'd been clawed from the skies and dumped in the gutter with nowhere to turn. He'd been standing with his mother at seven-thirty in the morning on the corner of Peel and Dorchester where the buses came in. She wasn't going to work that day, but she'd wanted to walk with him to the bus stop. She'd been bright and witty, her twenties not her thirties self, full of brittle talk and saucy opinion—the side he preferred, but couldn't fully respond to. It was easier to be the son of her sour, schoolteacherly side.

It had been a mushy morning in late March, with the night's fresh snow already crushed to slabs of silvered sherbet by the pre-dawn ploughs and now the rows of backed-up buses. Twenty different bus lines circled Dominion Square; buses were lined two abreast in the street and bumper-to-bumper along the curb. It was the sign of late winter, his mother observed, the number of lone male galoshes poking up from the puddles, sucked off by slush.

His bus, an express, sent up a wave of brown, salted ice as it slanted to its dock. Carrier was looking down at his feet, making sure of his footing, when his mother took his hand and said, 'There's something I must do,' and then pulled away and dove for the right front tire. The driver slammed his brakes so hard he mounted the curb, but his mother had already disappeared under the bus in the slushy, black pool of gutter water. A woman screamed at Carrier, '*Qu'est-ce qui s'est passé?*—What happen?' and he found himself pushed aside by policemen and drivers and some passengers who worked their way under the bus to pull his mother out.

At the inquiry it was determined that she must have slipped on the icy curb and been pushed forward by the surging crowd. Carrier did not dispute the finding, and for thirty years he'd accepted it. He concealed from everyone the letters she had left back in their rooms: a termination notice from the Protestant school board and, from the nearest town in Ontario, a notice from his father to file a Bill of Divorcement since Quebec did not permit divorces.

He was now standing at the spot. In front of him now was a six-lane Dorchester Boulevard and just down the hill the giant cheese-grater known as the Château Champlain Hotel. Windsor Station and the old Laurentian Hotel, profitable places for passing out peep-show leaflets, and the old Club Lido itself were gone, and Dominion Square was now an art park. The only survivors he could place from thirty years ago were the old grey mastodons: the Sun Life building and Marie-Reine-du-Monde. When he sat on the park bench the city fell away in bluffs and terraces down to the river. Cool air rose from the invisible water like a sea breeze, bringing the smell of fresh ironing.

Not the smell of ironing: the stench of it, the way all ripeness implies rancidness and rot. He could smell the stench of foul clothes right down to the sweat and sebum and the powders that lay against them. He could smell the scorch of cotton and, faintly, the odour of searing flesh.

Most children find the image of their parents' sexuality amusing if not ridiculous. Many children of older parents of his generation felt they were spawned in some awkward and accidental effort, never before attempted, never later duplicated. Porter had carried that feeling for many years.

But by the time he married and embarked on his own tenuous course, he began seeing his parents in heroic and tragic dimensions: his mother a frail Giacometti; his father a squat, fierce Rodin. He saw his father as the existential beast, his mother as the balance of restraining forces, consumed by contraries. He carried that image of their heroic decimation into his adulthood and into his writing. And his writing to date had been of himself, the adolescent yo-yo, the little rubber ball restrained by his mother's frail rubber cord, whacked by his father's paddle.

It was two o'clock on a July morning in the last fifteen years of the twentieth century. A different generation in a different city in a country he no longer recognized had taken over. The only continuity between that winter morning at this spot and this summer night were the defunct buildings and the diseased synapses in Porter's brain.

14.

She met him at the door of her apartment, dressed for summer in a wide straw hat and peasant skirt, Indian top and sandals. 'I thought we could drive up north,' she said, and she'd even packed a wicker basket with lunch and wine. They'd go to her mountain cabin near Ste-Agathe and spend the rest of the week in the cool air on a lake. In fact, she'd come back to town only for Corinne's party and to meet him. Friends had been using it; that's why he couldn't stay the night before.

Porter had walked over the mountain from Côte-des-Neiges and Camillien-Houde to near Côte-Ste-Catherine where she lived. It was a muggy day climbing to the nineties; the mountains were appealing, and a lake would be nice, but nothing could match a quiet air-conditioned apartment on a sidestreet on Outremont.

'Do we have to go?' he asked. And he followed her silently back through the living room into her bedroom where he lay on the bed and untied his shoes as she stood in front of the closet, slowly undoing her day's preparations. She laid the straw hat on a ledge, stepped out of the sandals and loosened the pearl earrings and placed them on the dresser. It was the slowest, most orderly undressing in Porter's long experience, as she took down the hangers, the hooks, for both their sets of clothes.

'Would you like to shower?' she asked, and yes, he said, he would. The serene lack of urgency was something new and unexpected, for last night, thinking of Madeleine Choquette as he lay awake in his tourist room, he'd all but phoned her at four in the morning, all but taken a taxi out and pounded on her door. Minutes later she slid the shower door open and stepped inside with him, and they stood wrapped together under the warm waterhead until it seemed to him that air and flesh and water were continuous and he had stepped out of his body altogether.

They were lying on the translator's bed, talking for the first time since last night. She'd been playing little translation games, confessing small confusions with English, even after twenty years of intimacy. 'There's a sign on the thruway going down to Albany,' she said, '"Trucks Under 40 Use Low Gear," and my first impression was, *How very old their trucks are!* Or last winter, the TV weatherman in Plattsburgh said, "Expect six quick inches of snow," and I panicked! What's a "quick inch"? Is that like a country mile? Even last night when you said you had to go straight back to New York, I first thought, well, I certainly hope he's not going to get *bent* first! You see what I mean? And then I hit sentences in your book like, "I spun my mental Rolodex and her name came up ..." How am I supposed to deal with that in French?'

He ran the palm of his hand up her body, resting it on her cheek, then back down. They had cooled off, returned to their separate bodies. 'Madeleine,' he said, 'help me.'

She pressed cool fingertips to his eyes.

'I'm lost,' he said.

'I'm here. I'm not going away.'

'I'm forty-six years old, Madeleine. By forty-six a man should have an ability to predict likely reactions. Utter ignorance should be pretty well eliminated. Total insecurity should be fairly unlikely ... you know what I'm saying?'

'Those are American expectations. I'm fifty-two and my life is exactly the same. I don't know anyone whose isn't.'

'My mother was fifty-two,' he said.

'Don't think I don't know. I was almost afraid to mention it.'

'My epilepsy has come back.'

'I know. I saw it last night at dinner.'

'I don't know how to treat it. Last time, the medicine slowed me down. I couldn't take that again. I don't know if it's a medical condition or . . . a message, you know? My mind is falling apart. I haven't written in over a year. I have a new family, but I don't feel like I belong to them. . . . I feel like a monster, sometimes.'

He felt like a blind man, trying to assemble a thousand-piece jigsaw puzzle.

'You were a Quebec Catholic once,' she said. 'Remember the consolations of melancholy.'

She lifted her fingers. She crouched over him, a full, immense woman of fifty years, her breasts whiter than milk, nearly touching his eyes. She was a smiling haze above him, grey hair without striking features. Then she buried her face in his, her lips on his, and the long, erotic nightmare of his life began to build. He was conscious of the presence of sin in what his body was doing, impurities linked to the dusty hallways of his childhood and adolescence and the dingy lights of de Bullion Street and none of it mattered. He would have handed over his soul at that moment for just twenty more minutes like this, fifteen, ten, and when it was over and they were lying still in one another's arms, he fell asleep believing that no condition, moral or medical, could have survived those last eruptions intact.

15.

He had a very active profile, cutting in and jutting out, like an ingenious edge to a jigsaw puzzle piece. Ageing was just a process of thinning here and thickening there, getting shorter, or stretching out. His hands were comparatively huge—arthritic, Porter supposed—and his forearms bulged like Popeye's, but the neck was frail and the cheeks were sunken. Porter would not have recognized him, and no one would have placed him in the same century, on the same continent, with his daughter.

He limped now—again, the arthritis, Corinne had mentioned on the drive out—and he hadn't worked since Paulette died. He was on disability, which paid the beer and the rent on a second-floor flat in Ville d'Anjou. He wasn't yet fifty, but he'd lost out on things.

It was Madeleine who'd persuaded him: see your cousin. 'I met him when I was translating your book. He's a little sad, but he sincerely wants to meet you again.' Then she'd said, 'You know what he told me? He said, "Knowing Phillie gave meaning to my life." How's that, eh?'

Whenever Corinne visited her father, the neighbourhood gathered. 'Coco, Coco,' people shouted, and lined the sidewalk hoping for a glimpse. There should be a documentary in this, Porter thought: the New Quebec, built on the bones of men like Dollard. With Corinne and Richard, Madeleine and Porter all out on the front gallery and with a case of beer at his feet, Dollard Carrier was the soul of volubility. He reminded Porter of an artificial-heart recipient, an affable soul utterly confused by all the attention. Now he was waving down to the passersby, toasting them with a beer at eleven in the morning, giving his daughter loud kisses and keeping one enormous paw on Porter's knee.

'Some times we had, eh?' he laughed, rolling a cigarette. 'Christ, this guy comes up from the States and steals my bed. Him and his parents, breezes into our little flat down in Hochelaga that was already jammed . . . goddamn, I hated him at first. Couldn't understand a word of English, of course. I must have made life hell for you, Phillie, I'm sorry. I never apologized. I'm not right sometimes. Stupid, that's what I am. No, no . . . you took it all like a man and surprised the shit out of me, I'll admit it. You were weak and twice as smart as anyone else, and I couldn't say it then but I'll say it now—I was damned proud of you.'

Corinne winked at Porter; Madeleine squeezed his arm. Richard asked. 'Did you hear him on Coco's show?'

'Naw, she knows about me. Can't understand her on the radio, speaks too high class for me to follow. Give me a base-ball game or a hockey match.'

'I was sorry to hear about Paulette,' said Porter.

'She was a good woman,' said Dollard, dipping his head. He held up a new beer; he was drinking alone.

'Dollard—' and now Porter moved closer and put his arm on his cousin's shoulder. 'My mother, you remember, killed herself?'

Dollard crossed himself. 'Terrible thing. A tragedy,' he muttered.

'I wondered if anyone ever talked about it. One thing was, my father wanted a divorce. She was carrying the papers with her when she died.'

'We don't believe in divorce,' he said. 'Everyone else is get-ting a divorce nowadays. Not me and Paulette. Twenty-three years married, praise her soul, six good kids. Already two of the boys—Coco's brothers, there—they got divorces. You understand what's happening, Phillie?'

'No, I don't.' If he could have answered he might have said, twenty years of intimacy is too heavy a burden for the human heart. What he said was, 'I was hoping for word of my father. You're the only person I can ask.'

Until he'd come back to Montreal, Porter had felt com-paratively young. Now he felt like the last of his generation, the last, along with Madeleine and maybe a few old priests and nuns, who remembered the bad, murderous and suicidal old days. It was a culture made for incongruities. Dollard and Corinne; Dollard and himself.

'Uncle Reggie,' said Dollard. 'My father always warned me about Uncle Reggie.'

'What happened to him, Dollard?'

'He was a restless man, Phillie. That's what my father always said.'

'Where is he?'

'It's a home—St. Justin's out in Laval. He's an old, old man. The sisters do what they can. Sometimes he must ask for me, and they come over and get me.'

'What does he say, when he asks for you?'

'Nothing. He forgets, or probably he never asked. They have to keep busy, too. I don't mind.'

'Does he ask about *me*? About his son?'

Dollard turned slowly and looked down at his beer. 'He doesn't have a son, not where he is.'

16.

They were lying in bed after another day of not making it past the front hallway of Madeleine's apartment. She had greeted him now three days running, freshly showered and crisply dressed, as though ready for tennis or a long afternoon in a rented punt, a picnic from straw hampers in a Impressionist glade. But she would close the door and move to her well-stocked closet and casually begin undressing. She scattered the hangers on the bed, and they hung up their clothes in silence. And they would lie together as though they'd already been out, taken their exercise and now were back for rest.

She made him feel he was on perpetual vacation in some tropical resort, passing his mornings in strenuous touring then stealing a few hours for drinks, sex and slumber while the rest of the tour was on a dusty bus visiting ruins. She was the oldest woman in his life; the only older woman in his life.

And then they would talk. About his parents, his childhood, her family, her children, his children; her adjustments to the States when her family had moved down there, his to Montreal; about her writing, his writing. Madeleine had left the States when her marriage failed ('Husbands can forgive their wives hating them, so long as they don't learn to love other men,' she said), but she'd gone to Paris and lived there ten years, working in publicity. She was going to stay, thinking that Quebec held nothing for her. She started writing in Paris. Quebec writers and singers were just beginning to catch on in France, after three hundred years of ridicule.

Her children were Americans, they'd stayed back in Boston with their English-speaking father. And why did she leave Paris? Something so small, really, but one of those potent moments that forced her to examine her irrelevance in France. 'A perforation in the fabric of indifference,' she called it.

'I was walking with my lover in the Bois de Vincennes, passing to the Parc Floral.' She named those places as though Porter had seen them, as though any cultured person knew them intimately. 'We had to take a subterranean passage under a stone bridge. There were unpleasant piss-odours, but that's not uncommon on the streets of Paris. No, it was the graffiti sprayed on the walls of the passage: *Mort aux juifs*, and *Violer les filles arabes* and *Purité aryenne*, and dozens of condoms, hundreds of them, slippery underfoot. My friend was roaring with laughter—he'd *brought* me there deliberately! It was all *funny* to him, you see. He was a very sophisticated, socialist lawyer, but he said he liked to come down there to 'get in touch with his feelings.'

'The obscenities weren't on the walls—they were in his politics, and I'd never appreciated that before. When I got upset he called me a typical reactionary Quebec cow. To him, the problem was I couldn't take a good joke.'

Porter had had no such moments, at least, none that he remembered. He envied people their moments of clear hate, knowing their own names and where they were born, their small perforations. He hungered for clear distinctions. What this visit had awakened in him was the realization of his fundamental Quebec Catholicism, the Jansenist belief that there is no end to the implications of a single act.

One day in Pittsburgh when he was twelve years old and living in utter harmony even with his epilepsy, his father went to work and learned he'd been fired without warning. 'My name was Phil Porter, my father was Reg Porter and we were Americans from Pittsburgh.

'Then in one moment my father hauls off and slugs the man sitting at his desk and runs from the store. I wake up the next morning without the parents I thought I knew, without the name I thought I had, without a city or a country or even a language I could speak! And because of that I become split down the middle, my mother kills herself and I'm sitting here in middle age and I'm still running.'

Madeleine ran her fingers over his shoulder, down his arm and flank. 'Why do you think you're epileptic?' she asked.

'I was battered by a baby-sitter's husband when I was three, in Cincinnati.'

'I know that's what you wrote.'

He gathered her fingers in a stunted bunch of carmine nails. 'Wasn't I?'

'Isn't it time to find out?'

'I don't remember any of it. The earliest memory I have is of sitting in the kitchen sink and being bathed. I remember Johnny Mercer singing "Don't Fence Me In" on the radio, and I sang along with him. And I remember sitting next to my father on the arm of his chair, and I fell off and broke my arm.'

'I'll tell you what I think, Philip. You're the one who's always so amazed by *mutations,* right? You keep looking at Coco and saying. "How did it happen?" like she's some kind of miracle. And you look at Dollard like he's a caveman or something—' 'A fish,' said Porter. 'I'm a mud-puppy.' 'Okay, whatever. But Philip, there's no such thing as a mutation here. Where's the transition between *your* father and *you?* It's your mother, right? and between Dollard and Coco—it's *you,* that's who. *We're* the transition, Coco's a transition, your little daughter who plays Chopin and Mozart, *she's* a transition. There aren't any permanent forms of *anything,* Porter darling. Where did you pick up that museum mentality? Listening to you is like going on a tour of Ste Anne de Beaupré or Lourdes or Brother André's Shrine—it's medieval! You look at life like it's some kind of before-and-after picture. Either it's totally damned or it's too good to include you. That's old Quebec Catholicism, darling. You're holding out for a miracle to come down and save you.'

17.

There are no permanent forms, except perhaps the styles of institutional Catholic architecture: schools, hospitals, convents, nursing homes. The muggy weather had begun to break when Porter made his way alone over the black river to the island of Laval. Maison St-Justin could be spotted from half a mile away, a battlement of yellow brick in the middle of unvarying fieldstone duplexes.

Grey Sisters ran the place; they made Porter nervous. St. Justin's seemed to be in a permanent state of renovation, like Olympic Stadium with its cranes, the result of insufficient public money beginning to supplant the church. Ladders and scaffolding, dropcloths, uncured drywall and brightly painted television rooms were jammed into dingy, cream-coloured corridors with varnished oak doors, set with stippled glass. The number of Greys thinned out on the upper floors; rough-looking orderlies with lips curled cruelly over hockey scars seemed to be in control. His father was listed on the fourth floor. Dozens of old men in striped hospital pyjamas lined the halls in wheelchairs. The opened doors of the wards showed only withered legs and bony toes pointing up at silent television screens.

He asked one of the orderlies for M'sieur Carrier's room. The young man snickered, but gave out a number. 'Reggie,' he winked. *'Reggie, l'américain!'*

And then there was no delaying it. He stood at the base of his father's bed staring the length of his father's body, from the bare feet up the shins and over the sleeping chest to the enormous nostrils, the flaring eyebrows, and the immense pink ears, caught by the pillow and spread out full. His mouth was open as he snored. The teeth were out; his father had become all cavities, air was claiming him.

Over the bed hung a crucifix.

He took a chair at the head of the bed. The plastic wristband around the bundle of purple veins read 'Carrier, R.' He remembered his father as a snorer and heavy sleeper. He held his father's hand and gave it a firm tug.

'Dad?'

The eyes were open. Porter thought he read panic. He cranked up the bed. His father didn't seem strong enough to sit up straight. 'Dad, it's me, Philip.'

No recognition. He wanted his teeth; his eyes told him that. He slipped them in without any problems, then cleared his throat. This was as long as his father had normally gone without a cigarette. Such a drastic change as that—what had it cost him? When had he done it? Who had suffered through it with him?

The male orderly came to the door, accompanied by a nun. 'M'sieur Carrier,' she said, 'there's much to talk about.' Fees? he wondered. He couldn't afford his father's care; didn't feel he owed it.

His father cleared his throat, smiled briefly, and fluttered his hand in the nun's direction.

'Sometimes we can't shut him up.' She repeated it louder, for his father's benefit. 'Eh, Reggie? He looks confused right now.'

'I thought, all these years . . .' Porter began, 'he was lost. Gone. Totally out of my life.'

He felt his French deserting him. Fear of the nun, back to the time when he was learning the language under the unforgiving tutelage of Soeur Timothée. She'd had a nickname; that too had deserted him. He realized he had never spoken French to his father, despite the fact that his father's Frenchness had helped destroy his life.

'He did not list you among his immediate family.'

'That is nevertheless my father,' said Porter. If this was a Catholic home, he didn't want to jeopardize his father's care by too much disclosure. 'My mother has been dead nearly thirty years. I went to the States and changed my name.'

'That's your business, of course. If all the papers are in order, we can release him to you,' she said.

'I can't look after him.'

'So you came here for what? Curiosity? Will you sign papers attesting to your refusal, then? It is required, now that he is a ward of the province.'

Porter signed. Bless socialized medicine; forms, not bills. He used his proper name, Philippe Carrier, *fils*.

'Dad? Do you know who I am?'

'This is your son, Reggie,' she echoed, louder. She glanced down at his signature. 'Philippe.'

'He knew me as Phil. We always talked in English, so maybe, if you don't mind. . . .

'Dad, I haven't seen you in thirty years. I want to talk to you. I want to find out what you've been doing, where you've been. . . . Do you understand me?'

There were flickers in his eyes, as though he might have understood and then immediately suppressed it.

The orderly had worked his way to the head of the bed where he was untying the bow of the old man's gown and slipping it over his head. His father slumped forward a little, and the orderly took out the pillow.

His father was obviously starving to death. What kind of man lets his father starve to death? Porter wondered. He probably weighed well under a hundred pounds, and the dead white skin was marked with bruises, nicks, veins and scars that Porter had never seen.

He must bruise like a peach, he thought.

'You might help us here, Mr Carrier,' said the nun. 'We try to account for as much of the medical history of the patient as seems relevant. Your father has had quite an extensive medical involvement.' She traced the still-red scars of abdominal surgery, indicated more whorls of stitching in his groin—'Hernia, we had to do that'—and then tipped him forward to show deep, smooth scars under the shoulder blades. 'A lucky man—lung-cancer operation, at least ten years old. We have a fairly complete record from your brother in Ottawa, but he couldn't tell us—'

'—my brother?'

'Yes, of course. He often visits, along with your sisters. They're much better than you've been, you'll forgive my commenting. Technically, your father should be moved to a more medically oriented facility—this is still for the ambulatory and continent, and you can see your father is not in that category.'

'I'll sign,' he said.

'And one more thing, just for our legal records. There's this scar on his back—' she tipped him forward like a slab of meat into Porter's arms and loosened the knot of his clean gown. 'What do you know of this?'

He had never noticed a scar; to him, his father was unblemished. His parents had never undressed in front of him, except for his mother that one time. And now, today. His father after thirty years smelled the same, the same powders, the same sweat, the same stale cotton odours, but with age the ripeness had turned putrid. My God, don't they bathe him here? Should *I* bathe him? He pulled his father closer, loosening the robe that melted from his dead-white shoulders. It was like baby's flesh rubbed in flour, red at the slightest touch, scabs clustered where his collar bone had nearly poked through. He knew even before he saw it what he would find.

It was an old, discoloured patch of skin, shaped like a shark's fin, a neat, purple parabola. It wasn't deep, but it was extensive, and it had withstood the shrinking of his body and the loosening of his skin. It looked like a decal ready to be pulled off.

'I don't think it gives him pain,' the nun said, 'but watch—'

She touched it with her ballpoint pen, and Porter's father lunged forward, hard against his chest. 'You see, there's sensitivity there—or maybe a memory of it, locked away. You could stick pins in the rest of his skin and he wouldn't feel them. His circulation is entirely gone—he can't move his feet, and they're like chunks of ice to the touch.'

'Don't you operate?'

'We must justify the expense, m'sieur. Your father is not likely to survive surgery—or live long enough to benefit from it.'

He could feel his father's breathing, his heart pounded fast as a bird's against his arm. He stared down his father's back at the patch of discoloured skin rising like a shark's pointed snout breaking water, and he felt a twist of terror.

'I think I know,' he said. 'It's shaped like an iron, isn't it?'

'What kind of man brands himself with an iron on his own backside? Your brother said he'd always had it.'

'A man like my father,' said Porter. 'A woman like my mother.' Then, savouring the words, 'My brother was always a particularly unobservant boy.'

He laid his father down, straightening the new gown and centring his head on the pillow. He could smell the ironed clothes, deep in his brain. 'My father remembers the iron, I'm sure, don't you?' He showed signs of wanting to speak, but again held back. Porter stifled an urge to ask for an iron and bring it close, and closer, to his father's face. Deep in the brain, the intruder ran from room to room, and Porter turned on the lights, chased, blocked the escape routes.

'That scar happened over forty years ago, when I was three years old. My mother was ironing clothes. My father was bathing me in the kitchen sink. And I started screaming. Why, I don't know.' But he remembered it vividly: the record playing 'Don't Fence Me In,' the water, and being lifted and dropped, lifted and dropped, and his head striking the porcelain partition between the sinks. 'I didn't remember it till this minute.'

The nun seemed not to notice.

He turned to her. 'Get me a sponge and some water, please.'

He gathered his father's head in his arms and pressed his lips on his forehead, his cheeks and then his lips. He stared into the grey eyes that gave nothing back, praying for just another sign of recognition, and then his father closed his eyes.

'Sleep, father,' he said. 'I have loved you all my life.'

18.

They met him in Poughkeepsie station and drove him home. He'd been gone just under a week, but they had news! Hannah had learned a new sonata that she wanted to play for Poppy that very night, tired or not.

'Have you learned some things, too?' Petra asked him as they cleaned the dishes later that evening.

'I'll see the doctor in the morning. He said he can dose me, so I'll let him try.'

'You didn't really believe in miracle cures, did you?'

'I'm afraid I did.' He took her into his arms. 'I've learned many wonderful things from many wonderful people, but I did not learn any miracle cure for epilepsy.'

She didn't struggle, as she often did. She even returned the hugs and lingered for a kiss. 'We've missed you. Well, Hannah's been too busy to really *miss* you, but I've missed you.'

When the dishes were dry, they moved to the living room and sat quietly as their daughter began to play.

MEDITATIONS
ON STARCH

POTATOES: Mr Spud opened at the local mall, and hired my high school boy for his first job. He was saving for a trip to Europe, where he has relatives.

He's been taught to do amazing things with potatoes. They're just a shell of their former selves. No longer prized for snowy yields, for understated contribution to stews, now they're just parka-like pockets waiting to be stuffed. It's the fate of blandness in the mall-managed world, I tell him, to be upscaled into glamour like pita bread and bagels, chicken and veal. Stuffed with yoghurt, sour cream and cottage cheese, spread with peppers, cheese and broccoli, topped with Thousand Islands dressing and bacon bits.

What wizard thought this up?

Mother!

I still like mashed potatoes. Even the name is honest and reassuring, after the *gepashket* concoctions with alfalfa sprouts and garbanzo beans. Butter-topped, cream-coloured bins of heroic self-indulgence, inviting a finger-dip the way a full can of white enamel compels a brush.

Is there a taste explosion in the world finer than the first lick of the Dairy Queen cone, the roughened vanilla from a freshly opened tub, the drowning in concentrated carbohydrate where fats and starches come together in snowy concupiscence?

CORN: My son never knew his grandmother, whose presence comes back to me as I stand at the Mr Spud toppings bar. She only exists in these sharpened moments, triggered by significant images that otherwise baffle me. 'Mother.' I murmur, 'what do you make of this?' Questions to my mother are questions to history, answers from her are brief parables of the twentieth century.

Don't you know? she tells me. The yearning for a clean, quick, anonymous bite is universal.

My mother found herself in Prague in 1933. Her art school in Germany had just been closed down. One of her professors offered escape with him to Rio. Many went to Paris and Brussels. These weren't the BigTime Bauhausers; New York and L.A. weren't in the cards. These were commercial designers ('but not designing enough,' my mother would joke). Shanghai, Istanbul, Alexandria, Stockholm, with the leaders taking off for Caracas and Rio. One got to Vera Cruz. Maybe eventually some of them made their way to America. My mother got to Montreal.

I was a stamp collector. I knew the tales behind those thick letters with the high-denomination stamps, the elegant handwriting in black ink turning to olive. Cancelled stamps are less valuable than mint, but I treasured them for the urgency of cancellation. My mother had known a time when the germ of genius was clustered in the back streets of Dresden and Weimar and Dessau, before the Big Bang flung it to tin shacks on the shores of Maracaibo.

The poles of her existence can move me to tears, the B. Traven world of artists from the heartland of order and austerity rotting in the rat infested tropics. She showed me photos of an art college, hand-painted signs on a tin-roofed shack,

Herr Professor in jodhpurs and bush shirt, teaching from a canvas deckchair.

'Poor old Dieter,' she'd say.

She'd wanted a career in fashion design. Her surviving portfolios from art school feature ice-skaters and ballerinas. She was the Degas of Dresden. But the faces of the skaters and dancers seem grafted on, dark and heavy, like hers. The eyes are shadowed, in the movie fashion of the day. They stop just short of grotesquerie, for those girls will never soar, never leap. She could get the bodies, but not the faces. I can't tell if it's Expressionism, autobiography, or mild incompetence. I don't know if these were the drawings she kept out of fondness, or the ones that didn't sell. Others found their way into magazines. The idea of my mother influencing the Prague Spring Collection of 1934 fills me with wonder.

Or do I read too much into those drawings, too much into everything about her? Had she somehow, secretly, read Kafka? The idea of her Europe, of pre-war Central Europe, tugs at me, the continent I missed by the barest of margins.

There was no concept of Eastern or Western Europe in those days—Warsaw and Prague were as western as Paris. Russia and Spain, of course, didn't count; they were Asian, or African. Budapest and Bucharest had reputations for pervasive dishonesty, deriving perhaps from the perversity of their languages. So the stories I grew up with and passed on to my son were of an *idea* of Europe that hasn't existed in eighty years, a Holy Roman Empire in which a single language and a single passport dominated all others and the rest of the world suffered paroxysms of exclusion for not being European, and specifically, German.

When he was twelve, I asked my boy what he wanted to be when he grew up. 'A European,' he answered.

In Prague she got a job painting commercial signboards to hang over doorways, like British pub placards. One of the first signs she painted was for something called 'Indian Corn'. A corn café! Nothing but stubby ears of corn, cut in half, standing in pools of butter. In Prague, in 1933.

She had never eaten corn. Her parents considered it servants' food, part of a cuisine beneath serious cultivation. Nothing that required labour in the eating—and corn on the cob looked like work—was part of their diet. My grandparents, whom I of course never met, favoured pre-nouvelle cuisine French cooking, which meant soft, smothered, simmering things, the mashed potatoes of their day, short on fibre, low on spices, long on labour and quickly digested. Much favoured were compotes and warm puddings, since they detested anything cold as well as anything hot. Worst of all were the still-churning, molten messes that had become chic in Germany with the rise of Mussolini. Upscaling the lowly pasta. My grandfather's response to history is summarized in a single gastronomic grumble. 'Why couldn't *il Duce* have been a Frenchman! At least we would have eaten properly.' My grandmother, no less patrician, responded, 'Be grateful. He could have been Hungarian.'

Of all the stories I want to know, of all the things my mother told me of the secret lives of complicated people, I remember only these ridiculous little lines. So she painted her cob—half a cob, and the cobs weren't big in those days—standing up like a stubby candle in its pool of butter. Each kernel was treated like a window in an apartment tower, radiating a buttery light. It wasn't easy, before acrylics, before the conventions of Magic Realism, being a German artist, to devote herself to a humble corncob.

'I didn't know anything at first. Or maybe I discovered it as I worked. It was love for America,' is how she put it. 'A craving for Indian corn saved my life.'

Franz Kafka had been living a few blocks away just a decade earlier. He'd written *Amerika* under the same mysterious craving, though it didn't save his life. Maybe America-worship was in the air, at least among those who professed no longing for Germany. For my mother, Prague was just another provincial German city with an interesting Slavic component to be respected, but faintly pitied. She couldn't imagine civilized discourse in any language but German, with the possible exception of French in well-defined circumstances. French and German divided the dignified world between them, the spheres of pleasure and labour, though her French years were still in the future.

Her boss had a son, named Jürgen Jaeger—a good movie name, and he had dabbled in films like many German-speakers in the '20s. He still thought of himself as a set designer, a property man ('but not a man of property,' he joked, and the joke has survived them all because my mother jotted it down). He also identified strongly with Hitler's Sudeten policy, feeling himself mightily abused by the majority Czechs with their dirty, mongrel ways. I am making him sound unappealing—a Hitler of sorts, another expansionist sign painter with acting ambitions, born on the rim of Germany—but my mother never did. His attitudes were too common to be evil. I'm sure most Prague-born German-speakers yearned for enosis with the Fatherland, all other implications of Hitler-rule to be put aside, temporarily.

This, then, was my mother's situation in 1933. She was thirty and unmarried, talented, attractive, and stateless. She had an admirer whose rechannelled ambition was to join the political and if necessary military services of the greater German state. I have seen his picture, the suggestive swagger, as I interpret it, of one leg up on the running board, elbow on the windshield, body tight against the touring-car's flank. No monocle, no duelling scars, but a leather coat, a self-regarding little blond moustache, and a short, elegant cigarette that can only be carried in a theatrical gold case. He strikes the pose of a big-game hunter, even on a Carpathian picnic in the summer of 1934. This is the man who must be eliminated before I can be born.

Pictures of my mother show her always smoking, though I never saw her smoke, nor empty an ashtray without a show of disgust.

I came into her papers five years ago. That's when I unwrapped the first of many portfolios she'd been keeping under her bed. I had never seen them, and she had shared everything with me, I'd thought, the only child, the late-born son, the artistic and sensitive man in the family. Some of these I had seen—my grandparents sometime in the late twenties at a resort in the mountains. Taking the Cure. All those faces, relaxing, carefree, getting away from business and the city and the nameless sickness that seemed to stalk them.

I look like my grandfather—her genes won out. The gene for baldness, carried through the mother. The gene for Alzheimer's disease—who carries that? My mother maintained a saving fiction all the years that she was able, that her parents could have left Germany in time, just as she had, there was an uncle in Montreal who would sponsor them all, but her father lost first the will, then the sense of all urgency. It was, in his case, a medical, not political problem.

'Who is this man?' I asked her, and she pretended to look, and to smile. 'He's very handsome, mama. Like a movie star.' Still no response. The photo is sepia, faded, and extremely small. If only it could be blown up, Jaeger and the touring-car, the mountains and forest in the background, I might understand just a little more. There are other pictures, equally small, taken from upper windows, overlooking city squares. Brno? Bratislava? Carlsbad? Prague, perhaps, or the view from a Carpathian resort hotel. Maybe Jürgen is standing at her side, whispering, 'Sehr schon'.

'Jürgen Jaeger, mama, does it mean anything?'

She held her hand out to appease me, her fingers now blue-edged tines, but she didn't look.

I can read German, speak it enough. Her old-style hand-writing is difficult. *I tell him he must do what he must do. His*

father has interests in Germany. They have relatives in Leipzig.
I read it out loud, looking at its author's face, which gives back nothing. She probably jotted down these notes in ten seconds, sixty years ago. Now, the simplest resurrected fact of her life embraces the world. If I don't take these boxes now, they will be lost. She is going away and won't be coming back, and we have decided we must leave Canada.

He says, 'Der Fuhrer may be a little crude for your tastes, but he's no fool! He knows who makes money for him. And with this Rosenfeld getting elected in America, well...'

There is another tiny, sepia street scene. It is the most precious picture in the box. For an artist, my mother took terrible pictures. A tram snakes off the top of the frame. Half of a bundled Frau crosses the street. Uniformed men—police, army, Czech, German?—fill the space at the corner, outside a coffee shop. There seems to be an *Apotheke* next door. Cold-looking children play a sidewalk game using chalk just outside its door. You would miss it if you weren't looking for it, the sign for *Korn* struggling for attention against much larger and fancier boards.

This is the picture to be enlarged, at any cost. I palm it and slip it away, knowing I am taking her soul, and fearing that something will slice through all the blown cells in her brain and reach out for it, and then destroy it.

Fly! Fly! Go west and don't stop. I tell you this as a friend, as someone who knows.

This on a worn sheet of airmail paper, initialled with what appears to be a double T inside a crest, with a swastika hanging below it. So strange to see, as it were, a sincere swastika and not some gangland graffiti.

J.J., Visa Clerk, Leipzig.

RICE: In my wife's culture, Usha is called a 'cousin-sister' which means any female relative approximate in age. Actually she is Anu's first cousin, daughter of my father-in-law's oldest brother. In the ancestral long-ago, they had lived in the same Calcutta house, the *jethoo-bari,* part of a joint family numbering forty.

She is married to Pramod, and both are physicists. But instead of staying in the university world and settling down on some Big Ten campus, Pramod had taken a position in Holland, setting up a lab, and the Dutch government had recommended him for similar work in Indonesia and Surinam and before too many years, he had found himself sidetracked into sophisticated, high-level nuclear management, the protocols of which led, inevitably, to international agencies. He is now with the UN's nuclear-monitoring agency in Vienna, and Usha works as a researcher in physics for the University. They have been in Vienna for fifteen years, their children are European, they own an apartment in the city and a garden house in Wiener-Neustadt. It's a comfortable life in a country where immigration and assimilation as we know them are impossible.

We are all together this night in Vienna, enjoying a huge Bengali banquet, cooked from locally gathered fish and rice and vegetables, simmered in spices brought back from frequent trips to London and Bombay. My son and I have our Eurail passes, Anu will be with us only three days before going on to India to visit her mother and sister.

It's this life we lead, I silently explain to myself, and to the ghost of my mother. Vienna was another of her cities, briefly. The world has opened for us, no fears of the unknown. My mother shrank from the very idea of India, but tried to disguise it with images of Gandhi and respect for ancient wisdom.

How under-defined I feel, at fifty, compared to Pramod; a father who has written some books, who teaches when he must, who dabbles in cultures that have their hooks in him.

We are talking of Canada. 'They've become like the British,' Anu says, spooning out rice to our son. 'Hateful little people.'

The Sens had visited Niagara Falls last summer, and been turned away at the border for an afternoon's visit. For pleasure trips they use their Indian, not UN passports. 'He said things to us I wouldn't say to a servant,' says Usha Sen. '"How do I know you will leave when you say? How do I know you own a house as you say?" They are very suspicious about Indians, I must say.'

'I told him to go to hell,' says Jyoti, the Harvard boy. 'Who needs the hassle? The Austrians are bad enough, but I always thought Canadians were better.'

I remember when it wasn't so, in our cosmopolitan refuge of Montreal, when my mother and I lived like Alexandrians in a large apartment in Outremont after my father's death. We had original paintings on our walls, French-Canadian artists only. My father was an old man even in my earliest memories, a lawyer nearing retirement, then dead two months after achieving it. I remember the visits of his grown-up children from an earlier marriage, of being the same age as his grandchildren, and of wondering what, exactly, to call our relationship. My son and Jyoti are, precisely, second cousins. Usha is his first-cousin-once-removed. He calls her *mashi*, aunt.

'Have more rice, please. There is plenty.'

'Mother, this isn't Calcutta,' says Tapati, the MIT daughter. Everything this evening is exquisite. There is no cuisine in the world that excites me like Indian, no painting that thrills me like Moghul miniatures, no city, for better or worse, like Calcutta. After India, Europe is a bore. I'm staying back for my son's sake, his ancient dream of being European.

Anu is explaining our move to the States. 'To be Indian in Canada was to be a second-class citizen no matter how good you were, no matter how Canadian you tried to be. At least if we're second-class in the States we know it's because we're just second-rate.' I wish I could sink into the rice, the dimple-topped pyramids of snowy rice scooped out for fish and vegetables. I want to grab handfuls of rice and smear them over my head and rub them in my face. I want to do something vulgar and extravagant in this apartment of excellence, among these diligent and exquisite people, out of my own shame, the accumulated guilt and incomprehensions of my life.

Tapati is asking our son, 'Is there anything special you want to see in Vienna? I can take you there.'

They are amazed that for who he is and what he represents to them—America, after all, the place and people they most admire—he speaks only English. Usha's children have been raised in Europe, but with Indian ways. Each of them speaks eight languages, but they have no country. Jyoti writes rock lyrics in German, plays in an Austrian band, studies economics at Harvard. Tapati has a Ph.D. and an MBA and now interns at the World Bank. Both are in America, but not of it—too exquisite for the mall-culture America I know.

'Anything,' he says. 'It doesn't matter.'

'No, there must be something.'

He looks to me for help. He wants Europe, he wants saturation, a way of entering. He's been studying German in high school, but it's the last thing in the world he'll admit here to his second cousins. He doesn't trust himself to understand a single word. He's heard Bengali all his life, but never thought it part of himself. He spent half his life in a French-speaking city and did his French exercises perfectly, like history. It's the legacy of the New World. Jyoti has already told him, he'd trade it all—the languages, the sophistication that dazzles his Harvard friends—for a simple work permit, for the chance to stay and work the summer at Mr Spud.

'And what about you, Uncle?'

'Berggasse 19,' I say.

'The Freud house?' Usha asks. 'Why that—there's nothing there, believe me.'

'Wasn't he a coke-head?' my son asks in all seriousness, and the question sails over the heads of all but Jyoti, who smiles and nods. A conspiratorial friendship is starting to grow.

'Berggasse is very near my lab,' says Usha. 'We can take the tram there tomorrow. But it's not what you think—it's just a couple of rooms with photos on the walls.'

'Bor-ring,' Jyoti hums, as my boy suppresses a grin. We're there at eleven o'clock the next morning, my son and I, and Jyoti who's brought his guitar along. He'll do Freud with us, and we'll do the music shops with him. He's promised us a tour of the lowlife dives of Vienna, the coffee shops where the punks hang out, the places where he spent his high school years avoiding expectations to be good and dutiful.

The first cousins have gone out for a proper Viennese lunch, *Kaffeeschlag mit Sachertorte*. Nothing that has to do with the man who once compared the ego—rational and altruistic—to Europe, and the libido—rapacious and murderous—to Asia, inspires my wife to sympathy. A foolish little man, racist and chauvinist, with bad science to justify it.

It is a sunny, summer day, cool but bright, sweater weather. Children are playing on the sidewalk of Berggasse, outside the corner *Apotheke*. Jyoti says to us, 'Watch this—you think the Austrians know anything?' He asks the oldest boy, 'Do you know the Freud house?'

'Did they just move in?' he asks.

'Get that?' he laughs, turning to us. My son translates it.

'You could ask anyone on this street. Old, young, it doesn't matter. One group wants to forget, and the other one never knew.' We cross over the narrow street, looking for brass plates outside the formal doors. Number 19 is just a flat, as it always was, squeezed between other flats and offices.

Usha was right, it's only an old doctor's office cluttered with photos. The second cousins browse respectfully, faintly embarrassed by all the fuss. It's all Jyoti can do not to unzip his guitar case and start banging out something scandalous for the Freud Museum. I don't know what I expected to find.

This is the room where all of them came, I want to say. Princess Marie sat there. And the young Viennese Circle—see their pictures!—met here, in this room. In this room, someone challenged the incomprehensible with bad science and bad politics, in the name nevertheless of reason. The smallest facts had the deepest gravity, chance events were all connected, public events were the ritualized form of private projection.

Son! Are you listening?

Someone dared to say our dreams had a pattern, our dysfunctions a cause, our beliefs a pathology. On the walls, the Holy Roman Empire surrenders, and Freud stands on the dais, Vienna's most honoured, most famous citizen, as the Austrian Republic is declared. Here, Freud is welcoming the President of the Republic and his cabinet on the quarter-century anniversary of *The Interpretation of Dreams*. His birth cottage is decked with bunting.

And it chokes me, suddenly, the realization that science and music and literature can be so advanced, and do nothing to influence a political culture in its infancy. Austrian democracy was younger than Ghana's when the Nazis crushed it. I want to turn to my son and remind him of the great despairing poems I've read to him, of Yeats, of Auden, and the vast literature of the Holocaust that radiates from this room and a thousand others in this city, and echoes off these grey, sunny streets. The tradition, however faintly, I belong to. Poems about the imbalance of what we are capable of feeling and thinking, and what we have inflicted.

They've gone.

'They heard music outside,' the ticket-seller tells me. 'They said for you to follow the music.'

At first I hear nothing. I watch the children across the street, and the old women slogging their way from shop to shop, carrying groceries in string bags.

Berggasse slopes downward, and I follow it a block, half-imagining a rhythm, a few high notes and a beat in the air. Turn right, twist left. People are in the streets now, following something.

Up ahead in a small square at the rim of a fountain I can see them, clowns juggling, and a small crowd clustered. The performers wear top hats and putty noses, their cheeks are reddened, and one of the boys is darker than all the others, in a borrowed top hat, crouched on one knee like Chuck Berry, cutting in front of the clowns and drummers, leading everyone in lyrics I can't understand. And at the edge of the fountain is my boy in a borrowed vest and putty nose, punching a tambourine and doing a snake-dance on the fountain's edge.

THE SOCIOLOGY
OF LOVE

MONSTROUSLY tall girl from Stanford with bright yellow hair comes to the door and asks if I am willing to answer questions for her sociology class. She knows my name, 'Dr Vivek Waldekar?' and even folds her hands in a creditable *namaste*. She has researched me, she knows my job title and that I am an American citizen. She's wearing shorts and a midriff-baring T-shirt with a boastful logo. It reads, '*All This and Brains, Too*.' She reminds me of an American movie star whose name I don't recall, or the California Girl from an old song, as I had imagined her. I invite her in. I've never felt so much the South Asian man: fine-boned, almost dainty, and timid. My wife, Krithika, stares silently for several long moments, then puts tea water on.

Her name is Anya. She was born in Russia, she says. She has Russian features, as I understand them, a slight tilt to her cheeks but with light blue eyes and corn-yellow hair. When I walk behind her, I notice the top of an elaborate tattoo reaching up from underneath. She is a walking billboard of availability. She says she wants my advice, or my answers, as a successful South Asian immigrant on problems of adjustment and assimilation. She says that questions of accommodation to the US , especially to California, speak to her. And specifically South Asians, her honours project, since we lack the demographic residential densities of other Asians, or of Hispanics. We are sociological anomalies.

It is important to establish control early. It is true, I say, we do not swarm like bees in a hive. 'Why do you criticize us for living like Americans?' I ask, and she apologizes for the tone of her question. I press on. 'What is it we lack? Why do you people think there is something wrong with the way we live?'

She says, 'I never suggested anything was wrong—' She drops her eyes and reads from her notes.

'—That there's something defective in our lives?'

'Please, I'm so sorry.'

I have no handkerchief to offer.

Perhaps we have memories of overcrowded India, when everyone knew your business. I know where her question is headed: middle-class Indian immigrants do not build little Chinatowns or barrios because we are too arrogant, too materialist, and our caste and regional and religious and linguistic rivalries pull us in too many directions. She hangs her head even before asking the next question.

No, I say, there are no other South Asian families on my street. My next door neighbours are European, by which I mean non-specifically white. I correct myself. 'European' is an old word from my father's India, where even Americans could be European. Across the street are Chinese, behind us a Korean.

That's why I'm involved in sociology, she says, it's so exciting. Sociology alone can answer the big questions, like where are we headed and what is to become of us? I offer a counter-argument; perhaps computer science, or molecular biology, or astronomy, I say, might answer even larger questions. 'In the here and now,' she insists, 'there is only sociology.' She is too large to argue with. She apologizes for having taken my name from the internal directory of the software company I work for. She'd been an intern last summer in our San Francisco office.

I say I am flattered to be asked big questions, since most days I am steeped in micro-minutiae. Literally: nanotechnology. I can feel Krithika's eyes burning through me.

The following are my answers to her early questions: We have been in San Jose nearly eight years. I am an American citizen, which is the reason I feel safe answering questions that could be interpreted by more recent immigrants as intrusive. We have been married twenty years, with two children. Our daughter Pramila was born in Stanford University Hospital. Our son Jay was born in JJ Hospital, Bombay, seventeen years ago. When he was born I was already in California, finishing my degree and then finding a job and a house. My parents have passed away; I have an older brother, and several cousins in India, as well as Canada and the US. My graduate work took four years, during which time I did not see Krithika or my son. Jay and Krithika are still Indian citizens, although my wife holds the Green Card and works as a special assistant in Stanford Medical School Library. She will keep her Indian citizenship in the event of inheritance issues in India.

Do I feel my life is satisfactory, are the goals I set long ago being met? Anya is very persistent, and I have never been questioned by such a blue-eyed person. It is a form of hypnosis, I fear. I am satisfied with my life, most definitely. I can say with pride and perhaps a touch of vanity that we have preserved the best of India in our family. I have seen what this country can do, and I have fought it with every fibre of my being. I have not always been successful. The years are brief, and the forces of dissolution are strong.

Jay in particular is thriving. He has won two Junior Tennis Championships and maintains decent grades in a very demanding high school filled with the sons and daughters of computer engineers and Stanford professors. As a boy in Dadar, part of Bombay—sorry, Mumbai—I was much like him, except that my father could not offer access to top-flight tennis coaching. I lost a match to Sanjay Prabhakar, who went on to the Davis Cup. 'How will I be worthy?' I had asked my father before going in. 'You will never be worthy of Sanjay Prabhakar,' he said. 'It is your fate. You are good, but he is better and he will always be better. It is not a question of moral worth.' I sold my racquet that day and have never played another set of tennis, even though even now I know I could rise to the top of my club ranks. I might even be able to beat my son, but I worry what that might do to him. I was forced to concentrate on academic accomplishment. In addition, public courts and available equipment in India twenty-five years ago left much to be desired.

Do I have many American friends? Of course. My closest friend is Al Wong, a Stanford classmate, now working in Cupertino. We socialize with Al and Mitzie at least twice a month. She means white Americans. Like yourself? I ask, and she answers 'not quite.' She means two-three-generation white Americans. Such people exist on our street, of course, and in our office, and I am on friendly terms with all of them. I tell her I have never felt myself the victim of any racial incident, and she says, I didn't mean that. I mean instances of friendship, enduring bonds, non-professional alliances … you know, friendship. You mean hobbies? I ask. The Americans seem to have many hobbies I cannot fully appreciate. They follow the sports teams, they go fishing and sailing and skiing.

In perfect frankness, I do not always enjoy the company of white Americans. They mean well, but we do not communicate on the same level. I do not see their movies or listen to their music, and I have never voted. Jay skis, and surfs. Jay is very athletic, as I have mentioned; we go to Stanford tennis matches. I cannot say that I have been in many American houses, nor they in mine, although Jay's friends seem almost exclusively white. Jay is totally of this world. When I mention Stanford or Harvard, he says *Santa Cruz, pops.* He's not interested in a tennis scholarship. He says he won the state championship because the dude from Torrance kept double-faulting. Pramila's friends are very quiet and studious, mostly Chinese and Indian. She is twelve and concentrates only on her studies and ice-skating. I am not always comfortable in her presence. I do not always understand her, or feel that she respects us.

We will not encourage Pramila to date. In fact, we will not permit it until she is finished with college. Then we will select a suitable boy. It will be a drawn-out process, I fear, but we are progressive people in regard to caste and regional origins. A boy from a good family with a solid education is all we ask. If Pramila were not a genius, I would think her retarded. When she's not on the ice, she lurches and stumbles. Jay does not have a particular girlfriend. He says don't even think of arranging a marriage for me. Five thousand years of caste-submission will end here, on the shores of the Pacific Ocean.

'So, you and your son go to Stanford to watch Mike Mahulkar?'

'Mike?' I must have blinked. 'It is Mukesh,' I say. 'My son models his tennis game on Mukesh Mahulkar. Some day Mukesh will be a very great tennis player.' Neither my son nor I would ever be able to score a point off Mukesh Mahulkar.

My father has been dead nearly twenty years. I think he died from the strain of arranging my marriage. Krithika's parents never reconciled to my father's modest income. In my strongest memory of him, he was coming from his bath. It was the morning of my marriage. His hair was dark and wet. We will never be worthy, he said. A year later, I was sharing a house with Al Wong and two other Indian guys. Jay was born that same year, but I was not able to go back for the birth, or for my father's funeral services. Fortunately, I have an older brother. My father was Head Clerk in Maharashtra State Public Works Department. In his position, he received and passed on, or rejected, plans for large-scale building and reclamation projects. Anywhere in Asia, certainly anywhere in India in the past twenty years, such a position would generate mountains of black money. Men just like my father pose behind the façade of humble civil servant, living within modest salaries, dressed in kurta and pajama of rough khadi, with Bata sandals on their dusty feet. They would spend half an hour for lunch, sipping tea under a scruffy peepal. But in the cool hours of morning or evening, there would be meetings with shady figures and the exchange of pillow-thick bundles of stapled hundred-rupee notes. They would be pondering immense investments in apartment blocks and outlying farmhouses and purchasing baskets of gold to adorn their wives and daughters.

But Baba was one of the little folk of the great city, an honest man mired in universal graft. He went to office in white kurta. At lunch, he sat on a wall and ate street food from pushcart vendors and read his Marathi paper. He came home to a bath and prayer, dinner and bed. Projects he rejected got built anyway, with his superiors' approval. He was seen as an obstruction to progress, a dried-up cow wandering a city flyover. So we never got the car-and-driver, the club memberships and air-conditioning. He retired on even less than his gazetted salary, before the Arab money and Bombay boom.

I suddenly remember Qasim, the Muslim man whose lunch cart provided tea and cigarettes and fried foods to the MSPWD office-wallahs. My father and Qasim enjoyed a thirty-year friendship without ever learning the names of one another's children, or visiting each other's houses, or even neighbourhoods. Dadar and Mahim are different worlds. We never learned Qasim's last name. But whenever I dropped in on my father on lunch or tea breaks, I would hear him and Qasim engaged in furious discussions over politics, Pakistan, and fatherhood. Qasim had four wives and a dozen children, many of them the same age, all of them dressed in white, carrying trays of water and tea. Qasim and Baba were friends. To me, they are the very model of friendship. You might find it alien. You might not call it friendship at all. If, as rarely happened, Qasim did not appear on a given day, my father would ask a Muslim in the office to inquire after his health. Once or twice in a year, when my father took leave to attend a wedding, a strange boy would appear at our door, asking after Waldekar-sahib. I'm certain my father expressed more of a heartfelt nature to Qasim than he ever did to his wife, or to me. In that, I am my father's son.

'My father, too,' says the blue-eyed girl in the T-shirt. *All This and Brains, Too.* Suddenly, I understand its meaning, and I must have uttered a muted 'ahhh!' and blushed. Breasts, not height and blondness. I feel a deep shame for her. Krithika reads the same words, but shows no comprehension. I have a bumper sticker: *My Son Is Palos High School Student of the Month.* When I put it on, my wife said I was inviting the evil eye. For that reason, we have not permitted newspaper access to Pramila. We are simple people. Our children consume everything. To pay for tennis and ice-skating lessons takes up all our cash. I could have bought a Stradivarius violin with what I've spent. When Pramila was ten years old, after a summer spent in Stanford's Intensive Mathematics Workshop with the cream of the nation's high school seniors, she wrote a paper on the Topology of Imaginary Binaries. It is published in a mathematical journal, which we do not display. I do not mention it, ever.

'My father says that if he'd stayed in Russia and never left his government job, he would be sitting on a mountain of bribes. Over here, he started a Russian deli on Geary Boulevard.'

'You have made a very successful transition to this country,' I say. *All this.* 'I personally have great respect for the entrepreneurial model.'

She takes the compliment with a shy smile. 'Appearances can lie, Dr Waldekar,' she says.

Krithika brings out water and a plate of savouries.

I am of the Stanford generation that built the Internet out of their garages. I knew those boys. They invited me to join, but I was a young husband and father, although my family was still in India waiting to come over, and I had a good, beginning-level job with PacBell. I would be ashamed to beg start-up money from banks or strangers. My friends said, *well, we raised five million today, we're on our way!* And I'd think *you're twenty-five years old and five million dollars in debt? You're on your way to jail!* I have not been in debt a single day of my life, including the house mortgage. It all goes back to my father in frayed khadi, and three-rupee lunches under the dusty peepals.

'I notice an interesting response to my question,' she says. 'When I asked if you've fulfilled your goals, you mentioned only that your son is very successful. What about you, Dr Waldekar?'

Krithika breaks in, finally, 'We also have a daughter.'

'I was coming to that,' I say.

'She is enrolled in a graduate level mathematics course,' says Krithika.

'That's amazing!'

'She is the youngest person ever enrolled for credit in the history of Stanford. She is also a champion figure skater. My husband forgot to mention her, so I thought you might per-haps note that, if you have space.'

'I believe I mentioned she is very studious,' I say. Suddenly my wife forgets the evil eye.

Anya breaks off a bit of halwa.

I rise to turn off the central AC. The girl is underdressed for air conditioning, and I am disturbed by what I see happening with her breasts, under the boastful logo. They are standing out in points. Krithika returns to the kitchen.

'I am content, of course.' What else is there on this earth, I want to ask, than safeguarding the success of one's children? What of her father, the Russian deli owner? Is he happy? What is happiness for an immigrant but the accumulation of visible successes? He cannot be happy, seeing what has happened to his daughter. Does the Russian have friends? Does he barge into American houses? Do Americans swarm around his? Who are his heroes? Barry Bonds, Terrell Owens, Tiger Woods, Jerry Rice? We share time on the same planet; that is all. We will see how much the Americans love their sports heroes if any of them tries to buy a house on their street. Mukesh Mahulkar is big and strong and handsome and he is good in his studies and I'm sure his parents are proud of him and don't fear the evil eye. He'll play professional tennis and make a fortune and he won't spend it all on cars and mansions. He will invest wisely and he will be welcomed on any street in this country.

'My father works too hard. He's already had two heart attacks. My mother says he smokes like a fish. Drinks like a chimney. He dumps sour cream on everything. Everything in his mouth is salty, fatty meat, and more meat, and cream, and cheese and vodka. Forgive the outburst.'

'We are vegetarian. We do not drink strong spirits.'

'So's Mike. Veggie, I mean. He's teaching me.'

'You mean Mukesh, the tennis player?'

'His name is Mike. He's my boyfriend, Dr Waldekar.'

The ache I feel at the mention of a boyfriend is like the phantom pain from a lost limb. If I could even imagine a proper companion for this Russian girl, he would be as white and smooth as a Greek sculpture, built on the scale of Michelangelo's David. The thought that it is a Mumbai boy who runs his hands over her body, under those flimsy clothes, makes my fingers run cold.

'I might as well come out with it, Dr Waldekar,' she says. 'We've broken up. His parents hate my guts.'

Good for them, I think. Maybe you should dress like a proper young lady. I knew a Mahulkar boy in Dadar. I knew others in IIT, but no Mahulkars of my generation in the Bay

Area. So many have come. Given my early advantage, the opportunities I turned down, I am a comparative failure.

'This is my honours project, but . . . it's personal, too. I love India and Indians, I love the discipline of Indians. No group of immigrants has achieved so much, in so little time, with such ease and harmony. I love their pride and dignity. I even love it that they hate me. I can respect it.' She is smiling, but I don't know if I should smile with her and nod in agreement, or raise an objection. She might be a good sociologist, but there is much she is missing in the realm of psychology. So she goes on, and I don't interrupt.

'But what I don't love is that Mike won't stand up to them, for me. You know what his father said? He said *American girls are good for practice, until we find you a proper bride.* When Mike told me that, we laughed about it. I'm friendly with his sister and I said to her, *your game's a little rusty. Think you need some practice?* and we laughed and laughed. Mike said he'd show me Mumbai, and I said I'd take him to Moscow. He's twenty-two years old, but the minute his father said to stop seeing me, he stopped. One day we're playing tennis, or at the beach or he's cooking Indian vegetarian and I'm learning, and then, nothing. Nothing.' She lets herself go, drops her head into the basin of her hands, and sobs. It is a posture I, too, am familiar with. Krithika rushes in from the kitchen, stops, frowns, then goes back inside. I will be questioned later: what did I do, say, what didn't I do, didn't say? She will suspect some misbehaviour.

So, I think, Mahulkar has found a bride for his son. This is very good news. Who could it be? Why hadn't I heard that the famous Mukesh Mahulkar was getting married? It means there is hope for every Indian father with a son like mine.

'Please, take water,' I say. I would be tempted to hold her, or pat her back, but my arms might not reach. It would be awkward, and perhaps misinterpreted. Now that she has pitched forward, I see deep into her bosom; she has a butterfly tattoo on one breast, well below the separation line. A girl this big, and crying, in my living room, wearing such a T-shirt, has brought chaos from the street into our life.

'I'm so sorry,' she says. 'That was inexcusable. You must think I came under false pretenses. Mike's getting married in Mumbai in three weeks. It's very hard, to be told, without warning, without explanation, that you're just ... unworthy.'

She has a beautiful smile. It's as though she had not been crying at all, or knew no sadness, or had a Russian childhood and a father with a mouthful of meat and vodka. I will ask around and discover the bride's name.

I stand. 'I must ask you quietly to leave. I must pick up my daughter from practice. My son will be home soon.' I do not want her defiling my house, spreading her contagion into our sterile environment. She has no interest in successful immigrants, or in me. 'I have no special Bombay advice to offer.' When I open the door, my fingers brush the white flesh of her back, just above the tattoo. I don't think she even feels it. She says only, 'You have been very kind and hospitable. Please forgive me.'

I could not go home for my father's funeral. I did not see my son until he was four years old and had already bonded with my wife's family. I think he still treats me like an intruder. So does my wife. It has pained me all these years that I permitted my studies and other activities to take precedence over family obligations. I have been trying to atone for my indiscretions all these years.

In three of the four years I shared a house with Al Wong and the Mehta boy who went back and a Parsi boy who married an American girl and stayed, I remained steadfast to my research. I got a job at PacBell, where they immediately placed me in charge of a small research cell with people like myself, debt-free, security-minded team players. Suddenly, I had money. I bought a car and a small bungalow in Palo Alto, suitable for wife and child. No one in the group knew I was already married, and a father. We were all just in our twenties, starting out in the best place, in the best of times.

In my small group there was an American girl, a Berkeley graduate. Her name was Paula, called Polly. Pretty Polly, the boys liked to joke, which embarrassed her. On Fridays, our group would join with others for some sort of party. I would allow myself a beer or two, since carbonation lessened the taint of alcohol. Those sorts of restaurants made vegetarianism very difficult; I was admired for my discipline. Polly was naturally less restrained than I, especially after sharing a few pitchers of beer, a true California girl from someplace down south. Watching closely, I could gauge the moment when a quiet, studious girl, very reliable and hard-working, would ask for a cigarette, then go to the bathroom, come back to the table, and sit next to someone new. She sat next to me. One night she said, 'You're a very handsome man, Dr Waldekar.' No one had ever told me that, and to look fondly at one's reflection in a mirror is to invite the evil eye. 'Take me home,' she said. 'I don't know where you live,' I answered. She punched me on the arm. 'Ha, ha,' she said, 'funny, too.'

It's that transformation, not the flattery, that got to me. All week in the office, she was a flattened presence. She totally ignored me, and I, her. I imagined she was one of the good girls, living with her parents.

The passion that arises from workplace familiarity is hotter than hell. It *is* hell, because one must hide certain feelings, erase recurrent images, must put clothes back on a girl you've been with through the night. Above all, it must be secret. On Friday nights, she must not sit next to me. 'May I call you Vivek, Dr Waldekar?' she would ask. After the first time, I told myself it was the beer, but I knew it wasn't. The sexual acts that had resulted in the birth of my son back in India, a boy whose pictures I now had to hide, had seemed, in comparison to Polly, a continuation of tennis practice, slamming a ball against a wall and endlessly returning it. She took drugs, expensive drugs, and I was helpless to stop her, or complain.

'Go to her, if that will make you happy,' says Krithika. 'I know your secrets.'

'What foolishness.'

'You were staring at her. You shamed me. You behaved disgustingly.'

'If you were interested in the facts you would know I threw her out.'

'Remember,' she mumbles, 'I get half.'

I reach out for her, but she pulls away. This is the woman, the situation, I left Polly for. Eventually, I left PacBell because of her, which has worked out well for me. Polly left California because of me. Al Wong is the only person I confessed it to; I think he's mentioned it to Mitzie because of the ways she sometimes scrutinizes me. *What do you think of her, Vivek?* she'll ask me, as though I have a special interest in attractive women, instead of Al. Maybe she's mentioned it to Krithika. The promiscuous exchange of intimacies, which passes for friendship in America, is a dangerous thing. It is the sad nature of the terms of a marriage contract that the strongest evidence of commitment is also the admission of flagrant unfaithfulness.

One night fourteen years ago, I went up to SFO to meet Krithika and Jay who were arriving in my life after a thirty-hour flight from Bombay. I got there early and pressed myself close to the gate, but Sikhs from the Central Valley, rough fellows with large families and huge signboards, pushed me aside and called me names. It was a time of deep tensions between Hindus and Sikhs. If I had stood my ground, they threatened to stamp me into the floor. The Indian passengers poured through, fanning out in every direction, pushing carts stacked high with crates and boxes. Waiting families ducked under the barriers to join them, and I waited and waited, but no wife, no child. The terminal is always crowded, but the number of Indians diminished, to be replaced by Mexicans and Koreans. Perhaps she was having visa problems, I thought, or the bags had been lost.

After two hours, just as I'd decided to go back to my empty house, I heard my name on the public announcement. *Please pick up the courtesy phone, Vivek Waldeker.* Your wife wants you to know that since you were not here to meet them, she and her child have gone to a safe address provided by a fellow passenger, and she will contact you in the morning.

Two days later, I got that call. Perhaps you forgot you have a wife and son, she said. Perhaps you no longer remember me. She has remained on friendlier terms with that generous family who took her home on her first night in America than she ever has with me.

At four a.m. when the streets are dark and only the dogs are awake, the rattling of food carts begins. Barefoot men and boys dressed in white khadi push their carts heavy with oil, propane, and dozens of spiced tufts of chickpea batter ready for frying, all prepared during the night by wives and daughters. Each cart is lit by a naphtha lamp; each man fans out to his corner of the city near big office buildings, under his own laburnam, ashoka or peepal tree. Qasim died one morning as he pushed his cart through the streets of Mahim. His son Waqus appeared the next day, with his father's picture and a page of Urdu pasted to the cart's plastic shield. Even Hindus knew what it meant. My father took his retirement a month later—his superiors were truly sorry to see him go, since he was the obstruction that enriched everyone around him. He arranged my marriage, I received my Stanford scholarship and went to America, leaving a pregnant wife behind. After three years of bad health, Baba died. And I didn't attend the funeral services because I was trying to please an American girl who thought starting a fire in my father's body was too gross a sacrilege to contemplate.

IN HER PRIME

TIFFY HU and I are passing by the hedges behind the tennis courts, headed to skating practice, when a horrible truth strikes me: life is eternal. There's no escaping it, not even in death. I'm scuffling my shoes over the concrete slabs, over tufts of grass and weeds and the anthills and dried snail shells. Dogs do their business under the hedges. Flies drop their eggs.

Smudgy little birds perch on the fence and hop through the thorny branches.

'You coming, Prammy?'

'I'm thinking,' I say. What goes on in her little brain? It must be like the birds, hopping and chirping. Actually, I do know. It's scx, scx, scx.

A year ago, towards dusk, I was walking by this same place. A gray veil, like a frayed blanket, had moved up from the gutter and across the sidewalk. Birds were dive-bombing. As I got closer, the blanket dissolved into moving parts. Hundreds of mice, or maybe moles, were making a dash up from the sewers and across the naked sidewalk to their burrows under the hedge. It reminded me of a nature film, like wildebeest on their migration, attacked by crocodiles, or hatchling turtles pecked by seagulls.

We die and decompose. We never return and we will never sleep with virgins in a perfumed garden, or go to heaven or hell no matter what our sins or virtues, or drop into the airless nirvana my mother prays for. But this afternoon, the combination of birds and ants and tufts of grass makes me see that something of us does return. Our chemical shell is reabsorbed. It's as simple as the Law of Conservation of Matter. The elements keep going on, and on, and on and they recombine randomly, making birds and mice, grass and trees, and sometimes, even, every few thousands years I guess, a dog or a human being. Life is a default position. Wherever the promise of sustainability exists, something will find a way to inhabit it.

'Prammy?'

How many lives before I'm a self-conscious person again? There's no end to it until the sun quits, but then our elements are blasted into space and we drift in the dark for a few million years, like dandelion fluff, and our cells start splitting and a few billion years later we slither onto alien rocks in a galaxy far, far away. Without a gram of religious feeling in me, I'm suddenly a believer in eternal life. This is seriously weird.

The ice surface is a polished pearl, and I start by laying down a long, lazy sum, the $\int$ from the Calculus, running the length of the rink, edge to edge. It's my signature: Pramila Waldekar was here. Nothing is hard if it can be reduced to numbers and everything, sooner or later, is just numbers. So long as I do my spins and axels inside the sum, I'll be safe. Today he's going to be hard on me, maybe because Tiffy is with me. 'My Gods, you are not Aeroflot taking off from SFO, you are artist. You must rise from nuthink. From ice. All rise coiled inside.'

And I wonder if there is not a coefficient that includes speed, drag, and vertical lift. It's a matter of directing energy.

Poor Borya thinks it's an invocation to the ʃ-hole on the top of a violin, a subtle dedication to his marvelous self. Back in Minsk, he played the cello. Sometimes he plays for me.

People are prime numbers, or they're not. The Beast is eighteen, which factors to 3x3x2, a perfect expression of his mental age. I'm thirteen: prime. Tiffy Hu is twelve, 3x2x2: what more to say? Borya is thirty-seven: prime. We are irreducible. Borya hasn't been prime since he was thirty-one and he won't be prime again till he's forty-one. What will I be like in my next prime, at seventeen? A fat cow, says Borya. A woman is never stronger than she is at twelve or thirteen. We are designed for our maximum speed and strength, before the distraction of breasts and hips. He only takes on girls between eight and ten; after that their contours change, their centres of gravity, their strength. That's Borya's philosophy, and I endorse it.

He also says a thirteen-year-old woman will never be more desirable. It's a Russian thing, maybe. I've read *Lolita*. On a normal practice day, after skating, we drive to his place in Palo Alto and do it in his basement apartment, in the house of Madame Skojewska. Madame is the widow of Marius Skojewski, a Slavic Studies professor at Stanford. Borya says Polish ladies are 'very tender, very sophisticated. Russian people very narrow, very brutal.' In order to explain my comings-and-goings in Palo Alto, I asked Daddy to pay for Russian lessons, which he was happy to do.

Borya was surprised I wasn't a virgin. No girl with a brother like The Beast can be a virgin. No one watching us at the rink, listening to Borya's berating, his picking apart of my motivation, my technique, my discipline, would think us anything but bashful student and demanding teacher. With Tiffy Hu watching and waiting her turn, it's only skate, skate, skate:

leap and twist and turn and spin, work up a sweat and then take her home with me for dinner.

The Beast is in. 'Tiffy Hu!' he shouts, charming as always. 'Hu's on first?' Tiffy doesn't get it. 'Or should I be asking, who's first on Hu?'

'Ignore him,' I tell her. 'How's your Russian?' I ask. It's a test. If he suspected anything about Borya and me, he'd ask, *how's yours?*

He's got a Russian secret-girlfriend, a big golden Stanford sophomore goddess, too good for his sorry UC-Santa Cruz freshman ass. I'm starting at Stanford next year, skipping the entire, doubtless illuminating, American high-school experience. I'll be the youngest they've ever admitted. I'll be thirteen years, ten months.

The Golden Goddess used to go with the big Stanford tennis player, Mike (that is, Mukesh) Mahulkar. The Beast used to be his lob-and-volley partner. The Beast was a decent high-school player—he even won the state finals. Golden Goddess would spread a towel on the grass and watch them slug it out. Those long, golden legs, those skimpy tops—I could see The Beast was a little distracted. Then suddenly Mike and GG were no longer a couple—Mike's parents said she was just another practice-partner—and Mike was engaged to a proper caste-and-class appropriate Bombay cutie. The Beast, just a senior in high school, started hanging out with GG. Our parents would have nailed his door shut if they'd known. At least it left me free to explore other options.

My father and The Beast think Mike Mahulkar is going to be the next Big Name in international tennis. No way, I say. I charted two of Mike's games. He's totally predictable. Backhand, forehand, lob, rush the net. So many balls to the net, so many deep volleys, side to side, in a sequence even Mike doesn't know is mathematically predictable. You can lure him to the net and set him up for a passing shot. Of course The Beast can't, and so far no one in the amateur and college ranks can, but some Swede or Russian will humiliate him. I showed The Beast my pages of calculations. 'Even you can beat him,' I said. 'Here's the probabalistic algorithm for beating Mike Mahulkar,' and he said to me, 'just go back to the ice.'

The Beast thinks the only difference between him and Mike is Mike's superior coaching and Stanford's weight room and flexibility training. Since we didn't have our own gym and staff of coaches, he doesn't stand a chance against the famous Mike Mahulkar. So Mike is strong and determined, but just forget that his game is boring and he'll meet someone out there who matches him in strength and sees into his game and sends him spinning back to country club status and an eventual MBA.

We sit in silence around the dinner table. We always sit in silence. I cannot remember a time when anyone spoke. We're not like Americans, grabbing a bite here and there, stuffing ourselves with processed foods, injecting our flaccid bodies with empty calories in front of a television feeding us empty images. Therefore we are better than Americans with beef blood dripping from their fangs.

We never miss a meal. We are family. We are Indian. We are vegetarian. Every meal is a small production. Chop-chop, spice and dice, then fry, always fry. Even our bread and desserts are fried. Our walls glisten from airborne globules. My forehead glows. We sweat it. We practically bathe in vegetable oil. Our lifetime vegetable oil consumption, expressed as a function of water-use, is rising.

Of course I am the only true American in the family. The Beast was born in Bombay. He conveniently forgets this fact. I have my sliced red pepper, celery and carrots. Tiffy is scarfing down on the fried food.

She breaks the silence. 'This is really good!' and my mother is pleased. This is the daughter she should have had.

'All we get at home is greasy soup with noodles and pieces of vegetables swimming around in it.'

I could say all we get is the same stuff, chopped and fried in the same spices, every day for all eternity. I stopped last year. His Lordship is drinking a beer. The Beast has a Coke; Tiff, Her Ladyship and I have iced tea.

'Chinese food is very good. I have many Chinese friends,' says His Lordship. So far as I know, all he has is Al Wong, his friend since graduate school, and Al and Mitzi come over once a month and they go to Al and Mitzi's once a month, and they play bridge.

'Chinese food very healthy,' says my mother.

'Especially deep-fried egg roll,' says The Beast. *Don't say it*, I pray, but out it comes: 'I mean egg loll and fly-lice.' He never disappoints. Tiff doesn't get it.

'Chinese people are like Indian people,' His Lordship explains. 'Very loyal to family. Children very loyal to parents, parents very protective of their children.'

Tiff looks to me for help. 'I never thought of that,' she says.

'I think we're very Greek, actually,' I say.

Mother says, 'Greek people eat meat wrapped in leaves.'

'Greek myths,' I say.

'What myths?' His Lordship weighs in. 'All European myths are comic book versions of Indian myths.'

'I was thinking of Atreus,' I say, to deafening silence.

On the walk back, Tiff asks, 'What's that Atreus thing you said?' Just the usual incest and slaughter, I answer. Gross, says Tiff. Then she says, 'your dad and Al Wong actually rented a house in Palo Alto? Lots of hot action, I'll bet.' Among Chinese, Al Wong is a little bit famous.

But she doesn't know my father. My father and hot action—in the linguistic interstices, all things are possible, I guess. And the third guy, a Parsi, went back to India. But then she says,

'You won't get mad if I ask a personal question?' My life is nothing but very personal secrets. 'Go ahead,' I say.

'You and Borya, you're getting it on, aren't you?'

'Getting it on? What does that mean, exactly?'

'I don't care if you are or if you aren't. I was wondering about, you know, his thing. How big is it?'

'Big, meaning long, or wide, or what? It's a meaningless question, Tiff. Big as a function of his pinky finger? Big as a function of his arm?'

'Forget about it,' she says. And I wonder if she already knows that she's next. And Tanya Ping is lined up, just after her. 'Just, what's sex like?'

It's like a puppy of some rough, large breed that just keeps jumping up and licking your face. It's shaped like a candle, without a wick. Of course, Borya's Jewish, so the shape's a little off. 'It makes you sleepy,' I say and Tiff nods, 'that's what I thought.'

347

Maja Skojewska was Maja Pinska. 'I grew up in a very liberal Jewish family,' she told me, in our informal Russian 'classes', and when I'm her age I'll probably be saying, 'I grew up in a Hindu family.' Madame's idea of Russian lessons is to talk of her life, in Russian, interjecting Polish and English and before too many weeks she says, 'See? You just asked me that in Russian!'

Her father was a schoolteacher, a great admirer of India. That's why she and her sister, Uma, have Indian names. When the Germans came to the school to get him, the priest said, we already turned him over. And there he was all along, working in the same school, only sooty black from shoveling coal. The Germans couldn't imagine a Jew working like a Pole, dirtying his hands like a Pole. Her husband-to-be was also a school-teacher, a Polish Catholic (not to be redundant) but after the war he went to university, then to Moscow State for more study and after two books, he was invited to Oxford, and that's when they made their escape. The idea that little Maja Pinska would be eighty years old and tending her garden in California is testimony, she says, to a kind of stubborn life force.

On her table are bananas so unblemished that I thought they were wax. 'That's the first thing I noticed when we got to England,' she says. Bananas! And the thrill of peeling a banana has never left her, after fifty years. And we sit a few minutes in silence, and she leans towards me and says (I'm sure it's in Russian, but it's as clear to me as English), 'You know, Borya will drop you.'

'I know,' I say.

'I don't approve of what he does, but then I say, it's better you learn from him than from these boys I see on the streets.'

'Yes,' I say.

Sometimes I think of Madame's life, and mine, and that it's all a kind of trigonometry of history. Her life is a skyscraper, mine is just a thimbleful of ashes, but our angles are the same. My adjacent side is just a squiggle, and my opposite side barely rises above the horizon. But the angle is there. I feel that I can achieve monumental things if I can just live long enough.

Even with all his money, it took Al and Mitzi fifteen years to leave their cottage in Cupertino and splurge on a twenty-third-floor apartment in downtown San Francisco. It's all glass, 360° panoramic views of the city, the Bay, the bridges, the Marin Headlands, Berkeley and Oakland. No interior walls, but for the bathroom and two bedrooms. They also have a country estate in Napa. Some evenings when the fog rolls in, we're suspended in a dream, disrupted only by bridge-table small talk. Other nights, the city sparkles. Al pours me a small glass of plum wine. Tonight, my father complains of his job. He's in nanotechnology, and his responsibilities are shrinking fast.

'Have you thought about something new?' Al asks. 'I mean really new.'

'Yes, I have,' His Lordship responds. It's the first time I've ever heard such a thing. He always defends continuity. His father spent forty years in Maharashtra State Government service. What really new thing could he possibly do?

Every now and then, when Mitzi and Her Ladyship are out of the room, Al Wong will say, 'What do you hear from our old friend?' He's got a needle, and he uses it. I can tell it's a jab to my father's self-esteem, but I don't know what it means. I think there's a lot of sado-masochism, not nostalgia, in their friendship. Sometimes it's good to be a quiet, studious, Indian daughter; I'm just furniture. Except for Borya and Madame, I'm accustomed to being ignored.

Most of the time, they just sit and complain, drink some wine and play their bridge. After half a glass, my mother will say, 'What was the bid? I'm feeling so light-headed!' Al and my father were in grad school together and started out at PacBell together, and my father's still there. Al decided to go entrepreneur, and bought a computer franchise. He sold that at just the right time and bought and sold a few more things at their peak, and then he bought a hotel in Napa. He built it up with spas and a gourmet restaurant and hiking trails, and then he opened a winery: *AW Estates*. The hotel is where young Bay-Area Chinese professionals want to get married, or at least honeymoon or go on weekend getaways. He says there are so many young Bay-Area Asians at his hotel that it's like a second Google campus. *AW Estates* pinot is what young Chinese professionals drink. He's even got a line of plum wine for the older folks, and a girl like me. Every thing he touches turns to gold.

I don't know how it started, but tonight there's an edge, an identifiable complaint, coming from my father. 'I've been thinking,' he starts, and he leans forward, perhaps aware that I'm sitting ten feet away. 'I'm thinking my children disrespect me.'

That's the news? Al says, 'Mitzi and I never wanted children.' Once they made that decision, she went to law school and now she's a major litigator.

'I blame this country,' says my father.

'It's in the culture,' says Al. He came from Hong Kong. 'We can't live their lives.'

'I believe my son is dating a person without my permission. I believe he is involved with a most inappropriate young lady.'

That's when Al says, maybe to break up the seriousness, 'By the way, guess who's back from the East? Now she's an accountant. I've hired her to do my books.'

And then, just from His Lordship's grimace, it all makes sense. There *was* someone in those days of hot action in Palo Alto. Tiffy Hu smelled it out, and I've spent thirteen years in a fog. It's so exciting, so unexpected, I want to jump up and pump my fist.

'I think . . .' my father says, then pauses, 'I think that we must leave this country.'

If furniture could speak, it would shout, 'What?!'

'Hey, man, that's an extreme reaction,' says Al.

'I'm not talking of that one. I have been a bad father. Things have been going on under my nose, outside my control. Asian children should never be allowed to stay in this country past their childhood. I may have already lost my son, but I can still protect my daughter. If I can save one from shame and humiliation I will at least have done half my job.'

I clear my throat. 'May I speak?'

His Lordship stares across the living room, as though an alarm clock he'd set and forgotten about had just gone off. Truly, I am invisible to him. 'Pardon me, but that train has left the station.'

'We're not talking of trains,' he snaps.

'Okay. That horse has left the barn.'

I never thought I would, under any circumstance, defend my brother. His Lordship, says, 'Kindly keep your opinions to yourself. You are not part of this conversation. This is about your brother.'

I'm up against something that is irrational. I can't argue against it. 'No, it's not! It's not about him. That genie is out of the bottle. It's about me, isn't it?'

Al Wong passes his hand between my father's frozen gaze, and me. 'Vivek,' he says, 'she has a point.'

Some day I want to ask Al Wong, what was it that happened in that house in Palo Alto? What caused my father to cast a lifelong shadow on this family?

'Go to your mother,' my father says.

I don't go directly to my mother. My fate in this family is, as they say, fungible. I approach the sofa where His Lordship is seated. 'Let me say one more thing. If you try to make me go back to India and if you stop me from going to Stanford and you try to arrange a marriage with some dusty little file clerk, I'll kill myself.'

Things have been frosty these past few days. The Beast is back in Santa Cruz. While I'm at work on my AP History, and my parents are watching a rented Bollywood musical, the phone rings and my father picks it up, frowns, then holds it out towards me. 'It's your teacher,' he says, and I expect a message from school, maybe an unearned day off, but it's Borya. He says, 'Madame is asking for you.'

I tell him I have no way of getting there. And why would she be asking for me?

'I am driving,' he says, an amazing concession. He is not a hop-in-the-car Californian. He's a skater, not a driver. I didn't even know he had a license.

Normally, I would never ask to leave the house after dark, but when I say, 'Madame Skojewska is asking to see me. Mr

Borisov will pick me up,' my father barely lifts his eyes from the television.

'Where will you be?' he asks.

I write down Madame's address and phone number. They don't know that Borya lives in her basement.

I recognize the car as Madame's, usually parked and dusty in her garage. She revs the engine once a week. It's been over a year since she bought a gallon. 'A gallon a year, if I need it or not,' she joked.

Borya starts out in English, 'We go to Stanford Hospital. Madame has . . .' he strikes his chest, 'heart.' Stanford Hospital is where I was born, but this doesn't seem a commemorative moment. And then, it must have occurred to him that we are not at the ice rink and that no one is watching, and that my months of Russian instruction permits adult interaction; he grabs my hand, kisses it, and says, 'you know how she loves her bananas. She walked down to Real Foods, bought two bunches, and on her walk back home she suddenly collapsed.'

When we arrive at the hospital, he says 'They said she was going, tonight.'

She's in the ICU, under a plastic tent. It reminds me of the flaps on baby strollers, the plastic visors, the baby warm, secure and sleeping while rain is pelting. Just like that, sweet mystery of life and death. One day we were chatting like old friends, *See, you just asked me that in Russian!* and I felt I belonged in a time and place I'll never see, *I've never had a student like you, you sit so quietly, you don't repeat words, you don't ask why we say it the way we do—you just start speaking it like a native, like someone reborn.*

A student like me is accustomed to praise from her teachers. But that's not the point; the point is, I impressed *her* and she's the only teacher I'm likely to remember. I remember years of teachers' meetings, standing alone at the edge of the classroom while a teacher pulls my parents aside. I see her gesturing, and my parents shaking their heads. *What did she say about me?* I ask when we're back home and my mother says, *Some nonsense,* and my father says *You have a good head, but you are prone to dreaming and you must work harder, or you will fail.* I know it's about the evil eye; I might accidentally hear some praise that will turn my head from proper feminine modesty.

'You know what she said about you, even today? Even this morning when she was headed out to buy her bananas? She said, "Borya, living long enough to teach that girl Russian is the greatest privilege of my life."'

We stand behind the glass and it seems that Madame's eyes are open, and shining. I raise my hand and flutter my fingers; it's all I can do. *Do svidaniya, Madame.*

I think I know what it was, back in that rented house in Palo Alto when my father and Al Wong and the Parsi guy were Stanford students and my mother and the baby Beast were still in India. Al knows, Mitzi knows, my mother knows. He wants to go back to India because someone from his past, a woman perhaps, has suddenly come back. Some long shadow of shame has shaped our lives. It's about him, not me, though I'm the one who will pay the price.

When Madame died, I started thinking of other teachers.

When I was very young—five, I'd guess, in pre-school—I discovered algebra. First, it was the word itself, it tasted good in the mouth, like something to eat or drink. Fortunately, I had a teacher, 'Miss Zinny' we called her (I think her good name was Zainab, and we were the only two South Asians in that class), who didn't laugh when I asked her what algebra was. The next day she brought her college math book and we spent my naptime working out the problems. I remember the excitement, the *freedom* in a phrase like 'Let p stand for . . .' or a declaration like 'Let $a=c+1$.' Solve for the value of c. The consolation of algebra; everything is equal to something else. It was something I couldn't explain, but it's what I felt a few years later when I learned about imaginary numbers. It's about seeing the nine-tenths of the iceberg, and not being afraid. What I remember is the equals sign. Everything in the world can be assigned a value, and has an equivalent. I went home and told my mother, 'Let P stand for potato. Let R be rice.'

'Then wash the rice, please,' she said.

DEAR ABHI

WATCHED HIM this morning juicing a grapefruit, guava, blood orange, mango, plums and grapes and pouring the elixir into a giant glass pitcher. Beads of condensation rolled down the sides, like an ad for California freshness. *Chhoto kaku*, my late father's youngest brother, is vegetarian; the warring juices are the equivialent of eggs and bacon, buttered toast and coffee. He will take tea and toast, but never coffee, which is known to inflame the passions. Life, or the vagaries of the Calcutta marriage market, did not bless him with a wife. Arousal, he believed, would be wasted on him and he has taken traditional measures against it.

Ten years ago this was all farmland, but for the big house and the shingled cottage behind it. No lights spill from the cottage, yet *Chhoto kaku* makes his way across the rocks and cacti to her door. *Don't go*, I breathe, but the door opens. Devorah was alone last night. Usually she comes out around eight o'clock with a mug of coffee and a cigarette, sometimes joined by one of her stay-overs. On our first visit she produced a tray of wild boar sausage that a friend had slaughtered, spiced, cooked and cased, after shooting.

Her hair changes colour. I've seen it green and purple. Today, there are no Mercedes or motorcycles in the yard, she was alone last night. She wears blue jeans and blue work shirts and she smells richly resinous, reminding me of mangoes. Her normal hair is loose and graying.

She told me the day after we'd moved in, 'your uncle is a hoot.' She calls me Abby, my uncle, Bushy. His name is Kishore Bhushan Ganguly. We call her Devvie, which in our language approximates the word for goddess. 'He looked at my paintings and he said, "you have the eyes of god." Isn't that the sweetest thing?' I count myself a man of science, so I must rely on microscopes and telescopes and X-rays to glimpse the world beyond. 'He said I see the full range of existence. He said, "I tremble before you." Isn't that beautiful?'

When I reported her assessment, Uncle said, 'I think she is an advanced soul.' I asked how he knew. 'She offered me a plate of cold meats. I told her meats inflame the passions.' Youngest Uncle is a Brahmin of the old school. 'So, she's giving up meats, is that it?' I asked. He said, 'I believe so. She said, "maybe that is my problem."'

Six months he's been with me, my cherished Youngest Uncle, the bachelor who put me and two cousins through college, married off my sisters and cousins with handsome dowries and set up their husbands, the scoundrels, in business. He delayed, and finally abandoned all hopes of marriage for himself.

When he was an engineer rising through the civil service, then in industry, there'd been the hope of marriage to a neighbour's daughter—beautiful, smart, good family from the right caste and even subcaste. Her father had proposed it and even Oldest Uncle, who approved or vetoed all marriages in the family, declared himself, for once, unopposed. Preparations were started, horoscopes exchanged, a wedding house rented. Her name was Nirmala.

I came home from school one day in my short pants, looking for a servant to make me a glass of fresh lime soda and finding, unimaginably, no one in the kitchen. The servants were all clustered in Oldest Auntie's room joining in the loud lamenting of other pishis and older girl-cousins. I squeezed my own limes then stood on a chair and from the kitchen across a hallway open to the skies, I had a good view into Youngest Uncle's room. He was in tears. He had been betrayed. In those years he was a handsome man in his middle thirties, about my age now, with long, lustrous hair and a thin, clipped moustache. Older Uncle had voided the engagement.

Something unsavoury in Nirmala's background had been detected. I heard the word 'mishap.' Perhaps our family had given her the once-over and found her a little dull, flat chested or older than advertised, or with a lesser dowry. It could have meant a misalignment in the stars, a rumour of non-virginity or suspicion of feeble mindedness somewhere in her family. Or Nirmala might have caught a glimpse of her intended husband and found him too old, too lacking in sex appeal. Every family can relate a similar tale. A promising proposal not taken to its completion is an early sign of the world's duplicity. My parents who married for love and never heard the end of it, did not call it duplicity. They called it not striking while the iron is hot, an image in English I always had difficulty picturing.

In time 'Nirmala' stood as a kind of symbol of treacherous beauty. In this case, the rumours bore out. She had a boy on the side, from an unsuitable community. They made a love match, disgracing the name of her good family and rendering her younger sisters unmarriageable to suitable boys. They had two boys before she was eighteen. The sisters scattered to Canada and Australia and had to marry white men. A few years later, Nirmala divorced, and once, I'm told (I had already left for California), she showed up at Youngest Uncle's door, offering her body, begging for money. Proof, as my mother would say, that whatever God decides is for the best. God wished that Youngest Uncle would become middle-aged in the service of lesser-employed brothers and their extended families and that he not spend his sizeable income on a strange woman when it could be squandered on his family instead.

You will see from this I am talking of the not-so-long ago Calcutta, and surmise that I am living, or more properly, was living until a few months ago—with my wife, Sonali, our sons, Vikram and Pramod—in the Silicon Valley and that my uncle is with us. You would be half right. My wife kicked me out six months ago. Not so long in calendar days, but in psychological time, eons.

My Christmas bonus eighteen months ago was $250,000. In Indian terms, two and half lakhs of dollars; multiply by forty, a low bank rate, and you come up with ten million rupees: one crore. My father, a middle-class clerk, never made more than two thousand rupees a month and that was only towards the end of his life when the rupee had started to melt. What does it do to a Ballygunge boy, a St. Xavier's boy, to be confronted in half a lifetime with such inflation of expectation, such expansion of the stage upon which we strut and fret? Sonali planned to use the bonus to start a preschool. She was born in California and rarely visits Calcutta, which depresses her. Her parents, retired doctors who were born on the same street as I, live in San Diego.

There are three dozen Indian families in our immediate circle of friends, all of them with children, all of whom share a suspicion that their children's American educational experiences will not replicate the hunger for knowledge and rejection of mediocrity that we knew in less hospitable Indian schools. They would therefore pay anything to replicate some of that nostalgic anxiety, but not the deprivation. She could start a school. Sonali is a fine Montessori teacher. Many of the wives of our friends are teachers. Many of my friends would volunteer to tutor or teach a class. We would have a computer-literate school to do Sunnyvale proud. She spoke to me nightly of dangerous and deprived East Palo Alto where needs are great and the rents are cheap.

If I stay in this country we would have to do it, or something like it. It is a way of recycling good fortune and being part of this model community I've been elected to because of the responsible way I conduct my life. You name it—family values, religious observation, savings, education, voting, tax-paying, PTA, soccer-coaching, nature-hiking, school boards, mowing my lawn, keeping a garden, contributing to charities—I've done it. And in the office: designing, programming, helping the export market and developing patents—I've done that, too. America is a demonstrably better place for my presence. My undistinguished house, bought on a downside market for a mere $675,000 cash, quadrupled in value in the past five years—or more precisely, four of the past five years. It is inconceivable that anything I would do not be a credit to my national origin, my present country and my religious creed.

When something is missing it's not exactly easy to place it. I have given this some thought—I think it is called 'evidence of things unseen.' Despite external signs of satisfaction, good health, a challenging job, the love and support of family and friends, no depressions or mood swings, no bad habits, I would not call myself happy. I am well-adjusted. We are all extremely well-adjusted. I believe my situation is not uncommon among successful immigrants of my age and background.

I went alone to Calcutta for two weeks, just after the bonus. Sonali didn't go. She took the boys and two of their school friends skiing in Tahoe. She has won medals for her skiing. I am grateful for all those comforts and luxuries but had been feeling unworthy of late. It was Youngest Uncle who had paid for the rigorous Calcutta schools and then for St. Xavier's and that preparation got me the scholarships to IIT and later to Berkeley, but I lacked a graceful way of thanking him. The bonus check was in my wallet. I would be in Calcutta with a crore of rupees in my figurative pocket. I, Abhishek Ganguly of Ballygunge.

Chhoto kaku is now sixty-seven, ten years retired from his post of chemical engineer. The provident funds he'd contributed to for forty years are secure. One need not feel financial concern for Youngest Uncle, at least in a rupee zone. He has no legal dependents. Everyone into the remotest hinterland of consanguinity has been married. He was living with his two widowed sisters-in-law and their two daughters plus husbands and children in our old Calcutta house. The rent has not been substantially raised since Partition when we arrived from what was then East Bengal and soon to become East Pakistan, then Bangladesh. *Chhoto kaku* was then a boy of eleven. I believe the rent is about fifteen dollars a month, which is reflected in the broken amenities. A man on a bicycle collects the rent on the first of every month. They say he is the landlord's nephew, but the nephew is a frail gentleman of seventy years.

It is strange how one adjusts to the street noise and insects, the power cuts, the Indian-style bathroom, the dust and noise and the single tube of neon light in the living room which casts all nighttime conversations into a harsh pallor and reduces the interior world to an ashen palette of grays and blues. Only for a minute or two do I register Sunnyvale, the mountains, the flowers and garden, the cool breeze, the paintings and rugs and comfortable furniture. And my god, the appliances: our own tandoori oven and a convection oven, the instant hot-tea spout, ice water in the refrigerator door, the tiles imported from Portugal for the floor and countertops. Sonali is an inspired renovator. You would think it was us, the Gangulys of Sunnyvale, who were the long-established and landowning aristocracy and not my uncle who has lived in his single room in that dingy house for longer than I've been on earth.

Youngest Uncle is a small man, moustached, the lustrous long hair nearly gone, fair as we Bengalis go, blessed with good health and a deep voice much admired for singing and for prayer services. He could have acted, or sung professionally. There was talk of sending him to Cambridge in those heady post-Independence years when England was offering scholarships to identify the likely leaders of its newly liberated possessions. Many of his classmates went, stayed on, and married English girls. He remained in India, citing the needs of his nieces and nephews and aged parents.

The tragedy of his life, if the word is applicable, was having been the last born in the family. He could not marry before his older siblings and they needed his unfettered income to secure their matches. And if he married for his own pleasure the motive would have appeared lascivious. This, he would never do. My father, that striker of, or with, hot irons, had been the only family member to counsel personal happiness over ancestral duty. He called his sisters and other brothers bloodsuckers. When my parents married just after Independence under the spell of Gandhian idealism, they almost regretted the accident that had made their brave and impulsive marriage also appear suitable as to caste and sub-caste. My father would have married a sudra, he said; my mother, a Christian, Parsi, Sikh, or maybe even a Muslim, under proper conditions.

I am always extravagant with gifts for Youngest Uncle. He has all the high-tech goodies my company makes: an email connection and a lightning-fast modem though he never uses it, a cellphone, a scanner, a laser printer, copier, colour television, various tape recorders and stereos. The room cannot accommodate him, electronically speaking, with its single burdened outlet. But the gifts are still in their boxes, carefully dusted, waiting to be given to various grandnephews still in elementary school. He keeps only the Walkman, on which he plays classic devotional ragas. He's making his spiritual retreat to Varanasi electronically.

I touched his feet in the traditional *pronam*. He touched my shoulder, partially to deflect my gesture, partially to acknowledge it. It is a touch I miss in the States, never giving it and never expecting to receive it. It is a sign that I am home and understood.

'So, *Chhoto kaku,* what's new?' I asked, the invitation for Youngest Uncle to speak about the relatives, the dozens-swollen-to-hundreds of Gangulys who now live in every part of India, and increasingly, the world.

'In Calcutta, nothing is ever new,' he said. 'In interest of saving money, Rina and her husband, Gautam, are here ...' Rina is the youngest daughter of his next older sister. Thanks to Youngest Uncle's dowry, Rina had got married during the year and brought Gautam to live in her house, an unusual occurrence, although nothing is as it was in India, even in polite, conservative, what used to be called *bhadralok*, Bengali society.

'Where do they stay, uncle?'

'In this room.'

There are no other spare rooms. It is a small house.

'They are waiting for me to die. They expect me to move in with Sukhla-pishi.'

That would be his oldest sister-in-law, the one we call Front Room Auntie for her position at the window that overlooks the street. She is over eighty. Nothing happens on Rash Behari Avenue that she doesn't know. The rumour, deriving from those first post-Partition years, is she had driven *Anil-kaku,* her young husband, my oldest uncle, mad. He'd died of something suspicious which was officially a burst appendix. Something burst, that is true. Disappointment, rage, failure of his schemes, who can say? It is Calcutta. He was a civil engineer and had been offered a position outside of Ballygunge in a different part of the city, but rather than leave the house and neighbourhood, Sukhla-pishi had taken to her bed in order to die. (I should add that modern science sheds much light on intractable behavior. Sukhla-pishi is obviously agoraphobic; a pill would save us all much heartache.) *Anil-kaku* turned down the job and she climbed out of bed and took her seat on the windowsill. All of that happened before I was born. There had been no children—they were then in their middle-twenties—so she became the first of Youngest Uncles' lifelong obligations.

'This is your house, uncle,' I said. 'Don't be giving up your rights.' As if he hadn't already surrendered everything.

'Rights were given long ago. Her mother holds the lease.'

I should say a few words about my cousin-sister Rina. She is most unfortunate to look at, or to be around. I was astonished that she'd found any boy to marry, thinking anyone so foolish would be like her, a flawed appendage to a decent family. We'd been most pleasantly wrong. He was handsome, which goes a long way in our society, a dashing, athletic flight steward with one of the new private airlines that fly between Calcutta and the interior of eastern India. We understood he was in management training. Part of the pre-marriage negotiation was the best room in the house, that would allow him to pocket his housing allowance from the airline while subletting the company flat, and his own car, computer, television, stereo, printer and tape recorder. He'd scouted the room before marriage since the demands were not only generic, but included brand names and serial numbers.

'I cannot say more, they are listening,' said my uncle.

It was then that I noticed the new furnishings in the room, a calendar on the wall from Gautam's employer. This wasn't Youngest Uncle's room anymore, though he'd lived in it for over fifty years. He'd sobbed over Nirmala on that bed. The move to the sunny, dusty, noisy front room, rolling a thin mattress on

Sukhla-pishi's floor, had already been made. Next would be Gautam's selling on the black market of all the carefully boxed, unopened electronics I'd smuggled in.

'Let us go for tea,' I suggested, putting my hand on his arm, noting its tremble and sponginess. I kept an overseas membership in the Tollygunge Club for moments like this, prying favourite relatives away from family scrutiny, letting them drink Scotch or a beer free of disapproval, but he wouldn't budge.

'They won't permit it,' he said. 'I've been told not to leave the house.'

'They? Who's they?'

'The boy, the girl. Her.'

'Rina? You know Rina, uncle, she's—' I wanted to say 'flawed.' On past visits I'd contemplated taking her out to the Tolly for a stiff gin just to see if there was a different Rina, waiting to be released. '—Harmless.'

'Her mother,' he whispered. 'And the boy.'

I heard precipitous noises outside the door. 'Babu?' came my aunt's query, 'what is going on in my daughter's room?'

'We are talking, pishi,' I said. 'We'll be just out.'

'Rina doesn't want you in there. She will be taking her bath.'

The shower arrangement was in uncle's room. His books, the only ones in the house, lined the walls but Rina's saris and Gautam's suits filled the cupboard. It was the darkest, coolest, quietest, largest and only fully serviced room in the house. Not for the first time did it occur to me that poverty corrupts everyone in India, just as wealth does the same in America. Nor did family life—so often evoked as the glue of Indian society, evidence of superiority over Western selfishness and rampant individualism—escape its collateral accounting as the source of all horrors. I suggested we drop in at the Tolly for a whiskey or two.

'I cannot leave the house,' he said. 'I am being watched. I will be reported.'

'Watched for what?'

'Gautam says that I have cheated on my taxes. The CBI is watching me twenty-four hours a day from their cars and from across the street. I must turn over everything to him to clear my name.'

'Kaku! You are the most honest man I have ever met.'

'No man leads a blameless life.'

'Gautam's a scoundrel. When he's finished draining your accounts, he'll throw you in the gutter.'

'They are watching you too, Abhi, for all the gifts you have given. Gautam says you have defrauded the country. We are worse than agents of the Foreign Hand. He has put you on record, too.'

All those serial numbers, of course—and I thought he was merely a thief. Every time I have given serious thought to returning to India for retirement or even earlier, perhaps to give my children more direction and save them from the insipidness of an American life, I am brought face to face with villainies, hypocrisies, that leave me speechless. Elevator operators collecting fares. Clerks demanding bribes, not to forgive charges, but to accept payments and stamp 'paid' on a receipt. Rina and Gautam follow a pattern. I don't want to die in America, but India makes it so hard, even for its successful runaways.

And so the idea came to me that this house in which I'd spent the best years of my childhood, the house that the extended Ganguly clan of East Bengal had been renting for over fifty years, had to be available for the right price if I could track down the owner in the three days remaining on my visit. It was one of the last remaining single-family, one-story bungalows on a wide, maidan-split boulevard lined with expensive apartment blocks. I, Abhishek Ganguly, would become owner of a house on Rash Behari Avenue, Ballygunge, paid for from the check in my pocket and my first order of business would be to expel those slimy schemers, Gautam and Rina and her mother, and any other relative who stood in the way. Front Room-pishi could stay.

Perhaps I oversold the charms of California. I certainly oversold the enthusiasm my dear wife might feel for housing an uncle she'd never met. Rina and Gautam would not leave voluntarily. Auntie would cause a fight. There'd be cursing, wailing, threats, denunciations. Nothing a few well distributed gifts could not settle. Come back with me for six months of good food and sunshine, I said, no CBI surveillance, and you can return to a clean house and your own room, dear Youngest Uncle.

Bicycle-nephew was more than happy to trade a monthly eight hundred rupees for ten million, cash. And with India being a land of miracles and immediate transformation as well as timeless inertia, I returned to California feeling like a god in the company of my liberated *Chhoto kaku,* owner, *zamindar* if you will, like my ancestors in pre-Partition East Bengal, of property, preserver of virtue and expeller of evil.

It is America, contrary to received opinion, which resists cataclysmic self-reinvention. In my two-week absence, my dear wife had engaged an architect to transform a boarded-over, five-shop strip mall in East Palo Alto into plans for the New Athens Academy, the Agora of Learning. Where weeds now push through the broken slabs of concrete, there will be fountains and elaborate gardens. Each class will plant flowers and vegetables in February and harvest in May. Classes will circulate through the plots. I can picture toga-clad teachers. New Athens will incorporate the best of East and West, Tagore's Shantiniketan and Montessori's Rome, Confucius and Dewey, sports and science, classics and computers, all fueled by Silicon Valley resources. She'd started enrolling children for two years hence.

And then I had to inform her—that outpost of Vesuvius—that my one-crore bonus cheque now rested in the account of one Atulya Ghosh, the very cool, twenty-year-old grandson of Bicycle Ghosh, nephew of old Landlord Ghosh, the presumably late owner.

One of the Ghoshes, it might have been Atulya's grandfather, had been the rumoured lover of a pishi of mine who'd been forced to leave the house in disgrace. She killed herself, in fact. Young Ray-Bans Ghosh was a Toronto-based greaser, decked out in filmi-filmi Bollywood sunglasses and a stylish scarf, forked over a throbbing motorcycle—all I could ask for as an on-site enforcer. He took my money and promised there'd be no problems: he had friends. Rina, Gautam, and Rina's mother deserved to share the pokey company flat bordering a paddy field on the outskirts of Cossipore.

Sonali wailed, she broke down in tears, sobbing, 'New Athens, New Athens!' she cried. 'My Agora, my Agora! All my dreams, all my training!' What had I been thinking? And the answer was, amazingly, she was right. I hadn't thought about her or the school, at all.

'You don't care about me. You're always complaining about our boys' education, you think I'm lazy, you only care about your goddamn family in goddamn Calcutta ...'

'I should return home,' said *Chhoto kaku*.

'Oh, no,' she cried. '*I* should return home! And I'm going to!'

She stood at the base of the stairway—I could rhapsodize over the marble, the recessed lighting under the handrail, the paintings and photographs lining the stairwell, but that is from a lifetime ago. And her beauty, I am easily inflamed. I admit it, and I will never see a more beautiful woman than Sonali, even as she threw plates at my head. 'Boys! Pramod, Vikram! Pack your bags immediately. We're leaving for San Diego!'

Chhoto kaku began to cry. I held him. Sonali went upstairs to organize the late-night getaway. The boys struggled to pack their video games and computers. The ever-enticing, ever-dangerous phenomenon of the HAP, the Hindu-American Princess, had been described to me by friends who'd urged me not to marry here, but to go back to India. Do not take on risky adventures with the second-generation daughters of American entitlement. Did I listen? Did she love me for my money, had she ever loved me? Was this all a dream? I sat on the bottom step, hiding my tears, cradling my eyes and forehead against my bent arm, while *Chhoto kaku* ran his fingers through my hair and sang to me, very low and soft, a prayer I recognized from a lifetime ago.

Well, enough of that. Justice is swift and mercy unavailing. The property split left Sonali and the boys in the big house and my uncle and me in this tiny rental. Last Christmas there was no bonus. My boss, Nitin Mehta, called me aside and said, 'bad times are coming, Abhi. We have to stay ahead of the wave. I want you to cut 20 per cent of your tech group.' So I slashed, I burned. Into the fire went everyone with an H-1B visa; back to Bombay with Lata Deshpande who was getting married in a month. Off to a taxi in Oakland went Yuri, who'd come overnight from Kazakhstan to Silicon Valley, thinking it a miracle. This Christmas there will be no job, even for me. Impulse breeds disaster, I've been taught.

In a month or two we'll be free to move back to Calcutta. Ray-Bans Ghosh informs me the 'infestation' has been routed. But Youngest Uncle has found a girlfriend in America. Kaku and the Goddess; my walls glow with her paintings. The turpentine smell of mango haunts the night.

In the summer of my fourteenth year, Youngest Uncle was given a vacation cottage in Chota Nagpur, a forest area on the border of Bihar and West Bengal. Ten members of the family went in May when the heat and humidity in Calcutta both reached triple digits. The cottage was shaded by a grove of mango trees too tall to climb. Snakes and birds and rats and clouds of insects gorged on the broken fruit. The same odour of rotting mango envelops the Goddess and the sharp tang of her welcome.

She is a well-known painter in the Bay Area and represented in New York. The first time we visited, Youngest Uncle said, 'You smell of mango,' and she'd reached out and touched him. 'Oh, sweeties,' she said, 'it's just the linseed oil.' She never seems to cook. On garbage collection days there is nothing outside her door yet she can produce cold platters of the strangest foods. She has an inordinate number of overnight guests who doubtless return to their city existence, trailing mango fumes. My uncle brings her sweet lassi, crushed ice in sweetened yoghurt, lightly laced with mango juice. I hope that in place of a heart she does not harbour a giant stone.

That summer in Choto Nagpur, I had a girlfriend. There was another cabin not so distant where another Calcutta family had brought their daughter for the high-summer school holidays. We had seen each other independent of parental authority, meaning we had passed one another on the main street of the nearest village, and our eyes had met—in my twenty-four years' memory I want to say 'locked'—but neither of us paused or acknowledged the other's presence. The fact that she didn't exactly ignore me meant I now had a girlfriend, a face to focus on and something to boast about when school resumed and the monsoons marooned us. I had the next thing to a wife, a Nirmala of my own. Knowing her name and her parents' address in Calcutta and trusting that she was out there waiting for me when the time would come, I was able to put the anxieties of marriage aside for the next five years.

When I was eighteen I asked Youngest Uncle to launch a marriage inquiry. I provided her father's name and address—I'd even walked by their house on the way to school in hopes of seeing her again and perhaps locking eyes in confirmation. Youngest Uncle was happy to do so. He reported her parents to be charming and cultured people with a pious outlook, whose ancestral origins in Bangladesh lay in an adjoining village to our own. Truly an adornment to our family. It seemed that the girl in question, however, whose name by now I've quite forgotten, was settled in a place called Maryland-America and had two lovely children. And so, outwardly crushed but partially relieved, I took the scholarship to IIT and then to Berkeley, met Sonali at a campus mixer thrown by outgoing Indo-Americans for nervous Indians, had my two lovely children, made millions and lost it and the rest is history, or maybe not.

All of my life, good times and bad, rich and poor, married and alone, I have read the Gita and tried to be guided by its immortal wisdom. It teaches our life—this life—is but a speck on a vast spectrum, but our ears are less reliable than a dog's, a dolphin's or a bat's, our eyes less than a bird's in comprehending it. I have understood it in terms of science, the heavy elements necessary to life, the calcium, phosphorous, iron and zinc, settle on us from exploded stars. We are entwined in the vast cycle of creation and destruction; the spark of life is inextinguishable. Today human, but who knows about tomorrow? We are the fruit and the rot that infects it, the mango and the worm.

Ray-Bans Ghosh now wants to put his crore of rupees to work in Toronto. Dear Abhi-babu, he writes, tear down this useless old house, put up luxury condos and you'll be minting money. Front Room pishi, who misses nothing outside the window, reports that she has seen evil Gautam in various disguises sneaking about the property. Dear Abhi, she pleads, come back, that man will kill me if he can and your cousin Rina and her mother will bury me in the yard like a Christian or worse, and please send my love to *Chhoto kaku* and your lovely wife and children, whom I've still not met.

Perhaps my Nirmala waits for me in Calcutta, perhaps in Tokyo or Maryland or the ancestral village in Bangladesh.

Youngest Uncle will stay here just a while longer, if he may, keeping my house clean and ready for whatever God plans. He has bought himself some brushes and watercolours, and takes his instruction from the Goddess who guides his hand and trains him to see, he says, at last. His old middle room has been vacant these past several months. It will suit me.

This life, which I understood once in terms of science—the heavy elements, the calcium, phosphorous, iron, and zinc, settled on us from exploded stars—is but one of an infinity of lives. The city, the world, has come and gone an infinite number of times. One day I expect my Nirmala, whatever her name, to come to my door wherever that door will be, our eyes will lock, and I will invite her in.

BREWING TEA
IN THE DARK

Y YOUNGEST UNCLE and I and a busload of other English-speakers were on a tour of Tuscany, leaving Florence at dawn, then on to Siena, followed by a mountain village, a farm lunch, another mountain village, the Leaning Tower of Pisa, and back to Florence after dark. I had planned to spread his ashes unobtrusively over a peaceful patch of sloping land, but each stop seemed more appealing than the one before, and so by lunchtime I was still holding on to the urn.

The mountain towns on our morning stops had been seductive. I could imagine myself living in any of them, walking the steep streets and taking my dinners in sidewalk cafés. I could learn Italian, which didn't seem too demanding. The fresh air and Mediterranean Diet could add years to my life.

The countryside of Tuscany in no way resembles the red-soil greenery of Bengal. Florence does not bring Kolkata to mind, except in its jammed sidewalks. My uncle wanted to live his next life as an Italian or perhaps as some sort of creature in Italy, maybe just as a tall, straight cypress (this is a theological dispute; life might be eternal, but is a human life guaranteed every rebirth?). Each time that he and his lady friend, Devvie, a painter, returned from Italy to California he pronounced himself more Italian than ever, a shrewd assessor of fine art and engineering, with a new hat, shoulder bag, jacket or scarf to prove it. He said Devvie was the prism through which the white light of his adoration was splintered into all the colours of the universe. (It sounds more natural in Bangla, our language). If that is true, many men are daubed in her colours. She taught him the Tuscan palette, the umbers and sienas.

At the farm lunch a woman of my approximate age—whose gray curls were bound in a kind of ringletted ponytail—sat opposite me at one of the refectory tables. She was wearing a dark blue 'University of Firenze' sweatshirt over faded blue jeans. In the lissome way she moved, and in the way she dressed, she seemed almost childlike. I am forty-five, but slow and heavy in spirit.

She dropped her voice to a whisper. 'I can't help noticing that urn you're carrying. Is it what I …'

I had placed it unobtrusively, I'd thought, on the table between the wine glasses. It was stoppered and guaranteed airtight, a kind of Thermos bottle of ashes. I was afraid that if I put him on the floor an errant foot might touch him.

'Very perceptive,' I said. 'It's my uncle.'

'Lovely to meet you, sir,' she said to the urn. Then to me, 'You can call me Rose.' *Call me Rose?* I must have squinted, but she said, 'You were talking to him back in Siena. You were sitting on a bench and holding it in your lap and I heard you. Of course, I couldn't understand what you were saying, but I'd never seen anything like it.'

'Why the mystery about your name?' I asked.

'You'll find out,' she said. Perhaps she changed her name every day, or on every trip, or for every man she met. I told her my name, Abhi, short for Abhishek.

The farm landscape reminded me of paintings on the walls of Italian restaurants: mounded vineyards framed by cypress trees, against a wall of purple hills sprinkled with distant, whitewashed villas. She moved like a dancer to the fence, then turned, and called to me.

'Why not right here?'

I walked over to the fence, but a goat wandered up to us, looking for food, and tried to butt me through the slats. Then he launched a flurry of shiny black pellets.

'Maybe not,' she said.

When we remounted the tour bus, the aisle seat next to me turned up vacant. 'May I?' she asked. She told me that my morning seatmate had also made a connection with the urn and a possible bomb, or shortwave radio. He too had seen me talking in a strange language in Siena, probably Arabic.

During the next leg of the trip, she opened up to me: 'You came here on a mission. So did I, in a way. I read that an old friend of mine was going to be in Florence for a Renaissance music festival. He plays the mandolin. And suddenly I wanted to see him again. Not to be with him—goodness, he has a wife and family—but I thought how funny it would be if we just happened to run into each other.'

I could not have imagined so much disclosure in a single outburst. I couldn't even understand her motivation. Funny? The impulsiveness of my fellow Americans is often mysterious to me, but I listened with admiration. We'd never met and we were on a bus in Tuscany, but she was spilling her secrets. Or did she consider me a harmless sounding post? Or did she have no secrets? And then I wondered had she—like me— been pried open by some recent experience? Perhaps our normal defences had been weakened.

'Maybe you had a wake-up call,' I said. 'The things we do that elude all reason, because suddenly, we have to do them.'

She seemed to ponder the possibility, then consigned it to a secret space for future negotiation. After a few moments she asked, 'Where are you from?'

Always an ambiguous question: where are you really from? India? Am I from Kolkata? California? Bay Area? She said, 'I work in a library in a small town in Massachusetts, two blocks from Emily Dickinson's house.'

She'd been married, but not to her mandolinist. She'd gone to New York to dance, she married, but she'd injured herself and turned to painting, and then she'd divorced and started writing. By her estimation she was a minor, but not a failed, writer. Like most Bangla-speakers of my generation, I've known a number of poets and writers, although most were employed in more mundane endeavours, by day. I had never considered them minor, or failed.

And then her narrative, or her confessions, stopped and I felt strangely bereft. I sensed she was waiting for me to reciprocate. What did I have to match her?

'Are you married?' she asked.

I began to understand that something thicker was in the air. 'Why do you ask?'

'You have an appealing air,' she said.

It is my experience in the West that Indian men, afraid to press their opinions or exert their presence, are often perceived as soulful. Many's the time I've wanted to say, to very well-meaning ladies, just because I have long, delicate fingers and large, deep-brown eyes and a mop of black, unruly hair, do not ascribe to me greater sensitivity, sensuality, or innocence, or some kind of unthreatening, pre-feminist manliness. Our attempts to accommodate a new culture are often interpreted as clumsy, if forgivable. I think my uncle and his painter friend enjoyed such a relationship, based on mutual misreading, but in his case all of the clichés might have been true. He was, truly, an innocent. Unlike him, I have no trouble saying 'fuck' in mixed company.

'Do you have children?' she persisted.

I have two boys, who stay with their mother and her parents in San Diego. In my world, the love of one's family is the only measure of success, and in that aspect, I have failed. I said only, 'yes.'

'I'm sorry,' she said. 'It's none of my business.'

My uncle was an afflicted man. He never married. His income paid for the education of all the boys in the family, and the dowries of all the girls. In a place where family means everything, and if part of the family is pure evil, even one's house can be a prison. Literally, a prison: he lived in a back bedroom, afraid even to be seen from the street. He was forced to pay his grandniece's husband ten thousand rupees a month, on the threat of his turning over certain documents to the CBI that would prove something. You ask why he didn't protect himself, why he didn't sue, why his passivity was allowed to confirm the most heinous charges? And I say, Indian 'justice' is too slow and corrupt. Cases linger before judges awaiting their bribes. Cases go on as lawyers change sides, as they win stay after stay.

That grim prison was the house of my fondest memories, the big family compound on Rash Behari Avenue that our family began renting the moment of their arrival from the eastern provinces, now known as Bangladesh. Our neighbourhood was an east Bengal enclave. We grew up still speaking the eastern dialect. We thought of ourselves as refugees, even the generation, like my grandparents', which had arrived before Partition. In soccer, we still supported East Bengal against the more-established Calcutta team, Mohun Bagan. It's the most spirited competition in all of sports, perhaps in the world.

Six years ago, I'd arrived for my annual visit, this time with a quarter-million dollars in year-end bonus money. It was the dot.com era nearing its end—although we thought it would go on forever—and I had been a partner in a start-up. When my uncle spilled out his story, and I could see the evidence all around me, I also had the solution in my pocket. I acted without thinking. No courts, no police, no unseemly newspaper coverage that would tarnish the family name. I simply bought the house and kicked the vermin out. But I had forgotten that my wife had a use for that money; a school she'd planned to start. I came back from Kolkata with my uncle in tow. She and the children left for San Diego a week later.

She slept on the long ride to Pisa. She slept like a child, no deep breathing, no snoring. I wished she'd turned her head towards me. I would have held her, even embraced her. It was the first time in years that I'd felt such a surge of protectiveness.

There is very little good I can say about Pisa. I'm of two minds about the Leaning Tower. It is iconic, but ugly. It's a monument to phenomenal incompetence, and now the world is invested in a medieval mistake. Actually, I'm not of two minds. It is an abomination. Preserving the mistake is a crime against the great Italian tradition of engineering. In the wide lawns around the Tower, various bands of young tourists, mostly Japanese, posed with their arms outstretched, aligning them for photos in a way to suggest they were holding up the crippled Tower.

We walked towards the Tower, past stalls of souvenir-sellers, most of them, if not all, Bangladeshi, hawking Leaning Tower T-shirts and kitchen towels. They called out to us in English, but I could hear them muttering among themselves in Bangla, 'It's an older bunch. Put out the fancy stuff.'

I stopped by, drawn in by the language. We may be one of the pioneering languages of Silicon Valley, but we are also the language of the night, the cooks and dishwashers and hole-in-the-wall restaurants and cheap clothing stalls around the world. Then they studied me a little closer. 'Hey, brother!' This came in Bangla. 'Something nice for your girlfriend?' They held up white T-shirts, stamped with the Leaning Tower.

'What kind of gift is that?' I answered back. 'She'd have to lean like a cripple to make it straight.'

They invited me behind the stalls. Rose came closer, but stayed on the edge of the sidewalk. I felt a little guilty—this was my call from the unconscious, the language-hook. I remembered my uncle, who had brought his devotional tapes to California, and many evenings I would return from work and the lights would be off, and he would be singing to his Hemanta Mukherjee tapes, and I would keep the lights off and brew tea in the dark.

Behind the display bins, the men had stored trunks and trunks of trinkets and T-shirts and towels and tunics, nearly all of them Pisa-related. On each trunk, in Bangla, they had chalked the names of cities: Pisa, Florence, Rome, Venice and Pompeii.

The three stall-owners were cousins. They introduced themselves: Wahid, Hesham and Ali, cousins from a village a kilometer from my grandparents' birthplace. They knew the town well, and the big house that had been ours, the zamindari house, the Hindu's house. Maybe their grandfathers, as small children, had worked there, or maybe they had just stolen bananas from the plantation.

'Then you are from the Ganguly family?' they asked me, and I nodded, bowing slightly, 'Abhishek Ganguly.' Hindu, even Brahmin: opposite sides of a one-kilometer world.

The buried, collective memory forever astonishes. Nothing in the old country could have brought our families together, yet here we were in the shadow of the Leaning Tower of Pisa, remembering the lakes and rivers, the banana plantation, my great-grandfather's throwing open his house on every Hindu and Muslim feast-day. In the olden days, in the golden east of Bengal where all our poetry originated, the Hindus had the wealth, the Muslims had the numbers, and both were united against the British.

My ancestral residence (which I've never seen; after Partition, my parents even tore up the old photos they'd carried with them), I learned, is now a school. The banana plantation is now a soccer field and cricket pitch. Wahid, Hesham, and Ali, and three remoter cousins—what we call 'cousin-brothers', which covers any degree of relatedness including husbands of cousins' sisters—have a lorry, and when the tourist season is over in Pisa they will strike their stalls and go to Florence and sell Statue of David kitsch, or to Venice and sell gondola kitsch. In the winter they will go to southern Spain and sell Alhambra kitsch.

But think of the distance these cheap but still overpriced T-shirts have traveled! Uzbek cotton, spun in Cambodia, stamped in China and sent to a middleman somewhere in the Emirates, to be distributed throughout Europe, matching the proper Western icon to the right city and the proper, pre-paid sellers. For one month they will return to Bangladesh, bringing gifts to their children and parents, and doubtless, enlarging their families.

The cousins had come to Italy four years ago, starting out by spreading blankets on the footpaths and selling China-made toys. Now they have transportable stalls and in a couple of years the six cousins will pool their money and buy a proper store, somewhere, and bring their wives and children over. Right now, they send half of their earnings back to their village, where the wives have built solid houses and the children are going to English-medium schools and want to become doctors and teachers. Their wives have opened up tea stalls and stitching shops. 'We are Bengalis first, then Hindu or Muslim after,' said Wahid, perhaps for my benefit. 'If anyone says he is first a Muslim or a Hindu, I give him wide berth. He has a right to his beliefs, but I do not share them.'

All of this I translated for my girlfriend, Rose. Then we sat at a sidewalk café and drank a glass of white wine, looking out on the Tower and the ant-sized climbers working their way up the sides, waving from the balconies. I was happy.

'I think you're a little too harsh on the Tower,' she said.
We reached Florence in the dark. There seemed little question that we would spend the night together, in her hotel or mine. Outside the bus-park only one food stall was still open. I

bought apples and a bottle of wine. The young man running it did all his calculations in Italian, until I stopped him, in Bangla. 'That's a lot of *taka*, isn't it?' and the effect was of a puppet master jerking a doll's strings. He mentioned the name of his village, this one far, far in the east, near Chittagong, practically in Burma. His accent was difficult for me, as was mine to him. 'Bangla is the international language of struggle,' he said.

The unexpected immersion in Bengal had restored a certain confidence. It was the last thing, or the second-last thing, I'd expected from a trip into the wilds of Tuscany. I was swinging the plastic sack of wine and apples, with the urn tucked under my arm, and Rose said, 'Let me take the urn.' I lifted my arm slightly, and she reached in.

'Oops,' she said.

My religion holds that the body is sheddable, but the soul is eternal. My uncle's soul still exists, despite the cremation. It has time to find a new home, entering through the soft spot in a newborn's skull. I felt he was still with me, there in Italy, but perhaps he'd remained back in California. The soul is in the ether, like a particle in the quanta; it can be in California one second, and Kolkata the next. But he'd wanted to find an Italian home, and now his matter lay in a dusty, somewhat oily mass on the cobblestones of Florence, amid shards of glass and ceramic. It will join some sort of Italian flux. It will be picked up on the soles of shoes, it will flow in the gutter, it will be devoured by flies and picked over by pigeons. If I am truly a believer in our ancient traditions, then it doesn't matter where he lies like a clot of mud while his soul still circles, awaiting its new house, wherever that house might be.

'It's all right,' I said. In fact, a burden had been lifted.

Her hotel was near at hand. This was an event I had not planned. It had been three years since any sexual activity, and that had been brief and not consoling. In the slow-rising elevator, she squeezed my hand. Sex with a gray-haired lady, however slim and girlish, lay outside my fantasy. How to behave, what is the etiquette? She'd taken off her glasses, and she was humming something wordless. Under her University of Firenze sweatshirt, I could make out only the faintest mounds, the slightest crease. Even in the elevator's harsh fluorescent light, I saw no wrinkles in her face.

As we walked down the corridor, she slipped me her keycard. My fingers were trembling. It took three stabs to open the door. The moment the door was shut, and a light turned on, she walked to the foot of the bed, and turned to face me. The bedspread was a bright, passionate red. It was an eternal moment: the woman's smile, her hands closing around the ends of her sweatshirt, and then beginning to pull it up. I dropped the bag of wine and apples. So this is how it plays, this is how people like us do it. Her head disappeared briefly under the sweater, and then she tossed the University of Firenze aside on the red bedspread and she stood before me, a thin woman with small breasts, no bra, and what appeared to be a pink string looped against her side.

'Now you know,' she said, and began kissing me madly. 'Come to my bed of crimson joy.'

What I knew was this: she was bald. Her wig had been caught in the sleeve of her sweater. The pink string was a fresh scar down her ribcage, then curling up between her breasts. But we were on the bed and my hands were over her scalp, then on her breasts and the buttons of her jeans, and her fingers were on my belt and pants.

There is much to respect in this surrender to passion. After sex, there is humour, and honesty. I poured the wine and she retired to the bathroom, only to reappear in her red 'Shirley MacLaine' wig. With her obviously unnatural, burgundy-coloured hair, there's a flash of sauciness atop her comely face and body. And so passion arose once again. 'I've got more,' she said. There was a black 'Liza Minelli,' and a blonde.

When we sipped the wine, she told me she'd been given a year, maybe two. But who knows, in this world miracles have been known to happen.

It is overwhelming, the first vision of the *David*, standing a ghostly white at the end of a long, sculpture-lined hall. An adoring crowd surrounds him, whatever the hour or the day. Viewed from afar, in profile, he is a haughty, even arrogant figure. His head is turned. He is staring at his immediate enemy, Goliath.

'That pose is called contrapposto,' Rose whispered. She was wearing her red Shirley MacLaine wig, and she looked like a slightly wicked college woman. *David*'s weight is supported on the right leg—the left leg is slightly raised—but the right arm is lank, and his curled hand cradles a smooth stone. The left arm is bent, and the biceps bunched. The leather sling lies on his shoulder and slithers down his back. Yet when I stood at his side, looking up directly into his eyes, the haughtiness disappeared. I read doubt, maybe fear. It's as though Michelangelo were looking into David's future, beyond the immediate victory. If I remember my Christian schooling, David would go on to become a great king and poet, the founder of a dynasty leading eventually to Jesus Christ, but he will lose his beloved son Absalom in a popular uprising against him and he will send a loyal general to his death in order to possess his wife. In the end, for all his heroism, he will grow corrupt in his pride and arrogance; his is a tattered regime. All of this I felt at that moment, and tried to communicate.

There is so much tragedy in his eyes. He knows he will accomplish this one great thing in the next few minutes, but regret will flow for the rest of his life. *David* is a monument to physical perfection, the antidote to the Leaning Tower.

And what about us? I wonder. She took my arm as we walked down the swarming sidewalk outside the Accademia. We passed through a great open square, near the Uffizi Palace.

Crews were setting up folding chairs for an evening concert of Renaissance music.

'Will you come with me?' she asked.

Of course I would. I would see her mandolinist. We would get there early and sit in the front row. I would stand behind her after the concert, assuming she could make her way to the stage against the press of admirers, and she would ask him, 'remember me?'

Maybe she would wear her gray ponytail wig. He would be more comfortable with that, more likely to remember her. In some way, I would learn more about her. '*Oh, Rose!*' he might exclaim. Or he might dismiss her with a flick of his fingers.

'If I'm still above ground next year, and if I came to your house, would you welcome me in?'

And I can only say, 'I will open the door.'

THE KEROUAC
WHO NEVER WAS

For my eleventh birthday, my brother Paulie turned over his paper route. He was entering high school and said he needed the two hours of extra sleep. He also admitted that still having a paper route in high school was a little humiliating. But he also said that getting up before dawn six days a week and pulling a high-sided sled down an icy sidewalk to the front door of Billy Marcotte's all-night gas station and clipping the wire around a stack of fifty papers labeled 'Frechette', stuffing in the ads and folding the papers the way he'd taught me and then delivering them all over Winooski would be the first great adventure of my life. I would learn Winooski by night, from the old tenement blocks down by the river to the empty mills and the creepy, hollowed-out office buildings downtown, up past the thick stone block of St. Francis-Xavier church and school, all the way to Lambert Park. I would learn what he called 'the workings of the world.' He said, 'At night it's a different world out there, Dickie.'

He said when a house light is on at five in the morning, hide behind a tree and just watch. You'll learn who's friendly and sober by day but a violent drunk at night, or the faithful Sunday communicant who beats on his wife on Saturday night. And the stuck-up goodie-goodies in school who sneak out and meet boys at night. People reveal themselves when they think they can't be seen. None of those revelations seemed too interesting. Avoid drunken hunters coming home at five in the morning with a bloody deer strapped to the hood. You'll see deer flashing across the streets. Avoid stags. Dogs might not be dogs. Don't get skunked. Avoid coons and possums—they might be sick. Don't stop and talk with Father Beaubien or Father Boyle even if they roll their windows down and call you out by name and offer a ride to wherever you're going. He could make simple words like 'five in the morning' sound threatening.

By day Paulie was slight and shy, and sunlight exposed him. In the dark, the world revealed itself to him. Paulie read serious books. He expected to go to college or maybe a real university like UVM or even Dartmouth and not live at home and go to St. Mike's. He was reading *Dr Sax*, which had just come out.

'The guy who wrote this book, he's one of us. He knows the Devil is following everyone in the parish. Kerouac's writing our life, Dickie.'

I tried reading a paragraph and I didn't recognize our life, or understand a thing. If that's our life, then our lives are too complicated, or they weren't worth too much. Kerouac: I didn't even think he was one of ours. Our names don't start with a K. I thought he was one of those Irish, like Kennedy or Kavenagh or something.

'It's Bréton,' Paulie said. ''Ker' means wall. I read it some-place.'

'You're always reading useless thing like Ker means wall in Bréton. Sweet bleeding Jesus.'

When Paulie tried to describe *Dr Sax*, our father said that writer sounded like a *doigt-en-cul*, someone who sticks his finger up his asshole and then complains that it smells like shit. Our father couldn't read.

'More like a man who sucks in smoke all day and coughs all night and blames bad night air,' said Paulie. He was fearless when it came to defending Kerouac. It's more like a *croûte*, Paulie told me later, a scab over a deep wound. We don't know what caused it, but we can guess. It's being French, and too Catholic, in America.

That first winter I saw nothing and learned nothing, but I became financially self-supporting. I could buy all the comic books and bubble gum with baseball cards I wanted. But in the spring, everything changed. The heaviness of winter lifted. It was still dark when I started, but by six-thirty, there'd be light. We were in mud season. Every morning the dingy tongues of old snow retreated by an inch or two, and sometimes after a strong rain, disappeared entirely. Even if we had a spring snowstorm the remnants would be gone in a day. I learned that life proceeds by increments. One morning the puddles were collared in ice, but the next day the collars never formed. I'd never appreciated nature in our corner of northern Vermont, until I got a paper route. I put away the sled and used my old wagon, repainted and axles greased.

I could make out the shadows of high school boys and girls making their way out of Landry Park, following the snake trail of their lighted cigarettes. Five o'clock in the morning, in the cold and mud, saying *sh-sh*, but giggling. 'Hey, little paperboy, you didn't see nothing, right?' I knew one of the girls, Linnie Robitaille, a pretty girl in Paulie's class, but the Robitailles were never around on collection night. Her younger sister, the beautiful Betsy, was in my class.

In April I got up even earlier, in order to study the overnight baseball scores. In those days, box scores didn't give up-to-the-minute batting and pitching stats—you had to wait for a Sunday paper for that, but *The Burlington Free Press* didn't publish on Sunday. I had to spend the first minutes inside Billy Marcotte's gas station just computing the latest earned run averages of Red Sox pitchers and updating the batting averages based on the previous night's box scores.

But there's something I did learn, and it's never left me. When you start the day twice, once in the cold dark with scary shapes, and then go home and catch some sleep and get up again, restart the clock in full daylight, get dressed again, eat breakfast, and head off down the same streets to school, you develop a sense of duality (as Paulie would put it). Which world is the true one? The day-lit world seemed bland and over-detailed; the night world was undefined and indistinct, and maybe for the rest of my life I never reconciled the two.

Just about everyone in our parish was *canadien*. The younger parents read *The Free Press* and their parents still spoke only French and probably couldn't read anyway. The language barrier made collecting hard when only the old folks were home. If they were alone they never answered the door. My mémère—my mother's mother—was that way. Why say *entrez* instead of *qui est-ce?* if you might be inviting the Devil in? As Paulie said, Dr Sax was out there, whatever you called him.

My parents had both left school in the first or second grade back in Canada. Rimouski. Winooski/Rimouski; sound Polish, but they're Indian words. Their huge families had been hollowed out by the Influenza epidemic in 1918. My mother had been the second youngest of twenty; my father was second youngest of sixteen. They each had lost ten siblings in a week. My father also lost his mother. *La Maladie* turned my father into an atheist, but made Ma into a more pious devotee. After another round of deaths, Ma ended up third oldest. Their families bounced around small towns and villages, and my parents ended up meeting in Montreal, getting married, and then heading a hundred miles south to Winooski.

My father hung drywall, using a special Canadian-made fire-retardant gypsum board. He was kept busy because the towns around us were growing, especially with chain motels.

My mother's parents were living with us. Ma and mémère attended mass every morning. Pépère was chair-bound and never left the back room, even for dinner.

From the kitchen banter between the women I picked up the old language or most of what I needed. I learned to make change and sweet-talk the old folks till I was paid. I spoke the old language; they called me a good boy.

Mémère was the kind of old-time Catholic who would weep if Good Friday dawned bright and sunny, or if resurrection Easter turned cold and drizzly. Evidence, said Father Beaubien, that God and the Devil were still locked in combat, and if Christ died on a day you'd rather go fishing, the Devil was winning. Her fear of cats proved that she was directly related to the Christian martyrs who were eaten by lions for their piety. Paulie said to me, 'hard to be a descendent of someone who was cat food two thousand years ago.'

We knew—Paulie and me and our father—that we were going to Hell. All the piety of our mother and grandmother could not outweigh our sins. My father's father had stormed out of the Church after his wife, four sons and six daughters died back in Canada, and my father never returned.

Back in Canada: we lived inside those words. That was the familiar beginning of many sentences, leading to many stories. Back in Canada, asbestos clumps rolled down the streets like tumbleweed; asbestos shards flecked the tree limbs like crushed glass, asbestos glinted like hoarfrost on winter days. *Back in Canada* was another way of dividing the world, like night and day. There was a Canada where our country cousins were poor and jobless and conditions were permanent, the clergy ruled and you stayed, and married, and died wherever you'd been born. And there was America where conditions weren't much different and we still clung to the church and the community, but an attitude had changed. Paulie and I were expected to better ourselves and not work with our hands and not cough our lungs out all night.

We all understood that 'Canada' meant only Quebec, and 'Canadian' meant only French. That expansive word, québécois, had not yet surfaced. Before there were 'Little Havanas' or 'Chinatowns' or 'Little Manilas' there were Little Canadas. I know: I was born and raised in one. I watched it fall, but I still carry it in my heart and memory. We disappeared in history's Big Gulp.

Many years later, when I became the Fréchette family's first college graduate, I read Nathaniel Hawthorne's *American Notebooks*, and noted that on his walking tours of the bottomlands of Salem, way back in the 1830s, he hadn't seen witches or women with scarlet letters, but he had noticed the huts of Canadians and Irish. 'Canadian' meant mill-workers with enormous families living in single-room shacks next to the similar huts of their co-religionist Irish with whom they often fought, and usually won. Those shacks were put up on a weekend for four dollars and sold for six when they returned to Canada. He admired the frugality of the Canadians, even as he lamented their Catholicism.

Three things happened that first year, one to me and one to Paulie, and one to the nation. I guess they qualify as life-changing glimpses of the workings of the world. The year started promisingly. In November, a New England Catholic overcame the dark forces of Hawthornean prejudice and was elected president of the United States. His wife could have been a movie star, and she was even French in some complicated way and rumoured to speak the language. (Paulie snorted, 'She'd cringe if she heard what we speak.') Our teachers had started classes with a prayer for his election ever since the nomination, and now that they had proof of its efficacy, Paulie predicted they would claim his success to our prayers. My mother clipped photos from *Life* magazine of the new first couple and taped them on the kitchen walls and in the parlour, over the credenza with its lighted-up, plastic sacre-coeur.

That winter, Paulie asked me an innocent-sounding question. 'When the sled handle is cold, does it give you any trouble?' What kind of question was that? Of course not. 'And what about the wagon? Any problems?' Again, I must have frowned a response. That was Paulie, always on to something mysterious.

When the spring outdoor track season was underway, Paulie made the 4x800 junior varsity relay team, third leg, between Danny Lévesque and the only non-*canadien* outlier on the squad, Bobby Cronin. Bobby ran the anchor leg and if he got a clean pass of the baton, he was unbeatable. Paulie was slight but reasonably fast and he trained, as our track and hockey coach, Father Drouin, said, as if his life depended on it. Even if he weren't the fastest it would go against Father's principles not to reward him. He liked to have a hardworking underdog on the team, just to keep the real athletes honest. Paulie trained through the fall and winter in order to get a letter to show he was 'well-rounded' enough to get into a good university. In the quarterfinals of the state Catholic eliminations, we drew a bigger school from Montpelier.

There wasn't a big crowd, just a scattering of parents. It was only JV track, and it was a cold, blustery day. Paulie ran a creditable third leg, losing maybe a few seconds, nothing Bobby Cronin couldn't make up. But when the baton transfer was underway, Bobby with his hand out, Paulie with the baton outstretched, we watched Bobby tug, and tug again, and it appeared a fight would break out with Paulie refusing to let go as the Montpelier anchor leg whizzed by. Finally, Bobby used the baton like a baseball bat, spinning Paulie to the ground, standing on his wrist and wrenching the baton free.

Our loss earned a column in the paper. A French boy, fighting an Irish—isn't the country beyond such nonsense? Didn't Kennedy's election mean anything?

We got a lot of angry, even threatening phone calls, mainly from kids, probably classmates. Paulie was distraught, locked in his bedroom and wouldn't come out. I was appointed guardian of the phone, an innocent child, obviously younger than the chief villain of the house. But one call was different, an adult male with a calm voice. 'Is this the Fréchette residence?' he asked. From the way he pronounced our name, I knew he was French. 'May I speak with Paul?'

'He's not talking. Who is this?'

'My name is Mario Séguin, from the neurological clinic at UVM Hospital.' At least he gave his name. My math teacher was also a Séguin. 'Perhaps I could speak to his mother?'

'She doesn't speak English,' I said.

'Cela n'importe. Je parle.'

My mother talked; I listened. From what I understood, Dr Séguin had read the article about Paulie and the baton, and he had a different interpretation. He'd like to run some tests. 'I don't think it's his fault,' he said. 'He wasn't involved in anything the papers said. Bring him to the clinic. It could be a medical condition we've been looking at.'

We'd had a long, cold spring. Then in early May came a sudden warming, long fingers of moist southern air seeking out the valleys and clinging tightly to the surface of the lake. The cold waters of Lake Champlain leeched fogbanks from the sticky air, fog so thick I couldn't see my feet or the porches where I normally tossed a paper. I was walking inside a wet cloud, *trempé jusqu'aux os,* my mother would say, drenched to the bones. Out on the street, I could hear cars hissing by, but their headlights barely smudged the fog.

I was down by the church when I felt a sharp jolt between my shoulder blades. 'Hey!—' I started. I turned, expecting to see one of the pre-dawn drunks with a loaded rifle and a blood-streaked face, but what I was looking at was a gawky, knobby-kneed moose calf, my height, who kept nudging me, now in my chest and when I turned, on my shoulder and in my ribs. 'Moose,' I crooned, dragging my hand down her long nose—if she was a she—like patting a horse, 'What have you done?'

This was the moment Paulie had talked about, a moment of the night that day people never saw. Why did she stay with me? Why hadn't she bolted, or pushed me aside?

She stretched her long neck high, looking over my head, down the sidewalk. She ignored me. Then she snorted in my face. She smelled of rotten vegetation. When she barged into me, I collapsed into her crop of thick neck hair. I knew the danger I was in. Moose were North Country killers; they were just too big for our tiny state. She might be bigger and stronger and more dangerous, yet I felt she was the endangered one and that I was her guide and protector. I slapped her shoulder with a rolled-up paper when she strayed from the sidewalk. If she stepped off the curb, she'd be killed and maybe the driver too. When she got ahead of me, she'd stop so I could catch up, then she would follow me, butting me from behind, other times laying her head on my shoulder and her snorts warmed my neck.

Up ahead, throbbing pink lights bounced against the fog bank and muffled voices mumbled in the distance, punctuated by the scratchy response of a police radio. Something big had happened. People were shouting but the fog muffled the words. The calf bellowed. I stood behind a tree. I could make out the bulk of Sgt. Teddy Bergeron, a one-time football star at UVM—'fastest back since Kerouac' they wrote of him—shouting into his car radio, 'Looks like the old queer met a moose. Didn't turn out too good for either one of them.'

Then the calf dashed out to the gutter to sniff her mother, or maybe nurse, and Teddy whirled with a loud 'oh, shit.' The calf was bent over, down on those knobby knees and Teddy pulled out his service revolver, stuck it in her ear and as I shouted 'No!' fired three shots. Then he spoke into the radio, 'Call Charlie Rouleau. Tell him there's a ton of twitching meat down here.' Rouleau ran a sausage factory, so the rumours were true. A pile of still fresh meat, and two attendants rolling a gurney with a dead body on it and lifting it into the back of an ambulance: a hell of a way to start my day. Up on the sidewalk was a familiar car with a crushed grill and shattered windshield.

Teddy leaned into his cruiser. Someone was sitting in the back. 'Go home, kid. If I catch you at this kind of thing again, I'll throw the book at you.' And out of the back came Paulie. 'You're one lucky little bastard, that's all I can say. Not a scratch on you and the priest gets his head sliced off.'

Paulie saw me. I can't say he smiled, but he could zone out like that, smiling slightly, bobbing his head slightly like he was in a charmed space, hearing music or voices but not humming or talking. You could talk to him but he didn't answer and later he'd deny the whole experience. Maybe it wasn't a charmed space at all, maybe he was epileptic and we never knew it.

I knew I was going to Hell when I realized I cared more about the dead moose calf who'd trusted me and I'd tried to protect but had led to slaughter than I did about the mangled corpse of Father Beaubien. In fact, I blamed him for killing a god who'd emerged from the fog. 'Move back, kid. Deliver your papers,' said Teddy Bergeron.

Paulie didn't go home. He walked with me, for old time's sake, he said, folding the papers and running them up to porches. I asked him what he was doing with Father Beaubien. 'Getting his advice,' he said, and I asked, maybe sneering, 'What kind of advice could he give?'

But he was serious. 'Remember that time I couldn't let go of the baton?'

I probably said who could forget it? 'Remember that doctor, Mario? He said I've got the beginning of something bad. Ma didn't believe him, especially when he said it's something the French carry—that got her really mad, like he was accusing her of passing it on like the flu.' We walked another block in silence. 'She doesn't understand. She said she'd pray it away. But it's in all of us. We'll never get rid of it.'

He said I might try reading Kerouac now. 'It's Dr Sax, Dickie—he's in my blood.' Pépère had finally died that winter, and mémère said she had nothing to do but die and our father was dying from the meso, growing up near asbestos mines and from hanging that special Canadian wallboard with the asbestos coating. Paulie said Father Beaubien had told him to pray. Coddle the credulous, that's what the Church does, and Father said he would put him in special priest-only prayers, but probably he'd committed some sort of sin to bring it on, a special kind of boy's sin. He said, 'Show me the sin you committed.' I told him I didn't commit any sin. He said, 'If I can't see it I won't know the right prayer. You know the kind of sin I'm talking about.'

Paulie snickered, 'crafty old goat. And then his head got ripped off.' Then he added, 'Mario said it's going to get a lot worse.'

'Does it have a name?' I asked.

'Yeah, it's got a name. Officially, muscular dystrophy, but I call it Dr Sax Disease.' Then suddenly he shouted into the muffling fog. 'The moose is God! The calf is Christ! Father Beaubien is Dr Sax! We brought all of them down from Canada!'

We kept on walking, but he was crying. And I said something really stupid, even for the kind of eleven-year-old I was, because diseases that killed children were part of Canada, sad stories with bad endings that parents told.

I said, 'Don't worry, Paulie. We're Americans.'

Clark Blaise, a Canadian and American citizen, is the author of twenty books of fiction and nonfiction. A longtime advocate for the literary arts in North America, Blaise has taught writing and literature at Emory, Skidmore, Columbia, NYU, Sir George Williams, UC–Berkeley, SUNY–Stony Brook, and the David Thompson University Centre. In 1968, he founded the postgraduate Creative Writing Program at Concordia University; he later went on to serve as the Director of the International Writing Program at Iowa (1990–1998), and as President of the Society for the Study of the Short Story (2002–present). Internationally recognized for his contributions to the field, Blaise has received an Arts and Letters Award for Literature from the American Academy (2003), and in 2010 was made an Officer of the Order of Canada. Married to fellow writer Bharati Mukherjee (1940–2017) for fifty-three years, he is predeceased by their two sons. He lives in New York.